From an exciting new literary voice comes the powerful novel
that has critics cheering and readers rejoicing. . . . You will
never forget the celebration of life and love captured in

BEFORE I GO

Colleen Oakley's wise and warm fiction debut is
A *People* magazine Best New Book
One of *Library Journal*'s Smash Winter Titles
Featured in *US Weekly, All You, Good Housekeeping*,
and *In Touch Weekly* magazines!

"Brilliant in its simplicity, beautiful in its sentiment, heartbreaking in
its honesty, *Before I Go* takes on one of life's ultimate cruelties, death
before one's time, and makes us believe."

—Susan Crandall, author of *The Flying Circus*

"The psychology of dying is one of the few great mysteries we have
left. But Oakley rises to the challenge, especially in the moments that
bring the reader closest to Daisy's thoughts. . . . With compassion and
humor, Oakley makes us feel for this dying woman and understand
her final wish."

—*Good Housekeeping*

"Touching. . . . Oakley expertly tugs at the heartstrings with well-rounded
characters and a liberal dose of gallows humor."

—*Publishers Weekly*

"It's not giving anything away to reveal that the book turns out to be more about living than dying. Or that Oakley wants us to come to that frustrating, funny, but ultimately most fulfilling realization right along with Daisy."

—*The Atlanta Journal-Constitution*

"Colleen Oakley takes on the big three—life, death, and love—and delivers a jewel. *Before I Go* absolutely glows with humor, wit, and compassion. I adore Oakley's fresh voice and could hardly bear for the book to end."

—Lynn Cullen, author of the national bestseller *Mrs. Poe*

"This emotional debut and its gutsy heroine will have you laughing through tears and staying up late until you've reached the final, fully satisfying page."

—Jennie Shortridge, author of *Love Water Memory*

"A big-hearted tale with a fresh take on a woman grappling with the inevitable. The characters are approachable, full of wit and humor and—above all else—touching sincerity."

—Suzanne Rindell, author of *The Other Typist*

"In *Before I Go*, Colleen Oakley addresses the oft-asked question: if you had only six months to live, what would you do? In her deft hands, what could easily turn maudlin becomes a funny and insightful journey."

—Catherine McKenzie, bestselling author of *Hidden* and *Forgotten*

"Oakley has set herself a tricky balancing act here, blending a comic sensibility with the depth and poignancy her subject requires. She pulls it off."

—*People*

"An affecting work that, while avoiding maudlin sentimentality, makes the reader care about Daisy and her determination to live while dying."

—*Booklist*

"Highly recommended for laugh-out-loud fans and the tearjerker set."

—*Library Journal*

"The emotion always rings true. . . . It's impossible not to feel Daisy's pain, confusion, and sadness as she thinks about what life will be like after she's gone."

—*Kirkus Reviews*

"[A] poignant debut novel. . . . Oakley tells this story with such confidence and grace that readers will find themselves fully invested in—and emotionally braced for—the unfolding tragedy."

—*Atlanta* magazine

"An emotional picture of what it means to live and die that will tug at the heartstrings through the final pages."

—*RT Book Reviews*

before
i go

Colleen Oakley

G

GALLERY BOOKS

NEW YORK   LONDON   TORONTO   SYDNEY   NEW DELHI

G̶

Gallery Books
An Imprint of Simon & Schuster, Inc.
1230 Avenue of the Americas
New York, NY 10020

This book is a work of fiction. Any references to historical events, real people, or real places are used fictitiously. Other names, characters, places, and events are products of the author's imagination, and any resemblance to actual events or places or persons, living or dead, is entirely coincidental.

Copyright © 2015 by Colleen Tull

All rights reserved, including the right to reproduce this book or portions thereof in any form whatsoever. For information, address Gallery Books Subsidiary Rights Department, 1230 Avenue of the Americas, New York, NY 10020.

First Gallery Books trade paperback edition July 2015

GALLERY BOOKS and colophon are registered trademarks of Simon & Schuster, Inc.

For information about special discounts for bulk purchases,
please contact Simon & Schuster Special Sales at 1-866-506-1949
or business@simonandschuster.com.

The Simon & Schuster Speakers Bureau can bring authors
to your live event. For more information or to book an event,
contact the Simon & Schuster Speakers Bureau at 1-866-248-3049
or visit our website at www.simonspeakers.com.

Interior design by Davina Mock-Maniscalco

Manufactured in the United States of America

10   9   8   7   6   5   4   3   2   1

Library of Congress Cataloging-in-Publication Data is available.

ISBN 978-1-4767-6166-4
ISBN 978-1-4767-6167-1 (pbk)
ISBN 978-1-4767-6168-8 (ebook)

For my parents, Bill and Kathy Oakley

Life is pleasant. Death is peaceful.
It's the transition that's troublesome.

—Isaac Asimov

february

one

THE KALE IS gone. I'm standing in front of the open refrigerator, allowing the cool air to escape around my bare thighs. I've pushed aside the stacks of Tupperware containing leftovers of dinners that we'll never eat. I've searched the crisper, even digging beneath the wilted celery (does anybody ever use an entire bag of celery before it goes rubbery?). There was some type of slime that had accrued on the bottom of the drawer. I added cleaning it out to my mental list of duties. I even pulled all the organic milk and juice cartons from the top shelf and looked behind them. No dice.

The kale is definitely gone.

Then I hear it. The high-pitched squeal of Queen Gertrude, our Abyssinian guinea pig, coming from the living room. And I know what's happened to my greens.

I feel anger bubble up inside of me like a bottle of Dr Pepper that's been rolling around the floorboard of a car—just waiting for the top to be taken off so it can burst free from its confined plastic.

It's just kale.

It's just kale.

It's just cancer.

My anger is supposedly grief wearing a disguise. That's what the therapist said in the one session I agreed to attend four years ago when I had breast cancer.

Yes, *had*.

But now I think my anger is just anger at the possibility that I might have breast cancer again.

Yes, *again*.

Who gets cancer *twice* before they turn thirty? Isn't that like getting struck by lightning twice? Or buying two Mega Millions winning tickets in one lifetime? It's like winning the cancer lottery.

"Morning." Jack lumbers into the kitchen, yawning, in a rumpled T-shirt that says STAND BACK, I'M GOING TO TRY SCIENCE and his green scrub pants. He pulls a travel coffee mug from the cabinet above the sink and places it under the spout of our one-cup coffeemaker. He pops the plastic cylinder of breakfast blend into the machine and presses start. I inhale deeply. Even though I don't drink coffee anymore, I love smelling it.

"Jack," I say, having moved from my recon mission at the fridge over to the counter where the blender is set up. I pour a cup of frozen raspberries into the glass pitcher.

"Yeah, babe." He walks up behind me and plants a kiss firmly between where my ear and jawline meet. The *swack* reverberates in my eardrum.

"Benny!" he says, also directly in my ear, as our three-legged terrier mutt skitters into the room. Jack kneels on the ground beside me to greet him. "There'sagoodboy. How'dyousleep? Ibetyou'rehungry. YouhungryBennyboy?" Benny's tail whacks the mauve tile on our kitchen floor repeatedly as he accepts Jack's morning nuzzles and ear scratches.

Jack stands and heads to the pantry to scoop a portion of kibble for Benny's food dish.

"Did you feed Gertie the kale that was in the fridge?"

"Oh yeah," he shrugs. "We were out of cucumbers."

I stand there, staring at him as he grabs a banana from the fruit bowl on the counter and peels it. Benny is munching his breakfast contentedly.

Jack takes a bite of his banana, and finally noticing the weight of my gaze, looks at me. Then he looks at the blender. He lightly taps his forehead with his banana-free hand. "Aw, damn. I'm sorry, babe," he says. "I'll pick up some more on my way home from the clinic tonight."

I sigh and jab the blender's crush ice setting, making my morning smoothie, sans kale.

Deep breath.

It's just kale.

And there are children starving in Darfur. Or being murdered in their sleep. Is Darfur the genocide thing? I can't remember. Either way, bad things are happening to kids overseas, and here I am worried about a leafy vegetable.

And the possible come-back cancer.

But Jack doesn't know about the cancer because I haven't told him yet. I know, you're not supposed to keep secrets from your spouse, blah, blah, blah.

But there are plenty of things I don't tell Jack.

Like the fact that you can't just pick up organic kale at the Kroger down the street. The only grocer that sells it is more than eighty-five miles away, almost to Atlanta. And the farmer's market that I've been getting my organic kale from this season won't be open again until Monday. There is a small produce stand in Monroe that sometimes carries organic kale, but it's only open on Saturday. And today is Thursday.

Jack doesn't know any of this because he doesn't do the grocery shopping. He doesn't do the grocery shopping because the one time I sent him to the store for dishwasher detergent and a lemon, he came home with $125 of stuff we didn't need—like three pounds of rib-eye steaks and a case of forty-two snack-size plastic cups of mandarin oranges.

"Don't worry about it," I say. "I'll get some next time I go. It's no big deal."

It's no big deal.

It's no big deal.

I pour my pink-but-should-be-green smoothie into a glass and walk over to the counter where I keep my to-do list. I pick up the pencil lying beside the pad of paper and write:

4 Clean out vegetable drawer.
5 Call monroe to check on kale for Saturday.

Then I scan the other three things I need to accomplish today in between classes.

1 make flash cards for gender studies exam.
2 Buy caulk for windows.
3 Work on thesis!

My thesis. For which I still don't have a topic. I'm in the second semester of my master's degree program in community counseling and I have chosen, researched, and then discarded roughly six different themes for my dissertation.

"Diorama!" Jack yells, jarring me out of my thoughts.

My eyes focus on him as I realize what he's just said. Relief washes over me, and I temporarily forget everything else that has been weighing on my mind—kale, cancer, thesis.

"*Yes!*" I reply.

He flashes his teeth at me, and I focus on his off-center upper bite. It's the very first thing I noticed about him, and I found the flaw devastatingly charming. That's how I knew I was in trouble. Because when you don't like someone, you just think, "He's got some crooked teeth."

Still smiling, Jack gave me a slight nod of his head, obviously pleased with himself that he had remembered the word that had eluded us three nights ago when we had been flipping through the channels and landed on *Jurassic Park*.

"God, this is the best movie," he said.

"The best," I concurred.

"I loved it so much that I used it for my fifth-grade science project—"

"—analyzing whether it was actually possible to resurrect dinosaurs from the dead using mosquito DNA. And you won first place in the Branton County science fair," I finished for him, playfully rolling my eyes. "I've heard."

But my husband was not to be deterred from reliving his nerdy glory days. "The best part, though, was that thing I built with all the miniature dinosaur models. Dang, what are they called? God, I kept that forever. I wonder if my dad still has it."

"Terrariums?"

"No, those are with real plants and stuff. This was with the shoe-box and you look in one end of it—"

"I know what you're talking about. I just can't remember, wait—cycloramas? No, those are circular."

"It's on the tip of my tongue . . ."

And on we went for another few minutes, both drawing blanks on the word.

Until now.

"Diorama," I repeat, smiling.

And it's not the liberation that comes with finally remembering a word that escaped recall that makes me grin. It's Jack. My husband, who blurts out words with absolutely no context in the middle of the kitchen on a Thursday morning. And makes my heart fill with the wonderment and satisfaction of our connection. I suppose all couples feel this way at some point—that their bond is the most special, the strongest, the Greatest Love of All. Not all the time, just in those few-and-far-between moments where you look at the person you're with and think: Yes. It's you.

This is one of those moments. I feel warm.

"Why do you still drink those things?" Jack says, eyeing my home-made smoothie. He's now sitting on the countertop across from me, slurping a spoonful of milk-laden Froot Loops out of an entirely-too-big Tupperware bowl. Jack loves cereal. He could literally eat it for every meal. "You had cancer four years ago."

I want to give him my canned response when he questions my boring all-organic, antioxidant-packed, no-processed-anything diet: "And I don't want it again."

But today I can't say that.

Today I have to tell him the secret I've been holding inside for nearly twenty-four hours since I got off the phone with Dr. Saunders yesterday morning, because I physically haven't been able to say the words. They've been stuck in my throat like one of those annoying popcorn hulls that scratch your esophagus and make your eyes water.

I search the corners of my brain for the right way to say it.

The results of my biopsy are in. It doesn't look good.

So, my tumor marker numbers are up. Want to meet for lunch today?

You know how we had that party last February celebrating three years of me being cancer-free and the end of my every-six-months blood tests? Whoopsies!

But I decide to go with something simple: the hard, cold truth. Because no matter how much the doctor tried to lessen the blow with his "we just need to run some more tests," and "let's not panic until we know what we're dealing with," I know that what he really means is one terrible, horrible, no good, very bad thing.

I clear my throat. "So, Dr. Saunders called yesterday."

My back is to him, but the room has gone silent and I know if I turn around and look, his spoon will be hanging halfway between his mouth and the bowl, as if he's eating cereal in a movie and someone paused it to answer the phone, or go to the bathroom.

"And?" he says.

I turn in time to see him lower his utensil into the still-half-full Tupperware. He's now in slow motion. Or maybe I am.

"It's back," I say at exactly the same time the Tupperware slips out of his grasp and a waterfall of milk and Froot Loops cascades down his leg and onto the floor.

"Shit," he says, leaping off the counter.

I grab the paper towels from the holder behind me and start rolling off sheets until I have a bouquet big enough to sop up the mess. Then I bend down and get to work.

"Let me," Jack says, kneeling beside me. I hand him a wad of paper.

We attack the puddle in silence—shooing Benny away as he tries to lap up the sugary milk—and I know that Jack is absorbing the information I've just given him. Soon he'll chide me for not telling him sooner. How could I sit on this for a full twenty-four hours? Then he'll ask me exactly what Dr. Saunders has said. Word for word. And I'll tell him, as if I'm relaying bits of neighborhood gossip.

He said.

And then I said.

And then he said.

But until then, Jack will absorb. Ponder. Digest. While we—side by side—do our best to clean up this big, ridiculous mess.

BEFORE JACK LEFT for the vet hospital, he pecked my cheek, squeezed my shoulder, and looked me directly in the eyes. "Daisy. It's going to be OK."

I nodded. "Don't forget your lunch," I said, handing him the brown paper sack that I had filled the night before with a tuna sandwich, granola bar, and baby carrots. Then I walked to the bathroom to get ready for my day as he left through the back door in the kitchen. The rickety screen creaked as it opened and shut behind him.

What he meant was: "You aren't going to die." But I know I'm not going to die. It's only been a year since my last clean blood work, and I can't even feel the tumor they found on the mammogram when I poke and prod my left breast, so I'm sure they've caught it early, just like the first time. And the tests they want to run tomorrow morning will just confirm that I have breast cancer. Again. But that doesn't mean everything will be OK.

I don't want to go through surgery again. Or chemo. Or radiation. And I don't want to have a year of my life taken away from me while I endure these treatments. I know I'm behaving like a petulant child—stamping my foot and clenching my fists, eyes squeezed tight against the world. I don't wanna! I don't wanna! I don't wanna! I know I should be grateful. As far as cancer goes, relatively, I've had it easy. Which is why I'm ashamed to even admit my greatest fear: I don't want to lose my hair again.

I know it's vain, and so very inconsequential, but I love my hair. And while I tried to be all "strong, bald woman" last time, it just honestly wasn't a good look on me. Some people can carry off bald. I am not one of them. My chocolate mane has just started grazing my shoulders again—it's not quite as thick or polished as it once was, but it's long. It's feminine. And I appreciate it more now after having lost it once. I sometimes catch myself petting it, nearly crooning like I do when I stroke Benny's wiry fur.

Good hair.

Nice hair.

Stay, hair.

I also adore my breasts, which is why I didn't let Dr. Saunders lop them off last time. A lot of women go for it. Just take them! Just to be safe! They're just breasts! But I was twenty-three, and didn't want to part with them. Why couldn't the cancer have been in my thighs or my never-quite-flat-enough stomach? I'd have happily given those up. But please, for the love of God, leave my perfect, C-cup, make-most-men-do-a-double-take perky tits.

It's not like I was making a bad medical decision. A big article in *Time* came out right after my diagnosis, touting the results of a large study in Houston that found women who opt for a preventative double mastectomy have about the same recurrence rates as women who don't. I never read *Time*. I saw the article on the way to my sociology of crime class while I was peering over the shoulder of the student seated next to me on the bus. It's an omen, I thought. And when I brought it up to Dr. Saunders, he agreed that while the study was preliminary, the findings seemed solid—the choice was up to me. Now, four years later, sitting here with cancer once again, the random sighting of a magazine article doesn't seem so much like fate as it does me just believing what I wanted to believe so I could do what I wanted to do. I should have let them take my breasts. I shouldn't have been so vain.

I finish brushing my teeth and take one last glance in the mirror.

My hair.

My perfect breasts.

I inhale. Exhale.

It's just cancer.

I LIKE THE still of the morning. I'm alone in the house but revel in the reminders that I'm not alone in the world. Jack is gone, but his presence is still palpable. The indent on the bed, where his body warmed the sheets, beckons me. Maybe I could crawl in just for a second, I think. What is it about an unmade bed that's so tempting? I resist the urge, pull up the comforter, and smooth out the wrinkles. Then I fluff Jack's pillow, erasing the evidence of a good night's sleep and leaving it fresh for tonight's slumber.

I gather three pairs of his worn socks from the floor beside the bed and drop them in the hamper. Then I glance over at the open suitcase on the floor beside our dresser. Every year Jack and I celebrate February 12, the day—after months of chemo and six weeks of radiation—that Dr. Saunders called and said I was officially cancer free. Last year, for the third anniversary, we planned a quiet dinner for family and friends at my favorite restaurant. Jack was supposed to reserve the private room at Harry Bissett's, but the morning of the party when I called to ask if we could bring our own champagne, the manager said there was no record of our reservation. Jack had forgotten to make it. **Seriously, Jack? No reservations at H.B. Call everyone and tell them the party is off,** I texted him, furiously punching out each letter on my innocent iPhone.

When I pulled into our driveway that evening, I was still so frothing with anger, I barely noticed the cars lining the side of our narrow street. But when I walked in the back door, a chorus of voices shouted "Happy Cancerversary!" and my wide eyes took in the buoyant faces of our family and friends. Not only had Jack invited everyone to our place for an impromptu keg party, he had even ordered a few trays of chicken fingers from Guthrie's and lit the Clean Cotton Yankee Candles that I only take out for company. "I love you," he mouthed from across the kitchen where he was pouring my mom a glass of white zinfandel—the only wine she'll drink. I nodded, my cheeks flush with heat and my heart full of affection for my absentminded husband who, like a cat, somehow always manages to land on his feet.

This year, Jack surprised me by announcing he had planned an overnight trip for us. It's rare that I get to spend more than a few hours alone in the company of my overworked husband, who's one of a few overachieving individuals who's concurrently getting both his DVM and his PhD in veterinary medicine, so I'm particularly excited. We leave in two days, and my side of the suitcase is neatly packed, sweaters rolled, jeans folded, underwear and socks tucked into the mesh pocket. Jack's side is empty. I've been reminding him to fill it every night this week, even though I know he'll wait till the last minute, throw everything in Saturday morning, and then inevitably forget something important like his toothbrush or contact lens solution.

I let out an audible sigh. Out of the corner of my eye, I notice a half-empty, sweating glass on Jack's nightstand. I pick it up, rub the water ring off the pressed wood with the palm of my hand, and walk the glass into the kitchen.

When we first moved in together, I balked at Jack's lack of order and cleanliness. We were a newlywed cliché, though we weren't even married yet.

"I'm not your freakin' maid!" I spat during a particularly heated argument.

"I never asked you to be," was his cool reply.

We were opponents on a battlefield, neither one wanting to lose ground. Jack's stance was that clutter and mayhem didn't bother him; he wasn't opposed to cleaning, he just didn't think about it. I argued that if he cared for me, he would think about it and pick up after himself. Every dirty plate that I came across, every jacket or pair of shoes that didn't make it back into the closet, was a tangible insult. "I don't love you! I don't care about your feelings! I'm purposefully leaving my coffee cup on the bathroom sink to get under your skin! Ha! *Ha-ha-ha!*"

But like most people who decide to stick it out for the long term, I slowly learned to accept that his messiness was just that—

messiness. It wasn't a personal attack. And Jack made a halfhearted effort every now and then to straighten the mountain of papers on his desk in the study that threatened to avalanche onto the scuffed wood floor—and on really good days, he even remembered to return used dishes to the kitchen.

But they never quite make it into the dishwasher.

A cool draft greets me as I pour the dregs of multicolored milk from Jack's impromptu cereal bowl into the sink and load it into the dishwasher. I look up at the row of windows over the faucet, admiring their aged beauty while lamenting their inefficiency. Not only do they have the original glass panes from 1926, the year our house was built, the wooden frames around them have been painted so many times that many of them don't close all the way, leaving cracks where air sneaks in. They need to be completely replaced, but until we can afford that costly solution, I've just decided to caulk them shut. Job number thirty-seven on my interminable list of tasks to keep our Spanish bungalow from being deemed unin-habitable.

When we were house hunting two years ago, I immediately fell in love with its rounded doorways, red-clay-tile roof, stone front porch with black ironwork handrails, and yellow stucco exterior. I pictured myself lazily eating hunks of Manchego cheese and drinking wine under the large olive tree in the backyard. Jack wasn't as charmed.

"That's not an olive tree," he said, shattering my fantasy. "And this house needs a lot of work. The townhome was move-in ready. Fresh paint and all."

I shook my head, thinking of the arched nook in the hall and the antique phone I would find at a flea market to set on the recessed shelf. "This is it."

"I'm not going to have the time to do everything this house needs," he said. "You know what my schedule's like."

"But I do. I have time. You won't have to lift a finger. I promise."

He tried again. "Did you see the yard? I don't think there's a blade of grass to be found in all those weeds."

"I'll fix it," I said quickly. "You'll see."

He sighed. Jack knew me well enough to know once I set my mind on something, I wouldn't be deterred. He shook his head in defeat. "Only you," he said.

I smiled and snaked my arms around him, pleased with my victory.

"It will be perfect," I said.

But it was not perfect. Shortly after we moved in, I realized what Jack had first intuited (though I never would admit he was right)—it wasn't just a little TLC that the house needed. It was a lot. After I painted all of the interior cake-icing walls, got new air filters, pulled weeds in the yard, pressure washed the exterior, hired a handyman to build a new set of stairs on the back deck, and scrubbed, polished, and dusted everything in sight, our heater exploded. Into flames. Five months later, the air conditioner followed. Then a pipe burst, flooding the basement, and that's when we uncovered a mildew problem that had just been lying in wait behind the walls. And after putting out all those fires (literally, in the case of the heater), I still have a laundry list of little tasks I need to complete that I keep on the door of our fridge, like hiring an electrician to come install GFCI outlets, putting a new backsplash in the kitchen, buffing the original hardwood floors, and of course, caulking the won't-shut windows.

I finish loading the dishwasher and sponge down the counters. Then I grab a bag of baby carrots out of the fridge along with the lunch I had packed the night before and my daily to-do list and put it all into my shoulder bag, which I ease over my head and sling across my sweater-clad chest. Winter has behaved more like an early spring this week, so I leave my favorite black down coat in the hall closet, even though it's February.

I exit the house the same way Jack did, opening first the heavy wooden door with the handle that sticks and then pushing my way out the screen door. I let it slam behind me, delighting in the squeak of the rusted hinge, as I do every day. It sounds like summer, which has always been my favorite season.

I walk down the back steps to our one-car driveway. Whoever gets home last has to park on the street—usually Jack. I glance next door to Sammy's house. Her porch light is still on, so she probably stopped somewhere for breakfast after her shift. I'm a little relieved, because as much as I like her, she talks a blue streak, and a simple hi always turns into a fifteen- or twenty-minute fairly one-sided conversation (hers). And today I have just enough time to drive to campus, park my car, catch the university bus, and make it to the psychology building before class starts.

I navigate my Hyundai Sonata through the backstreets of my tree-lined neighborhood until I get to the baseball stadium. In the spring, if we're in the backyard, we can sometimes hear the crack of leather meeting wood and wonder if it was one of our Georgia Bulldogs or the opposing team that swung the bat. Neither one of us cares about sports enough to ever check and see who wins. It's one of the first things I loved about Jack—that unlike every other guy in this town, he didn't spend his Saturdays in the fall tailgating and guzzling beer and saying things like, "Coach has got to stop running that blitz every third down."

Like most other southern universities, Athens is a football town. It's also a college town by every sense of the definition. The thirty-five thousand students who attend the university make up a third of the city's population. When summer comes and the students pack up their belongings to head home or to study abroad in Amsterdam or the Maldives, the frenetic energy that fills every coffee shop, bus stop, and bar from September to May dissipates. The city seems to breathe, luxuriating in the space it has to stretch its arms until school is back in session.

But today, the energy is full and present as I slowly drive past throngs of kids loping to their classes, filling sidewalks, haphazardly crossing streets. I marvel at how young they look. At twenty-seven, I'm only a few years apart from the seniors, so I can't explain why it feels like lifetimes. Is it marriage that's aged me? The cancer? Or the realization and acceptance of mortality—something most college kids haven't quite wrapped their still-developing brains around?

Fortunately, I'm not the oldest in my master's program. A graying forty-something woman named Teresa sits near me in my Advanced Theories of Stress Management class. I imagine she's a divorcée and this is her *Eat Pray Love* experience. She's going back to school! Getting her counseling degree! Making something of herself! Jack says that's unfair. That maybe she just lost her job in the recession and is trying out a new career path.

Whatever the reason, I guess everyone has their story for why they are where they are. Mine, of course, has to do with the cancer. I started chemo right after graduating, and deferred my acceptance to my master's program for a year. But the next fall, when my treatment had long been finished, I still wasn't ready. My body was tired.

"Take a few years off," Jack said. "We'll get married. Have some fun."

That's how my husband proposed to me.

I accepted.

Then I got a job at a credit card call center where I wore a headset and flipped through psychology medical journals to pass the time. When a tone beeped in my ear, I pleasantly said, "Thank you for calling AmeriFunds credit." My job was to help people make balance transfers onto a new credit card with zero percent APR for twelve months. "After twelve months, the variable APR will be fifteen-point-nine-nine percent to twenty-three-point-nine-nine percent based on your creditworthiness," I explained to faceless voices on the other end of the line.

But my favorite part of the job wasn't really part of the job at all. Or it wasn't supposed to be. It was when customers would explain why they were opening the new credit card, giving me a glimpse into their lives. There were the happy clichés: "My daughter just got engaged. There goes the retirement fund!" And the abruptly sad: "My Herman usually took care of this kind of stuff. But he's gone now." I wasn't supposed to veer off the script, but if a supervisor wasn't hovering, I'd probe deeper ("How old's your daughter?" or, "When did he pass?"). And it occurred to me that most people just want to talk. To be heard. Even if it is by a stranger. Or maybe, especially if it's a stranger. I felt like I was doing a public service. Or that's what I told myself in order to feel better about my menial minimum-wage job. Either way, I liked it. The listening.

Until then, I had been going through the steps in becoming a psychologist. Checking off boxes on the life plan I had made when I was thirteen years old and watched *Prince of Tides* for the first time. I wanted to be Barbra Streisand, in a cushy chair and expensive diamonds, unlocking the mysteries of men's brains and irresponsibly falling in love. It all seemed so grown-up and glamorous. And though, like most thirteen-year-olds, I already thought I was the former, I desperately wanted to be the latter, as well.

After two years, when my manager wanted to promote me to the other side of the call center—the one that actually placed calls, instead of received them, I decided it was time to go back to school. I didn't want to be "a goddamned telemarketer" (my mother's term). I wanted—really wanted—to be a therapist.

I get to Gender Studies with five minutes to spare. I slide into a desk and take a pack of empty index cards out of my bag so I can fill them with concepts that I need to memorize for the exam we have next Tuesday. I delight, as I always do, at the idea of crossing something off my to-do list. But before I can put pen to paper, my cell buzzes.

It's my best friend, Kayleigh, who's a kindergarten teacher and isn't technically supposed to be using her cell phone during school hours while children are in her class. But Kayleigh doesn't give a fuck. In fact, when she dies, I'm 90 percent sure that's what her gravestone will read: "I don't give a fuck."

I silence my phone, sending Kayleigh to voicemail, because I do care, and because my professor, Dr. Walden, a tiny woman who's five feet tall on a good day, has taken her position at the front of the classroom and cleared her throat. I smile, anticipating what Kayleigh's message will say. Probably a diatribe about the nineteen-year-old UGA basketball player she's inappropriately sleeping with, or a bitch-fest about her goody co-teacher, Pamela, who wears pearls and sweaters with animals on them. Then I frown, because I have this feeling in the bottom of my stomach, like I've forgotten something. Did I turn the stove off? Did I remember to grab my lunch from the fridge? Is my car overdue for an oil change?

And then it hits me all at once, and I can't believe that I forgot, even for a second.

My cancer is back.

two

I'M NOT INDECISIVE. If someone asked Jack to pick out four adjectives from a list of characteristics to describe me, that would not be one of them. Stubborn? Yes. Organized? To a fault. Independent? Of course. Indecisive? Absolutely not. Which is why it's baffling that I have yet to decide on a thesis topic for my master's degree. I blame it on my adviser.

"Pick something that interests you," she said while I was trying to decide if I should tell her she had lipstick on her coffee-stained teeth. "You'll be eating, sleeping, and breathing it for a year."

Instead of being helpful, it paralyzed me. A lot of things interest me, but enough to garner my attention for a year? How do I choose?

That evening, I'm contemplating this for what feels like the thousandth time and mowing through a plate of roasted root vegetables on the couch when I learn from *PBS NewsHour* that a decorated soldier, who returned home to Wisconsin from Afghanistan with one less leg than he deployed with because he threw himself onto an IED saving the lives of two Afghani boys and their dog, is now in prison for shooting his wife and her sister in the head three times each. As Judy Woodruff interviews a psychiatrist on the effects of PTSD, I pause midchew. That could be an interesting thesis topic. PTSD and soldiers? No, I'm not especially interested in the military. But PTSD and its effect on children's cognitive development? Maybe. I like kids.

The familiar creak of the back door opening interrupts my thoughts. Benny, warm against my thigh on the couch, lets out a yip, but then lays his head back down, too comfortable to greet the intruder.

"Jack?" He's rarely home during *NewsHour* and my heart does a middle-school skip that I might get to see him before I expected tonight.

"Nope, just me," I hear before I see Kayleigh's wild spirals of hair and hunched shoulders fill the door frame of the den. Kayleigh rarely knocks, even though I've told her that one of these days she could regret it.

"Why?" she asked. "I might walk in on you and Jack mopping the kitchen floor with your naked bodies?"

"Maybe," I said. We actually did have sex in the kitchen once. I was boiling water for tea and Jack came in looking for a snack. It was right after we moved in and Jack had joked it was our homeowner's duty to consecrate every room of our house.

"Don't you mean consummate?" I asked him. He smiled and slipped his hand down the front of my jeans, and I let him, no longer caring about vocabulary or the kettle screaming at us from the stove.

"Ew," she frowned as if she, too, could see the memory replaying in my mind, and then: "When his car's here, I'll knock." But between his classes, clinic, and volunteer work, his car was rarely here.

"Oh," I say, sliding my empty plate onto the coffee table. "Hey."

"Nice to see you, too." She plops onto the couch beside me and props her skinny ankles next to my dirty plate. Everything about Kayleigh is geometric, from her cylindrical hair to her right-angle elbows and stick-straight parallel legs. In middle school, when curves sprouted on my body like an unwanted fungus, I envied her still-flat chest and protruding hipbones.

We sit in a comfortable silence that only people who've known each other for most of their lives can share, while the news show moves on to a story about vaccines.

"Do you have any microwave popcorn?" Kayleigh asks on a commercial break.

"Are you serious?" I look at her. "Do you know how terrible that stuff is for you?"

"Oh, Jesus, here we go," she says, and rolls her eyes.

"It's got this chemical, diacetyl, that causes lung scarring. The factory workers who make it? They get this disease called popcorn lung from working around the fumes all day."

"I'm not planning on huffing it," she says, shaking her head. "You watch too much news."

"Whatever. Hey, can you still take care of Benny and Gertie this weekend?"

"Yes! You've already asked me three million times. I promise I won't forget." She picks up the remote and clicks off the TV. "So, you'll never believe what Pamela did today."

"She took off all of her clothes and ran from classroom to classroom screaming 'the British are coming!'"

"No."

"Then you're right. I'll never guess."

"Do you have scotch?"

I nod toward our bar in the corner of the room. "Help yourself."

She stands up and pads over to the liquor cabinet, forgoing the Dewar's for Jack's good bottle of Glenlivet, and then starts in on her coworker's latest misdeed. "She found some conference in Kansas on this teaching method she's all obsessed with. Reggius? Reggio. I don't know. And she suggested to Woods that all the kindergarten teachers should go. To Kansas. What the fuck do I want to go to Kansas for? Why can't these conferences be in someplace awesome?" She takes a thoughtful sip of the scotch. "Like Vegas. I would totally go to Vegas."

As she's talking, I sit back in what Jack calls my "therapist pose" and wonder if Kayleigh's projecting: Freud's theory of rejecting your negative personality traits and attributing them to others. But Pamela's personality traits don't seem to be that negative. She's kind of a go-getter. Maybe a little bit of a suck-up, sure. But she's passionate and obviously loves her job. Of course, I don't say any of this to Kayleigh because Kayleigh hates her, which means I should hate her, too, out of solidarity.

That's something Kayleigh's good at. Not hating people, but loyalty. In the second grade when I had the chicken pox, she came over and watched *Karate Kid* with me over and over until her mother called and made her come home. It was summer, which meant she could have been out riding bikes or lying in her backyard trying to turn her ghostly pale skin pink and then red (she never tans), but she was holed up with me and Ralph Macchio. And when I had cancer, she was there again. While most of my friends faded away during the treatments—just like the cancer books and blogs had warned me—Kayleigh showed up more often, armed with gossip magazines and details of her latest torrid affairs to keep my mind off the pain.

Shit.

The cancer.

"Kayleigh," I say.

"I know, I know, it could be worse," she says. "I could be unemployed, the grass is always greener, blah, blah, blah—"

"My tumor markers are up," I say. Then I laugh a little, because it feels like I'm playing *The $25,000 Pyramid* and the answer is "How many different ways you can tell people you have cancer."

Her head snaps toward me. "What?" The word comes out of her mouth like a dart.

"They think it's back."

"Seriously?"

"Yeah."

"Wait, they *think*? So it might not be, right?"

"Well, I guess they know. Just not how . . . much. I have more tests tomorrow."

"Jesus."

"Yeah."

"What can I do?"

"Nothing, really," I say, and then, because neither of us has ever been big on sappy displays of emotion, I pick up the remote. "Can I watch my show now?"

"Yeah, of course," she says, pouring more scotch into her empty glass. The move comforts me. It means—like always—she's here to stay.

"OH MY GOD," Jack says, stretching his long arms above his head as he enters our bedroom. "I'm exhausted."

"I bet." I glance at the clock on my nightstand. "It's midnight."

Kayleigh left about an hour earlier and I got in bed to read and wait for Jack to get home.

I slide a bookmark between two pages to hold my place and set the book beside me on top of the duvet. Jack takes it as an invitation to crawl onto the bed and lay down directly on top of me, his full body weight distributed over mine.

"You're smushing me," I say into the side of his scratchy face. I inhale his evening scent—it's mostly Jack muddled with his lingering woodsy antiperspirant, a sharp contrast to his morning smell, which is all soapy and fresh and tingles my nose. I like the evening Jack best— even on days when he's had a surgery and smells faintly antiseptic.

"Good," he replies. It comes out muffled and his breath is hot on my neck. "Mmhungry."

"Did you eat dinner?"

He's silent and I know he's thinking about it.

"Seriously, Jack. I don't know how you forget to eat. Doesn't your stomach growl?" I push at his hips, heavy on my thighs. They don't budge. "Get off. I'll go warm you up something."

"No, it's fine," he says, rolling off me. "I'm too tired to eat."

He sits up and begins his nightly ritual of peeling his socks off one by one before shoving his feet under the covers and rolling up tight like a burrito in our sheets.

"What time is your appointment tomorrow?"

"Ten," I say, and before he can offer, I add: "You don't need to come."

Although I'm not sure he would have offered. Jack's on the ortho-pedic surgery segment of his clinical rotations this week, and tomor-row he's observing a hip replacement on a German shepherd. Except when he told me about it on Monday, it sounded more like: "AND I GET TO WATCH A HIP REPLACEMENT ON A GERMAN SHEPHERD."

"I can if you want," he says.

"No," I say. "You've got that hip thing."

"It's a dog. I can see that anytime."

"Don't downplay it. I know you're excited," I say. "Besides, it's just going to be a long day of sitting in the waiting room between tests, and I won't even be getting the results. Trust me. It will be mind-numbingly boring."

"Well, I can come and entertain you with my fascinating wit and intellect," he says, smiling.

I roll my eyes at him, but can't help returning his smile. "Really, it's not a big deal," I say, reiterating what I've been telling myself since I got off the phone with Dr. Saunders yesterday.

He stares at me for a beat and his eyes turn serious. I know he's trying to decide if he should push once more. He doesn't. "OK," he says, leaning over and nuzzling me just beneath my ear. I hear him inhale my skin through his nose and I wonder if I smell dif-ferent in the morning and evening, too, and which one he likes best.

"If you change your mind, I'll drop everything and come straight over," he says.

"Don't drop everything," I say. "What if you're holding the dog?"

"Ha-ha," he says, leaning away from me to switch the light on his nightstand off. And then, almost as an afterthought, he turns his head back toward me and crinkles his brow. "Have you called your mom?"

My body tenses. I had been meaning to. No, that's a lie. I had been doing everything I could to avoid it, really.

"Daisy," Jack chastises.

"I know! I know," I say. "I will."

Click. He turns out the light and I lean back into my pillow and try not to think about my mother or the come-back cancer.

I fail at both.

THERE ARE SEVEN cracks separating the large square cement blocks of the sidewalk leading up to the automatic sliding glass doors at Athens Regional. In four years, I have never stepped on any of them. Today is no exception. I slip through the silent doors and turn left toward the cancer center. I nearly run smack into a wrinkled woman supporting an elderly man down the hallway.

"I'm so sorry," I say, veering around their path.

She looks at me with kind eyes, then turns her attention back to her shuffling husband. That's love, I think. And for a split second I wish I had let Jack come with me.

A new receptionist greets me at the front desk. I nod to her as I sign in. "Is Martha on vacation?" I ask.

"Retired," she says. "Bought a motorcycle with her boyfriend and they're going cross-country."

"Good for her." I try to picture the gentle, white-haired, grand-motherly woman who had been my longtime liaison for paperwork, insurance questions, and scheduling appointments on the back of a Harley.

I pick an open chair in the waiting room and settle into it, avoiding eye contact with the other patients. It's something I've done ever since my very first visit when I accidentally met a man's gaze and he regaled me for forty-five minutes with his "cancer journey." He ended with an invitation to his weekly support group. All my life, I've been a joiner. In high school, it was Honor Society, Drama Club, SADD, Pep Squad. In college, Phi Kappa Phi academic fraternity, Students for a Free Tibet, intramural soccer, and LeaderShape. But this—this cancer crowd—this was a club I didn't want to belong to.

Magazines litter the side tables, but I stare straight ahead at the clock, willing time to tick faster. I want to fast-forward to tomorrow, my romantic weekend rendezvous with Jack, where I can pretend to be cancer free one last time before I get my sentence on Monday. While my mind is on the future, the fingers on my left hand begin tracing my past—the jagged scar that runs from the crease of my right elbow to midbicep. The wound has long since healed, but it's as if the skin was sewn back too tight. It often itches—and at the most inopportune times, like when I'm giving a presentation in class or waiting for sleep to overtake me at night.

It's a good conversation starter at parties. "Oh, this? This is the six-inch cut that saved my life." Wait for requisite gasps from my audience, and then "How?"

I'm glad you asked. It was finals week my senior year and I was having a study group over to my apartment for a class in which the professor was notorious for including ridiculously minute details of the lives of cognitive development theorists on his tests. I was planning to make homemade chicken enchiladas—the ultimate study comfort food. I reached up to the top shelf of my open kitchen cabinet where I kept my glass casserole dishes and *BAM!* An avalanche of Pyrex and CorningWare tumbled down on top of me. A dish must have broken in midair because when it made contact with my extended arm, it sliced it wide open, like a fisherman gutting a trout.

In the ER, when the doctor was reviewing the film of the X-rays to make sure there were no fractures, he noticed something not in my arm but in my breast, which had been captured in the edge of the picture. "See that small mass?" he asked, pointing to the film hanging from the light box. "It's probably nothing, but you ought to get it biopsied just in case." Turns out, it wasn't nothing. It was cancer. During the surgery to remove the tumor, they found it had already spread to my lymph nodes. Fortunately, it was nothing a little chemo and radiation couldn't handle. But if I hadn't broken the dish that cut my arm that led to the X-ray, they may never have caught it in time.

In this retelling of my tale, I don't mention the three panic attacks I had while waiting for the results of the biopsy. I don't mention the two surgeries I had to endure—thanks to a positive margin (which sounds like a good thing, but isn't) and a high ratio of cancerous sentinel lymph node cells after the first lumpectomy. And I don't mention that chemo and radiation were actually my only choices in treatment, thanks to my diagnosis of triple-negative breast cancer, meaning it tested negative for all three receptors that respond to the well-known and highly effective hormone therapy treatments like Tamoxifen and Herceptin. When it comes to cancer, people like the happy ending, not the boring details.

When I'm done with my story, audience responses vary. "Amazing." "God is good." "Talk about fate." "That is one lucky scar." I'm not sure who's right—whether it was fate, luck, or some divine intervention. But I am glad that when my mom was helping me unpack the kitchen in my new apartment, I ignored her advice to put the casserole dishes in the bottom cabinet instead of the top. "They're so heavy," she said. "It's dangerous for them to be up so high. What if they fall?"

"Daisy Richmond." A large black woman with a clipboard calls my name.

She leads me to an exam room, and I hesitate at the door. It's the exact same room where Dr. Saunders gave me the bad news four years ago—using his red dry erase marker on a whiteboard to detail the position of the tumor in my breast, explain the lumpectomy the surgical oncologist would perform, and teach me about margins and how radiation would work. By the time he was done with the lecture, the board was bleeding with his sketches, diagrams, and poor penmanship.

Is this a bad omen? Should I request a different room?

I sit down in the same uncomfortable blue chair near the door and stare at the blank white board hanging on the wall across from me.

My cell vibrates in the front pocket of my bag announcing a text message. I pull it out. It's from Kayleigh.

Sure you don't want me to come up there when school's out?

I'm fine! I want to shout. *It's just a few tests. It's no big deal.* But I know she's just being a good friend. And I know this tiny display of concern is nothing compared to what my mother would be doing right now. Even though Jack was right, and I should have called her, I'm glad that I didn't. Because no matter how many times I said, "Mom, that's all the information I have right now," she would have still peppered me with at least forty questions that I didn't have the answers to, and then she would have gotten overly dramatic and weepy and immediately made the hour-and-a-half drive from Atlanta to Athens so she could sit anxiously next to me all day, asking me every five minutes how I was feeling. Sometimes, it's just nicer to be alone.

I'm sure, I tap out to Kayleigh. As soon as I hit send, the door to the exam room opens and Dr. Saunders shuffles in.

"Daisy," he says warmly, and I'm instantly at ease. If there were a Zagat for doctors, Dr. Saunders would get five stars for bedside manner. Even though he called with every test result, I haven't actually seen him since I finished my radiation therapy three years ago. Nurses were the ones who drew the blood and squished my breast between the cold metal plates. I realize, strangely, that I missed him. As he engulfs my hand in his cozy bear paw, I quickly assess the discrepancies between my memory of him and the flesh and blood in front of me. He has a little less hair on top of his head and a little more girth in his midsection, but his eyebrows are the exact same as I remember them—large and furiously unruly, like two gray and black woolly worms resting above his wire-rimmed bifocals.

"Just couldn't stay away, could you?" He sets a folder on the counter beside my chair and starts flipping through it.

"Last time was so much fun, I wanted to do it all over again."

He chuckles, then looks up from my chart and claps his hands together. "OK, so like I told you over the phone, the biopsy from the little tumor they found on the mammogram came back positive. But your tumor markers and liver enzymes are a little more elevated than I'd like to see for such a small mass, so let's go ahead and get a PET scan and an MRI, just to make sure it's confined to the breast. You haven't had anything to eat or drink today, right?"

I agree that I've followed the orders that were given to me, and then, because I've never been good at waiting for anything, I ask: "Will I have to do chemo again?"

He puts his hand on my shoulder. "Let's just make sure we know what we're dealing with before we discuss treatment."

"Oh, and I saw a thing about a trial they're doing in Canada that condenses the radiation down to just one week, instead of six. Would I be a good candidate for something like that?"

"Still trolling the Internet for medical advice, I see." His lip curls on one side. His hand is still on my shoulder and he pats it reassuringly. "One thing at a time, Daisy. Any other questions?"

Only about a million. I bite my lip, shake my head no.

"Great," he says. "Rachel and Lativia will take care of you." He touches my shoulder a final time. "I'll see you Monday."

I dread the MRI the most, so I'm glad that the nurse says we're doing that one first. I keep my eyes shut for the entire forty-five minutes that I'm lying in the capsule and try to pretend that I can sit up and get out of it anytime I want. When the magnets *bang bang bang* overhead, I attempt to drown them out by going over to-do lists in my head.

Price wood-flooring refinishers.

Bang!

Take salmon out of freezer for Sunday dinner.

Bang!

Wash sheets and towels.

Bang!

Buy caulk.

Bang! Bang! Bang!

I grit my teeth. I didn't get a chance to buy caulk yesterday. When I called the farmer's market about the kale, the guy said he had a few heads and that I didn't have to wait until Saturday to get it. So after my last class, I drove to Monroe, and by the time I got back to Athens, I had to go directly home to let Benny out and make dinner.

After the MRI, the tiny exam room feels absolutely cavernous and I don't mind the two-hour wait between tests. I use the time to review my Gender Studies flash cards. Finally, a nurse comes into my room with a syringe and asks me to roll up the sleeve of my sweater. "This is the sugar solution for the PET scan." I nod. I remember from last time. "It will help us see where any cancer cells might be congregating." I follow her to yet another room and lie down for the second time that day in a machine that's far more open—and far less scary than the first.

Then, at the end of the long day, I'm free. I make my appointment for Monday with the new receptionist—"Does four thirty work? He's filled up solid until then"—and step out into the cool air. The sun is setting behind the pine trees that surround the parking lot, casting long shadows over the sidewalk. I let my eyes adjust to the dusk before I walk to the car, so I don't accidentally step on any cracks as I leave.

WHEN I WALK into our bedroom that night, after *NewsHour* and long before Jack gets home, the suitcase that awaits our overnight trip still sits on the floor near our dresser. Jack's side is still empty. I resist the urge to pack it for him and crawl into bed, exhausted from the day.

three

ON SATURDAY MORNING, I can see my breath when I run out the front door to get the newspaper that was thrown haphazardly in the dewy grass. It's as if winter decided it wasn't quite done yet and elbowed the brief respite of spring out of the way. I shiver in my cotton pajama pants and long-sleeve T-shirt and hurry back inside, even though it's not much warmer in our house of slightly cracked windows.

I snuggle into the couch, tugging a crocheted afghan I bought from a thrift store around my shoulders. I put my slipper-clad feet up on the coffee table, making the legs on the right side touch the ground. A significant hump runs the length of the floor in the den, causing the coffee table to act like a seesaw—if one side touches the ground, the other side hovers about half an inch above it. When we first looked at the house, Jack was concerned it was water damage that had warped the wood, but the inspector assured us it was just normal settling of the foundation on a house this old.

I pull the paper out of its plastic sheath and unfold the front page. Jack made fun of me when I called to order the *Athens Banner-Herald* delivery service shortly after we moved in. "You do know all of those stories are online, don't you? For free?" I tried to explain that curling up on the sofa with my computer didn't quite have the same soothing effect. That I enjoyed the gray smudge of newsprint on my fingers. That the slightly acidic, slightly musty smell of the pages reminded me of weekends in my childhood spent tracing the comics with a pencil on notebook paper while Mom read Dave Barry and hooted. If it was a really funny one, she would cut it out with the good scissors and affix it to the fridge door with a magnet, where it would stay until the paper turned yellow and the edges curled. Jack didn't understand any of this. He just shook his head at my purchase. "Only you."

"T minus forty-five minutes to departure," Jack announces from the doorway between the living room and the kitchen.

"Aye, aye, Captain," I say without taking my eyes off the headlines I've been scanning. Benny jumps up onto the cushion beside me and I scratch his ears. For Jack, forty-five minutes doesn't really mean forty-five minutes, so there's no urgent need to budge from the indent I've settled into on our worn couch.

"Daisy," Jack says.

This time I look up at him. And find that he's naked. Holding a mug full of steaming coffee. I burst out laughing. He leans against the door frame, nonplussed, crossing his right ankle over his left.

"Happy Cancerversary," he says with a clever grin. I jolt at the C-word. I was asleep when he got home last night, so when we woke up this morning, Jack immediately grilled me about the doctor visit and my tests, as if he could somehow glean the unknown results from every minute detail ("Did Dr. Saunders sound hopeful or worried?" "How did the technician look at you after the scan?"). Finally, when he was out of questions, we agreed we wouldn't discuss my tests or the possible results for the entire weekend so as not to put a damper on our time together. But the irony that the purpose of the trip was to celebrate me being cancer free wasn't lost on either of us. He pulls the cup to his lips with his left hand and takes a sip of the breakfast blend. The hot vapor fogs up his glasses.

"Jack, it's freezing in here!"

With his empty hand, he casually scratches the back of his shaggy scalp and I notice he's overdue for a haircut. He yawns. "That's why I was just about to take a hot shower. Thought I could use some help."

"Did you?" Jack and I rarely shower together. It's nice in theory, but someone is always left out of the water stream, standing like a wet dog in the freezing air. But I quickly dismiss the downside of the practice because Jack looks so devilishly cute. "You must be *really* dirty," I say, playing into his charade.

His smile spreads wider. "You have no idea." He casually crosses his arms, and in the process sloshes hot coffee onto his bare stomach. I swear I can hear it sizzle when it touches his flesh, but he doesn't flinch.

I suppress a laugh. "That really hurt, didn't it?"

"Immensely," he says, still not giving in to the pain.

I stand up and walk toward him, holding his gaze. When we're parallel, I reach my hand out to the now-red skin on his stomach and gently wipe the dripping mocha liquid off his abdomen. Then I lean close to his face, so close that I can see the soft downy fuzz on his cheeks, and whisper in one quick burst, "First one to the bathroom gets to stand under the showerhead." I take off like a shot and can hear Jack lumbering behind me. Just as I get to the bathroom door, his arm encircles my waist, throwing me off balance, and I shriek. We stumble to the ground, both laughing, Jack's naked hindquarters landing with a smack against the hardwood floor. Out of breath and still laughing, he leans over to kiss me. My T-shirt disappears over my head and Jack cups my left breast with his hand. He rubs the pad of his thumb over the small scar.

And though I don't believe in ESP, I know we're both thinking the same thought: Somewhere in there is another tumor. Olly olly oxen free. Come out, come out wherever you are.

Then Jack's thumb moves slowly to my nipple and I sharply inhale, grateful for the distraction.

Later, when I'm in the bathroom alone, pulling my hair up into a ponytail elastic to create a messy bun, I hear Jack in our bedroom next door, cursing. "Have you seen my jeans?" He owns three pairs, but I know he's referring to the only ones he wears in public, a dark blue wash from American Eagle. A purchase he made when I finally dragged him to the mall after trying to explain to him for months that holey, ripped-up jeans might have been a good look in high school when he was listening to "Smells Like Teen Spirit" on cassette single, but now it just makes him look homeless.

"In the dryer," I call back. I cringe thinking of the drawers that I'm sure he's rifled through and left looking like a half-off bin at Ross. It amazes me that as smart as Jack is, it never occurs to him to check various places in the house when he's searching for something. Isn't laundry the next logical step if you can't find an article of clothing in the dresser?

Jack passes the bathroom in his boxers and thunders down the rickety wooden steps to our dungeon of a basement in search of his pants. I take one last glance in the mirror and then walk into our room to start refolding all the clothing that's askew. A few minutes later, Jack returns wearing his freshly laundered jeans. "Babe, stop it," he says when he sees me. "I'll do that. You go relax." He takes the T-shirt out of my hands, and I have to physically stop myself from snatching it back from him. Jack doesn't fold shirts. He kind of rolls them up like individual sleeping bags and stuffs them haphazardly into the dresser.

I turn and perch myself on our king bed, trying to ignore Jack's imprecise method. "Did you pack your razor?" I ask.

"Yep."

"Boxers?"

"Uh-huh."

"What about your—"

"Daisy," he cuts me off. "I got everything. You worry too much."

After he pulls his socks on and stuffs his feet into a pair of scuffed brown boots that he's owned for as long as I've known him, he leans over to kiss my cheek.

"I'm gonna take our stuff to the car," he says. "You ready to go? Meet me out there?"

He leans over to zip the suitcase and hefts it out of the room.

As soon as I hear the back door creak open and slam shut, I hop off the bed and open the drawer where his shirts are smushed together like bulging Tootsie Rolls. One by one, I quickly pick them up and crease them in the exact center, then make a series of near-origami folds until each shirt is a perfectly rectangular cotton parcel. Satisfied, I close the drawer and grab my shoulder bag from the hook on the closet door. In the hallway I pause at the bathroom, then duck inside and pull back the shower curtain. I scan the tub, the vanity, and then open the medicine cabinet. And that's where I spot it. Jack did remember his toothbrush and razor, but his contact solution stands like a lone soldier left on the battlefield. I tuck it into the side pocket of my sack and yell "Coming!" when Jack calls to me from the back door.

"ARE YOU GOING to tell me where we're going?" I ask from the passenger seat of the Ford Explorer Jack has been driving since he got his license thirteen years ago. The air coming out of the vents hasn't warmed yet, so I tuck my cold hands under my thighs.

"It's a surprise," he says.

"Did you get a cabin in Ellijay?"

He laughs. "OK. Maybe it's not a surprise."

"You left the Web page up a few weeks ago." And then, even though I promised myself I wouldn't ask, that I would trust Jack to plan everything out, I say, "What are we doing for food?"

He drums his thumb against the steering wheel to the beat of the song coming through the speakers. Something by the Lumineers.

"Daaaaa-isy," he says, drawing out the "a" like he does when he teases me. "It's under control."

His BlackBerry sitting in the cup holder between us starts buzzing. He turns down the volume knob on the CD player in the dashboard.

"This is Jack," he says, holding the phone up to his ear.

My shoulders immediately tense as I recognize the formality of Jack's professional voice. *Please don't let this be an emergency*, I silently plead. This is the first time I've had Jack all to myself for a weekend in months and I don't want anything to ruin it.

"Do you have her on her stomach? OK, clamp your hand on her muzzle . . . Now start rubbing her back. Is she sucking?"

He exhales a breath. "Good. Now, if she sneezes, you'll need to clear the formula out of her nose. It means she's eating too fast . . . OK, call me if you need anything else."

He hangs up and runs his hand through his in-need-of-a-haircut mop.

"Is everything OK?" I ask.

"Yeah, that was Charlene. I literally *just* explained to her step-by-step how to feed Roxanne yesterday afternoon. I don't understand how she's made it this far in the program."

Jack belongs to the Wildlife Treatment Crew, a volunteer group for vet students at the university. When he was on call last weekend, someone brought in a baby raccoon after they had accidentally killed its mother with their car. Jack immediately dubbed it Roxanne and has been nursing it back to health at the vet hospital— feeding it every three hours, weighing it daily, and keeping it warm with heating pads. I had stopped in to bring him dinner one night and seeing him with the bottle, cradling the little creature, made my ovaries hurt.

"Well, it was sweet of her to take over for you while we're gone," I say, aiming a vent, now full of hot air, so that it blows directly on me.

"I just hope she doesn't screw up."

After driving for a few hours, Jack turns the car into the cracked parking lot of a strip mall desperately in need of renovations. He pulls into a parking spot in front of a glass door with a sign that reads: Sky Blue Cabin Rentals. The parking brake screeches as he sets it with his foot, then he turns to me and nods his head in the direction of the Ingles next door. "Do you want to run in and stock up while I check in and get the keys to the cabin?"

"Ah!" I say, vindicated. "I should have known that 'under control' meant I was going to be getting the food."

He smiles and leans toward me, pecking me on the nose. "That's just because you're so good at it."

I sigh, because I can't deny the truth.

While pushing my squeaky-wheeled cart full of questionable chicken breasts, half-wilted vegetables, and a four-pack of toilet paper—who knows what the cabin stocks and doesn't?—I'm cursing Jack under my breath for not giving me a heads-up so I could have properly prepared and packed a cooler full of my organic, healthy foods. In the spirits aisle, I pick up a dusty bottle of pinot noir. It appears that the locals don't drink too much fine wine in these parts. I wipe it with my sleeve and place it into the cart next to the only three zucchini I could find that weren't rubbery to the touch.

"Daisy!"

I start and am grateful that I had just put down the wine or I would've dropped it.

"What, Jack?" I say, irritably.

"Don't be mad."

"Oh, Jesus. What is it?"

"Promise you won't be mad."

"Fine." I put my hand on my hip to wordlessly convey that my promise actually means nothing.

"They can't find our reservation."

"*What?*" I roar. "Why not?"

"Well"—he drops his head and averts his eyes from my direct gaze—"I may have kind of forgotten to make one."

I open my mouth to speak and then close it. I'm not mad. I'm furious. That's two years in a row he's forgotten to make a reservation on my Cancerversary, but now we're two and a half hours from home, in a backwoods mountain town without organic vegetables, oiled shopping carts, and—most important—a place to sleep. I look at Jack and silently wonder if he can see the steam coming from my nostrils.

And that's when I realize that he's laughing.

"What. Is. So. Funny." My teeth are clenched so tight I can almost feel the enamel wearing off them.

"Man, you should see your face." He holds the cabin keys up at my eye level and jingles them. "Daisy, I'm joking. We're all set. I can't believe you bought it."

I tilt my head and cock an eyebrow at him. The tension has fled my body, but my stomach is still roiling.

"OK, I guess it's not that unbelievable," he mutters.

Even though the trees are naked skeletons from their winter slumber, the view of the Blue Ridge Mountains from the cabin's cold wall of windows is still striking. Jack is crouched in front of the fire, knocking the hot embers around with a metal poker. Flames pitifully spit from between the lengths of wood. "Wonder what I'm doing wrong," he says, half under his breath. He's palming his BlackBerry in the other hand, studying the screen where he's Googled "how to make a fire."

I smile at the back of his frustrated head from the couch, where I'm sitting on my feet and cupping a goblet of wine. I often revel in Jack's inability to grasp such simple, everyday tasks because his advanced intelligence intimidated me so greatly when we first met. So much so that in preparation for our third date, I had mentally practiced an entire soliloquy based on Dr. Helen Fisher's science of love research that I had just studied in my Psychology of Human Sexuality class. I wanted so desperately for Jack to find me his intellectual equal.

"It's really fascinating," I said. We were sitting close on a worn velvet couch in an independent coffee shop, our mismatched china touching on the tiny table in front of us alongside a half-eaten cranberry muffin. His thigh was pressed against mine, and it unnerved me in the best possible way. "Using functional magnetic resonance imaging, she studied the brains of people in love and found that it's actually just this heady mix of chemicals. Dopamine floods the posterior dordate causal—"

"Dorsal caudate," Jack corrected me, smiling his crooked smile.

Heat crept into my face. "Right, that's what I meant. And, um, the prefrontal cortex." I was flustered from my mistake, and groped for the right words, determined to impress him. "It's really a motivation, or reward system—not an emotion. Like a drug addiction. In fact, the brain chemistry of those in love is the same as people who are on cocaine. It stimulates the same neurotransmissions."

"Transmitters," he said gently.

"What?"

"Neurotransmitters."

Ugh. Why did his undergrad degree have to be in biology? And what was I doing on a date with a double-doctoral student anyway? I was a lowly junior majoring in psychology—a degree I had realized most people settled on when they didn't know what else to do because it sounds good—and I didn't even know what a neurotransmitter was, exactly.

I took a sip of my coffee, hoping that my shaking hand wouldn't betray me and slosh the hot liquid over the side, although I was already positive that I had ruined my chances for a fourth date. I steeled myself and took a deep breath. I might as well finish my speech, I thought. There wasn't much more damage I could do. Except when I searched my brain for all the other scientific terms and interesting factoids I had memorized, they weren't there. My cheeks were positively on fire at this point, so I just sort of waved my hand and concluded my botched minilecture with this: "So basically, it's not real, you know."

Jack tilted his head, obviously amused—and confused—by my stupidity. "What isn't?" he asked.

"Love." I couldn't look at him as I said the word. I was afraid the definition of it was written all over my face.

He was silent, and I felt rather than saw his body lean closer to mine. He smelled clinical, like someone who spent the day in close proximity to formaldehyde would, and I found it intoxicating. I glanced up at him and thought wildly for a second that he was going to kiss me, and my stomach flipped at the anticipation alone. Our second date had ended with our first kiss, and I was eager to pick up where we had left off. But this time, he stopped inches from my lips. "You have a crumb," he said, wiping the side of my mouth with his thumb. He sat back, and I put my fingers up to my face where he had touched it.

"Thanks," I said weakly. I looked up at him and he was grinning, as if he were having a secret laugh at my expense. My embarrassment flared, and an irritable "What?" escaped my lips.

"Nothing," he said, shaking his head. "I just think Dr. Fisher might not know what she's talking about."

"Why's that?" I asked, still fuming.

"Because," he said, taking a bite of the muffin we were sharing, an avalanche of crumbs cascading down his shirtfront. But instead of finishing his thought, he changed the subject to something he had studied that day—influenza in fish or something equally ridiculous—and left me reeling with the notion that I had just blown it with him. It wasn't until months later that he confessed it was at that moment he knew he loved me.

My belly warms at the memory and I call to my husband from my perch. "Leave it. It's plenty cozy in here." He doesn't turn and I know that he hasn't heard me. Like a caveman, he is singularly focused on conquering fire.

Later, at the pine farm table in the kitchen, when I'm a little woozy from my two glasses of wine and so much unadulterated time with my husband, Jack interrupts our comfortable silence.

"Are you worried? About the cancer?"

The air leaves the room, like he's announced "Voldemort!" in the middle of Hogwarts.

I stare at him and we have a mini conversation with our eyes.

So we're talking about this? mine ask.

We're talking about this, his answer.

I take a deep breath. "A little," I say, and I'm relieved to admit it, since I've spent the last three days pretending otherwise.

"Me, too," he says. He runs his index finger around the rim of his wineglass and stares into the plum liquid. I wait, and let him put his thoughts in order. When it comes to serious topics, Jack doesn't like to speak until he knows exactly what he's going to say. He takes a deep breath. "I know the lumpectomy isn't a big deal, but what if you have to do chemo again? I graduate in three months and I thought we were going to finally start trying for a"—he clears his throat and looks at me—"a baby."

Maybe Jack can surprise me, after all. "You did?"

"Yeah. I want a little dude to buy telescopes for and rocket kits and ant farms."

"Or little dudette," I say, raising my eyebrows at him.

"Or dudette," he concedes, sighing heavily.

I laugh and the full sound comes straight from my gut.

A baby. Jack and I had always talked about becoming parents in that vague way that most couples do—"One day when we have kids . . ."—but we had never pinpointed a date. I assumed that Jack didn't really think about it. That he had enough on his plate getting both his DVM and PhD concurrently. And then I thought when he graduated, he would have another checklist of excuses to delay parenthood—*Just let me get board certified. Maybe you should finish school. Let's wait and see about the tumor.* Or maybe those excuses are mine.

But the thing is, sitting across from Jack and seeing the sweet eagerness in his eyes, the justifiable reasons to not have children melt away, and all I can see is a phantom tot with Jack's flat feet and erratic wisps of my chocolate hair, Jack's eagerness to laugh, and my eagerness to line up matchbox cars in parallel rows.

"That sounds . . . perfect," I say. "I mean, everything but the ant farms."

And we sit smiling at each other like two kids who have been locked in an FAO Schwarz overnight.

We make love again after dinner on a queen-size bed directly underneath a startled deer head. Then, as I brush my teeth at the bathroom sink, Jack rifles through our shared toiletry case. "Your contact solution?" I ask, knowingly.

"Yeah," he says.

"In the side pocket of my shoulder bag."

He grins and playfully swats my naked bottom as he strolls past me. "You're going to be a great mom."

four

Buy caulk. I underline the sentence seven times to give it weight on the page. So now when I look at my list, it shouts at me: *buy some effing caulk! Calm down,* I silently tell it. *Life is good. I'll get the caulk.*

But you have cancer, the paper says.

Whoa. Mind your own business. I slide the list back into my shoulder bag and pull out my iPhone. I'm sitting in the Tate Student Center, killing the free hour between my Monday classes. I abhor this sixty minutes—it's too short to go off campus and actually do anything productive.

I Google flooring companies in Athens and call the first one that pops up. A man who sounds like he's been smoking longer than I've been alive says he can come to our house on Tuesday afternoon to give me a free estimate. I thank him and hang up, and then add the appointment to my calendar app.

That settled, I return my phone to its pocket and take my flash cards out of my bag. I stare at my black block handwriting on the index card: Matrixial Trans-Subjectivity Theory. The name of the psychoanalyst comes to me quickly: *Ettinger.* But I blank on the details. The only thing my brain seems to want to recall is the weekend spent with Jack. I'm still all pie-eyed and swoony for my husband, who now so wants to be a dad. And the only obstacle standing in the way to the rest of our lives is a doctor's appointment.

I make it through the rest of my classes—nervous energy escaping my body through toe tapping or knee jiggling—and find myself at the end of the day sitting, once again, in the uncomfortable blue chair in the exam room waiting for Dr. Saunders. I swallow down the guilt at not letting Jack come with me for this either.

"If you come, that means we expect it to be bad," I reasoned to him in bed last night.

"That's ridiculous," he said. "You're not even superstitious."

"It's not superstition!" I protested. "It's like that book—*The Secret*? We have to put out into the universe what we want to happen. If I go alone, I'm announcing to the world that it's no big deal. I'm conjuring good results."

"What, are you Wiccan now? Seriously, Daisy, I'm coming," he said.

I switched tactics. "You can't miss clinic. If you miss too many days, Ling won't let you graduate and I'm not going to have that on my shoulders."

That, at least, was partly true—Jack had been working on his dual degree for seven years and I'd be damned if I was the reason he didn't graduate on time. But the real reason I was fighting him so hard was that I hated to be seen as weak—especially by Jack. It's why I didn't let anyone go with me to my chemo appointments the first time around and why I preferred to be left alone when puking into the toilet or the plastic bucket beside my bed if I didn't make it to the bathroom. "Shut the door!" I'd yell out between dry heaves to whoever was on sick-patient duty—Jack or Kayleigh or my mom.

"I think Ling will understand," he said.

I switched back to my original argument, telling him if he did come with me, he was basically saying he wanted the results to be awful.

"You're unbelievable," he said, but I could tell I was wearing him down.

I shrugged. "It's how I feel."

Now, even though Jack was right and I don't really believe in *The Secret* or superstition, I silently repeat the positive thoughts I've been harboring.

Tiny tumor.

No chemo.

Tiny tumor.

No chemo.

My stomach growls, but before I can reach into my bag for the carrots I brought, the door opens. I look up. Instead of woolly worms, I see the perfectly arched and plucked brows of the nurse who did my PET scan. Her name tag reads LATIVIA. "Follow me," she says. "Dr. Saunders wants to speak with you in his office." This is strange because I've never been to Dr. Saunders' office. He must not need the whiteboard in the exam room this time, which can only mean that everything is better than expected. Sick people have to be in exam rooms. Healthy people sit in offices. But if that's the case, why does it feel like I'm walking through air as thick as mud, as if I'm nine and have been summoned to the principal?

Lativia stops outside an open office door. The placard on the wall beside it announces:

Dr. Robin Saunders
Radiation Oncologist

I pause because I had never noticed before that Dr. Saunders has a girl's first name. Then I walk in without the nurse and she closes the door behind me. Dr. Saunders is sitting in a large leather captain's chair. He doesn't look at me.

"Daisy," he says, taking off his glasses and setting them on the desk.

"Dr. Saunders," I reply, sitting down across from him.

Then his eyes make contact with mine and I see that they're sad. They're sad in the way that other people's eyes are blue or brown or green. Dr. Saunders' eyes are the color of sad. And that's how I know what he's going to say before he even says it.

"It's not good."

I feel heavy, as if all the clothes I'm wearing have been soaked in water.

He turns his computer screen toward me. "This is a normal PET scan," he says. The image on the screen looks like a dark blue neck pillow with a few blurry patches of yellow, green, purple, and orange. It's like a Rorshach test in color. Dr. Saunders picks up a pencil from his desk. "Picture the human body as a sliced loaf of bread—the PET basically shows us images of each piece. So this one happens to be a cross-section of the lungs." He uses the pencil as a pointer. "Here's the spinal cord, the lungs, the breasts." He hits a few buttons on the keyboard in front of him and the image changes. "We can move up and down through the body section by section. See how the heart is glowing in this one? All the cells in your body typically eat some form of sugar. The hungriest ones eat the most, so the sugar molecules we injected into your body congregate where the hungriest cells are—like the heart, kidneys, and any areas where there are tumors or cancer cells." He pauses and looks at me to make sure I'm following. I don't say anything.

"So like I said, this is a normal PET. The heart is orange and yellow, but there's not much in the lungs, liver, brain, etcetera." He manipulates the keys again and another image pops up. "This," he says, "is your PET scan."

I stare at the screen. It looks as though it's on fire.

"Daisy, the cancer is everywhere. You've got mets in your liver, a few in your lungs. Your bones. And even . . ." He falters for a minute, and this sliver of emotion reminds me that he is delivering this news to me, about me, and not just teaching a class on PET scans. He takes a deep breath, punches some more keys, and the image changes into a clear cross-section of a brain. There is a large glowing orb at the bottom of the picture. "You have a tumor in the back of your brain the size of an orange."

My hand reaches up to the back of my skull. I prod the skin beneath my hair, looking for a piece of fruit. I don't feel anything.

"I don't understand," I say sluggishly. My mouth feels like I've been chewing molasses. "It's only been a year. All my six-month checks were clear."

He shrugs and slowly shakes his head. "I'm so, so sorry. Unfortunately this happens sometimes. A patient goes from six-month check-ups to annuals and the cancer sneaks in. Yours is particularly aggressive."

Aggressive. The word triggers that football cheer and I can't help but silently chant: *Be! Aggressive!* You've got to be *aggressive!*

Brains are funny that way. The memories they conjure. The tumors they grow.

"Daisy, I know this is a lot to take in, but it's not all bad. You're asymptomatic, which is a good thing. It means you feel good, and you could continue feeling good."

He's wrong. I don't feel good.

"And the tumor is in a good spot. Easily removable. Of course, neurosurgery has its own dangers, so you'll want to talk to the surgeon and weigh the risks. Then, if you want, we could do radiation, make sure we zap any other cancer cells in the brain. For the rest, we can try chemo, see if anything responds to that. We'll look into clinical trials—"

"You're saying I can be cured, that you can cure"—I wave toward the glowing screen—"all this?"

He puts the pencil he's been playing with back on his desk. "I don't—" He stops. Tries again. "I'm not—" Another break. He sounds like a skipping record. "No." He scans his desk with his eyes, as if the words he wants to say are written on a piece of paper somewhere and he just needs to find it. "I'm saying we can . . . prolong things."

"Prolong things." I have become a parrot. "For how long?"

"It's hard to say," he says.

"How long if I don't do anything?"

"Hard to say."

"There must be statistics."

"I don't work in statistics," he says. "You're not a statistic."

"Dr. Saunders." I will him to look me in the eyes. "Tell me how long."

He takes a deep breath and puts his glasses back on. "Textbook for stage four is 20 percent survival rate." He pauses, glances at me, then back down at his desk. "Yours is fairly . . . advanced. If I had to guess . . ." He looks at me again.

I nod.

"Four months. Maybe six."

I quickly do the math. June. Or August.

"But listen, people can live for years. It's not unheard of. And of course there are complementary therapies, diet, meditation—"

I stand up and he stops talking. I need to leave the room, but my legs suddenly feel hollow, like two straws holding up a potato, and I don't think they'll support my weight. I sit back down.

I stare at Dr. Saunders' furious eyebrows, while the last two words he spoke run on a loop in my head. Diet. Meditation. Diet. Meditation. Diet. Meditation. I tried that already, I want to say, but I don't have a voice. So I think it instead. I list out all the things I've done the past four years to prevent a moment exactly like this one. Yoga. I hate yoga. Roasting, broiling, steaming, and sautéing every vegetable known to man. I hate vegetables. Breathing exercises. Preparing 1,467 smoothies. Give or take. Drinking 1,467 smoothies. Give or take. Eating blueberries. Eating pomegranates. Drinking green tea.

Drinking red wine. Taking fish oil. Taking coenzyme Q10. Avoiding secondhand smoke like the plague.

And yet, here I am.

I stand up again on my straw legs. Dr. Saunders stands, too. Reaches out to me.

"I need to leave," I say.

"Daisy, let me call someone. Jack. You shouldn't be alone right now."

I shake my head. Jack. There's not enough space for him in my brain right now, so I push his name away and try to focus on the information at hand.

An orange.

Four months.

So, so sorry.

"Daisy," Dr. Saunders tries again. He's now standing, too, and he reaches for the phone.

"Don't," I say. I glance at my watch. 5:52. This day is almost over, but there is still so much I need to do. I mentally force steel into my extremities, lift my chin up, and sling my shoulder bag across my chest. Then I meet Dr. Saunders' gaze and say: "I have to go buy caulk."

I STIFLE A giggle all the way to the parking lot, and when I finally slide into the front seat of my car, I let out a loud guffaw. Though I'm looking at my steering wheel, I can only see Dr. Saunders' face—his bushy brows forming half-moons over his bulging eye sockets, his mouth a perfect O. His countenance was hilariously frozen. Shocked into silence by my declaration.

He thought I said "cock" instead of "caulk."

The word hung in the air, and when I realized the source of his bewildered confusion, I mumbled something about my won't-shut windows that were really quite beautiful but completely impractical and quickly walked out the door of his office, closing it behind me.

My shoulders convulse uncontrollably and I feel a rivulet of tears meander their way down my cheeks. This sets off another wave of laughter, because I'm crying but not really crying. Not the way I'm sure most people would cry after getting the news I've gotten.

The cock/caulk conundrum has caused me to be the very definition of hysterical.

And all I can think is: "I can't wait to tell Jack."

HERE'S SOMETHING THAT I didn't know until today: The Home Depot offers a gratuitous selection of caulk. I stand in front of the display, staring at the labels.

All-purpose
Latex Acrylic
Clear Door & Window
Silicone Kitchen & Bath
White Window & Door
Supreme Silicone

If I look at them hard enough, maybe one of the tubes will jump out into my hand. Or reveal itself in a quiet but urgent whisper: *Daisy! I'm the one for you!* When it becomes apparent that won't happen, I start to get annoyed. What is the difference in the recipe of each caulk that warrants an entirely new product and label? It's the same way I feel when I shop for toothpaste. Why are there so many goddamned choices?

"Can I help you, miss?" A man in an orange apron is staring at me. He has crinkly eyes and a full mustache-and-beard combo. My dad had a mustache-and-beard combo. Before he was hit by a pickup truck at an intersection while riding his Cannondale. The collision caused his head to mop the pavement, which removed his ill-fitting helmet, and then most of his skin and facial hair. I was three when he died. A faint memory of him resurfaces at times—a man is nuzzling my neck, his sour breath familiar, his wiry whiskers scratching my chin.

I look at this man's face and wonder if his beard would feel the same against my skin. I take a step toward him. Then I stop myself.

"I need caulk," I say.

"Excuse me?"

I register the look on his face as one of confusion, and wonder if he, too, thinks I've said "cock."

Then I realize that I didn't say caulk at all. I actually said, "I need toothpaste."

And I may have added "Dad." As in: "I need toothpaste, Dad." A giggle bursts out of my mouth and I clasp my hand over it.

"Are you OK, ma'am?"

I consider his question. No. I'm not OK. And I feel compelled to tell him the reason why. To explain my erratic behavior.

"I'm hungry."

WHEN I PULL into the driveway at 8:37, Jack's car isn't there. My phone has rung seven times—eight? Ten? Really, I've lost track—since I left Dr. Saunders' office, but I've been letting the tune play on, nodding my head to the rhythm of it, as if it's just another familiar song on the radio. I jam my foot onto the parking brake, step out in the chilled, hollow night and walk around to the trunk, where the bagboy at Kroger helped me stash more groceries than Jack and I could possibly eat in a month.

There's a movement in the bushes to my left.

I look over, trying to make out the shape of a squirrel or possum, but I'm blinded by our porch light and can't see into the pitch black untouched by its glow.

Then a hulking form comes into view and I gasp.

"Daisy."

"Holy shit, Sammy." I put my hand over my rapidly beating heart "You scared the heck out of me."

"Sorry," she says. "I thought you saw me when you pulled up."

"What are you doing out here in the dark?" I ask, noticing that her house is shrouded in shadows. Not one light is on.

"I just got home from my shift," she says, and now that my eyes have adjusted, I can see her shiny bike locked up to the railing of her porch steps. "Must have forgotten to leave some lights on. I was in a hurry when I left this morning 'cause mom called and she just talks and talks and talks. Never can get her off the phone. Finally, I was like, 'Mama! Gotta get to work.' She still talked for at least ten or more minutes. Luckily, boss was out of the office when I finally got to the station."

She steps closer and I take in her uniform—government-issued blue cargo pants, black shoes, gray short-sleeved button-up with a patch on the arm that reads: Athens Clarke County Police Department. A belt cinches at her waist, and she looks like a gray and blue snowman: three round segments stacked atop one another to create a person. Sammy's a cop. Well, a bike cop. I don't know if that means she's a full-fledged police officer, or a junior one—like a Cub Scout who hasn't graduated to Boy Scouts yet. I've never had the heart to ask her. She spends most of her time ticketing drunk college students, and arresting them if they're underage. I asked her once after she handcuffed someone how she then transported them to the station. She said that she called for a backup patrol car, but all I could picture was her somehow strong-arming these inebriated kids onto her handlebars and joyriding them all the way to their incarceration. The comical image has stuck with me.

"Having company this weekend?" she asks, eyeing the plastic shopping bags nearly spilling out of my open trunk.

"Nope." I scan my purchases and I can't recall even one thing that I bought—as if I were on Ambien and sleep-shopping. I scramble for an explanation. "I went to the store without a list." As I say it, it hits me that I have never gone shopping without a piece of paper dictating what I will buy. Ever. This tiny rebellion thrills me.

"Ah," she nods. "I make the same mistake when I go to the store hungry, which seems to be every time I go. Doughnuts, fried chicken, those little peanut-butter-stuffed pretzels . . . I just buy everything in sight." She gestures to her doughy figure and grins. "Obviously."

Sammy comments on her weight often, as if she learned as a chubby kid on the playground that survival skill of getting to the punch line before anyone else could. Typically her self-deprecation makes me cringe. I never know what to say—should I laugh along with her? Placate her with denial? I often just change the subject to smooth over any awkwardness I might feel.

Tonight I just return her smile. "Then I broke the two cardinal rules of grocery shopping."

She hooks her thumb in the waistband of her pants and tugs back and forth, adjusting the fit. It's a movement her hand makes unconsciously and often, much like my hair petting. "I'll help you carry them in," she says, her sausage fingers already reaching to scoop up a load of bags, like the claw in that arcade game grasping for stuffed dolls. "So you know how I was hearing that scratching noise in my walls at night?"

I grab a few bag handles and lead her up the back steps of my house while she launches into a story about flying squirrels. At least I think that's what she said. I'm only half paying attention. I set my haul down at the top of the landing and fish for my keys in my shoulder sack. I hear Benny whining and scratching at the other side of the door, and guiltily realize he hasn't been out since I left for school that morning.

As I open the door, a ball of fur shoots past us and down the steps.

Sammy takes a break from her narrative to comment: "Little guy's quick on those three legs," then she picks back up with her tale. A high-pitched shrieking assaults us from the direction of the living room. I put the groceries on the counter and reach into my bag for a few of the carrots that I had packed that morning but not eaten. I walk into the living room and slip them through the bars of Gertie's cage. I know that I've been rude, leaving right in the middle of Sammy's story, but there's a disconnect in that knowledge and the emotion that's supposed to accompany it. "Here you go, girl," I coo quietly. "I bought you some cucumbers, too. Your favorite." She twitches her ears in appreciation and begins munching on a carrot. With her squealing silenced by food, the house is quiet and I wonder for a moment how long I can stand exactly where I am, not making a sound. Maybe Sammy will just leave. Maybe she already has.

But when I return to the kitchen, Sammy's coming back in the door with another load of groceries, Benny at her heels. She seems unperturbed by my bad manners and continues with her story, presumably where she left off. It takes us two more trips to get all the groceries in from the car, and the bags cover nearly every inch of floor and counter space.

"And then the exterminator is telling me—get this—that they don't really fly. Not like bats or whatever. They don't have wings or anything. They glide. They should be called gliding squirrels, he says. And I said I don't care what you call them, I just don't want them in my house, you know?" Her deep belly laugh causes the corners of my mouth to turn up perfunctorily. I'm like Pavlov's dog. Someone laughs, I smile in return.

But Sammy's not looking at my response. She's already started to unload purchases, opening cabinets, the pantry, the fridge, placing things at random according to where she thinks they should go. When she places a Styrofoam package of chicken on the third shelf of the fridge, I open my mouth to tell her that meat goes in the drawer above the vegetable crisper. Then I close it. I don't have the energy.

I pick up a box of Cheez-Its from a bag on the counter. The unnaturally orange crackers pictured on the red cardboard beckon me. I used to love Cheez-Its. I slip my finger under the tab on the box top and peel open the plastic bag inside. I stand in the middle of my kitchen eating one cracker after another, while Sammy works around me.

"I don't know how you eat all this stuff and stay so skinny," she says. I look up to see her holding a package of Oreos and a can of whipped cream. It's Kayleigh's favorite snack—eating the two together. I've watched her carefully squirt the foamy cream onto each cookie and stuff her maw with the entire concoction at least a million times, all while turning my nose up at the processed, sugar-laden, additive-and-chemical-riddled treats.

"I walk a lot," I say. I should tell her that I don't typically eat like this. I don't want her to think I'm one of those girls who flips her hair and says, "Oh, I've just got good genes." Instead, I add: "And do yoga."

Sammy plucks the thought out of my head. "Must be genetic." She puts the Oreos on a shelf in the pantry and then tugs at her waistband. "'Cause I ride my bike every day and can't seem to drop a pound."

I crunch another Cheez-It and pretend to think about this. But I'm really staring at her breasts and thinking how they look like two soft fluffy pillows, her stomach a cloud. I'm suddenly tired. Oh so tired. And I wonder if I can lie on her. Just for a minute.

"Daisy?" She's looking at me strangely. "Are you OK?"

I wish people would stop asking me this. What does OK even mean? It's not even a real word. It's unacceptable in Scrabble.

"I'm just tired," I say.

"Oh, you poor thing," she says. "And I've been going on and on. Let me get out of your hair. I got to be up early anyway. I told Carl I'd take his shift tomorrow morning—he has some NRA meeting or something or other. Anyway, he's taking my Saturday night. Happy to trade with him. College kids are the devil on weekends."

I vaguely wonder if I'm supposed to know who Carl is.

After Sammy leaves, I realize that I forgot to thank her for helping me with the groceries. This oversight makes me unspeakably sad. She was so kind. I wonder if I should go back outside and knock on her door to thank her, but the forty steps between our two houses feels like miles.

I set the box of Cheez-Its back on the counter. Nearly half of them are now in my stomach, but I'm still ravenous. And then I remember the steaks I bought at the butcher counter. Big, red T-bones with thick white bands of fat. My mouth waters. I can't remember the last time I ate red meat. I open the fridge and remove the white paper bundle that Sammy had placed on the second shelf and not in the meat drawer.

With a *click click click,* the gas burner turns into a flame, and I cover it with a cast-iron skillet. I leave the steaks to sizzle and pop in the hot pan and I go into the living room. I want music and vodka. Not necessarily in that order. Vodka was my go-to drink in undergrad. Vodka Red Bull. Vodka cranberry juice. Vodka and Rainbow Sprite. But tonight I pour the Absolut that we keep for company straight into a highball glass that has an R etched into it. The set of four was a wedding gift from Jack's aunt.

I take a mouthful of the clear liquid and cough and sputter as it burns all the way down my throat.

"Daisy?"

Jack is standing in the arched doorway between our kitchen and living room. I didn't hear him come in.

"Are you making steaks?"

I nod, my eyes still watering from the vodka.

His face falls, and all I can think is: he knows. I don't know how, but he must know what happened to me today. The fiery PET scan. The four months. All the Cheez-Its I just ate. Maybe it's because our connection is that deep, our bond that strong. And it's a relief, because until that moment I had given no consideration to how I was going to tell him.

But I don't have to think about it anymore because he knows.

"O-kaaaay." He furrows his brow. "What'd the doctor say? I've been calling you for the past three hours."

He doesn't know.

I take another sip of my drink. It tingles less this time.

He stares at me, and I know he is trying to piece together the puzzle he has walked into—why his wife who hasn't eaten red meat in four years is suddenly sautéing T-bones at 10 P.M. on a Monday night. That's what his brain does. It's always working, figuring things out. His brain is the reason he won first place at the Science of Veterinary Medicine Research Symposium the last three years in a row. His brain is good at numbers, and reasoning, and calculations. My brain, apparently, is good at growing tumors.

As I ponder how to respond, I suddenly remember the cock/caulk miscommunication and I tell him the story.

He laughs, as I knew he would.

Then I tell him the other stuff Dr. Saunders said in one long breath. Or maybe I'm wrong. Maybe I don't breathe at all as I speak. He stops laughing.

And besides the stunned silence, our home fills with the scent of seared flesh burning. I forgot about the steaks.

five

I WAKE UP AT 2:58 A.M. with a mouthful of cotton and an intense stabbing pain behind my right eye.

Water. I need water.

I get out of bed and grope my way to the kitchen in the darkness, feeling for the refrigerator handle in the dark. When I open the door, the bright light momentarily blinds me.

I squint and the throbbing in my head gets worse.

Stupid vodka. I drank two more glasses while Jack had me repeat everything Dr. Saunders said verbatim three times. Jack has never encountered a puzzle that he couldn't crack, so I knew he was just trying to get all the pieces of the equation so he could solve for y.

"Well, of course you'll do the surgery," he said, more to himself than to me. "And the chemo. What did he say about the clinical trials again? Which specific ones?"

When I started slurring my words in response, Jack finally stopped talking and opened his arms to me on the couch. I crawled into them, laid my head on his chest, and closed my eyes. He smelled like a raccoon.

I chug an entire glass of water and then refill my glass with the plastic pitcher from the fridge. I put it back on the top shelf, and then let go of the door. It slowly closes with a *thhwwuck*.

Even though it's drafty in the kitchen, and I'm only wearing a long T-shirt and underwear, I'm unbearably hot. The floor beckons me like a pool on a hot summer day and I let my body sink into a puddle. I stretch out and lay my cheek against the cold tile.

Salmon. That's the color the real estate agent called it. "Very authentic to Spanish design," she said. "It's not Saltillo, but it's a good imitation." Jack laughed when we got back to our apartment that night. "The kitchen is pink," he said. "We're buying a house with a pink kitchen."

Moonlight filters through the windows above the sink. I stare at the dark crevice beneath the cabinets where dirt and old cereal flakes and wisps of Benny's hair accumulate until I banish them with my broom once a week. I spy an orange Froot Loop. Jack must have dropped it at breakfast this morning.

Orange. I gingerly touch the back of my head where Dr. Saunders says an orange-sized tumor sits. Maybe he said an orange Froot Loop and I just didn't hear him. Or maybe that's what he meant to say and he accidentally left off the words "Froot Loop." I might be able to believe that I have a tumor the size of a cereal O, but a piece of fruit? It's unbelievable. And I don't say that lightly. I think the word unbelievable is overused. People say "That's unbelievable!" for things that really aren't. Like Skype. My mom thinks it's *unbelievable* that you can see someone across the world in real time as you're talking to them. "It's just like in the Jetsons!" she typed to me in an email when she discovered the video chat system four years after everyone else in the country. But Skype was really just the next logical step in the advancement of technology. It wasn't implausible, or something that came out of the blue.

Me with a tumor the size of citrus and cancer all over my body? That's the very definition of unbelievable.

Far-fetched.

Preposterous.

Unreal.

Like soap-opera-story-line-babies-switched-in-the-hospital-at-birth unbelievable.

My brain pauses, considering this.

Babies *are* actually switched in the hospital at birth sometimes. In fact, doctors make mistakes all the time. A few months ago, I read a story in the *Athens Banner Herald* about an Atlanta man suing Fulton Memorial for amputating the wrong foot. His right foot was supposed to get whacked off due to a bacterial infection, but nurses accidentally prepped the left one instead. When the surgeon entered the operating room, he didn't double-check the chart; just went right ahead with the procedure.

I sit up.

If something that big can happen, then surely a few test results can easily get mixed up. Right? *Right?* Right.

That must be it. Dr. Saunders showed me the wrong PET scan. And MRI. And one of his other patients laid her head on her pillow tonight thinking she just has a small tumor in her breast that will be taken care of with a simple lumpectomy.

Something loosens in my chest and I breathe a deep sigh of relief. I should wake up Jack and tell him.

I make an effort to stand up, but the burden of what I've just discovered pushes me back down. My hands start shaking and the throbbing in my head revs up in earnest. Sweat pushes its way out of my pores. I'm overcome with sadness for the poor woman who's blissfully asleep, unaware of this life-altering mistake.

I'll call Dr. Saunders in the morning. He'll fumble for words. "I have no idea how that happened, Daisy." This time his apology will turn up at the end with a happy exclamation, instead of a somber period. "I'm so, so sorry!" And then he, too, will get quiet, as he realizes what this means for a patient I've never met but am now intertwined with in a horrific twist. And we'll both be thinking the same thing: though the news is wonderful for me, somewhere out there is a woman who is on the shit-end of Newton's law. For every action, there's an equal, opposite reaction.

I'm going to live.

Which means she's going to die.

JACK IS A sound sleeper. I often tease him that if our house were lifted off the ground in a *Wizard of Oz*–esque tornado, he would snore right through it. But tonight as soon as I tap his arm, his eyes pop open.

"Daisy," he says.

His skin is warm from sleep, and I leave my hand on his shoulder as I whisper, "What if it's a mistake?" As soon as it's out of my mouth, I realize how childishly desperate it sounds. And the conviction I felt on the floor of the kitchen leaves me as quickly as the wind leaves a boxer who's been punched in the gut.

Jack struggles to sit up, and when his back is firmly against our white paneled headboard that I found at a yard sale shortly after we moved in, he reaches for me. "Come here," he says. I snuggle into his armpit for the second time that night. And because I tell Jack almost everything, I tell him my theory.

The amputated foot.

Switched-at-birth babies.

The other woman, sleeping peacefully.

When I'm done, Jack holds me tighter. "Maybe," he whispers into my hair, but not because he thinks it could be true. He says it because what else is there to say?

And I realize that even though I didn't believe it—not really—I desperately wanted Jack to. I wanted him to jump up and clap his hands together and confirm that *Yes! Of course!* This is all just one terrible mistake. Not one that we'll laugh at ten years down the road. God, no. But one that we'd think of when terrible shit happens to us, like getting laid off, or both of our cars breaking down in the same week or our basement flooding (again), and he'd look at me and say, "It could be worse. Remember that time we thought you were *dying*?"

I mask my disappointment and force a chuckle. "It was worth a try."

And then, even though Jack and I have never been big cuddlers at night, I don't move from his embrace—even when my arm starts to fall asleep; even when a slick of sweat forms between my neck and his naked shoulder; even when the sun peeks through our window blinds.

I WAKE UP in our bed alone, the digital clock announcing 10:37 in big red figures. Groggy and confused—I never sleep past seven—I call out into the still house for Jack.

I'm surprised when he responds.

"What are you still doing here?" I yell, sitting up and swinging my legs over the edge of the bed. "You're late!"

He appears at our bedroom door. "I'm not going in today."

"*What?* What about clinic? What about Rocky?"

"Daisy," he says, and the ache in his eyes reminds me of Dr. Saunders and everything comes screaming back at me like a freight train.

"Oh. Right." And suddenly I wish Dr. Saunders had given me a pamphlet like I got from the dentist the time I was diagnosed with gingivitis: "You Have Lots of Cancer: Here's What to Do Now."

"Well, what are we supposed to do?" I ask Jack. "We can't just sit around the house. What about school?" Shit. Gender Studies. "I have an exam today. And what about you? You're about to graduate. You can't miss clinic."

He comes to sit next to me on the bed and puts his hand on my thigh. It feels heavy. He says I should email my professors. He says he's already called his vet clinic director, Dr. Ling, and that he understood. He says that he's going to take the rest of the week off while we sort this out. And I wonder if my cancer is something that's just been placed in the wrong pile at a garage sale.

THE FIRST THING I see when I walk into the kitchen is the half-empty box of Cheez-Its on the counter. I cringe. I can't believe I let myself eat those fake, processed crackers. I pick up the box, walk it over to the trash can, and let it drop with a satisfying thud into the plastic liner.

I open the refrigerator and nearly gasp. All of my bad impulse purchases stare back at me. They lay chaotically on the shelves, like a group of children who have had assigned seating all semester and are suddenly given free rein of the classroom. Wrinkling my nose, I reach behind a six-pack of artificially flavored cherry Jell-O and grab the organic cranberry juice. I shut the fridge door. I'll reorganize it later.

As I pour the red liquid into a glass, my eye is drawn to the errant orange Froot Loop under the cabinet. I should get a broom and sweep it up, but I don't have the energy. Is it the cancer? Would I start feeling symptoms so quickly? No, that's ridiculous. And to prove it to myself, I retrieve the broom from the hall closet, take it back into the kitchen, and aggressively stab it under the cabinets, directing the Froot Loop and other debris into a neat pile in the center of the tile floor.

I transfer the mound into the dustpan and deposit it in the trash and then stand in the middle of the kitchen. See? I'm fine. I used a broom just like someone who doesn't have Lots of Cancer. And that niggling, hopeful thought sneaks into my mind again. Maybe, just maybe, I don't.

I look at the counter where I plug my cell phone into the wall every night, but the end of the white cord is empty. I must have left it in my shoulder bag. I walk down the hall to our bedroom and hear the water running. Jack's in the shower. I move faster. I can probably call Dr. Saunders before he gets out and he'll never have to know.

I retrieve my phone from its pocket and see that I have three missed calls and two text messages from Kayleigh. One of them says: **Are you alive?**

I clear the screen and dial the main office line at the cancer center. My heart thumps in my chest as it rings. *Dah-dump, dump dump. Dah-dump, dump dump.*

"Athens Regional Cancer Center," a woman's voice says. I ask to speak to Dr. Saunders.

"May I tell him who's calling?"

"Daisy Richmond."

"Hold, please."

The line clicks and flowery music fills my ear.

After a few minutes, Dr. Saunders' voice breaks in. "Daisy," he says. "I'm glad you called."

I'm a little surprised that it's him. I didn't really expect that I would get to speak with him simply by asking for him. Doctors have an elusiveness about them; almost celebrity-like. You can talk to their handlers and they'll set up an allotted time for you to be in their presence, but you can't call them directly whenever you want. They're much too important for that. But then, Dr. Saunders has always been a bit different. More accessible.

"Yes, well, I had a quest—"

"Can you come in this afternoon?" He cuts me off. "I'd like to talk with you about something."

My grip on the phone tightens. Oh my God. Maybe the diagnosis really is a mistake and he already caught it. Maybe he wants to tell me about it in person; make sure I don't intend to sue the hospital for mental distress. My heartbeat speeds up. *Dah-dump-dump-dump-dah-dump-dump-dump.*

"Daisy?"

"Yeah, yes. Of course. But, um . . . Can't you just tell me over the phone?"

You screwed up. Say it. *Say it.*

"I'm sorry, I have to run. I have patients. Stay on the line. Martha will set up a time."

Martha? Martha doesn't even work for you anymore, I want to shout, when the classical music starts up again. Then my flare of irritation settles into self-satisfaction. I am downright smug. Because if Dr. Saunders can't even remember that his receptionist retired, then it's all too conceivable that he could confuse a couple of test results.

The receptionist suggests 2:30 and I agree, because my day is inconceivably devoid of activity. As I hang up, Jack walks into the room, a towel around his waist, his hair still wet. He shivers.

"Who was that?"

"Dr. Saunders," I say. "He wants me to come in this afternoon."

"Did he say what for?"

I shake my head no. And then, instead of telling Jack about my successful handling of the broom, or Dr. Saunders' inability to remember that Martha no longer works for him, I leave the room, because all at once I've turned into a seven-year-old who doesn't want Jack to tell me there's no Santa Claus.

THE LAST TIME Jack and I stood in the Athens Regional parking lot together was right after my final radiation treatment more than four years ago. He surprised me with an obnoxious number of balloons—so many that I thought he might get whisked into the sky if a strong wind blew. "Did you miss the turn for the circus?" I asked him.

"I don't think so," he said, nodding at my bald head. "Aren't you the strongman?"

"Very funny," I said. We stood there grinning at each other. I had known Jack for only two years then, but he had stuck by me through all the cancer stuff, and we had made it to the other side. "You're done," he said. "I'm done," I agreed. He uncurled his fist that was holding the balloons and they started floating upward. Then he held out his hands to me. "Let's go."

Today we head toward the entrance in silence. I slip my hand into his and we walk through the parting glass and down the corridor to the heavy wooden door of the cancer center. Not-Martha looks up as I sign in. "Dr. Saunders is running a few minutes behind today," she says. I nod and go sit down next to Jack.

He picks up a *Sports Illustrated* and I start to rifle through a *Highlights for Children*, but it's clear that neither of us is actually reading the words on the pages in front of us. I'm mentally practicing what I'm going to say to Dr. Saunders when he admits to the mistake. I try angry: "How *dare* you? Do you know how freaked out I've been?" Or I could be happily surprised: "Really? Are you sure? Oh thank *God!*" And then, of course, there's kind understanding: "These things happen." I'd nod. "I just feel so sorry for the other woman. That poor thing."

Lativia finally calls my name and we both stand up and follow her through the waiting-room door and down the hall to Dr. Saunders' office. Before we walk in, I decide to go with kind understanding, because really, I like Dr. Saunders, and it is just a tragic situation for everyone.

He stands up behind his desk when we enter and sticks his hand out to Jack. "Been a few years, huh?" he says.

"Yes, sir," Jack says, shaking Dr. Saunders' bear paw.

"I'm glad to see you, though I wish it were under better circumstances," he says, addressing both of us.

I bob my head in a move that I hope oozes with somber empathy, so he knows that I'm ready to graciously accept his news. Jack and I sit down in the chairs across from him and wait.

Dr. Saunders removes his glasses and sets them down on the desk between us.

"Daisy, I know it's not even been twenty-four hours since you were here last, and that's not a lot of time to process the information I gave you, but I'd like to start with any questions you may have."

I look at him, confused. I feel like Dr. Saunders and I are actors in a play, and he's embarrassingly forgotten his lines. I need to prompt him.

"I do have a question," I say, glancing at Jack. "Are you sure those are my test results? I'm thinking they may have been switched with another patient."

He doesn't even wait a beat before responding, and I get the feeling I'm not the only person to have ever thought this. "Yeah, I'm sorry Daisy, but no. We have a system. We're very careful with that sort of thing."

I open my mouth to ask how he's certain, but Jack clears his throat and sits forward, cutting off my thought. "So what's the plan here? Daisy said something about brain surgery?"

Dr. Saunders leans forward and steeples his fingers, elbows propped on the desk. "I can refer you to a neurosurgeon. He'll want to look at the film and discuss the risks. I only recommend it, though, if you're going to go whole hog on treatment—chemo, radiation. Some people in, uh, Daisy's situation choose not to."

He drones on, repeating more or less the information he gave me yesterday and Jack pipes up with questions every now and then. I hear them speak, back and forth like a tennis match, but they might as well be discussing irrigation systems in third world countries. This is how little it feels that their conversation is about me. And I sit in my chair, simmering. The theory that the test results are not mine is a dead horse, and I have the inexplicable urge to beat it. Dr. Saunders didn't even pretend to double-check. Just like the surgeon in the operating room didn't double-check before lopping off the wrong foot. Stupid, arrogant doctors think they're so infallible, but they're not. They make mistakes all the time, goddamn it, and they need to start owning up to it.

"YOU DIDN'T EVEN KNOW THAT MARTHA HAD RETIRED!" The words erupt from somewhere deep down in my gut. And then the room goes absolutely still. Dr. Saunders and Jack both turn to look at me. My back is ramrod straight and my fingers are gripping the arms of the chair so tightly that my knuckles have turned white. And I have no idea what to say next.

Dr. Saunders breaks the silence. "I know this is hard," he says, his voice gentle. "But really, nothing about you is different today than last week or last month. You just have this new information now. And like I was saying, if you choose this clinical trial, it could give you another six months, a year—maybe even more."

I look up. "What clinical trial?"

"Daisy," Jack says, laying his hand on my arm. "The one Dr. Saunders was just talking about."

I turn red. "I wasn't listening."

Unruffled, Dr. Saunders repeats himself. He says a professor at Emory is researching a new drug, BC-4287, that in a lab has shrunk tumors in cancer-ridden rats. He says it's in phase one of human testing, and I'd be a perfect candidate. He says I couldn't pursue other treatments while taking it.

But all I'm hearing is "another six months." I realize that I'm supposed to be happy about this—ecstatic that my life expectancy could jump from four months to possibly twelve, but all I can think is: what a shitty negotiation. I want fifty years, and all I get is a few extra months? It's like asking your boss for a five-thousand-dollar raise and he nods and says, "I can give you ten cents."

"We'll think about it," Jack says and stands up, my cue that the conversation is over.

JACK ONLY SAYS one sentence on the drive home: "We're getting a second opinion." The rest of the time he spends casting me long side-ways glances, as if he's the zookeeper and I'm an elephant that could snap at any second and crush him with my sandpapery tree trunk of a hoof. Or maybe he's just looking at me to make sure I'm still there, and I'm grateful I'm not the only one concerned that I might abruptly dis-integrate, pieces of me drifting up toward the sky like those balloons so many years ago.

When we pull onto our narrow street, a brown van is occupying the space in front of our house where Jack typically parks. As Jack maneuvers the car into the gap behind it, I read the logo on the back door: "Prices so low, you'll be simply *floored*."

Shit. The flooring estimate.

I get out of the car and walk up beside the van to the driver door, ready to apologize for being late, but the seat is empty. I look around, but Jack and I are the only people in sight on our street. Then I hear our front door open and I turn toward the house. A burly man with hairy arms, wearing a dingy white T-shirt that leaves an inch of his potbelly exposed, walks onto our stone front porch. The same porch that's slowly pulling away from the house due to the weight of rainwa-ter that collects in it and needs to have a new drain installed in the center of it. It's on my to-do list.

A number of questions pass through my head at once. Did we leave our house unlocked? And even if we did, what kind of contractor just lets himself in? Is the weight of this guy going to cause our porch to buckle once and for all? Do fat people just not feel the cold? This guy looked comfortable in short sleeves, and tucked into my favorite black parka, I was still shivering.

Sammy appears in the open door behind the floor guy. At first I'm equally surprised to see her, and then a few answers click into place.

I gave her a key when we first moved in, because she gave us one and then stared at me until I had no choice but to reciprocate.

"There you are," she says, waving her sausage fingers in my direction. "This guy was standing on your porch in the freezing cold. Thought I'd let him in. That's what I love about small towns—don't you? Being neighborly. Couldn't ever live in Atlanta or New York. Heck, even Savannah's gotten too big for its britches. A cousin lives down there, says there's more shootin's than borrowin' sugar these days." She hooks a thumb in her belt loop and tugs back and forth.

Jack and I reach the porch steps. "I'm going to go let Benny out," he says, squeezing past Sammy and the floor man. He disappears into the house.

"Well, where have you two been? I never see Mr. Smarty Vet during daylight. Thought he was a vampire when y'all first moved in." She laughs at her own joke. Adjusts her pants again.

"At the doctor," I say, then turn to the floor guy. "I'm sorry I'm late. Did you get all the measurements you need for the estimate?"

He opens his mouth to speak, but Sammy cuts him off. "The doctor?" Her eyes are bright and shiny. "Don't tell me. Are you two . . . oh, I shouldn't ask. It's none of my business." My mind is still foggy, which is why it takes me a second before I horrifically realize what she's thinking.

Don't say it. *Please* don't say it.

She says it, her chubby cheeks swelling into a smile. "Is it a baby?"

I freeze, just now realizing the other implication of the Lots of Cancer. Jack will not be buying ant farms. I will not be a mother.

I slowly shake my head and the floor guy takes advantage of the silence. He says he's measured all the rooms. He says he doesn't often see original wood floors from the twenties. He says they're beautiful. He says he can easily restore them to a high-gloss shine for $1,875, including materials and labor but not including sales tax. Then he asks if we've noticed the hump that runs lengthwise through the den and the kitchen.

"May be the sign of a structural problem," he says.

I look at him.

"You know? Something wrong with the foundation? I'd get that checked out. Don't want the whole house to crumble down on you while you're sleeping." He chuckles.

He holds out his business card.

I take it.

And then I start to cry.

JACK DOESN'T COOK. The first time I spent the night with him, he offered to make me breakfast. The eggs were runny, the toast was burned, and the bacon was chewy. Perched on a stool at the granite island, fork in hand, I was poised to tell him that it looked delicious but I just wasn't all that hungry. He bit into the black, crunchy bread and put it back down on his plate. Looked at me. "Waffle House?" I smiled, relieved, and quickly ticked off my mental list of what I had learned about Jack in the past twenty-four hours: great in bed. Not great in the kitchen.

So that evening, when Jack says he's going to make me dinner, I'm not surprised when he presents me with a piping-hot bowl of chicken noodle soup. Even though it's not organic, and strictly against my diet, I keep a few cans in the back of the pantry for when I'm sick. I'm actually looking forward to the salty broth, rubbery chicken, and mushy noodles. It's what I used to make for myself when I stayed home from school, feverish, and the nostalgia is like a warm hug when I need it most.

Sitting on the sofa, staring at the blue TV screen but not really watching it, I stick my spoon into the bowl, only to find the texture is gelatinous—more like a porridge than a soup. Something in me snaps. I look up at Jack, who's positioned by my side like a maître d' at an expensive restaurant, ready to fulfill my every need. "You have a PhD, for Christ's sake!" I explode. "How do you not know that you're supposed to *add water* to *canned soup*?" Then I start crying again.

It's not my finest moment.

That night, Jack holds me until he nods off, lightly snoring in my ear. When I'm sure he's asleep, I scoot out of his arms and lie on my back staring at the ceiling fan. It looks like a starfish: my ceiling, the ocean floor.

And I think about dying.

In high school, I used to lie awake at night, overwhelmed by the notion. It wasn't the idea of actually expiring that struck terror into my heart, it was what came after that—the not being. Not existing. The Big Expanse of Nothing in the Great Beyond. Panic sped my heart until I could feel it beating in my ears and I would have to sit up and turn on the light, rid my room of the thick darkness that made it so hard to breathe.

My senior year, a couple of girls in my high school were killed in a drunk-driving accident. Wrapped their truck around an oak tree. I didn't know either of them, only vaguely recognized their faces as ones that I had passed in the hall. But the quickness of their deaths overwhelmed me. One minute they were here, the next they were gone. A catastrophic magician's trick.

And now I wonder, is it better that way? The not knowing? What would they have done differently if someone had tapped them on their shoulder and said, "You're going to die tomorrow." Probably nothing, because who would believe that? Considering death is one thing when it's intangible, an event in the far-off future. But when it's breathing down your neck? Impossible.

I have Lots of Cancer and I am going to die. I repeat it in my head, wondering when the panic will set in, the grief, the acceptance of my fate. But my heartbeat remains unhurried. And I know this is more than denial. It's Darwinism. My survival instinct has been woken from its slumber. You're on deck, my brain tells it. It steps up to the plate and roars.

I cannot die.

I will not die.

Then I look over at Jack in the darkness. The comforter rises and falls in time with his slow breathing. And as much as I try to keep the thought at bay, push it out of my head as I stare at my sleeping husband, like a seasoned thief, it sneaks in anyway.

But what if I do?

SIX

WEDNESDAY MORNING, MY to-do list has only three items:

1 Research options
2 make appt. with structural engineer to come look at
    floor hump
3 Find doctor for second opinion

As I press my pen to the paper to underline task three, Jack walks into the kitchen. "I made an appointment at the Northeast Georgia Cancer Center for tomorrow. They can do all your tests and give us the results by the end of the day."

Instead of underlining, I cross it off.

My to-do list has only two items.

"Can I get you anything?" he asks, his brow fixed in what now seems like a permanent wrinkle of concern. His constant attention the past twenty-four hours has been sweet but is starting to feel like a too-tight turtleneck.

"I'm fine," I say, a little too sharply. I concentrate on softening my words. "Why don't you go try to get some work done? I'm sure you have a lot to do, and I don't want you to get behind."

He studies me for a minute and then nods. "I'll just be in here if you need me," he says, gesturing down the hall to his office, and I fight the sarcastic rebuke lying on my tongue. *Where else would you be?* I sigh. I know it's not him I'm irritated with.

Once I hear the office door close, I settle in on our couch, prop my laptop on the sofa's arm, and open it. Out of habit, I check my email first.

Subject: Wednesday

Hi Hon,
Haven't heard from you this week. Did you get the cat pictures? Aunt Joey forwarded them. I thought they were funny! Also, don't buy anymore apple juice. Full of arsenic! Poison!! It was on the *Today Show*. Mixxy misses you! Left a dead bird on the porch this morning. Just a house sparrow! Nothing exciting. Have to run to work!! Hugs to Jack.

Love,
Mom

If I had to describe my mom in a couple of sentences, it would be these: she misuses exclamation points. She still wears pants with pleats. And she spends a lot of her time with a pair of worn binoculars around her neck spying on feathered creatures in her backyard and then logging the species she finds on eBird, an online birding community founded by researchers at Cornell that Jack made the mistake of telling her about one Thanksgiving. She tends to overstate to strangers how much she's contributing to science.

And she cries. A lot. When I was growing up, most of her crying was done in her room; a solitary activity that she thought she was concealing from me. "Daisy-bear," she'd say, emerging from her room with bloated eyes and a fake, ill-fitting grin that looked affixed to her face like a pair of false eyelashes. I often wondered if her makeup drawer had a collection of smiles lying next to the tubes of drugstore lipsticks and eye shadow palettes.

But now she cries in the great wide open—and not just when she's sad.

Progress, says the therapist in me. She's conquering her decades-long battle with depression, embracing life and all its messy emotions. But the daughter in me cringes—both at the overly expressive demonstration and my selfish and secret desire that she take it back behind closed doors.

I hit reply and then stare at the cursor blinking perpendicularly on the white screen. It was a reflex, but I obviously can't respond. What, I'm going to tell her my cancer is back via email? *Oh, and give Mixxy my love.*

And it reminds me, the first time I had cancer I learned that there's only one thing that's worse than actually having cancer, and that's having to tell people you have cancer. Never mind close family members, like a mother who will weep so uncontrollably that you think she may pass out from the effort of it.

But it's the acquaintances, the people who are in your life by circumstance—coworkers, neighbors, your hairstylist—that are the worst to break the news to. The pity is a given. But then comes the advice. And it always starts with "my great-aunt Ethel" or "my best friend's husband's cousin"—because everybody knows somebody with cancer. And then you have to sit through their Lots of Cancer story and all the treatments they underwent. Everyone's a sudden expert. And it's exhausting.

My cell phone abruptly comes to life on the coffee table, jarring me from my thoughts.

Kayleigh. It's the umpteenth time she's called this week and I know I can't put her off any longer.

"Daisy," she hisses into my ear when I pick up. "*Where* have you been?"

I hold the phone closer to my ear, straining to hear her. "Why are you whispering?"

"I'm in the arts and crafts closet," she says. I picture her huddling among shelves of Popsicle sticks and canisters of tempera paint in primary colors and plastic-handled safety scissors. And then as if imagining it has transported me back into elementary school, I start to faintly hear children's voices singing.

"Are the kids still there?"

"Yeah," she whispers. "Pamela's doing circle time. I told her I had a papier-mâché emergency."

"What's wrong?"

"With the papier-mâché ? Nothing, it's fine."

"No, with you. Why are you calling in the middle of a school day?"

"Oh. Right. Harrison came by. The school. I think he's stalking me."

I don't say anything, trying to remember who Harrison is.

"The nineteen-year-old? Basketball player?" Kayleigh prompts.

"Oh, Jesus. Of course he's stalking you. You're a cougar who stole his virginity."

"He was not a virgin!" She pauses, and I know she's chewing on a nail. A nervous tic she's had as long as I've known her. "I don't think. Anyway, where have you been? And what happened at the doctor? I've been trying to call you all week."

The normality of our conversation had sucked me into an alternate universe for a brief second. A pre-second-round-of-cancer universe where I could breathe without a steel plate pressing down on my chest. But her question pops the bubble and I thud back down to my reality.

I tell her what happened at the doctor.

"Holy fuck," she breathes.

"Yeah," I say. It's something I've always liked about Kayleigh: her honest brevity.

AFTER I HANG up, I turn back to my computer and open Google.

I type: *stage IV breast cancer*.

My throat closes when the first page I click on reiterates what Dr. Saunders has already told me: *There is no cure*.

Hearing it was numbing; seeing it's a vicious punch to the gut.

I move on. According to WebMD, chemo and radiation are options but have better success in early stage IV, when the cancer has spread to only *one* place outside of the breast. I count up the body parts my tumors have spread to. Brain, lungs, bone, liver. *Four*.

Then a link grabs my eye. A *New York Times* story about a woman who has lived for seventeen years with stage IV breast cancer. Hope surges. I click the link and scan the article. Her cancer had spread only to her bones. And hormone therapy worked. My triple-negative breast cancer doesn't respond to hormone therapy. Hope recedes.

I spend the rest of the day surfing the tangled web of Internet breast cancer information. I read really personal blogs of people who are dying. I tear up when I notice that the date on the last entry of my favorite one is more than two years ago. I pore over miracle stories where people claim to be cured by vitamin C infusions, hyperbaric oxygen tanks, a diet of Chinese pearl barley. I take notes on those, so I can ask Dr. Saunders about them. I sift through hundreds of medical journal articles and ongoing clinical trials.

By nightfall, my back is stiff, my eyes are bleary, and I am emotionally overwhelmed. There's so much cancer research that I could spend ten years reading it, and it would be the equivalent of taking one step in a marathon. I laugh at my arrogance. Thousands of scientists have dedicated their lives to finding cures, saving lives. And I thought that after a little Google research, the answer to my predicament would just pop up? Oh, *this* is what's going to fix you. *This* is the answer.

I know Jack has been making the same futile effort. When he wasn't on the phone with Dr. Ling or his fellow vet students, trying to vicariously catch up on what he'd missed that day, or checking in on Rocky, I heard him click-clacking away at his computer in the study.

As I close my laptop and slide it onto the coffee table, I hear Jack coming down the hall. His footsteps stop at the door. I look up.

"Permission to enter?"

"Granted," I say, stretching my arms overhead.

He sits next to me on the couch and reaches down for my calves, swings my legs up into his lap so he can rub my sock-clad feet. I let out a little moan and lay my head on the cushion behind me, closing my eyes.

"Have you eaten dinner?" he asks.

I shake my head no.

"Guess you don't want soup."

I snort with laughter, open my eyes. The parentheses that bookend his mouth deepen, and all I can think is: I love his face. A study came out a few years ago citing symmetry as the defining factor in attractiveness. The researchers examined and measured the mugs of the celebrities in a magazine's Most Beautiful People issue. The one thing they had in common? Facial symmetry. Jack doesn't have that. His right eye is slightly bigger than his left. When he's inquisitive, he can only cock his left eyebrow. He can't grow a full beard. The one time he tried, patches of hair on his face just didn't come in, making it look like he had a stroke when he was shaving. Then there's his off-kilter bite. But all of these imperfections add up to something magnetic. Jack's face is quietly disarming. And even though I've studied every inch of it over the years we've been together—memorized every line, freckle, and flaw—it still has the ability to warm me like the sun; I bask in its glow.

"Why do you put up with me?" I ask, lifting my head off the cushion and burying it in his chest.

"The snorting," he says, squeezing me to him. "It's terrifyingly sexy."

LATER, WHEN JACK is out walking Benny, I know that it's time; I've put it off for long enough.

I pick up my cell phone and instead of scrolling to her name, I punch out each number that I know by heart, my finger's staccato bringing me closer to the one conversation I've been dreading to have.

She picks up on the first ring.

"Mom?" I say.

"Daisy-bear!" she says. "The most amazing thing just happened. This hawk—huge! must have been a broad-winged or maybe a Ferruginous? I couldn't be sure—landed on the fence post in the backyard. Looked right at me. I tried to get my camera but it flew away right as I went to snap it. Most beautiful wingspan. So I guess, yeah, probably a broad-winged."

I nod, even though she can't see me, and then I take a deep breath and tell her about the cancer. How it's back. And that it's everywhere.

She's silent for so long that I wonder if I've lost the connection, but right when I start to take the phone away from my ear to check, I hear her demand "Where, everywhere?" as if I am somehow responsible for the cancer's placement.

I tell her.

"That's not possible!" her voice says, an octave higher and on the precipice of hysterics. I lower my tone to counterbalance. She peppers me with questions and I answer them, trying to focus on the positive. "Right now, it's asymptomatic so at least I feel good!" and "Dr. Saunders really thinks this clinical trial might work!"

But nothing I say can stop the tidal wave of emotion that I've unleashed.

So eventually I stop talking and clutch my phone so tightly my knuckles get sore while I wait.

And wait.

And wait some more.

For my mom to stop crying.

seven

"YOU REALLY FEEL fine? No headaches? No noticeable lack of energy?"

Jack and I are sitting across from a thin black man in a lab coat who doesn't look much older than us, in an office across town from Dr. Saunders'—but may as well be in the room next to his, as similar as they are. The light reflects off his shiny bald head and his thick lips part while he stares at the results of my second PET scan and MRI. He doesn't even attempt to hide his bewilderment as he looks up at me.

I shake my head no. He mimics the movement, like we're playing that acting class mirror game, and continues to scrutinize me as if I'm some medical miracle. Maybe I am. Maybe I'll be the first person to surpass the expected survival rate for Lots of Cancer. Maybe my tumors will form some kind of symbiotic relationship, instead of a parasitic one, and we'll all live happily ever after.

He tries again. "No pain or discomfort of any kind?"

He's so incredulous that I start to second-guess myself. *Have* I felt any pain, and I just can't remember it? Or I chalked it up to something else? And then I remember a special I saw years ago on Discovery about a girl who didn't feel pain. She could put her hand on a hot stove, and leave it there, the skin searing and blistering, but she didn't feel a thing.

Maybe I have that, I think.

And then I remember slamming my hand in the car door when I was five, and the excruciating *pop* when I rolled my ankle in high school and the white open sores on my throat during chemo and the two toenails that fell completely off and the headache just two days ago on the floor of my kitchen. I do feel pain.

"Is that a good sign? That she doesn't have symptoms?" Jack asks.

"It doesn't mean her condition is any less serious, if that's what you're asking. And it's kind of unfortunate—she might have come in months ago if an unusual pain had prompted her to seek medical advice."

"So what do you recommend? Chemo? Radiation?"

He looks at Jack. "Frankly?" And then pauses, as if he really expects Jack to respond, "Yes, please be frank."

I almost laugh at the near Abbott and Costello of it all.

"I think it would be a waste of time. There's just . . . too much of it."

He then asks if we've looked into supportive care, and gives us a card with the number for hospice services and a pamphlet titled "Coping with Terminal Cancer."

In the Zagat of doctors, this guy would have zero stars.

AT HOME, JACK throws his keys onto the kitchen counter. They skid across the laminate and stop just inches before the sink drop-off. He walks to the fridge and yanks open the door. Grabs the cranberry juice, takes three gulps directly from the bottle, sets it in an open space in the door that's strictly just for sauces and salad dressings, and slams the door closed.

He's mad. It happens so rarely that I just watch him, like he's a curiosity—the three-headed lady or the alligator boy in a traveling state fair. I once asked him if he ever got furious, ever worked up to the point of throwing something or growling with rage. He shrugged. "I'm from the Midwest."

His back remains toward me, his hand still resting on the fridge door. I gently pick up his keys and place them on the hook by the door.

We stand there in silence, not moving, like kids who have just been touched in a game of freeze tag.

And then Jack speaks: "That doctor was an idiot." His voice is gruff, worn.

I nod, even though he can't see me.

The silence is back and it hangs in the air between us. A privacy curtain to hide our true thoughts.

Jack breaks it again. "I'll be in the office," he says, but the word "office" cracks in the middle in a way that makes my breath catch.

I nod again, even though he still can't see me.

He leaves the room and I wait until I hear his footsteps retreat down the hall, the door to his office closed. Then I walk over to the refrigerator, open the door, and move the cranberry juice back to the top shelf where it belongs.

AFTER REARRANGING EVERY item in the fridge and tossing my bad impulse purchases into the trash, I sit at our tiny kitchen table for two. I drum my fingers on the glass surface, leaving smudge marks that I'll just have to buff out later. Good, I think. It will give me something to do.

And that's when it dawns on me that for the first time in my life, I don't have *anything* to do; I don't have a plan. The first time I had breast cancer, everything moved so quickly. There was a sense of ur-gency—we caught it, let's cut it out, chemo it, radiate it, get rid of it. Go! Go! Go! I barely had time to think, process what was happening. Now, there's too much time. And what's happening is not something I want to contemplate.

I know there are decisions to be made, but no one is pressur-ing me to make them. And I realize it's because my choices are rather like asking someone on death row if they'd like to die by fir-ing squad or electric chair. That's effectively what the second-opin-ion doctor said today. You can have chemo and radiation and die. Or, you could just die.

Now, the way Dr. Saunders was pushing the clinical trial is mak-ing more sense. He was giving me a third option—the only one where dying didn't have to be an immediate side effect.

Dying.

A laugh bubbles out of the side of my mouth. Is that what I'm doing? The very idea seems ludicrous. Dying is for old people and or-phaned children in Africa with distended bellies and dads who get struck down by cars when they're on their bicycles in the wrong inter-section at the wrong time of the day. It's not for twenty-seven-year-old women who just got married and want to have babies and feel fit and healthy and not even in a little bit of pain. I feel like I'm at a restau-rant and the waiter has brought me the wrong dish. Dying? No, there's obviously some mistake. I didn't order that.

But I can't send it back. And now I'm looking at four months or six months or one year, and what am I supposed to do with that?

On our fourth date, Jack and I went to Barnes & Noble and slowly browsed the shelves, petting each other's arms like only two people who are first falling in love do. We played a silly game where we would take turns picking up a random book and then reading the first line of it—or making up one of our own. Then the other person had to guess if it was real or not. While playing, we stumbled on a book called *If: Questions for the Game of Life*. Sitting in the middle of an aisle, we fired questions at each other for hours. Stuff like: *If you had to get rid of one limb, which would you choose?* (Jack: left leg. Me: left arm.) *If you could only eat one thing every day for the rest of your life, what would it be?* (Jack: his mom's chili spaghetti. Me: guacamole.)

But the one that I can't stop thinking about, even though I can't remember who actually asked the question: *If you knew you were going to die in one month, what would you do?* I said something like: *pack a suitcase, book a transatlantic flight, rent a house on the Amalfi Coast, and stuff my face with loads of authentic Italian pasta and wine.*

Now all I can think is: how naively ambitious of me. I'm a little embarrassed by that self-assured twenty-one-year-old who didn't let the prospect of death get her down. She'll just *carpe diem!* over a bottle of red until she draws her last breath. Silly girl. What did she know?

But there is something I admire about her: at least she had a plan.

ON FRIDAY, THE structural engineer who comes to inspect the hump in our den doesn't have much better news.

"It's a lacka support," he says, chewing on a toothpick. "That central beam in your basement looks like it was installed five, ten years ago. Just a Band-Aid."

"But our home inspector said the hump was fine—normal settling of a house this old," I say.

He shrugs, ignoring Benny's incessant whines at his feet for a head scratch. "You gotta bad one. Happens."

"So what do we do?" I bend down to scoop Benny up with one hand and he rewards me with tiny sandpapery licks all over my jawline.

"Y'need 'bout seven, mebbe eight new beams." He takes the toothpick out of his mouth and holds it in between two fingers like a tiny cigarette. "But that ain't cheap."

"How much?"

"You looking at two hundred a beam, so fourteen, sixteen hundred bucks."

I thank him, shut the door behind him, and then lean my back up against it. I put Benny's wriggling body back onto the floor and he scurries off toward Jack's office. If my mom were here she would recite one of her clichéd mantras, like "When it rains it pours." Or "Every cloud has a silver lining." Why does every quote about bad stuff happening have to do with weather? And are there any about tsunamis? Because that feels like the more appropriate meteorological condition for my life right now.

I glance at my watch.

Nine thirty-two.

I need to caulk the windows.

I need to figure out how we're going to pay for the new beams in the basement.

I need to call Dr. Saunders and see how to get on that clinical trial.

I take a deep breath, leave my post at the door, and walk down our scuffed wood hallway. I turn right into our bedroom, with every intention of pulling up the comforter, smoothing the pillowcases, and leaving my tidy bedroom to start my day.

Instead, I crawl onto the mattress, burrow under the covers, and promptly fall asleep.

The weekend passes in a blur wherein I find myself looking at mostly three things—the starfish ceiling fan, Jack's concerned face peering in at me from the bedroom doorway, and the back of my eyelids. At times, I wake to find pieces of fruit—apples, bananas, oranges—on my nightstand that Jack has left for me like offerings to

Pomona. I eat them without tasting them to keep the rumblings in my stomach at bay. In one of my more lucid moments of consciousness I notice the pamphlet that the second-opinion doctor had given us lying next to a cluster of grapes. I can't remember if I left it on my nightstand or if Jack has placed it there. Slightly annoyed, I stuff a pillow behind my back so I can sit up a bit and flip through it while I munch on the orbs of green fruit.

The title, "Coping with Terminal Cancer," is plastered onto a picture of a storm cloud where the sun is just barely peeking through. The literal silver lining. I roll my eyes.

Inside, it announces there are seven stages to grief. My irritation lessens when I see it's in list format. Lists, I get. Lists, I understand. I read number one.

Shock & Denial

Yes! I have experienced both shock and denial. I feel like I'm fourteen and taking a quiz in *YM*. I have gotten this answer: correct! Next.

Anger & Bargaining

Anger, yes. Bargaining?

You may try in vain to negotiate with the powers that be: "If you just heal my cancer, I'll spend the rest of my life volunteering and giving back to charities."

Hmm. Incorrect! I skipped that step, which makes me uneasy, because I don't like to leave anything undone. I decide to come back to that. Moving on.

Depression

This stage may not set in until even months after diagnosis, but is typically accompanied by a long period of sad reflection and isolation. You may feel lethargic and may not even want to get out of bed.

Now I'm downright smug. I was diagnosed less than a week ago and I'm already at stage three. I'm an Advanced Griever. If there was a class in grieving, I would be an A-plus student.

I put the flyer back onto my nightstand, roll over, and go back to sleep.

On Saturday night—at least I think it's Saturday night—the familiar clink of metal flatware hitting a bowl floats in from the kitchen and I know that Jack is eating cereal for dinner. I have the urge to get up and cook a proper meal for him, but it passes as quickly as it comes. I close my eyes again and drift off for the fifth or sixth time. I've lost count.

By Sunday morning, the thought of sitting up doesn't overwhelm me, so I do. Then I stand. My legs are a little wobbly and blood rushes too quickly to my head, but it feels good to stretch. I head down the hall and am sniffing my sour armpit when Jack walks toward me holding a clementine. He pauses midstride when he sees me.

"You're up," he says.

"I need a shower."

"Bathroom's that way," he says, and points with his left hand. He's wearing a ridiculous grin.

"I want a drink of water first."

He steps to the right, blocking my path. "I'll get it for you," he says. "You go on into the shower."

"What's your deal? Move," I say, brushing by him. "I'm not an invalid."

I enter the kitchen with Jack and Benny both at my heels and when I stop short and suck in my breath, Jack nearly topples me over from behind.

"Daisy—wait."

To call the kitchen a disaster would not do it justice. I scan the room from left to right and top to bottom, taking in the bowls, Tupperware, and mugs peppering the counters, containing dregs of milk and bits of swollen cereal, and various levels of what I assume is now-cold coffee, the fluffs of Benny's dog hair that roll like tumbleweeds on the fake Saltillo tile, the square cardboard box with grease spots and the words "Hot fresh pizza" on the side sitting on the glass kitchen table. I don't have to lift it to know that my finger smudges from Thursday still mar the surface beneath.

The first question that comes to mind is: How long have I been asleep?

I give voice to my second: "Why are the cabinet doors beneath the sink open?"

Jack sighs. "I've been trying to fix it."

"Fix what?"

"There's a clogged pipe somewhere," he says, scratching the back of his head. "Everything's backed up."

And that's when I notice the stench. And the dirty rags and tools that litter the pink floor in front of the sink.

Jack is many things, but a handyman is not one of them. When he attempted to put up the ceiling fan in our bedroom, he forgot to turn off the breaker and electrocuted himself. "Just a small buzz," he says, annoyed whenever I tease him about it. "It wasn't a big deal." I hired an electrician to finish the installation.

I close my eyes.

I need to call a plumber.

I need to add it to my list.

But my list is all the way across the room on the counter.

And I am going back to bed.

THE MOVEMENT OF the mattress from Jack's body weight sinking into it wakes me up later that night.

"What time is it?"

"Eleven." He brushes my matted hair off my forehead. "Sorry. I didn't mean to wake you."

"It's fine." I sit up a little.

He reaches under the covers and rolls his socks down past his hairy ankles and off his feet, one at a time. Then he pulls them out from under the sheets and drops them on the side of the bed. "I called Dr. Ling to let him know I'm not coming in again this week," he says, and reaches up to the lamp chain on his nightstand. He pulls it and the room goes dark. He leans toward me and his lips land somewhere between my nose and cheek. "G'night," he whispers.

I lie there for a minute, paralyzed. Jack is less than four months away from graduating with a degree he's worked more than seven years to obtain. He's already given up an entire week of clinic in his final semester while I've been fully absorbed in my (albeit accelerated) seven-stage grieving process and not even considering how my Lots of Cancer has affected him.

I reach over for the chain on my lamp and yank it. Light fills the room again.

"You have to go," I say. "You have to graduate."

"Daisy," he squints, holding his hand up to shade his eyes. "I'm not going to leave you."

"It's not like you're jetting off across the country. You'll still be here."

He doesn't say anything.

"Jack, seriously. You've worked too hard for this. *We've* worked too hard for it. I want you to graduate." And then in a smaller voice: "I need you to." And as I say it, I realize it's true. Jack continuing clinic, graduating, means life goes on as normal. The steady rhythm of our days can resume like a couple in a ballroom competition that trips, but picks back up with their waltz. Last week we stumbled, but now we must carry on.

"OK," he says, resigned. "I'll go."

"Thank you." I give a curt nod and reach for the chain again.

"But only if you'll go, too," he says. My hand freezes midair.

"What?" I picture myself following Jack around the vet school hospital like one of the animals on a leash. It's such a ridiculous notion that I almost burst out laughing.

"You have to go back to school, too. Tomorrow."

Oh. *My* school.

This triggers a flood of phrases: My degree. My Gender Studies exam. My thesis. My *career*. All of which I have given absolutely zero thought to in the full week since I was sitting in Dr. Saunders' office. But now that I am thinking about it, I have a bizarre urge to laugh and cry at the same time. It all seems so . . . pointless.

"Isn't that what Dr. Saunders said the first time?" he says. "That you should keep working, stick to your daily routine. It helps."

"Jack, this isn't like the first time," I say quietly.

He folds his arms across his chest. "That's my deal," he says. "I'll go if you go."

I consider this. I'm sure if I keep arguing I could win. He obviously hasn't thought it through—the amount of school I'll be missing for doctor appointments and the apathy I feel (that *anyone* would feel) about working toward a degree I'll never likely get to use. But I'm just so tired. And really, what else am I going to do with my time? Suddenly, the vast amount of unfilled, unplanned hours and days looming in front of me feels overwhelming—even if there are only four to six months of them left. "Fine," I say.

Jack's eyes get big, and I realize he wasn't counting on me giving up so easily. I reach up to turn off the light and leave him to enjoy his victory in the dark.

The mattress shifts as he rolls himself into his burrito of blankets, and after a few minutes I hear Jack's breathing slow and deepen. It's one of the things that drives me crazy about him—how he can fall asleep within seconds of closing his eyes. Once, I tried to get him to teach me how to do it. I wanted to learn the secret to overcome my all-too-often insomnia. "I don't know," he said. "I just kind of let my mind wander and next thing you know, I'm asleep." When I let my mind wander, sleep is the last thing that overtakes me.

Tonight as I lie there, my thoughts drift to Jack in his cap and gown, a proud grin on his face. My husband, a doctor twice over. And the pride I feel for him in that moment is almost enough to overcome the loss I feel at my own unrealized dreams. Almost. And then an idea sprouts in my brain, and as much as I try to push it aside, it grows like kudzu, overtaking every happy image I've conjured: *what if I'm not here to see it?*

I swallow. Breathe. I will be. Of course I'll be here. I have to be. *Please. Please let me be here to see Jack graduate. I'll do* anything.

I don't know who I'm talking to: gods, fate, some divine being that believes in me, even if I don't believe in it (isn't that what those WWJD people are always saying?) or just myself. But I feel better, if only because my grief journey is now more complete: I'm bargaining.

Jack shifts beside me and groans. "Daisy?" he whispers, his voice thick with sleep.

"Yeah?"

"Scratch my back?" His face is half smushed into his pillow and it takes me a minute to register what he's asked me.

I reach over and feel for his body in the dark. My hand brushes against his warm, bumpy skin—Jack has a moderate case of bacne. I ordered him that body Proactiv from the infomercial more than a year ago, but I don't think he's used it once. The bottle sits full in the shower, mold threatening to form a ring around the bottom of it if I didn't scrub beneath it once a week.

I slowly run my fingernails over his back near the length of his protruding spine.

"To the left," he mumbles.

I acquiesce.

"Higher."

I move my hand to just beneath his shoulder blade.

"Little lower."

I oblige.

"Ah." A sharp intake of breath. "R'there."

Having found X on the treasure map of his back, I scratch the spot as I would Benny's belly, with gentle vigor. After a few seconds Jack mutters something like "thanks" and I feel the tension leave his body as he settles back into his sleeping position.

I slip both hands between my head and my pillow, palming my skull, and lie on my back, wide awake. Something has just cut loose inside of me, like a snagged thread on a sweater threatening to unravel the entire hem, but I can't put my finger on it.

It's something to do with Jack, I know. Maybe I'm still shook by the thought of not being there for his graduation. But no, that's not all of it.

And then it hits me.

I'm shook by the thought of not being here—at all.

And not because of my lingering existential high school fear of death. It's not about what's going to happen to me.

With sudden clarity, I realize my fear, deep down, is what will happen to Jack.

And the dirty socks on the floor beside our bed.

Early in our relationship, I asked him why he doesn't remove them near our dresser, where he stands to peel off the rest of his layers from the day and deposits them all in the hamper, where dirty clothes belong. He said he doesn't like his feet to get cold, so he leaves them on until he can snuggle them deep under our comforter for warmth. I once bought him slippers for Christmas, hoping he could pad over to the bed in those and leave his socks safely in the hamper, because really, is there anything more off-putting than a naked man clad only in socks? The slippers sit unused on the floor of our closet.

But that's not what bothers me. In the morning, Jack leaves his socks, gray-soled and rotting on the floor, only to be joined by another pair of used socks that night. This goes on until the stench or the sight of so many socks motivates me to action, and I pick up the whole dingy mess and dump them into the laundry basket. Jack sometimes mentions it, especially if it was a particularly unruly pile, with an offhand, "Thanks for picking those up. I would've gotten to it eventually."

I take "eventually" to mean "when I run out of socks." Although something tells me that even in that circumstance, Jack would go to Target and buy a package of Fruit of the Loom in bulk rather than launder the ones beside our bed.

Now I wonder—with not just a small degree of panic—what would happen if Jack were left to his own devices? I picture the pile of socks growing exponentially until it teeters dangerously toward the ceiling and spreads like a fungus to each corner of the room. Jack would fall asleep every night in a sea of socks, until the one night he'd choke and sputter on the noxious odors and eventually suffocate under the oppressive weight of thousands of pairs of knitted footwear.

This is what happens when I let my thoughts wander. And this is why my heart is flapping wildly like the wings of a baby bird just kicked from its nest and why my face is hot and dry air is trapped in my lungs, unable to come or go.

If I die, who's going to pick up the socks?

If I die, who's going to scratch the itch just beneath Jack's shoulder blade?

When I die, who's going to caulk the windows and call the contractors and sweep the floors and pack the lunches and find the jeans and load the dishwasher and go to the store and make the bed and make sure that Jack doesn't eat *goddamned* cereal for every *goddamned* meal?

I bolt upright in bed, my ears ringing now with flat-out terror.

I have Lots of Cancer. I'm going to die. And then—then—what is going to happen to Jack?

Breathe, Daisy.

I need to make a list. I have at least four months, maybe six. Maybe even a year, if the trial works. That's plenty of time to get the house in order, maybe teach Jack how to cook. I could make him a cleaning chart.

My heart seizes. No, he'd never follow it.

I could hire a maid.

But she probably wouldn't make his favorite tuna salad with hard-boiled eggs for lunch. Or be able to tell him where his scrubs are when he's running twenty minutes late for work. Or scratch his back in the middle of the night.

The corners of my eyes sting as I picture Jack alone in our bed. In our tiny dark bedroom that suddenly feels cavernous and empty and sad. The thought is enough to break me in half. To kill me long before the cancer does.

Jack needs me.

I shake my head.

No, Jack needs *somebody*. A warm body. A body without Lots of Cancer that can take care of him and love him and pick up his dirty socks when he doesn't get around to it.

And suddenly, what's clearer to me than the glowing orb on that PET scan is that this is now the number one thing on my to-do list. Take that, twenty-one-year-old me who would frolic off to Italy. I, too, have a plan.

Jack needs a wife.

And I am going to find him one.

WHENEVER A TORNADO ravages some flat Midwest town, the news images of the damage always contain at least one shot of a home untouched—unmarred by the destruction—while every other house in the neighborhood is nothing but a few splinters of wood emerging from unrecognizable rubble. And in many ways, it's the still-standing house that's far more shocking than the one that's not. The house that hundreds of people passed every day and never gave a second thought to has transformed into a marvel overnight, even though—or precisely because—nothing about it is different.

Everything about my Monday morning is like that still-standing house.

I watch Jack shove his legs one at a time into his green scrub pants.

He eats Froot Loops; I make a smoothie.

He kisses my cheek good-bye.

I dutifully drive to campus in my Hyundai Sonata.

A tornado has ravaged my life, but everything around me—from the throngs of students loping to class to the sturdy brick buildings rooted to the ground—remains untouched. Everything is different, but nothing has changed. This paradox flummoxes me.

I walk into Gender Studies and head toward my usual seat in the front, but at the last second I turn and walk toward the back of the class, sliding into a desk in the last row, if only to prove to myself that not everything is the same.

"Good morning!" Dr. Walden chirps as she enters the door, clutching a travel mug of coffee with her right hand, a manila folder bursting with papers stuffed under her armpit. A few students respond with mumbled greetings.

She deposits her belongings on the old wooden teacher's desk at the front of the room and straightens her tiny frame. Her eyes scan the class and light on me. If she's surprised to see me—or at my change in seating—she doesn't show it. "Welcome back, Richmond," she says, with a smile. "See me after class to schedule your makeup exam." She moves toward the desk and picks up the thick folder that she just set down. "As for the rest of you, I've finished grading the tests—and let's just say some of you are lucky we're on a bell curve. You can come get them at the end of class." She sets the folder back down with a thud. "OK, let's talk about Julia Kristeva. Who can tell me about her?"

This is the point in class that I would typically raise my hand or open my laptop to studiously take notes, but the tornado has changed everything. Now, even though class and Dr. Walden are the same, I'm different. And how can she just be casually discussing the theories of a Bulgarian feminist philosopher as if I'm not sitting in the back of the classroom actively dying?

My eyes burn. What am I doing here? Why did I promise Jack I'd come back to class, resume playback in my life as if nothing had changed? I take a deep breath and scan the room, taking in the backs of women's heads (there's only one guy in the class, a lone crew cut in a sea of curls, messy buns, and Beyoncé-like weaves) and wondering how many people would notice if I just slipped out the door.

But where would I go? What would I do?

My heartbeat revs and my hands are shaking like they did the first time I took the car out by myself at sixteen and narrowly missed being flattened by a semitrailer while merging onto the highway, swerving at the last second and slamming the brake with both feet, screeching to a halt in the emergency lane. The desk/chair combo I'm sitting in suddenly feels constrictive. Why does the chair need to be attached to the wooden tray? It strikes me as some Communist one-size-fits-all design, and I desperately want to saw through the metal pole that joins the two pieces and push the chair back to allow for more breathing room.

I'm like an eighteen-year-old boy breaking up with a girl for the first time: I need space.

Dizzy, I stand up, forcing the metal pegs on my chair to scrape the linoleum, emitting a short high-pitched squeak into the air. A few heads turn. Dr. Walden frowns at me but continues her lecture. I glance at the door again, but my feet are glued to the floor.

I sit back down.

Tears spring to my eyes and I'm furious at Jack. For pushing me to go to class. For wanting everything to go back to normal, when everything is *not normal*.

There was a tornado! I want to shout. To tell the back of everyone's heads, to slow their typing fingers and quiet their glowing computer screens. *Didn't you see the tornado?*

I reach down into my shoulder bag on the floor, blindly groping for my cell phone. I need to text Jack. To tell him I can't do this. I can't just pretend that nothing has changed.

And then I stop.

Jack.

Who's only back at clinic because *I* pushed *him* to go. Because he has to graduate. Because he has to keep living.

Even after I'm gone.

I slip my phone back into the pocket of my bag and straighten my spine.

Jack.

Who can't scratch the middle of his back. Or remember to eat dinner.

Jack.

Who doesn't separate whites and colors. And leaves half-drunk coffee cups on floors and bathroom counters.

I pull my laptop out of my bag and open it on top of my Communist desk. I open a Word document and stare at the cursor blinking on the white page. A slew of adjectives fill my head: kind, funny, smart, thoughtful—but those are a given. You never ask somebody what they're looking for in a partner and they say "dumb and uncaring."

So I dismiss the obvious and settle on the first couple of characteristics that are a must for Jack's new wife.

1 Organized
2 Likes to cook
3 Loves animals

I ponder the third one for a minute and then add the word "all," especially the ones people usually don't love, like rodents, because Jack often comes home with lab rats and mice—and one time even a snake—after his colleagues are done conducting experiments with them. That's how we got Gertie.

While I read over the short phrases I've tapped out, I exhale a long stream of air from my lungs.

My heartbeat slows.

My hands unclench.

Lists always make me feel better.

march

eight

I'M ORANGE.

As in, the color of an Oompa Loompa.

I stare at my skin in the mirror and my face stares back at me with a look that's a cross between horror and keen curiosity. Like I'm witnessing a science experiment that's gone badly awry.

Last night when I went to bed, I was a normal shade of pink.

Now . . . now. I run the pads of my fingers over my cheeks. Gently at first, and then harsher, scrubbing the skin with my nails, as if I can rub this strange color off and return it to normal.

I wonder if Jack noticed it when he was fumbling around in our shadowy bedroom this morning looking for his keys and trying not to wake me. But then, that's probably something that's worthy of waking someone up to tell them. "Psst. You are orange."

I run into the kitchen and grab my phone off the counter to call him, but I hesitate when I see the time: 9:06. Jack's in surgery this morning to help remove a spoon from an overeager rottweiler's stomach—the first big procedure Ling is letting him scrub in on since he went back to clinic two weeks ago—and I don't want to bother him.

So instead, I scroll to Dr. Saunders' name and wonder how many other people have a radiation oncologist's cell number on their speed dial. He gave it to me right before Jack and I left his office. "Call if you need anything," he said, his eyebrows thick with sympathy. "Really. Anything." Most people would probably be comforted in the knowledge that their doctor is at their disposal twenty-four hours a day, seven days a week. All it did was remind me how dire my condition was.

But now I'm glad to have it.

He answers on the third ring.

"Dr. Saunders," I say. "It's Daisy. Richmond."

"Daisy. What can I help you with?"

"Well, um," I stutter, not sure what to say. "I woke up this morning and my skin is—it's not right. I look kind of . . . orange."

It sounds ridiculous to say it out loud, and I wonder if I'm exaggerating. Maybe it's not as bad as I thought, or maybe I'm just not fully awake. I walk back into my bathroom, cradling the phone to my ear and stare into the mirror. I blink back at myself. Once. Twice.

Yep. I am definitely orange.

"Mm-hmm. I see." He clears his throat. "Sounds like jaundice. The met in your liver has probably blocked a bile duct."

"OK," I say, as if this is a perfectly reasonable explanation, but I have no idea what a bile duct is or what happens when it's blocked. Except, apparently, you turn orange.

"Any itching?"

"I'm sorry?"

"Your skin, does it itch?"

"No," I say, and then my hand travels to my right arm. "Well, my scar, sometimes." I'm not following the significance of this line of questioning.

"Good," he says. "Where are you with the clinical trial? Have you gotten your workup yet?"

"Yes," I say, flashing back to last week when I drove down to Emory and met Dr. Rankoff for what she called my "screening visit," which was just a fancy term for another MRI, CT scan, and getting poked and prodded with a thousand needles and metal instruments. My mom came with me, but only after I made her promise she would leave the room anytime she felt like crying. She did surprisingly well. So well that at one point I felt myself wanting to scream, "Mom! I'm dying! Why are you acting so calm?"

"When will you start the medication?"

"Dr. Rankoff said if I'm a good candidate, I could begin next Friday."

"A week from today?"

I nod. "Yes."

"OK, I'll check with her, but I think getting a stent won't preclude you from the study."

"A stent?"

"Sorry, a plastic tube inserted in the duct to open it up. I can set you up with a gastroenterologist next week. It's a quick procedure and it'll relieve your jaundice."

Next week. Which means I will remain orange for the foreseeable future, which includes Jack's annual spring awards banquet for the veterinary school.

Tonight.

My head is spinning.

I could stay home from the banquet. Of course I could. Except I can't.

Jack's new wife could be there.

OPPOSITES DON'T ATTRACT. The notion that they do is one of those culturally imbedded ideas that's actually not true at all, like the old wives' tale that going to bed with wet hair will bring on a cold. I know this because for the past two weeks I've been poring over my back issues of *Psychology Today* and *Journal of Social and Personal Relationships,* studying what makes a marriage work. It would have been faster to go on the Web and type "marriage" into the search engine on livescience.com, but it felt like cheating. Too easy. I'm searching for a life partner, not a pair of shoes. It deserves a marked effort.

On my breaks from thumbing through the monthly tomes and squinting at the black print, I've been haphazardly going to class— partly because I promised Jack I would, but mostly because there are hundreds, maybe even thousands, of available women on campus at any given moment. I've begun to feel like an anthropologist, studying their actions, trying to attach meaning to them. Reapplying a dark burgundy lipstick to your pout while waiting for the bus— high maintenance. Checking your smart phone every three minutes—clingy, desperate. Wearing flannel pajama pants to class— too immature. Wearing heels to class—too much. I assign faults and pass judgments as if I'm a Manhattan prep school queen bee, deciding who to let in my clique with the point of a finger and flick of my hair.

After days of studying women in the flesh, at night I'd dig back into my stacks of journals, trying to get into their brains and discover what makes someone a good mate, what the defining characteristics of long-term healthy couplings are.

Turns out, my near-master's in psychology isn't useless after all. Though I do wonder if I should have been more proactive in this research before Jack and I said "I do." In the eyes of science, we're not a picture-perfect duo. For instance, according to a study by Florida State University, fighting makes for a happy marriage. It's unhealthy for couples to internalize their anger, the researchers concluded— which is really all that Jack does. Getting him to talk about his feelings is like trying to make it rain on a cloudless day.

But dwelling on Jack's shortcomings wasn't going to get me any closer to finding him a wife, so I tucked that nugget of info into the far back of my brain and added to my growing list of qualities Jack's wife should possess. Number twenty-four? Someone who has similar personality characteristics to Jack, because studies show that people who are alike have lower divorce rates. I need a nerd. One who's logical, even-keeled, and looks before she leaps. And where better to find someone who's like Jack than at his veterinary school? All those cerebral, doctors-to-be gathered in one place.

I look over my list one last time and close my laptop. Then I stretch my neck and slip my feet into a pair of red heels. I'm hoping the pop of color in contrast with my black dress will attract people's attention downward—away from my carroty skin.

I hear the screen door in the kitchen creak open, then slam shut, and Benny goes scurrying out of the room to greet Jack. Gertie chimes in with her own squeaky salutation.

Seconds later, Jack fills the door frame of our bedroom and stops.

"Beautiful," he says, almost under his breath.

I look up at him, ignoring his mandatory compliment, and meet his gaze. It took me a few days to get used to the new intensity with which Jack's been looking at me. As if he's memorizing every detail of my face and filing it away for later. Later is, I realize, when he won't be able to see it anymore, but neither one of us has given voice to that inevitable future.

"Better or worse than you thought?" I had texted him a warning of my new appearance after getting off the phone with Dr. Saunders.

He walks closer and rubs his fingers over my bare shoulder. "Better." His lips curve up, but the delight doesn't reach his eyes. They remain serious. Focused. "Sexy, actually. In an *X-Files* kind of way."

He pulls me to him. "We don't have to go. You know I hate these things."

I move out from his embrace. "Of course we're going. It's your big night."

Jack's getting an award for the research he presented to the Science of Veterinary Symposium, as well as being the first recipient of the Donald J. Hook research grant.

He steps toward the closet while pulling his T-shirt off over his head.

"Is my suit clean?" he asks, rummaging through the hangers.

I don't answer, as I see that his hand has found the plastic dry-cleaning bag encasing his sport coat and neatly pressed pants. I perch myself on the edge of our bed and smooth my dress over my thighs.

"Have you told people?" I ask. I don't add "about the cancer" because for the past few weeks Jack and I have abided by an unspoken agreement to not say the word—or discuss what the word is slowly doing to my body, our marriage, our happily ever after.

"A few," he says, buttoning up a crisp white shirt. I notice slight yellow stains at the pits and make a mental note to order him a new oxford online.

I nod. I don't want to get pity looks all night long, but I also don't want to have to explain why my skin is glowing like the sun.

As if reading my thoughts, Jack adds, "We'll just tell everyone else you spent too long in a tanning booth?" He pulls his pants up each leg, then stuffs his feet into a pair of black loafers with shiny silver buckles.

"Nobody goes to those anymore. Well, unless you live on the Jersey Shore," I say.

Jack looks at me blankly.

"You know, like JWoww? Pauly D?"

"Who?"

I laugh at his almost nonexistent pop culture knowledge. "C'mon, grab your jacket, we need to go."

He glances at the clock. "Relax, we have almost an hour."

"Jack," I say, rolling my eyes. I should have realized he probably never even glanced at the invitation. "It started thirty minutes ago."

I LOVE WALKING into a room with Jack. His towering height commands attention, literally turning heads most places we go. I wasn't blessed with model-good looks, so it's the closest I've come to knowing what that might feel like. With him, I turn heads by proxy, and the exhilaration that comes with it rarely gets old. But Jack hates it. If it were up to him, he would be a chameleon, blending into the walls and carpet everywhere he went. Jack suffers from a moderate case of social anxiety. He finds most conversations with strangers awkward and uncomfortable and often relays to me in bed at night the stupid things he's said or done in the company of others, which I find deliciously charming.

But tonight, for the first time, I wish he wasn't quite so noticeable. Heads turn from the speaker when we attempt to sneak in the door at the back of the hotel ballroom, and I feel myself start to burn under the scrutiny. "Where are our seats?" I hiss at Jack, trying to fold my shoulders in on themselves, making my body as small as possible.

He spots them across the room, and we weave in and out of tables, trying not to trip over handbags and chair legs and people's feet. What feels like hours later, I gratefully slip into my seat and pick up the goblet of water in front of me. Sweat has broken out on my forehead and I wonder why I didn't just take Jack up on his offer to stay home.

"Am I bright red?" I whisper to Jack, because my face is absolutely on fire. Then I realize what I've said, and we both burst out laughing, which garners some irritated glances from the other people sitting at our table.

Jack leans his mouth closer to my ear. "More of a yellow, actually, if that's possible. Must be the light in here." I stifle another giggle, as a man in gloves and a white jacket sets a plate with a gravy-covered chicken breast and four limp stalks of asparagus in front of me.

I compose myself and cut small bites of the cold food as the man at the podium talks about the year in veterinary science.

". . . and who could forget the woman who brought in what she thought was an injured house cat but turned out to be a *bobcat*? Thank god for Dr. Lichstein and his quick reflexes with the Diazepam."

Polite laughter titters through the audience. I laugh again, too, and sit back in my chair feeling light and airy and happy to be sitting next to Jack.

"Finally, before we move on to the awards, I'd like to congratulate this year's PhD and DVM candidates, who might just be the hardest-working, most innovative thinkers in the area of veterinary medicine that we've ever had." He pauses, then waves his hand toward the audience. "I know, I know. I say that every year. Congratulations on your achievements and I look forward to handing you your diplomas in May."

Applause fills the ballroom. I lift my hands to clap but find that they're frozen in my lap.

May.

It's as if someone placed an obnoxious alarm clock in the middle of the table and it's ticking right at me, time hurtling toward the future.

Jack's graduation.

Summer.

Four to six months.

And then I remember a gag gift I saw once in one of those Sky-Mall magazines or Brookstone catalogues that counted down the days until you die and I was thinking how morbid that was. But now I wonder how many days mine would say I had. Twenty-five? Sixty? One hundred?

"Jack Richmond."

Beside me, Jack scoots his chair back, then leans over to kiss me before standing up to walk toward the podium and I realize I've missed the entire lead-up to his award. I plaster a smile on my face and watch the back of his lanky body as it strides through the maze of tables, his jacket neatly hanging from his shoulders, his pants perfectly creased from the dry cleaner.

And I know that no number of days is enough.

When Jack gets back to the table, he sets his wood and gold plaque where his plate used to be and reaches out to take my hand. He leans in close and I think he's going to kiss me again, but instead he whispers in my ear, "Are you OK?"

I nod, even though I feel clammy and shaky and a little sick.

I take a deep breath.

Focus.

I just need to focus.

I squeeze Jack's hand reassuringly and smile at him, and when he turns his head back toward the speaker, I begin scanning the tables, though I'm not really sure what I'm looking for. Single women, for starters, but it's harder than I thought it would be to tell who's with a date and who's just sitting next to a classmate, professor, or friend.

Some of the faces are familiar—people I've run into when taking Jack lunch at the lab or met at other veterinary college events.

My eyes light on a woman with a sensible blond bob. I stroke my own thick brown locks, smoothing the ends around my fingers. Jack likes long hair. Regardless, she looks smart in her square-framed glasses. Responsible. Organized. And better still, she looks to be alone. I take in the top of her blue strapless gown that's splayed across her bosom like a cloth accordion—she's a little flat-chested, but not in an unflattering way. When my gaze travels back to her face, I notice that she's staring at me. She gives me a small smile before I dart my eyes back to the stage.

Later, people stand in clusters holding sweating beverages, watching a few daring bodies clumsily jerk their limbs on the small square dance floor set up in front of a four-piece band. Jack has left my side to get us wine from the bar, but he's being stopped every couple of feet with congratulatory handshakes and slaps on the back.

I stand with my hands clasped in front of me and then fold them across my chest. Then I put one hand on my hip and let my other arm dangle by my side. Even though I'm standing on the periphery of the party, I'm as self-conscious as if a spotlight is shining directly on me. I urge Jack to move faster through his admirers so I can take comfort in his shadow once again.

"Hey."

I'd been staring so intently at Jack's back I didn't notice the blue-frocked woman with glasses approach me.

"Hi," I say. Up close I can see that she's a natural, not bottle, blonde. Her hair is thin, wispy, and her skin is so pale it's translucent. Veins shine through like a roadmap of highways and rivers on her chest and cheeks. She looks fragile and I frown. I need Jack's new wife to be sturdy. Durable. She opens her mouth to speak and I notice she has a piece of asparagus wedged in her upper teeth.

"You're Jack's wife."

I nod.

"I'm Charlene," she says.

Charlene. The name clicks.

"You took care of Rocky when we were in the mountains," I say, remembering Jack's irritation at her seeming ineptitude. OK, so Jack's not terribly impressed by her veterinary skills. But she is responsible. And thoughtful. And she gave up her entire weekend so Jack could spend time with me. That's a pretty big favor.

"Thanks so much for doing that."

"Of course," she says, and then clears her throat. "Jack told me about . . . your situation."

"He did?" I'm surprised by this. That day in the car is the only time he's mentioned this woman, yet he knows her well enough to tell her something so personal? Although he did say he had told some of his colleagues, so, then again, why not her? It's not like he has a lot of close friends at work. People like Jack, but it takes a lot for him to open up. Even his best friend from high school, Thom, who still lives in Indiana, he only sees once a year, and talks to just a handful of times more than that.

"Yeah, it's kind of my research field," she says. "Cancer in dogs. Golden retrievers. I'm trying to find out why they have a higher incidence of it than other breeds."

Ah. Now it makes sense. Jack would want to collect data from all available resources—even if said source is dealing with canines.

"They do?" I ask.

"Yeah. About one in three dogs gets cancer, but in golden retrievers it's 60 percent." She brightens when she says this, and I know it's not because she's happy that dogs are riddled with tumors, it's because she's like Jack—invigorated by her work.

Like Jack. My heart trips over itself, quickening. So what if her skin is see-through? It's what's inside that counts.

"Do you cook?" It just tumbles out of my mouth and I wish I could reach up and grab the words with my fist and stuff them back in.

She tilts her head and narrows her eyes behind her glasses. "Huh?"

Great. Now I'm the *crazy* cancer patient. Maybe I can mumble something about the brain tumor and slip off into the crowd. But before I can formulate an explanation for my unexpected turn in conversation, a woman comes up behind her.

"Hey, Char."

She turns. "Hey!"

"Melissa, meet Daisy. Daisy, this is Melissa, my roommate."

I find it a little strange that a nearly-thirty-year-old woman getting her PhD would have a roommate, but maybe times are tight. Or maybe she doesn't like living alone.

I smile at Melissa and as she returns the expression, I notice a slight widening of her eyes as she takes in my sallow complexion. She quickly masks it, and turns back to Charlene. "Can we get out of here soon? I'm beat."

"Yeah, that's fine. Let me grab my coat." She looks at me. "It was good seeing you. Please tell Jack I said congratulations."

"I will."

She begins to walk off, and then hesitates and leans in closer to me and touches my arm. "Yun zhi mushrooms," she says in a quiet voice.

Now it's my turn to be confused. I wonder if it's a bizarre response to my equally bizarre cooking question, as in, "I do cook. Mushrooms."

Then she adds: "U Penn just found that they increased survival rates for dogs with hemangiosarcoma. Look it up."

I nod, struck by the kindness in her eyes. Even though I search for it, pity is nowhere to be found, and it makes me like her even more.

ON THE DRIVE home, Jack drones on about a professor that he spent most of the night talking to and his ideas regarding Jack's research on treating hip dysplasia with a blue-green algae derivative.

"The spirulina is effective, obviously, but Kramer thinks we could combine it with other compounds—make a supersupplement of sorts . . ."

I know he's speaking more to himself than to me—it's how he organizes his thoughts, because God forbid he would actually write any-thing down—so I tune him out and think more about Charlene. She has a lot in common with Jack, but is it too much? Is she scatter-brained like him, or organized? Maybe she wouldn't even notice an unruly pile of dirty socks because she'd be too busy thinking about mushrooms or sarcomas or her latest golden retriever patient. I won-der how she is to live with—maybe I could track down her roommate and try to get some information out of her. Melissa, was it? And then the thought that tugged on me when Charlene introduced us fully formulates itself in my brain.

"Is she a lesbian?" I say out loud, not even realizing I'm talking over Jack, until the words are out of my mouth.

He stops midsentence and looks at me, taking his eyes off the dark road leading up to our street for longer than I think is safe. His eyebrows furrow, and his mouth forms an O: "Who?"

"Charlene," I say, and then point to the windshield. "Watch the road!"

He resets his gaze forward and shrugs. "Um . . . I don't know? I've never really thought about it."

I nod. "Do you think she's pretty?"

The crease in his forehead deepens. "Daisy," he says. My name is a statement. "Are you OK?"

Great. My husband thinks I'm a crazy cancer patient, too. "I'm fine," I say, waving off his scrutiny. "Tell me more about Kramer."

But he doesn't. After a few beats of silence he asks me how class is going. "You haven't said much about it recently."

Which I could tell him is because after I got a D on my makeup Gender Studies exam, I decided to stop taking tests altogether. I don't do the reading assignments, I haven't written any papers, and my pro-fessors and I seem to have an unspoken agreement that I can just drop in on class like a socialite choosing which fancy parties she feels like going to.

But instead, I say, "It's good."

He waits for me to elaborate.

I don't.

As he sets the parking brake, he turns to me. "Hey, do you want to go to Waffle House in the morning?"

I unbuckle my seat belt and look at him. "Don't you have PetSmart tomorrow?" Jack volunteers the first Saturday of every month with the Athens Small Dog Rescue during their adoption day at the local pet store.

"Yeah, but I can skip it."

"You've never skipped," I say. "Besides, you know I don't eat that stuff." I open the door, bracing myself for the cool night air that's sure to bite my bare legs.

He mumbles something and doesn't move from the front seat.

"What?" I fold at the waist and stick my head back in the car to better hear him.

"You used to." The side of his mouth turns up and his crooked tooth peeks through his lips. "Remember the morning after the first time you spent the night with me?"

I cock my head at Jack's nostalgia. He's not the sentimental type.

And then I let out a tiny sigh as I think of that morning. Of course I remember. His bed-tousled hair. The chewy bacon. But that was before the Lots of Cancer. That was even before the Little Cancer the first time. And I am not the same girl who could throw caution to the wind and eat whatever she wanted. And Jack knows that. Or he should.

We stare at each other. Seven years of memories swim between us, and lighting on the same one strengthens the current. I swear I can feel it tugging on my heart. "Come on," I say more gently while straightening my bent spine. "Let's go inside."

nine

THE TEMPERATURE OF the hot yoga class at Open Chakra studio is a stifling and humid 105 degrees. For the past two years, I've suffered through the 8 A.M. Saturday morning sessions with Bendy Mindy and her weird southern Buddhist hybrid way of speaking ("Namaste, y'all!"), after reading a study that the practice helps rid your body of toxins and can possibly reverse the cancer process, effectively preventing tumors from growing in the body.

Now, even though I know it effectively does not, I still find myself perched on my organic jute mat, conqueror breathing in unison with eight other women—one of whom could be Jack's wife.

"Now, again," Bendy Mindy instructs. "Inhale deeply. From your beer guts, guys and gals!"

The hissing sound of our collective exhale fills the room like a band of angry cobras in a wicker basket and I glance around, wondering if Bendy Mindy has noticed that there are no men in her class. A woman with a Jamie Lee Curtis pixie cut in the back of the room locks eyes with me and quickly looks away, and that's when I notice a few other classmates boring holes into my skin.

Yep, I'm orange. Get over it, I silently tell them and then close my eyes to try and forget about their curious stares and find my Zen.

Except I've never really been good at finding my Zen. While everyone else is silently repeating mantras, I'm the one silently repeating items on a grocery list or psychological theories for an upcoming exam.

We move into downward dog and a bead of sweat runs from my forehead down the length of my nose and drips onto the floor. My hands slide a little on the slick mat and I concentrate on keeping my balance. I'm struck by how this simple pose seems more difficult than usual. Maybe because I haven't been in a few weeks?

My head goes light and I squeeze my eyes shut to combat the wave of dizziness that threatens to overtake me.

I breathe in.

Exhale.

Better.

"Knees down. Now slide back to ooh-tan-uh shee-sho-san-uh," Bendy Mindy directs in her soft twang. "And just let go of your week. Whatever you're holding on to—anger, stress, you're irritated that your favorite singer got kicked off *The Voice*—" She waits for a response and receives a titter of polite chuckles from two women. Satisfied, she continues: "Breathe it out. Let go of the anger."

It feels like that word-association game where someone says "door" and you say the first word that pops into your mind and it surprises you, because at the word "anger" the first thing I think of is . . . Kayleigh.

And as soon as I think it, I know it's true.

I'm mad at Kayleigh.

It's been almost three weeks since I told her about the Lots of Cancer on the phone, and though we've texted, she hasn't come over. She hasn't just shown up at the back door and let herself in and put her shoes up on my coffee table without being invited. And even though that's what used to irritate me, now I'm irritated that she hasn't done it. And until this moment, I've been trying to ignore it.

The little voice in my head has been making excuses: She's busy! I'm busy! We've gone longer without seeing each other! Quit being so needy!

But now the little voice in my head is wondering if maybe, even after all these years, I've miscalculated her. Maybe she isn't as strong as I thought. Maybe she's avoiding me like all my other "friends" who fell away the first time I had cancer because they didn't know if they should ask how the chemo was going or pretend I wasn't having chemo and talk about the weather or the latest episode of *Revenge* instead. So they just didn't talk to me at all.

Freud would say I'm displacing. I'm pissed about the cancer and I'm taking it out on Kayleigh. That's the problem with being a psych major. I can't just have feelings like normal people. I have to try to *understand* them. It's exhausting.

I sigh and give my head a gentle shake as Bendy Mindy directs us into the bridge.

God, it's hot. Is it always this hot?

"Concentrate on your breath, y'all."

I close my eyes again and exhale and try to let go of Kayleigh and my displaced anger or whatever it is. I need to be thinking about Jack anyway.

And his new wife.

We stand up for warrior pose and I try to discreetly survey the room again, but turning my head makes me decidedly more dizzy, so I look toward the mirror at the front of the room and try to focus on myself. Is my body aligned correctly? My back toes perfectly perpendicular with my front heel? Sweat drips in my eyes, blurring my vision, and as I lift my hand to try and rub it out, I feel my body swaying.

"Daisy?"

I hear my name, but it sounds far away and kind of singsongy, like when my mom used to serenade me with my favorite nursery rhyme over and over when I couldn't sleep. And then the song is on a loop in my head.

> *Dai-sy, Dai-sy, give me your answer, do!*
> *I'm half crazy, all for the love of you!*
> *It won't be a stylish marriage,*
> *I can't afford a carriage,*
> *But you'll look sweet*
> *Upon the seat*
> *Of a bicycle built for two!*

I open my eyes, smiling a kind of dumb, childish smile as if the song has transformed me into my three-year-old self, and I'm a little confused because all of these faces are staring at me and it takes me a minute to realize I'm on my back.

"Are you OK?" says the mouth of a woman who has hard, sinewy arms but a soft, dewy face and I feel like the duckling in that book: "Could you be Jack's wife?"

And then I notice that my head is pounding and I roll to the side just in time to throw up what's left of my kale smoothie on the sinewy/soft lady's bare feet.

And that's when I decide that I'm done with yoga.

JACK'S NOT ROMANTIC. At least not in the conventional way. At least that's what I tell people when they ask *What did Jack get you for Valentine's Day/Christmas/your birthday?* and they expect me to say *a bouquet of tulips* or *a sapphire bracelet* or *a box of truffles*. But instead I say, "Oh, Jack's not romantic in the conventional way," which leads them to believe that he *is* romantic in some other supersecret way. But he's not.

Jack's logical. Which isn't to say he isn't sweet and thoughtful, because he can be, but he can also be royally clueless, as if he's never seen a Meg Ryan movie in his life. I learned early in our relationship that if I wanted to be wined and dined, I was going to have to make the reservations—or specifically tell him that I want to go out to eat, which night I want to go and that he should wear a sports jacket and tie.

Which is why I'm shocked when Jack comes home early on Monday night and asks me to go out to dinner.

"A new restaurant just opened up downtown," he says. "Wildberry Café. It's one of those farm-to-table deals. Thought we could check it out."

"Tonight?" I ask, looking down at the same pajamas I've been wearing since I woke up this morning. I had planned on changing before Jack got home, so I could pretend that I had been to class, but it's only 5 P.M. and he never comes home before eight. I hope he doesn't notice.

"Yeah," he says. "I just gotta change." Benny at his heels, he walks back toward the bedroom, pulling his T-shirt off over his head as he goes.

"I'm not really hungry," I call after him, and snuggle tighter into the divot my butt has made on the couch. My cell buzzes on the coffee table and I know it's my mom, because she's texted me seven times in the past hour confirming her arrival Thursday morning to drive me to my stent procedure. It's taken her seven texts because she just learned to text a month ago and she accidentally hits send too soon or she leaves out an apostrophe or she wants to make sure I've gotten the text and that it's not floating in cyberspace somewhere or has erroneously (and miraculously) been zapped to someone else's phone, even though I've explained to her that that doesn't happen.

I pick up my phone. This one says: **Should I bring shedts? Or do you have? Can't remember.**

I know she means sheets. And I know I'll get another text message clarifying that when she realizes that she's misspelled it.

Minutes later, Jack reappears in a burgundy polo and looks at me expectantly.

"C'mon, go change."

So he has noticed my pajamas.

"What are you doing home so early?" I ask.

"I told you," he says slowly, as if I'm the crazy one. "I want to go to dinner."

I sit with this information. First it was the Waffle House and now this, and I couldn't be more baffled than if Jack had told me he was quitting school to be a trapeze artist. Part of me knows I should be thrilled. Isn't this what I always told Jack I wanted? To be caught off guard by a romantic dinner invite? Except when I told him that last year in a fit of restlessness because we'd only been married a year and I thought maybe we were lacking some of the spine-tingling excitement newlyweds are supposed to revel in, he said: "It's just not me. I don't think about stuff like that." And though I was disappointed, I knew he was right.

It's not him.

So instead of being elated, I feel something else, even though I can't immediately put my finger on it. It's like a sweater that used to hug my curves in all the right ways, but then shrunk in the dryer. This new Jack doesn't fit right.

"I don't want to go," I say, and I know that my voice is laced with irritation and I know that's not fair, because Jack is doing a nice thing. A Romantic Thing. And I'm ruining it. But I'm orange. And I'm in my pajamas. And I haven't felt right since throwing up in yoga, even though I didn't mention that particular episode to Jack because I didn't want him to look at me with any more concern than he already does.

"Are you sure?" he asks.

"Yeah," I say, keeping my eyes trained on the television. I can hear him breathing behind me and I know he's debating, calculating whether he should push or not. Try one more time. I try to tamp down my irritation. *Now* you want to be romantic? And then I'm jealous, because what if this really is the new Jack? What if this Lots of Cancer has flipped some switch in him and he's become Romantic Jack and then I die and some other girl gets to bask in his swashbuckling, poetry-spouting romanticness?

And then I try to look on the bright side, because his being more romantic is really just going to help when I *do* find his new wife, so at least it could make things easier.

And then I'm exhausted from the vast range of conflicting emotions I've experienced in the past ten seconds and I wonder if maybe the orange-sized tumor in my brain is to blame.

Remaining quiet, I hold my breath until I feel rather than hear him leave the room and I know he's retreating to his office. I can't help but feel a little relieved.

I pick up the remote and flip to a show with bespectacled scientists hypothesizing the top-ten ways the Earth could meet its demise in the next century. A man looking a little too pleased at the prospect discusses the possibility of a colossal black hole swallowing our entire solar system into its gaping maw. And I know I should be horrified by the idea, but a tiny selfish part of me kind of hopes that this will happen.

My cell buzzes again, and I sigh.

Preferably before my mom gets here.

ten

ON THURSDAY MORNING, a picture of Charlene stares pleasantly at me from the computer screen as I read her short bio on the university's veterinary medicine Web site. My eyes glaze over the first few titles of her published journal articles: "Digital Squamous Cell Carcinoma in Golden Retrievers," "Incidence of Malignant Mammary Tumors in Female Canines." I look back at her head shot and try to find some telltale sign of her sexual orientation. It's a pointless exercise, not only because identifying gayness from a picture is ridiculous, but because Jack doesn't appear to be remotely interested in her in any way. I click back to the directory of DVM candidates, and a sea of studious men and women in white lab coats look back at me. I start analyzing photos, and then laugh at myself. What can one possibly glean about someone from a single snapshot? And even if I could decipher that a woman would be a good fit for Jack, then what? Send her an email that says "Hey, Do you like my husband? Check yes or no."

I shut my laptop in frustration when I hear a knock at the back door.

I head into the kitchen, where Benny is crouched on the floor, coiled like a spring, a growl reverberating from somewhere deep in his throat.

I open the door for my mom, and then reach down for Benny's collar, scooping him up in my arms. "You brought Mixxy?" I ask.

Mom stands in the middle of the kitchen with the cat carrier in her right hand and her small rolling overnight bag in her left.

"Hi, sweetheart," she says, huffing from her walk up the back stairs. "Yes, I'm so sorry. I was hoping Jack could look at a cut on her paw. Poor little thing has been licking it all week. I texted you. You didn't get it?"

"You texted me the letter 'V.'" Benny struggles against me, so I walk with him toward the back door and fight with the stuck handle until it finally swings open and set him on the landing. "Go! Play!" I command him, letting the screen door *thhwap* shut between us. I turn back to my mother.

She's set both the carrier and the suitcase at her feet and is holding her flip phone at arm's length, squinting at the screen.

"I don't have my glasses. Darn thing." She makes a clicking sound with her tongue. "I don't know why they have to make it so complicated."

"Mom, it's fine," I say, eyeing her keys that are splayed on the counter. Benny's plaintive whimpers at the back door fill the air and I put my fingers to my temple. It's the second time I've had a headache this week, and I make a mental note to drink more water. I bend down to get Mom's belongings.

"Leave that," she clucks again. "I'll get it. You're in no condition—"

"I'm fine." Except I've already said fine twice and she hasn't been here for longer than three minutes. I take a deep breath and exhale as I carry her suitcase and Mixxy down the hall to the office, where I've blown up a twin-size air mattress on the floor.

I contemplate crawling onto it. I'm not really "fine." I've been so tired the past few days, I've been asleep before Jack even gets home from work.

"What time's the procedure?" Mom's voice from the doorway startles me and I straighten my shoulders.

"Three."

She glances at her wristwatch, holding the tiny face of it between the fingers of her right hand and squinting. "Great! Anything you want to do for the next few hours?"

Yes. Sleep. But I don't want Mom to worry about me any more than she already is. She may be in fake-cheerleader mode, but I know underneath flows a river of anxiety.

"We could take a walk?"

She brightens. "That's a wonderful idea. Fresh air will do us both some good."

As I scoot past her, mumbling that I need to get my sneakers, Mom squeezes my still yellowish-orange-hued bicep. "You look great," she says through a smile so wide I can see the gunmetal-capped molars in the back of her mouth. "You really do."

I glance into her eyes—red-rimmed and swollen—and I know it's not me she's lying to.

THE GASTROENTEROLOGIST HAS a mole the size of a pencil eraser on her chin, with three long hairs sprouting from it. This is what I focus on as she repeats the same questions I was just asked moments before by the nurse.

"Are you currently taking any prescription, over-the-counter medicines, herbs, or supplements?"

"Just essence of yun zhi," I say. The bottle of mushroom tablets arrived the day before in a yellow package with Chinese characters all over it. I'd already taken three.

She narrows her eyes and pens something on my chart.

"How's your throat feel? Getting numb?"

The nurse had sprayed a tangy anesthetic in my mouth and instructed me to swallow.

I nod. It is definitely working.

"Great," she says. "Can you lie back on your right side? We'll give that just a few more minutes to take effect and then we'll slip this scope in"—she holds up a plastic tube—"and get started."

She clicks a button on the intercom next to my bed. It beeps. "Tonya, we're ready to go when you are."

I assume Tonya's the nurse. She hadn't introduced herself before she started jabbing the IV needle into my wrist when she came into the room earlier. So much for bedside manner.

Dr. Jafari turns back to me. "Who did you bring with you today?"

"My mom," I croak. My tongue is thick in my mouth and my throat feels papery. Parched.

"Ahh. No one takes care of us like Mom can, right?" She's shuffling through papers on the counter next to a box of latex gloves and a cross-section of a plastic intestine and stomach, and I know that her comment is practiced. A canned response that's meant to relay a sense of comfort or camaraderie between doctor and patient. She's not looking for a real answer, so I nod.

There was a short time in my life when I thought that was true. That Mom took care of everything. After Dad died, she worked two jobs to stifle the endless flow of bills in our mailbox. I felt safest right by her side, so after school I would wait at home in our den, watching my taped cartoons until moonlight shone through the windows. Sometimes I'd wait up for her. Other nights, I would crawl into her tangle of sheets, and when I finally heard the car pull into the carport, I shut my eyes tight, pretending to be asleep so she wouldn't make me get into my own cold bed. It worked most nights.

It was life, and I thought it was normal until the day I realized it wasn't. I was eight. And I was wearing my favorite Rainbow Brite shirt that had a real red ribbon sewn into the cotton fabric at the end of her long yellow braid. A girl in my class, Angela, was riding the bus for the first time that day—she usually stood in the car pickup line, but her mom had some kind of appointment and couldn't make it. I knew that because she announced it loudly when she boarded the bus, as if it was imperative she let us know that just because she was riding with us that one time, she was still different, better in some intangible way. Her mother was standing on the sidewalk waiting to meet her. I got off first and ambled to my house, the front door key on a piece of purple yarn around my neck. I reached the front stoop and pulled the key up through the neck of my T-shirt. I was about to put it into the lock, anticipating the snack I would make for myself once inside—butter on saltine crackers—when a voice cut into my thoughts.

"Sweetheart?"

I turned to see Angela's mother looking at me with concern. Her thick bangs stopped an inch above her eyebrows. I wondered if she cut her hair herself, like my mom did, and accidentally cut one lock too short, forcing her to make the rest of her bangs match. They were sharp. And judgey. And I didn't like the looks of them. Angela stood at her side, peering at me, too, and I had a fierce, overwhelming feeling like I was being caught breaking some unwritten rule that no one had told me.

I fingered the ribbon on my shirt and looked at her.

"Darling, is your mother home?"

Lying was wrong. This I knew with the righteous fervor possessed by every eight-year-old. But I also knew somehow that it was currently my only option.

Still mute, I nodded.

She took a step into our small yard that seemed to be perpetually brown, though the grass in the lawns that flanked our house was a vibrant green.

"Can I speak with her, hon?"

My mind raced and I opened my mouth to voice my first-ever real lie to an adult. "She's asleep. She sleeps in the afternoons."

Angela's mom was now standing on my front stoop with me, Angela tight against her leg as if she were attached to it. I felt cornered.

"Maybe you could wake her up," she said. "I'd like to talk with her."

I realized this woman wasn't going to go away. There was no escape route and my young mind was struggling to come up with one on the fly. I slowly turned the key in the lock and opened the door.

As I stepped into the hallway, Angela and her mom on my heels, I cringed, seeing our house for the first time through the eyes of a stranger. The hallway light was a single bulb. The glass fixture meant to encase it sat on the fake wood floor beneath it, covered in dust. It didn't make sense to reattach it, my mom said, when you just had to take it off every time you needed to change the bulb. I stepped over it and glanced at the five uneven, teetering stacks of newspapers lining the wall leading into the den making the hallway feel even narrower. They were meant to be recycled, but there never seemed to be any time to take them to the dump.

The den was worse. Old plates with crusts of stale bread and plastic cups a quarter full of leftover Crystal Light or Diet Coke sat scattered on our sticky end tables. Mold had started to grow in one of them, and I checked it every afternoon when I got home, curious to see what new spores—and colors—had developed while I was gone. In the corner of the room, the litter box for Frank, a cat that my mom had found in the parking lot of the drugstore she was working at one night, overflowed with black turds and urine-soaked lumps of gray grit. I thought of the cleaning chart mom put up on the fridge when school started. I was supposed to do my chores and check them off as soon as I got home. The first few weeks, she had been hawkish, making sure I was following the rules. But that had been months ago, and the cleaning chart had long since been

covered up with magnets holding straight-A report cards and cou-
pons for two-for-one pan pizzas at Little Caesars and yellowed Dave
Barry columns.

Angela's mother's wide eyes scanned the scene, her lip curled up
in disgust. She put her hand on Angela's bony shoulder, willing her
not to move.

"Um, stay here," I said, turning away from her. "I'll go get my
mom."

I ran down the side hall that connected three boxy bedrooms and
a bathroom, and entered the door that belonged to my mother's room.
Her bed was unmade, the white sheets grimy and yellowed from years
of use and limited washings. My heart raced and I had no idea what I
was going to do. *Think,* I commanded myself. I took a few deep
breaths and that's when an idea came to me. I left her room and
ducked into the bathroom. I reached into the shower and turned on
the water full blast.

Then, I calmly walked down the hall to face Angela's mother's
bangs.

"She's in the shower," I announced as soon as I stepped foot in
the den. "She says if you leave your number she'll call you when she
gets out."

Angela's mother furrowed her brow and I knew she didn't believe
me. She glanced at her watch, and I was terrified she was going to say
she'd wait. But she didn't.

She nodded, as if she had made a decision about something,
grabbed Angela's hand, and gingerly stepped her way back to the front
door. Then she turned around. "You tell your mother that I'll be back,"
she said, and narrowed her eyes at me. The thinly veiled threat hung
in the air between us.

When she shut the door behind her, the heat of shame blossomed
up my face and I looked around at the den, seeing it with Angela's
mom's eyes—unable to see it again through my own.

I spent the entire afternoon scrubbing and vacuuming and washing dishes and dusting and bagging newspapers and laundering sheets. I even moved a chair into the hallway, and standing on my tiptoes on the seat of it, I was just barely able to screw the light fixture back into place.

When my mother got home that night, long after the moon had made its appearance, she entered the house through the door between the carport and the kitchen. I heard her keys clatter on the now-glistening countertop.

"Daisy-bear?"

"Yeah," I called from my perch on the couch. I beamed, waiting for her to shower me with gratitude and praise for our new, sparkling house.

"Did you do your homework?" she called out.

"Yes," I said. Maybe she hadn't looked up yet. Maybe she was still flipping through the mail that she carried in with her each night.

She appeared in the doorway of the den and looked at me. The purple circles under her eyes were more pronounced in the evening. "Did you have a good day, sweetheart?"

I nodded. I knew I should tell her about Angela's mother. Ask her what I should do if she came back. But Mom looked so tired. And I couldn't bear to burden her with one thing more.

"I'm so glad," she said, giving me a weak smile. Her eyes scanned the room, and I waited for them to brighten, for her to be overcome with the marked difference between now and when she left it that morning. "You picked up," she said.

I nodded again. If I were a dog, my tail would have been thumping the floor in rapid-fire succession. "You're a good daughter." There they were—the words I'd been waiting for, the reward for my hard work—but the emotion behind them was flat. And I couldn't understand why, instead of brightening, her face appeared even more defeated. She walked behind the couch, leaned down, and kissed the crown of my head. "Go do your teeth. It's bedtime." She padded off down the hall and I stood up. But instead of following her, I walked the opposite direction into the kitchen. I got a hammer and a nail from the junk drawer, and with my tiny fingers, I gently tapped the nail into the wall beside the door. Then I picked up Mom's keys from where they were splayed on the counter and hung them on the new metal peg.

"ALMOST DONE." A voice jerks me out of my past.

I open my eyes and focus my gaze on the long tube protruding from my mouth. I know it's jammed all the way down my throat and—even though I can't feel it—I fight the urge to gag.

A hand rests on my shoulder. "It's OK," the nurse says. "Relax." Her tone is warm, soothing, and I feel bad for thinking poorly of her before. She sounds nice.

I notice a slight pressure to the right above my abdomen and then nothing.

"There," she says, patting me again. "All done."

I try to raise my eyes to look at her, but my lids feel heavy and I have the absurd thought to prop them open with my fingers. I resist the impulse.

"Tired?" the nurse asks. "We gave you a light sedative. It should wear off shortly."

As she threads the plastic tubing backward out of my throat, Dr. Jafari's voice cuts in from beside me. "You did great. Tonya here will wheel you to the recovery room, go over a few postop details with your mom, and then you'll be on your way home in no time."

I want to say OK or thank you or something to acknowledge that she has spoken, but I can't make my voice work in conjunction with the opening of my mouth, so I shut it and don't say anything.

In the recovery room, Tonya rattles off instructions from a clipboard. "You may notice some discomfort where we placed the stent over the next few days, but if your stomach gets hard or swollen or you start vomiting, call us immediately. Ditto if you have a fever, chills, or any severe pain."

I nod like an obedient child but I'm not really listening to her. She has nice hair. Big soda-can-size curls that she obviously spent some time perfecting in a mirror before she left her house that morning. And she's a nurse, which means she's good at looking after people and disinfecting things. I wonder if Jack would find her attractive—her hips are wide and round.

Childbearing hips.

The phrase enters my mind, unbidden. I need to add to my list—a woman who wants children. And doesn't mind ant farms.

Just as I've decided that yes, Jack would like her, Tonya hands over the postop checklist and the diamond-studded gold band on her left ring finger neutralizes my thoughts. Great. So far my contenders for Jack's wife are a maybe-lesbian, a few smiling head shots of Jack's colleagues whom I've never met, and a woman who's already married.

On the way home, Mom reaches over and pats my leg. "How are you feeling?"

"I'm fine," I say, inching away from her and closer to the door.

"But do you—"

"Mom! I said I'm fine."

She nods and we ride in silence for a few minutes until she begins to fill the empty air with tales of Mixxy and the latest Giada recipe she re-created ("It was too tomatoey. And I don't think I like capers.") and the ending of the Mary Higgins Clark book she just read. Then she tells me that she's recently joined the Atlanta Audubon Society and she's going to attend her first bird-watching field trip this weekend. "I really only leave the house for work," she says. "I need to get out more."

I murmur a reply, but sit up a little straighter. That's it.

If I'm going to find Jack a wife, I need to get out more. I need to widen my net. I'm not going to meet anyone by staring at strangers on campus or going to the same yoga class I've been going to for years or getting procedures done at the doctor's office. I don't know why I didn't think of it before, but then it occurs to me that I've never had to date before. Not really. I met Jack when I was twenty. A baby. And he was the first real adult relationship I'd had—unless I count Adam, my "friend with benefits" who lived in the dorm beside mine my freshman year. My roommate assured me that this was what everyone did in college. But after a few short weeks, when I realized I knew how Adam curled his lip and whinnied like a horse when he came, but had no idea what he ate for breakfast, I ended it.

I need to get out. But it's more than that. I need to know where to go. And whom to look for. And what to do.

I need to learn how to date.

And I know, as much as I hate to admit it, that there's only one person who can help me.

I need Kayleigh.

eleven

TURNS OUT MIXXY'S cut is infected. Jack says he needs to run her up to his clinic to bandage her paw ("She has to stop licking it if it's going to heal," I overheard him instruct Mom in the living room) and pick up a round of antibiotics.

"You'll be OK?" he asks, sitting beside me on our bed. He rubs the back of my hand with his thumb.

I shrug him off. I'm only lying in bed because Mom won't let me get up, not even to do a load of laundry. I tell Jack this, adding a smirky: "Doctor's orders." I sigh. "I'm so glad she's leaving in the morning."

It's a sentiment I would have never voiced in elementary school, when I swallowed envy as other moms sewed costumes for school plays and made pineapple upside-down cakes for bake sales and were chaperones for field trips to pick-your-own berry farms and art museums. I nearly shook like a timid puppy with my own desire to have her reassuring hand smooth my hair or to put my head in her lap on the rickety seat-belt-less bus that we traveled in to our destinations. But I never told her that. There wasn't enough room in our tiny house to hold all of our sadness, so I did everything I could to alleviate hers and basked in the attention I received for my efforts. "I don't know where she came from," I overheard Mom whisper to Aunt Joey on one of their ritual Sunday-night long-distance phone calls, her voice cracking. "She's just so . . . responsible."

By high school, we had evolved into something resembling roommates more than mother and daughter. While my peers were fighting for later curfews and driving privileges, I was essentially running a house—ironing Mom's pleated pants, trying new recipes for dinner from her Weight Watchers cookbook, admiring the parallel vacuum lines that I etched into the carpet every second Saturday that I spent deep-cleaning, and reminding her every three thousand miles to get her oil changed.

"You worry too much, Daisy-bear," she'd say to me, but the unorthodox role reversal worked for us—until she met George. He was a car mechanic with a handlebar mustache, skinny arms, and a round belly. And the first time I saw him make Mom smile was like seeing the sun after living underground for ten years. George moved in with us when I was in the tenth grade and encouraged Mom to go back to school for her two-year degree—which is exactly how long their relationship lasted. "Not everyone's meant to be together forever," she said when I asked her why he was leaving. I was worried she'd revert back to her old self, but she never did. He had changed her. Or she had changed herself. And that changed us.

It was like some dormant momness had been jolted awake inside her, and like a peacock, she felt the overwhelming urge to display it all at once. On the Richter scale of parenting, she was suddenly a ten, insisting on driving me up to UGA for my first semester of school and decorating my dorm room with Target pillows and lamps and picture frames, then calling every day to make sure I was studying and not partying too hard or sleeping with inappropriate boys. I didn't resent it as much as I just didn't know how to respond to it. It was like we had been doing the fox-trot our entire life and Mom suddenly switched to the tango. I didn't know the steps. So I ignored most of her phone calls and her advice, while continuing to navigate my life the only way I'd ever known how—alone.

And then I got cancer. And I had no choice but to finally let her be the mother she had so desperately been trying to be, because for once I couldn't completely take care of myself and I didn't think it was fair to depend entirely on Jack and Kayleigh. So I let her come drive me to a few appointments and slather my dry skin with lotion, but I drew the line at spoon-feeding me broth and holding my hair when I threw up.

And now, here we are again—with her trying to squeeze in as much mothering as I'll allow, leaving me to believe it's no coincidence that only one letter changes the word to "smothering."

"She is leaving?" Relief floods Jack's face. "She was just saying something about staying the weekend."

I sigh again. "I already told her that wasn't necessary."

"I can see how she would think it might be," Jacks snaps. "She probably thinks I'm the worst husband ever. You should have let me take you today." Since I didn't let him come down to Emory for my trial workup, he had been single-minded in his determination to accompany me to the stent procedure. But I was just as determined not to let him miss any more clinic and jeopardize his chances of graduating on time.

I shake my head. "School comes—"

"—first," he finishes. "Yeah."

He stares at me and I feel like a glass slide in his lab, beneath his microscope lens. The sensation that I could break at any second under his gaze is constant and exhausting. At least he's given up trying to be romantic. After my rebuff of his uncharacteristic dinner invite, Jack's been working his usual hours—maybe even more than usual, and I wonder if it's because he wants a break from playing the concerned husband as much as I want a break from being the pitiable, dying wife. I'm relieved when Mom pops her head into view, declaring that I have a visitor.

Kayleigh steps into the room, her neon-pink shirt as loud as her voice. "What the hell? I have to get announced around here? It's like getting an audience with the queen." She curtsies at the foot of my bed.

"Hey, Kayleigh," Jack says, acknowledging her presence without really looking at her. When I first started dating Jack, I had a naive wish that he'd love Kayleigh as much as I did and the three of us would seamlessly become best friends, taking cross-country road trips and finishing each other's sentences like some kind of NBC sitcom. But it didn't exactly work out like that. "Does he ever, like, actually speak?" Kayleigh asked after first meeting him. I tried to explain about his social anxiety and that he warmed up after you got to know him. "She's a little, uh . . . in your face," was Jack's assessment, destroying the last vestiges of my perfect-friend-triangle fantasy.

Since then, they've learned to tolerate each other, even though Jack still sometimes questions our friendship after spending extended amounts of time with her. "You guys are just so . . . different." I've given up trying to explain that what we have in common is our whole lives.

Now he stands up, his right knee—the one that he had to have ACL surgery on in high school, not because of sports, but because he tripped *up* a set of cement stairs—popping, at the same time that Kayleigh crawls up onto the bed and sits cross-legged on Jack's side, facing me.

"I'll be back soon," Jack says. "Yell if you need anything."

Mom follows him out of the room. "No more than thirty minutes, Kayleigh," she calls over her shoulder. "Our patient needs her rest!"

I roll my eyes and lean into the stack of pillows supporting my back.

Kayleigh and I stare at each other, and the anger that I lit on in the yoga studio comes rushing back.

"Where have you been?"

"You just texted like ten minutes ago. I came right over."

"Not *today*," I say, annoyed. "For the past three weeks."

"What do you mean? I've asked if you want me to come over and you keep saying you're busy."

Technically, that's true. But she always texted right when I was el-bows deep in my wife research or in the late evening when I've been too tired to respond. And besides, that's not the point.

"So? You've never asked before."

"Excuse me for trying to be polite," she says.

"That's the thing!" I sit straight up to allow the irritation to rise up from my belly and out of my mouth. "You're not polite! You've never been polite!"

"Daisy, calm down," she says, glancing at the door as if we're eleven and she doesn't want her mom to catch us watching soap op-eras when we're not supposed to have the TV on. "Look, I was just trying to give you and Jack some space."

I nod. My body's suddenly weak from my small outburst. I lean back into the stack of pillows and take a deep breath. "I don't want space. And I don't want to go to the Waffle House."

At this, she scrunches her nose and tilts her head at me. "The Waf—"

I wave my hand to metaphorically erase what I just said. "Forget it. I just want everyone to stop acting so weird."

"OK," she says.

"OK," I say. But the air around us feels stretched thin, like a chewing gum bubble that's getting ready to pop. I know it's bad when I start wishing my mom would come in to check on me, just to break the silence.

But she doesn't, and finally Kayleigh speaks.

"You really were not kidding about your skin," she says. "You look like George Hamilton. I thought the stitch was supposed to fix that."

Relief washes over me. She's back.

"Stent," I correct her. "It will. Doctor says it may take a few days."

She nods. "How do you feel? Did it hurt?"

"No. It was nothing. I don't know why Mom's acting like I just had brain surgery."

"She just cares about you," Kayleigh says, waving her hand. "You're all she's got."

The words fall on my chest like a wrecking ball, and it takes effort to push them away. I'm not all she's got. She's got Mixxy. And Aunt Joey in Seattle. Or Portland. Somewhere near where those vampire movies were filmed. I can't ever remember. Oh, and her bird club. She's getting out more.

I smooth my hair over my shoulder, eager to change the subject. "How's work?"

Our eyes meet and I realize she's just as relieved as I am to discuss something normal. Neutral. Unrelated to Dying and Cancer. She launches into a rant about her annoying co-teacher, Pamela, and the upcoming kindergarten open house. "She's overhauling our entire classroom as if Bill Gates himself is coming to judge her teaching skills. And Pinterest. Oh holy God, the things she's finding on Pinterest. I don't have time to make sandpaper letter cards or any of the forty-seven stupid crafts she thinks will"—Kayleigh makes air quotes with her fingers—"enrich the learning environment."

We ease into the rhythm of our years-long friendship, bantering back and forth like two lumberjacks gliding a saw through a felled tree trunk. I take the lead, guiding the conversation toward the reason I invited her over.

"Are you still seeing the nineteen-year-old?"

"Harrison?"

"Is there more than one nineteen-year-old?"

"No!"

"OK, then."

She chews her thumbnail and mumbles. "I may have been at his house when you called."

"Kayleigh!"

"*What?*"

"It has to stop. We need to get you back out there."

"I know! I know."

I nod, pleased that I've steered our chat in the exact direction I wanted it to go. Pleased that I'll be able to get the information I want from her without revealing why I want it. I thought about telling her the truth, but every time I practiced saying it out loud, it sounded crazy. Even to me. "OK. Where do you go to meet guys?"

She shrugs. "I don't *go* anywhere. I just meet them when I'm out."

I lean forward a bit. "Out where? Where was the last place you met one?" Then I add, to clarify: "A man. Not a man-child."

She pauses, thinking, and spits a piece of her nail out of her mouth. "The dog park."

It's my turn to pause. "You don't own a dog."

"I know. I took Benny. That weekend you were in the mountains."

Oh, right. I brighten. The dog park. Why hadn't I thought of that? Not only will there be a lot of women there, but they will love dogs, which means they'll have something in common with Jack.

"Great. Let's go back. This weekend?"

"You're going to help me find a man? This should be good. You find something wrong with every single guy I date."

"Not true!" Although it is kind of true. But only because Kayleigh has the worst possible taste in men (and men-children) ever. She always has, dating back to middle school when she was obsessed with Chris Poland, a skater boy who spent more days in in-school suspension than out of it and sent her a love note with her name spelled incorrectly. And though my plan hadn't really been to help Kayleigh find a guy, I might as well help her at the same time I'm helping Jack.

God knows she could use it.

That night when Jack gets home and crawls into bed and rolls his socks one at a time off his feet and adds them to the pile on the floor, I watch him. I've spent the time since Kayleigh left in awe of the effort it takes to meet potential partners. With Jack it was so easy. I think about the day we met—when I didn't know he was my husband, when he was just a fellow student waiting for the university bus. I flinched when I saw a hand come at me from my peripheral vision.

"Sorry," a voice said. "There was a bee."

I had heard the buzzing, even seen the furry insect, but I hadn't been concerned about it.

"I thought those big ones were friendly," I said. "They don't have stingers, right?"

"Common misconception." He smiled, and I swear his face competed with the sun above us. My eyes lit on his crooked tooth. My stomach dropped to my toes. "They can actually sting more than once because they don't have barbs like honeybees."

I marveled as if this was the most interesting thing I had ever heard. Maybe it was.

In bed, Jack pulls me to his naked chest and I burrow my head into it, his wiry curls scraping my cheek, and I gather more memories into my growing pile. Jack memories. The terrible poem he wrote me one Valentine's Day, using the word "zaftig" to describe me. "It means curvy! You're curvy! Beautiful." I laughed. "Next time just use beautiful." Or driving to my mom's for Thanksgiving and the wreck he nearly caused on I-85, screeching to a halt and jumping out of the car to save a box turtle that was attempting to cross all six lanes of the highway. Or when he first kissed me, my lips trembling with nerves, and he pulled his oversized sweatshirt over his head and swallowed my small frame with it, allowing me to keep up the pretension that it was the air causing me to shiver.

I stack each memory in the suitcase of my brain side by side like neatly folded T-shirts, like I'm going on a trip and I don't want to leave them behind.

I suppose I am. And I don't.

Jack squeezes me tight and water fills my eyes, threatening to spill over.

"What are you thinking about?"

I want to tell him.

About the poem.

The turtle.

The sweatshirt.

And how these memories act like kerosene on the fire of my love for him. They engulf me. Scorch the innards of my being.

But I open my mouth and none of this comes out. I shut it. Swallow. Curl tighter in his embrace. Then open my mouth again.

"Did you lock the back door?" I ask.

"Yes," he murmurs, brushing his lips on the top of my head.

I thank him, and the two words hang in the air, until his breathing grows even and his heartbeat keeps the slow time of a metronome beneath my ear.

ON SATURDAY, IT'S raining. Not a drizzle, but thick, pelting sheets of water, as if the gray sky is as angry as it appears and is taking it out on the earth below. It's also the first official day of my clinical trial. I drove to Emory yesterday to pick up my vial of BC-4287, the miracle shrinking-rat-tumor pills and a list of instructions regarding how and when to take them (two every twelve hours on an empty stomach) and how often to come in (every two weeks for blood work and a CT scan).

The black writing also boldly instructs me not to take *any other medicines or supplements, prescription or over-the-counter, as doing so could compromise the integrity of the study and/or the efficacy of the drug.*

I turn the paper over so it won't judge me as I swallow my two pills along with an essence of yun zhi supplement. I feel guilty for undermining—and possibly ruining—a scientific study. But I'm dying. And I need all the help I can get to postpone that.

I stand at the kitchen sink, staring at the rain as it beats against the single-pane windows and—GOD-BLASTED MOTHER OF MARY. Water is seeping in through the small cracks where the windows won't shut.

Caulk. Tubes of it are still sitting where I left them in the Home Depot plastic bags in the basement. And I really need to get them out and caulk the windows.

I walk over to the fridge and affix the trial instructions to the door with a magnet, right next to my list of keep-the-house-from-falling-down tasks. Most of the entries are neatly typed—the original list that I compiled when we first moved in—like *Caulk the windows* and *Fix the back door lock* and *Plant hydrangeas and verbena in front flower bed.* The newer additions are in my tight loopy cursive at the bottom like *Beams for the basement.* I pause. A thought is flitting at the periphery of my memory, but I can't pin it down. There was something else I was supposed to add to this list, but I can't remember what it was. I absolutely hate forgetting things, which is why I keep so many lists.

I'm still attempting to turn my brain inside out when the back door bangs open and Kayleigh walks through it.

"Holy fuck," she says, her galoshes squeaking with each step on the tile.

"Morning to you, too."

"That door sucks. And it's crazy out there."

before i go 147

"I know. I need to fix the handle. Right after I stop my windows from leaking."

"How are you planning to do that?"

"I need to caulk them."

"Now?"

I turn to look at her. Rivulets of water are dripping down her raincoat, and even though her hood is up, black coils of hair are plastered to her face. The floor beneath her is a Jackson Pollock of mud and water and leaves and debris.

"No. Sometime," I say. "Soon."

She nods. "You ready to go?"

I sigh. "Yeah. Let me just mop up real quick."

Twenty minutes later, Kayleigh is backing her Jeep Wrangler ("total man magnet," she said when she first bought it) into a parallel parking spot in front of Jittery Joe's Coffee. Since the park idea was out, she swore this was the second-best place to pick up single men.

"So I've been thinking," Kayleigh says once we're inside and seated at a table, my chamomile tea cooling in front of me next to the sack of two cranberry muffins I bought to take home to Jack. I start scanning the small shop, looking for single women around Jack's age.

"Stop," Kayleigh hisses. "You can't be so obvious about it. Act normal. Just talk to me."

"Sorry." I dart my eyes back to the table. "What were you saying?"

"I think you should sign up for that Make-a-Wish thing."

I look at her, confused. "What? That kid's charity?" I sneak a furtive glance at the door, where a woman has just walked in.

"Oh, it's just for kids?" she asks.

"Yeah, what did you think?" I turn back to her, even as it dawns on me exactly what she thought. "You thought they did it for *adults*?" I start laughing. "Yeah, OK, I've always wanted to go to Disney World."

I slap my knee and a snort slips out. But then I start to think about it. They should do it for adults. They should totally do it for adults.

I grin at Kayleigh. "You should start that. Make-a-Wish for grown-ups."

"Maybe I will," she says, puffing her chest. She takes a sip of her coffee, her lips pursed to brace for the heat. I look back up at the woman, who's now paying for a bagel at the counter. Her legs are impossibly long in a pair of black leggings that disappear into high-heeled ankle boots, and I hate her for a second until I remember that she could potentially be Jack's future wife. And then I hate her even more.

Kayleigh sets her cup back on the table. "What would you wish for?"

I think about it. About how I answered Jack so flippantly on our fourth date, when dying seemed like something that happened to other people: Italy. I'd go to Italy. But now, dying is happening to me. And yes, I've always wanted to go to Italy, because who doesn't want to go to Italy? But I've also wanted to go to Greece. And Burma. And Ibiza. And New Zealand. And Seattle.

Seattle.

I've never even been to freakin' Seattle.

I once saw this show on The Travel Channel or PBS about Seattle and its weird tourist attractions, like the wall of chewing gum and the tree that grew around a bicycle on some island because a kid chained it there, like, seventy years ago and then never came back for it. And at the time I thought how I'd like to see those things. How I *would* see those things. How I had plenty of time in my long life to go and look at those weird things. Because that's what you think when dying is one of those things that happens to other people.

But dying is happening to me. And then Jack's going to be alone. And who has time to go to Seattle and look at wads of old chewed-up gum?

I sigh and glance up at Kayleigh. She's looking back expectantly, and I realize she's still waiting for an answer. But I can't very well explain how my greatest wish is to see a bicycle stuck in a tree on some island in Washington State.

I chew my lip and force a smile. "To have sex with Ryan Gosling."

She scoffs. "That would be everybody's. He couldn't have sex with four thousand dying women."

The long-legged woman settles into the velvet couch in the back of the tiny shop and it jars me that it's the same couch Jack and I shared on our third date, our knees generating an abnormal amount of heat where they touched.

I tune back into Kayleigh, who's midsentence: "—have to pick someone that no one else would, to be sure that it would happen. Like Kevin Spacey."

I pull a face. "Who would want to have sex with Kevin Spacey?"

"I don't know. He's kind of hot in *House of Cards*."

I gaze back at the woman one last time, and wonder what I'm actually looking for. With Charlene, I knew they had the vet thing in common. I was drawn to the nurse because she was a natural caregiver. How do I pick out a wife for Jack on sight alone? What should she look like? I realize I haven't given it any thought. I've been searching for a woman in the exact opposite way most men do—trying to decipher personality and compatibility before taking note of physical attractiveness. Does Jack have a type? Am *I* his type? Should his new wife look like me or would that be too weird? The woman eating the bagel looks nothing like me. Her hair, a vibrant honey chestnut, is straight, sleek. Everything about her is finished, like a puzzle that's been shellacked. In fact, her nails, which I'm pretty certain are acrylic, actually have been shellacked. I can't picture Jack with a woman who has fake nails.

"Do you know her?" Kayleigh's voice cuts into my thoughts.

"Who?" I turn back to my tea.

"Uh, the woman you've been staring at since she walked in here?"

"No," I say, thinking quickly. "I just like her . . . nails."

"Mmm. That's a totally normal thing to say."

I give her a weak smile.

"Daisy," she says, and then she looks at me in the same way she looked at me on the first day of second grade when she told me that her dad was the president of a company, which meant he got to fire people with a gun and then asked what my dad did and I told her I didn't have a dad. She takes a deep breath. "Do you want to talk? You know . . . about stuff? I mean, you obviously didn't come here to help me pick up guys."

I crease my brow, not ready to let go of my ruse so fast. "Why do you say that?"

She nods her head at a table toward the front of the shop. "That dead ringer for Bradley Cooper has been in here since we walked in and you never even noticed."

I steal a glace in his direction. He did kind of look like Bradley Cooper. Smaller nose, less hair. But still. I sigh and lean back into the curled ironwork of my uncomfortable parlor chair. The gurgle of steamed milk turning into foam blasts from the direction of the counter. A cell phone rings from a sofa behind me. Bits of conversation float through the air like miscellaneous dust particles. I stare at Kayleigh, measuring her, weighing the strength of our friendship like gold coins in my palm. I decide it's enough. And let the truth burst free in one long stream of words.

"I'mtryingtofindJackawife."

She stares at me, unblinking, and I wonder if she's heard me. If I need to repeat myself. Instead, I launch into an unprepared explanation. "For when . . . for after . . ." I trip over the words, not sure how to elucidate something that seems so obvious to me. I settle on: "I need to know that he's going to be OK."

I hold my breath, wondering if I've miscalculated her. Us. The possibility of her unspoken responses bark in my ear: "You can't be serious." "Who does that?" "That's the most ridiculous thing you've ever said." Or worse still—peals of laughter.

But the silence between us stretches like taffy. I long to break it. A clean cut. I open my mouth to laugh and tell her that, obviously, I'm joking, when she snaps her head to look at me.

"OK," she says with a curt nod. Understanding pools in her eyes like spilled ink. And then a grin slowly finds her lips. "But you can't seriously be considering *that* girl." She gestures to the shellacked woman on the couch. "She is definitely not his type."

I release the breath I've been holding and let my thoughts start tumbling out, grateful to have ears to receive them. "That's the thing. I'm not sure what his type is. I know I need someone responsible and organized like me, and driven like him, but I have no idea what she should look like. What he's really attracted to."

She attacks her pinky nail with her teeth, thinking. "Who's his celebrity crush?"

"It varies. Natalie Portman. Sarah Jessica Parker. He loved Demi Moore in *G.I. Jane*—he watches it every time it comes on TBS—but I don't think he likes her now."

"Everyone loves Demi Moore in *G.I. Jane*." She sits back and crosses her arms over her chest. "You need to find his porn stash."

"Ohhh-kay," I say, rolling my eyes at the very Kayleigh-like habit of taking everything one step too far. I change the subject. "Let's get back to you. Are you going to go talk to Bradley Cooper?"

She sighs. "I don't know. I've been doing a lot of thinking lately."

"That's dangerous."

She ignores me. "Maybe I'm not ready for a relationship. Maybe that's why I keep choosing unavailable men."

"Boys."

She shoots me a look. "Eric was a man."

"A very married one."

"They were separated. Whatever. I'm just saying that maybe I'm not ready to settle down."

I know that she's right, but I'm surprised at this flash of self-awareness. When we were in high school, and even college, I used to be jealous of Kayleigh's carefree attitude, how she seemed to meander on no particular path, going this way or that, while I stayed on the straight and narrow—choosing studying over partying or going to class over sleeping in. But as we got older, her enviable spontaneity began to morph into pitiable flailing, and it was diffi-cult to watch. Like how she majored in education just because she accidentally got sent to that orientation our freshman year and de-cided it was easier to stay there. When she graduated, she took her LSAT on a whim, though she'd never expressed any desire to be a lawyer. I didn't point out that this sudden career choice just hap-pened to coincide with her older, do-gooder sister's acceptance of a job as a financial analyst at JP Morgan—or that as much as she tried to deny it, she obviously craved the accolades her parents so easily bestowed upon Karmen. But then she flunked her LSATs and her pride refused to let her retake them. She took the first teach-ing job in Athens she could find (because what else was she going to do with an education degree?), even though she wasn't really pas-sionate about it. I'd been pushing Kayleigh to retake the LSAT or go back to school—to go after *something* with the same gusto she goes after nineteen-year-old boys.

But the last time I brought it up she snapped at me and I don't want to risk triggering her ire again. So instead, I strike my armchair therapist pose, tilt my head, and simply ask her: "Why don't you think you're ready?"

Before she can respond, a shadow darkens our table. We both look up at the Bradley Cooper doppelgänger, who's staring intently at Kayleigh. "Hey, uh . . ." he says. "Do you, like, go to school here?"

I cover my mouth with my hand, to prevent the laughter from escaping.

He doesn't look a day over nineteen.

LATER THAT AFTERNOON I stop by the vet hospital to take Jack the cranberry muffins. The building is modern, linear—all angles and glass. I've often thought it too cold, a contradiction to the warm and furry bodies that occupy it on a daily basis. As I open the see-through door to the entrance, a shrill wail pierces the air. I tense, darting my eyes first to the glass walls, as if they might shatter from the sharp arrows of sound waves berating them, and then to the culprit of the noise. A girl. No more than seven or eight, with a mop of uncombed curly brown tendrils framing a face that's all mouth. Or appears to be, because it's wide open and emitting the offensive sound without pause.

Her mother is frantically trying to embrace her rigid little body, unclench her furled fists, stop the tears sprinting from her eyes in midflow. But nothing will soothe her. The woman gives up, wraps her arms around her daughter's tiny shoulders, and carries the girl, still screaming, to the front entrance. I move to let them pass, and when the glass door gently closes behind them, overwhelming quiet fills the still lobby.

I walk toward Maya at the reception desk with wide eyes. "What. Was. That?"

She looks up from the manila file folder she's writing in. "The girl?"

I nod, wondering what other crazy spectacles occur in this lobby to leave her so nonplussed.

"Dog died. Mom asked us to cremate him, and that's when she really lost it." She goes back to writing. "I think Jack's in his office. You can go on back."

"Thanks," I say, still shaken from the intensity of the screams. But as I follow the linoleum path to Jack's office, something else starts to niggle its way into my thoughts.

Something Maya said. Something I haven't thought about at all. Until now.

"Should I get cremated?" I ask when I enter his tiny ten-by-ten square feet of space. Jack looks up from where he's standing, hunched over a stack of medical records, open journals, and God knows what else in the piles of stuff that look just like the piles of stuff on his desk at home.

"You brought food," he says, shifting his gaze to the brown paper bag in my hand. "I'm starving."

I drop the sack in front of him and plop down into the plastic molded chair. I wonder if he heard me. I wonder if I said the question out loud or just thought it. No, I said it. I can still taste the words. Is that possible? Do words have flavor? I wonder if I am actually going crazy.

"Jack?"

He digs into the bag and starts devouring the first muffin, a waterfall of crumbs landing on the documents he's still studying. He brushes them off. "Hmm?" he asks without looking up, his mouth full of cake.

I don't want to repeat my question. I didn't even know I was going to say it until it was halfway out of my mouth, the consequence of a seven-year habit of giving voice to my inner thoughts when I'm with Jack. But now. Now, things are different. It occurs to me that even though Jack's been looking at me as though I might disappear any second and his typical "Hey babe" greeting has morphed into "How are you feeling?" we haven't specifically discussed what's happening. What's *really* happening. And at first I thought it was because Jack was being naively hopeful.

But now I think Jack's in Denial, which after reading my grief brochure seems like a place you go to, like the beach or Target or the dentist, for an indefinite amount of time. I went there once, but because I'm an advanced griever, it was a short visit. It appears that Jack packed a bag before he left. The psych major in me wants to help him—ask him probing questions about what he'll do when I'm gone, get him to ponder the future without me in it—but I've taken enough classes to know that he has to deal with it at his own pace.

I pull my feet up and tuck them underneath my thighs in the uncomfortable bucket seat. The frayed hem of my favorite jeans is damp from my trudge through the wet parking lot. "How's the possum?" I ask.

He looks at me then, and I'm not sure if I'm imagining it, or if it is relief that's shining in his eyes. He smiles. "Good as new. A dog got him, nearly bit right through its leg . . ."

Jack relives the details of the case, slipping into medical jargon, which is when I'd typically stop him with an "English, please," or "What the hell's a pectoral girdle?" but this time I just let him talk. My mind has already left the conversation and is pondering the pros and cons of turning my body into ashes.

twelve

W HEN WE WERE thirteen, Kayleigh convinced me that I should ask my three-year crush, Simon Wu, to the eighth-grade dance—even though he had shown no apparent interest in my puppy-dog-like presence at any point in our entire middle school career. "What's the worst that could happen?" she reasoned. Emboldened by her confidence, I approached his table in the cafeteria, where he was involved in an intense pencil war with his friends, and stood beside him, waiting for him to acknowledge me. When he finally looked up, I whispered my query. "What?" he asked, bidding me to repeat myself, one eye still on his friend who was pulling back the wooden pencil and about to let it fly. "Do you want to go to the dance with me?" I said loudly, causing a ripple of snickers to flow outward through the adolescent boys. His eyes widened, and without preamble or explanation, he opened his mouth to release one word—"No"—before turning back to his game.

When I returned to Kayleigh at our lunch table with slumped shoulders and tears threatening to spill down my cheeks, she assured me that Simon had bad breath and a funny cowlick that would have looked ridiculous in the pictures. She also promptly dumped her date,

Ken Wiggins ("He has a stupid last name," she said), and came over to my house the night of the dance to eat Oreos and watch *The Bodyguard* for the umpteenth time.

Still, I've been wary of her advice ever since.

But she did have one good suggestion regarding my wife hunt as we were leaving the coffee shop Saturday: "Try a bookstore. There are a ton of nerds there."

On Monday morning, as soon as Jack leaves for clinic, I pour my smoothie into a plastic to-go cup, turn the handle on the back door a few times before it finally unsticks, then walk down the stairs to my car. Out of habit, I glance at Sammy's house and am surprised to be greeted by the two khaki-clad moons of her full derriere, staring up at me from the ground.

I suck in my breath and begin tiptoeing, hoping she didn't hear the creak of my back door shut. I had run into her the day my mom and I took a walk, and had no choice but to explain my orange appearance. Overrun with pity and embarrassment, she had launched into a lengthy discourse on everyone she had ever known with cancer, including her pet gerbil when she was a kid. I don't want to get stuck in a never-ending conversation this morning, but realize that she's going to hear me open the car door anyway. I could pretend that I didn't see her until then, but either way, I'm going to end up having to speak with her.

"Sammy!" I say as I step off the last stair and onto my driveway, but it comes out all wrong. Too cheerful. Too fake.

From her kneeling position, she turns her head and looks at me with a smile, but the exact same expression of pity. I wonder if she's been walking around with that countenance since the minute I told her, as if that mother's threat to a child—"If you cross your eyes, they'll stay that way!"—has actually come true.

"Daisy," she says, peeling off her gardening gloves as she struggles to shift her hefty frame upright. "How are you?" She emphasizes the "are," which is another thing that people do when they know you have cancer. "How are you?" becomes a loaded question instead of a simple greeting.

"Oh, you don't have to get up," I wave her back down. "I'm actually running late."

She gets up anyway and starts walking toward me, while nodding her head knowingly. "Doctor's appointment?"

"No," I say, but then I can't think of anything else I'd be running late for. I glance around, searching for a lie, and my eyes fall on the plastic pots of flowers surrounding the ground where Sammy had been digging. I give up trying to find an excuse and opt for a change of subject. "What are you planting?"

"Oh, whatever the guy at the Home Depot talked me into. I got a couple of azaleas and some sweet alyssa? Or something like that. Said it's for ground cover. A few pansies. My thumb is not green." She holds up the thick digit on her left hand and wiggles it as if to prove its beige color. "You'd think with an onion farmer for a granddaddy, it'd be in my genes or something." She makes a clicking sound with the side of her mouth. "I can't even keep cactuses alive."

I smile and resist the urge to tell her that the plural of cactus is cacti. Then I make a commiserating, I-know-what-you-mean comment about my mess of a flower bed, gesturing to the weeds overtaking the patch of yard in front of my porch.

Her eyes brighten. "I could do it for you," she says. "I've got the whole day off, and I should be done with this by lunch. I'm happy to help."

It's sweet of her to offer, but I can't help but feel like the charity case I know she now views me as. "Oh, no, that's not necessary," I counter. "I have a big plan for it. Hydrangeas, some verbena, a stone edging. I'm excited to tackle it." I'm not, actually. It's just become one more thing on my never-ending list that I don't have time for now that

I need to find Jack a wife, but she's like a dog who's picked up a scent and I'm hoping this will call her off.

"Wow. Sounds like you should be doing mine, Miss Gardening Guru." She laughs her big round laugh.

I muster a canned chuckle. "Yours will look great. Can't wait to see it when I get back." I say, cueing my exit as I take a step toward the car and open the door.

"Yes, sorry," she waves me on. "Didn't mean to hold you up." But she doesn't move from her spot where the edge of her yard meets my driveway, and I see the hesitation in her eyes before she calls out: "Maybe I could buy the hydrangeas at least." She frowns. "I don't really know what verbenas are, but I could ask for them. Or I could bring you guys dinner one night or watch Benny if—"

I slam the car door shut and wave at her through the window. "No, thank you," I say, loud enough for her to hear me through the glass. Then, through my gritted smile, I whisper: "Everything is under control."

THE BARNES & NOBLE near the mall is nearly void of people, barring the few navy-polo-shirted employees who are restocking shelves and manning cash registers. I suppose I should have realized that Monday morning isn't a prime shopping time for book buyers.

"Can I help you?" asks an eager salesman with a head of curls that are burnt orange—one of those hair colors that just look unfortunate on a man but that women spend years trying to reproduce with the help of a box.

"Just looking," I say. I don't tell him what for.

With one eye on the door, I scan the tables at the front of the store. New releases by John Grisham, Danielle Steel, Nicholas Sparks, Stephen King. It seems like the names on display never change, just the covers. And I wonder if these prolific authors will ever run out of stories to tell. If one day they'll just turn off the computer and say, "That's it. I've told them all."

A cowboy on the cover of a Nora Roberts catches my eye. I pick it up and stare at his bare, plastic-looking chest. When I was growing up, my mom had a stack of these types of books on her nightstand. It seemed like such an adult thing to have, like a travel coffee mug or a checking account, that when I pictured myself twenty years in the future, as an adult, I invariably knew that my nightstand would also be covered with my own stack of lusty books. But when I got older, romance novels never interested me. I eschewed them for psychology textbooks and Jodi Picoult dramas and the latest *New York Times* best-sellers that everyone buzzed about. Now, holding it, I realize reading romance novels was something I always assumed I'd pick up, like crocheting or flower arranging, when my hair grayed and my skin wrinkled.

But my hair won't gray. And my skin won't wrinkle. And I may die without having ever read a romance novel. Without ever knowing what the fuss is about. And this—*this!*—is what causes water to spring up and fill my lower lashes, blurring my vision.

And it occurs to me if I were to write a "Coping with Terminal Cancer" pamphlet, *this* is what I would cover. Not the obvious stuff about anger and bargaining, but the ridiculous moments like crying over bodice rippers in a suburban strip mall at 10 A.M. on a Monday morning.

I wipe my eyes and glance around to make sure no one has noticed my silly tears, and then tuck the book into the crook of my arm, realizing that I'm equally concerned to be spotted buying such drivel. But its weight on my elbow—and the knowledge that it will be on my nightstand tonight—is absurdly comforting.

I straighten my spine and lift my head, trying my best to emulate a normal shopper and not a blubbering, dying woman who is looking for a wife for her husband. The bell at the entrance chimes and I look up and see a short woman struggling to push a baby stroller through the glass door. I close the gap between us and grab the edge of the door, holding it open for her.

She smiles at me, revealing two deep dimples just below her cheekbones. It instantly reminds me of the time I tried to draw dimples on my face with my mom's Maybelline eyeliner in the third grade because I so desperately wanted to look like Heather Lindley, a fifth-grader with long blond ringlets who wore white tights and large bows in her hair and brought Lunchables to school every day, which is how I knew that her family had money because my mom always said they were too expensive.

"Thanks," says the woman. "I'm convinced the people who design doors like these are men who have never had children."

I smile back at her but can't think of anything to say in response other than "I like your dimples," which would be ridiculous.

She points her stroller in the direction of the children's section and I walk back the way that I had come in my best fake shopping mode, while I'm secretly marrying this woman—Heather Lindley's grown-up doppelgänger—and Jack in my mind. I picture them with a pack of dimply, blond children following them like waddling baby ducks. And then I let the image disintegrate.

She has a baby, which means she's probably already married.

I slowly stroll past the bargain books, the racks of magazines, and the self-help section, where imperatives yell at me from the covers:

Get Rich Now!
Stop Panicking!
Lose Your Baggage, Lose the Weight!

And then I stop short. Eight words jump out at me from a book jacket, and my hand is reaching for it before my brain has given it permission.

Preparing for the Death of a Loved One, by Dr. Eli Goldstein.

A sticker on the cover declares: WORLD-RENOWNED PSYCHIATRIST AS SEEN ON DR. PHIL.

I flip through the pages without really reading the words; I know that I'm buying it for Jack on the title alone, as casually as I would pick up the latest Michael Crichton or a pair of Dockers on sale at Macy's.

Saw this.

Thought of you.

Then I hesitate. What happened to letting Jack deal with his grief at his own pace? My hand moves to put the book back on its shelf.

But he's not dealing with it.

He will! At his own pace.

But maybe he just needs a little push, a little help. Maybe he needs to be forced to confront it. Like ripping off a Band-Aid instead of waiting for it to become grimy and useless, falling off on its own from days of wear.

In the end, I add it to the Nora Roberts under my arm and decide I'll just leave it on his nightstand the way my mom left *Our Bodies, Ourselves* on my nightstand when I was twelve. Wordlessly, and without preamble.

What's the worst that could happen?

As I turn to leave the aisle and pay for my new books, I notice the stroller woman standing at the opposite end of the self-help section. I chuckle—a little bitterly—to myself. What could she and her perfectly towheaded son need assistance with? *Help! My life is too ideal.*

I stop my silent, callous sarcasm when I notice that she, too, is looking at the grief books. Sad. I wonder if she's looking for something to help a friend deal with the loss of a grandmother, or an aunt or a brother. That's something Heather Lindley would have done. She was the girl who had a smile for everyone—even Darrel Finch, who nobody liked because he wore the same pair of Levi's every day and smelled like sour milk—and she brought extra number two pencils on test day in case anyone forgot, and when she sold the most World's Finest Caramel Bites and Mint Meltaways for the annual chorus trip to Disney World and won a hundred dollars for her efforts, she decided to donate it to a family at her church whose trailer had burned down. Which is why I couldn't hate her, even though her hair bows always matched her socks and she could afford Lunchables and I couldn't.

I look back at the woman, who's now intently reading the back of the book she's holding and gently rocking the stroller back and forth with her free hand.

Maybe it's not for a friend. Maybe *she's* lost a friend. Or a grandmother. Or an aunt. Or a brother.

Then I notice that the hand she's moving the stroller with is her left hand. And there's no wedding band on it. And that's when my heart starts racing, as I begin to piece together that she's obviously a widow who lost her husband in a tragic car accident when she was eight months pregnant and her therapist suggested a few books that could help guide her though the pain of losing him so suddenly and leaving her with just the memory of him every time she looks at her son's chocolate eyes and tiny ears.

And then, even though I never pictured Jack's wife already having a kid, or being a widow, or having dimples like Heather Lindley, it strikes me all at once that maybe all of the above should also be added to my list.

I inch closer to her, trying to think of an opening line, something that could engage her in conversation so she can open up to me about her dead husband and how hard being a single mom is and then I can tell her my sob story and we'll bond over chai tea in the tiny coffee shop while we hatch a plan to introduce her to Jack.

I'm so close now I can see the raw skin around her fingernails, where she has chewed and bitten them down to the quick, and I nod, understanding that her grief has driven her to that. She looks up at me and there are tears in her eyes. I clutch my chest with sympathy for her.

"Are you OK?" I say, my voice filled with concern.

"Yes," she says, her voice squeaky in return. She runs the back of her hand across her dripping nostrils and sniffs. "I'm sorry."

I smile gently at her, wanting to share that I was just crying in the bookstore, too. That we can bond over this embarrassing display of overemotion. That I get it. But I just wait, allowing her to take her time in unburdening her grief.

"It's just—" She takes a deep breath, and I think maybe she's pulling it together, but a few more sobs tumble out. "Oh, Max," she breathes.

I nod. Her husband's name was Max. It's a good name. A strong name. I instantly imagine a man with equally deep dimples and straight teeth, his dark locks contrasting with her blond. And then I realize I'm picturing the man on the Nora Roberts book I'm holding.

A high-pitched wail startles me, and the adult Heather Lindley wipes her eyes and leans down to pick up her squawking baby. "Shh," she croons. "It's OK." Like magic, the crying stops and the boy snuggles his downy head into his mother's neck.

"Was Max your husband?" I prompt, not wanting to break the moment we seemed to be having.

Her eyes grow large as she looks at me. "Oh, no. No," she says, and she stops jiggling the baby for a second so she can dig into her jeans pocket for a ratty Kleenex. "Not my . . . he's my"—she dabs at her nose—"well, *was* my . . ." The tears start flowing again and I wait expectantly. So Max wasn't her husband, but still, she doesn't have a wedding ring and she's good with kids, and those dimples—

"My cat," she says, then blows her nose into the tissue. Her son briefly opens his eyes at the commotion and then closes them again.

"Your cat?"

She nods. "He was sixteen. I got him in middle school, and when he was a kitten he would suck on my hair and knead his little paws onto my chest while I slept. And then . . ."

The woman continues delivering the eulogy for her beloved feline while I peer more closely at the book she's holding: *Losing a Pet, Losing a Friend: Coping with the Death of Your Animal Companion.*

My first thought: That is a really long title.

I voice my second thought. "So are you married?"

She stops midsentence and I realize I've interrupted her.

"Um, no," she says, assessing me and my strange line of questioning. I chide myself for not being more patient, for not trying to glean the information I'm seeking in a more subtle way. But really, time isn't something I've got in spades right now. "Not really," she continues, still sniffling. "Tristan's father and I don't believe in marriage. You know, just a piece of paper and all that. We're like Susan Sarandon and Tim Robbins."

I nod, more irritated at myself than at her for jumping the gun. But I'm irritated at her, too. At her perfect dimples and magic baby-calming powers and her son who will probably never be the kid in the cafeteria who can't afford a Lunchable.

"You know they broke up," I say.

"Oh," she says, stepping back as if this news is an extra weight that I've handed to her. "I didn't know that."

And then I feel bad because it's not her fault that Max died or that her boyfriend is alive or that one of Hollywood's oldest power couples couldn't make it after all or that I have cancer all over my body.

I take a step back, too, cradling my books as if they're a peaceful baby with blond feather wisps of hair, and say with as much heart as I can muster: "I'm really sorry about your cat."

WHEN JACK GETS home from work just after nine thirty, I'm already in bed, half reading the Nora Roberts and realizing that it wouldn't be quite so sad to die without having finished one. That perhaps I should concentrate on going through the classics that I always meant to read someday. Like *Lady Chatterley's Lover* or something by Proust. I dog-ear the corner of the page that I've reread three times and close the book, sliding it onto my night table. Jack shrugs off his jacket and slings it over the back of the blue velvet wing chair in the corner. His shoulders are curved over his long frame and when he looks up at me his eyes are bloodshot.

"Rough day at the office?" I say, offering him a smile.

He groans. "Yeah, if you consider three back-to-back surgeries and then staring at a computer screen for eight-plus hours trying to compile as much research as I could find about equine prosthetics for Ling a rough day. I don't even think I scraped the tip of the iceberg."

He peels off his T-shirt. "How was class?"

"Fine," I say, swallowing down the guilt at my little white lie. I do still go to class sometimes, but not nearly as often as Jack thinks I'm going.

"What else did you do?"

I shrug. "Not much. Bookstore. I ordered you a few button-ups online. Called and got some quotes for the beams in the basement."

He raises his eyebrows in question.

I shake my head. "You don't want to know. Let's see . . . what else? Took Benny for a walk. I should've started caulking instead but it was too pretty outside."

Jack doesn't respond and suddenly I'm self-conscious about my lack of interesting activities or news to share about my day. I used to have intelligent things to say about my classes or stories that I couldn't wait to share with him when I got home. I search the crevices of my brain for something noteworthy or fascinating that happened that I can comment on, engage my husband in some way.

Oh, and I consoled a crying woman at Barnes & Noble who I thought you could marry because she had just lost her husband, but it was her cat. She was totally crying over her cat.

It's one of those awkward social moments that Jack would have found entertaining, but I can't exactly explain why I was talking to her and I'm afraid the mention of death will just make Jack's shoulders tense even more, so I stay silent.

Naked, except for the tube socks that hug his calves, Jack walks over to his side of the bed. I hold my breath as he glances down at the self-help book I left on his nightstand. What will he say? Will he be irritated? Intrigued? Will the words leap out at him off the cover and shake him out of his denial? Will he throw himself into my arms sobbing "I can't lose you" while I knowingly brush his hair off his forehead and whisper "Shh" and "Everything will be OK"? I quickly dismiss this option, knowing it's just a scene that I saw in a movie once. Jack has no penchant for drama.

I watch Jack's eyes graze the cover and wait for his reaction. But there isn't one.

His expression doesn't change as he lifts the comforter and sits down on the mattress, stuffing his legs under the blankets. He removes his socks, drops them on the floor, sets his glasses on the nightstand—on top of the new book—and reaches for the lamp.

"G'night," he says, leaning over and kissing my shoulder. "Love you."

He rolls over and within sixty seconds, his breathing deepens and I know he's asleep.

"Night," I whisper to his back as I let out the breath I was holding.

I pick up my Nora Roberts from the nightstand, blink a few times, shake my head, and resume trying to get lost in a world of ripped bodices and sweaty cowboys.

thirteen

Now that I'm dying, the sky seems larger. Or maybe it's that I feel smaller. Or maybe it's just that dying or not, when you really stop to look at the expanse of blue hanging above us, you can't help but feel inconsequential. Overwhelmed at how meaningless your tiny life is in the grand scale of things.

I tip my face to the sun and let it warm my skin, closing my eyes and leaning into the bench Kayleigh and I are sharing. The dog park is full, people shaking off their winter inertia and embracing the first weekend of temperate weather.

"She's pretty, in an urban hipster kind of way."

I open my eyes and look in the direction Kayleigh is staring. A paisley scarf engulfs the neck of a diminutive woman in a white tank and skinny jeans, her head topped with a fedora. A large mutt—some type of pit bull mix—trots beside her on a leash.

"Too trendy," I say. "And she looks young."

"I think she just has one of those faces. I say twenty-five, maybe twenty-six."

I close my eyes again. Inhale the grass-scented, earthy air. The smell used to make me tingle with anticipation—a presage reminding me that the long, alluring days of summer were near. Now that feeling is mixed with something else. A sense of time tumbling out of control. Wasn't it just winter? How did spring unfold so quickly? The urgency with which I used to live life suddenly seems gratuitous. Always yearning for something—for Jack to graduate, summer to get here, Fridays. Now I long for Mondays that last all week and sun rays that refuse to surrender to moonlight.

"So," Kayleigh starts, then pauses as if trying to find the right words. "What are you going to do when you actually find someone?"

"What do you mean?" I reach down and scratch Benny behind the ears. He strains at the leash, whimpering for freedom to sniff other dogs, tree squirrels, find a dead bird and roll ecstatically in its decaying carcass.

"I mean, what's your plan? Your opening line?"

I avoid her gaze and continue stroking Benny. I'm embarrassed to tell her I haven't gotten that far. I had been spending so much time on my list, choosing the specific qualities that Jack's perfect wife should have and not much time on what I would actually do when I find her. *If* I find her. As evidenced by my encounter with the woman in the bookstore, finding someone is proving to be more difficult than I anticipated. And apparently I've become terrible at making conversation with strangers.

"You don't know."

"I don't know *yet*," I say, not ready to admit to the multiple holes in my plan. While I'm more convinced than ever that I need to find Jack a wife—particularly as I try to quell the rising anxiety that with each passing day, I get a day closer to leaving Jack completely and utterly alone—I've realized that knowing it and doing it are two completely different things. I know exactly what I'm looking for—my list is solid. But what if I don't find her? Or what if I do? Then what? How do I introduce them? And what if Jack doesn't like her? Or she doesn't like Jack?

"You should practice. Go talk to that woman."

"The fedora girl?"

"Yeah."

"No. That's stupid. I'm not going to waste time talking to someone that's not even his type."

We're interrupted by a strain of Lionel Richie singing *"Hello . . ."* then four slow chords on an eighties synthesizer . . . *"is it me you're looking for?"*

Kayleigh digs into her pocket for her cell phone and silences it.

"Harrison?" I raise my eyebrows.

"No," she shoots back.

"Who was it?"

She mumbles something.

"What?"

"Bradley Cooper," she enunciates.

"You're kidding." Benny starts yipping furiously. I tug the leash to rein him in. "The guy from the coffee shop? I thought you were done with nineteen-year-olds."

"He's twenty-one," she sniffs. Then shrugs. "And he's hot."

"You. Are hopeless," I say, though I'm happy to have a respite from thinking about my problems.

"Whatever. Oh, before I forget, I need you and Jack to come to open house and pretend to be prospective parents."

"Um—no."

"No, seriously. You have to. I'm supposed to bring five parents and I don't even have one. Pamela's already got eight." She rolls her eyes, but I notice she's only half involved in our conversation. Her thumbs are furiously typing a text. I try to ignore it.

"So claim some of hers."

"I can't. It doesn't work like that. Will you please come?" She hits send and slides her cell back into her jeans. Then looks at me. "Pretty please? I don't want to look like I totally don't care."

"You don't."

"I know. But I don't want my principal to know that."

I sigh. "I'll think about it."

"Great," she says, smiling and sitting back into the bench, because we both know that I'll go. That I can't ever say no to Kayleigh.

I lean back again and look up at the sky. An airplane that looks like a small sparrow, it's so far away, streaks across the blue, leaving a trail of white smoke in its wake. A sudden urgency grips me. I want to be on that plane. I think back to the question Kayleigh asked me in the coffee shop about my biggest wish. Why *didn't* I travel more when I had the chance? Study abroad or backpack around Europe. Or go see that bicycle in Seattle. How hard is it to get to Seattle? And I know it's because of Jack. He never had the time to take off and I didn't want to go without him.

But he promised we'd go on vacation to celebrate his graduation. We'd been talking about it forever, tossing out ideas of where we could go. Realistic destinations: Seaside, Savannah, Miami, mixed in with unrealistic ones: Capri, Mykonos, Bora Bora. Where we ended up didn't really matter to either one of us. We were just in awe of the idea that we'd get to spend seven full days together. Jack's school finally behind us. Our entire lives ahead of us.

Now I realize that since my diagnosis, neither one of us has mentioned the trip. No tickets have been booked. No new bathing suits have been bought. And I realize that maybe that's because I won't be around to take it.

I shake off the thought and turn to Kayleigh: "You should be a flight attendant," I say. "Or a pilot."

"Ah, no," she says, digging the toe of her boot into the dirt at our feet. "Flying terrifies me."

"Really?" I say. It's hard to picture Kayleigh being terrified of anything. "Well, have you thought about—"

"Daisy," she cuts me off and shoots me a warning with her eyes.

"Sorry," I mumble. It's not the first time I've made career suggestions to her and I know it irritates her. And I know she has to figure it all out on her own timetable—that something, someday will inspire her, or point her in the right direction—but I can't help but try to encourage her to pick up the pace sometimes.

"Oh, did I tell you Karmen got a promotion?" she asks, and I know she doesn't mean it in a I'm-so-happy-for-my-sister way, so I don't say anything in response.

We stare in the direction of the fedora girl, who's now engaged in light banter with a skinny guy in Ray-Bans and a vintage concert T-shirt.

"You snooze, you lose. Dude beat you to it," Kayleigh says.

"She wasn't Jack's type!" I say, annoyed. "Look at that guy. Now he's totally her type."

"Yeah, they probably met at Goodwill buying vests."

"Or at the tailor making their skinny jeans even skinnier."

"Or on, like, Fuck-the-Mainstream-Match-Dot-Com."

I laugh. And then I stop laughing. Because that's it. And I don't know why I haven't thought of it until now. The one place where there are more single women looking for partners than anywhere else on earth—the Internet.

KAYLEIGH'S APARTMENT STILL smells like fresh paint even though she moved in two months ago. Once inside, I immediately walk over to her windows and begin opening them.

"What are you doing?"

"You don't smell that?"

"What? Did I forget to take out the garbage?"

"No, the paint," I tell her, explaining that it's full of VOCs, a major cause of cancer. "I know the management didn't spring for the ecofriendly kind. It's like fifteen dollars extra a can."

Kayleigh just stares at me, the same expression I get from Jack when I turn my nose up at conventional fruit or nonfiltered water. I know they think I'm crazy, but now that I know all of this stuff, I can't not know it.

"I'll go get my laptop," she says.

For the next forty-five minutes, Kayleigh briefs me on the merits and pitfalls of the seven different dating Web sites she has personally used.

"Seven? How are you possibly still single?"

"I'm picky," she retorts.

I scoff, but she shoots me a look, so I refrain from bringing up the slew of college boys she is decidedly not being picky about.

We narrow it down to Checkmates.com, where potential daters must pass a background check before being allowed to join the site, and Loveforlife.com, which guarantees you'll find someone in six months or your money back. I ask Kayleigh if she actually asked for a reimbursement, since it obviously didn't work for her. She explains she had to cancel her subscription after a month because a guy she met started stalking her.

"Crazy Mike?" I ask.

She shakes her head. "Weird Cal."

"You met Weird Cal online?" It catches me off guard because I've known Kayleigh so long it feels like there's nothing I don't know about her, and it's unlike her to be secretive. "I had no idea."

"I wasn't hiding it. I just don't think I dated him long enough to share all the sordid details."

In the end we go with Checkmates, because I think Jack's future wife is going to be cautious about meeting strangers online. I know I would be.

"OK, we're in," Kayleigh says, handing me back my credit card.

"Great. First question?"

Kayleigh stares at the screen. I wait. Her computer must be running slow.

Thirty seconds pass.

"Kayleigh?"

"Um . . ." She turns the computer to me.

What's your relationship status?

Single

Divorced

Separated

Widow/er

The word "widower" jumps off the screen and slugs me in the gut.

Widowers are supposed to be hunched, with unruly eyebrows and nose hairs. They wear Mr. Rogers cardigans and shoes with thick rubber soles and smell like boiled chicken. Widowers do not have thick brown hair and firm abs beneath a cotton T-shirt and smell like summer grass just after it's rained.

I look up at Kayleigh and notice the water rimming her lashes. "I'm sorry," she says, putting her hand up to her mouth. "It just . . . it hit me."

"That's OK," I say, careful not to touch her, knowing that any contact will shatter us both. "It hits me all the time."

I grab the edge of the computer screen and slide it closer to me. Then I run my index finger over the mouse pad, click "Widower," and move on.

AROUND SIX, I pull the car into our driveway. But instead of tapping the gas to accelerate to the end of the slab of concrete, my right foot slams the brake pedal, jerking my upper body forward. I barely notice. I gape at the front of my house, my mouth poised to catch flies. My flower bed. It actually has flowers in it. Hydrangeas and . . . I squint. Is that a stone edging? It is. A beautiful, natural river-stone edging. I put my car in park and leave it where I stopped—not bothering to ease it the last ten yards where I usually park by the back door—and get out. I walk toward the freshly mulched, beautifully manicured garden that now borders my front porch. Small blooms of purple verbena sprout from between the larger hydrangea bushes. I'm dumbfounded. Struck speechless, which hardly matters since there's no one around to talk to. It's as if garden gnomes sprang to life while I was gone and created this masterpiece. It's exactly how I pictured it, exactly how I had explained it to . . . Sammy. I tip my head back and laugh. Sammy. Of course she would take it upon herself to dig up my unsightly weeds, even after I told her not to.

And even though I didn't think I wanted the charity, I can't help but be touched by her thoughtfulness, the obvious hard work she put into this flower bed that I probably never would have gotten around to doing, if I was being honest with myself. I lean over, inspecting it closer, staring at foliage that I don't recognize. Hosta? The name comes to me from nowhere. I hadn't planned on hosta, but it does make for perfect ground cover between the two flower shrubs. I smile, wondering if the man at the Home Depot had recommended it to her. And then I wonder, though the chances are small, if it was the same man who helped me pick out the caulk. He had nice eyes.

I stand rooted in my front yard, soaking in the last warm rays of the day—and the unexpected feeling that there are people in this world who still have the ability to surprise me.

fourteen

I'M NOT SURE how people who date online have time for anything else. For the past five days it's like I've been sucked into a black hole—one that's wallpapered with hopeful women's head shots and swimming with statistics: height, weight, eye color, religion.

From the moment I get up in the morning until the time I crawl into bed at night, I've been wading through pages and pages of profiles. I feel like a headhunter searching for the perfect job candidates, which I guess in a way I am. I'm fascinated by what people will share about themselves, and I wonder how much of it is true. Are the majority of women really "spontaneous and fun," or do they think that's what men are attracted to? Wouldn't most women prefer at least a few days' notice before being whisked away on a romantic beach trip so they could stop eating carbs, shave their bikini areas, and pick up new underwear?

By day three, I started rereading profiles that I've read before.

By day five, I've received forty-two "nudges" and twenty-three messages (four don't count as they're from women who don't have a firm grasp on the English language and/or appear to still reside in eastern Europe).

I'm not surprised Jack's gotten so much attention. According to

Kayleigh, Athens is a "buyer's market" for guys. For every decent man with straight teeth and a car, there are hundreds of hot, intelligent coeds. "You can't throw a rock without hitting one," she said. "And believe me, I've been tempted."

I also used my favorite picture of Jack—he's staring straight at the camera, a broad crooked grin punctuated by the deep smile lines carved around his mouth, his eyes, one slightly bigger than the other, bright and magnetic. The collar of his shirt and sport coat are visible just below his neck, but his tie is unknotted, emphasizing his casual, devil-may-care attitude that I fell in love with; the same attitude that at times wiggles under my skin and sits there like an itch I can't scratch. This photo is Jack in all his imperfect glory—on our wedding day.

It was a Friday in July at the Athens-Clarke Courthouse. And my heart erupted with joy when the judge looked at me and said "wife." It was the kind of manic happiness that confuses your nervous system, and I giggled and cried in turns, not caring how foolish I appeared. I was foolish. And I was in love.

"Please tell me you see the irony in using a picture of your husband on your wedding day to try and help him score chicks," Kayleigh said when I grabbed it off my Facebook page.

"Not chicks, plural," I said, uploading it to the Web site. "Just one."

Now, staring at my husband on the computer screen staring at me, my heart pings. I do want him to find a wife and I even hope he'll be able to find that joy again, on another wedding day in the future. But I also secretly hope that while that day will be lovely and warm and good, that it's not quite as bright as the sun that once shone down on a girl and boy kissing on the hot brick steps of a courthouse on a Friday afternoon in July.

Maybe it will rain.

I click off Jack's profile and read through a few of the new emails I've gotten.

A new message from CatLady63

Subject: Hi!

I have three cats. You're a vet. Match made in heaven? Ha-ha. Just kidding. What do you like to do for fun? I'd love to learn more about you.

Madeline

A copper curly-headed woman peers at me with squinty eyes. Her mouth is small. Ratlike. Meh. She's not overly unattractive, but I don't trust cat people. Maybe it's the inside knowledge of growing up with one, but I think they're often like the animals they love—unpredictable and emotionally unstable. You never know when they'll be aloof and distant or senselessly desperate for your affection.

A new message from GoodLuckCharm

Subject: Hi there

New to online dating. Be nice! I see that you like Micheal Critton. I thought the Stand was a really great book.

Oh, no. No, no, no. Where do I begin? Spelling. Ignorance about classic modern literature. I hit delete. The next four emails are no better. Maybe Kayleigh's right and I'm too judgey. Maybe I look for things to find fault with. But I'm choosing a wife for my husband, and if that's not cause for being picky, then what is?

I need a break. I open Facebook and get lost in other people's whitewashed versions of their lives. With social media, I'm a voyeur, not a poster. It weirds me out to think that people would be interested in what I had for dinner or how long I waited in line at Kroger or "Oh, hey, I have cancer now." As personal as it is, it seems so impersonal.

After scrolling through the news feed for a few minutes, I click a new tab and check my regular email. Of course, there's one from my mother.

Subject: Friday

Hi Hon!
How are you feeling? Are you sure you don't want me to meet you up at Emory tomorrow? Ron says I can take a long lunch break! Also, what do you want for dinner? Aunt Joey gave me a new Guy Fieri recipe (that's the guy who wears his sunglasses backward) that she says is to "Die For"! But I don't like his show. I told her that and she said to "stop being such a fuddy-duddy and trust her." So, we'll see! I have my bird club meeting tonight. Did I tell you last week a man asked for my number? Me! Of course I didn't give it to him. He has a tattoo of a sandpiper on his neck, and I just don't know what to make of that.

Love,
Mom

Huh. Maybe I should tell Kayleigh to join the Audubon Society to meet men. I tap out a quick response to my mom (*Don't come to Emory. Whatever you make will be fine. Guess bird club isn't as boring as I expected.*) and then navigate back to Checkmates.com and my search page of women.

I scroll through a sea of familiar faces until one catches my eye and I stop. Have I seen her before? No, I'd remember. She's stunning. But not in an unapproachable way. And I wonder if she's the elusive girl next door who everyone talks about but doesn't ever really live next to. Her wide smile makes you want to tell her things because you know she'll listen. And her toffee-colored hair looks like it belongs in a Pantene commercial. She's the girl in high school that I would have hated because I wasn't more like her, and then I would have hated myself even more for hating her.

I click through to her profile, ready to be disappointed. Ready for misspellings and exclamation points and no depth.

PW147

Height/Weight: 5'5", 130 pounds
Age: 29
Have kids? No
Want kids? Definitely

About me: Honestly, I'm a little bit of a nerd. But I hope it's in a cute, endearing way and not in a "That girl can recite the entire periodic table in less than 3 minutes" kind of way. (Disclaimer: I can.) I'm a little overorganized. OK, a lot. But I won't hyperventilate if you leave your dirty dishes in the sink. I'll just wash them and put them away (and probably rearrange your cabinets) when you're not looking. I love dogs. Deal breaker if you don't. And I love pie. Bonus if you do. (But get your own piece. That's something I won't share.)

I lean back into the couch cushion, a jumble of emotions coursing through my veins: excitement, relief, a little leftover high school jealousy of the girl I always wanted to be but never quite measured up to. She's perfect. OK, nobody's perfect. I know that. But she is. Perfect for Jack, anyway.

I click on Send a Message, and a blank email pops up on the screen. I wait to be inspired, struck with the gift of eloquence. I just knew that when I found the right woman, I'd know exactly what to say to her.

I was wrong.

I stare at the cursor blinking on and off, taunting me, until my eyes are bleary.

Until the room grows dark.

Until my husband comes home.

I close my laptop and click on the TV as Jack walks into the den.

"Hey," he says.

"Hey."

"Whatcha watching?"

"Nothing."

He nods and slips out of his loafers right in the doorway. I know that's where they'll stay until he decides to wear them again or I move them into the shoe rack in our closet.

"Can I watch with you?"

"Sure," I say, and then grope for other words to break my new monosyllabic speech pattern, but there are none.

He pads over to the couch and scoops up Benny, who's resting comfortably beside my thigh, and sits down beside me, rearranging Benny in his own lap. "That'sagoodboy," he croons, scratching him under the chin. Benny thumps his tail appreciatively.

There are a few inches of space between our legs, but the distance feels larger somehow and I wonder where this palpable tension has come from. Has it been steadily growing and now it's big enough for me to notice? Or did it just pop up like an uninvited stranger and plant itself between us on the couch? Does Jack feel it, too?

Like a girl on a first date, I purposefully move my knee until it bumps his, closing the gap, leaving no room for the tension, but now my leg is just awkwardly touching his. Then he palms my thigh casually with his left hand and I let out a breath I didn't realize I had been holding.

Jack nestles closer. "Mmm," he says, his cold nose grazing my neck. "You're warm." His hand begins to slowly creep up my thigh, and I freeze. Jack hasn't touched me like this in weeks, I assumed because the word "cancer" has been as much a libido killer for him as it's been for me.

Until now.

"Do you want to . . ." he whispers, gently squeezing the meat of my leg, like he's analyzing a peach for ripeness.

And a small part of me does want to. If for no other reason than to push this tension—this uninvited stranger—out once and for all. Or at least for a few freeing minutes.

But my body isn't interested in that chain of reasoning and remains rigid, uncooperative. I place my hand over his, gently stopping its upward motion.

"I'm sorry," I say. "I'm just really tired."

He sits up and clears his throat. "No, of course," he says, patting my thigh one last time before putting his hand back on Benny's wiry fur.

I immediately regret my response, not because I want sex, but because I miss the weight of him, the warmth of his body on mine. I long to wrap myself in his arms, but I don't want to give him the wrong idea, so I sit there, wondering if all too soon his arms will be wrapped around someone else.

Someone with toffee-colored hair.

fifteen

BEFORE LEAVING FOR Emory Friday morning, I read PW147's profile again. It's a pointless exercise, considering I studied it so many times yesterday, I memorized the entire thing. I close my laptop and vow to compose a pitch-perfect email in my head while driving today.

Grabbing a basket of vegetables that I picked up at the farmer's market for Sammy as a thank-you for the flower bed, I head out the back door. It doesn't hit me until I'm halfway down the stairs that something is different. The handle on the door didn't stick. I look up at the sun and wonder if it has something to do with the change in temperature. Did the handle get a reprieve from sticking last spring? Maybe it's something about cold air and expansion or contraction that makes some days worse than others. Some physics lesson that I never paid attention to. I can't recall a time that it didn't ever stick at all, though. Maybe I just never noticed.

I walk through Sammy's front yard and leave the basket on her front porch, on top of a natural fiber doormat that says "Welcome Y'all" in black script. I had wanted to thank her before now, but I've been holed up in the house in front of the computer. Better late than never. I straighten the index card that I tied with a ribbon to the handle: "Thanks for being a good neighbor." Then I get into my car and turn on the radio, ready to make the ninety-minute drive to Atlanta.

By the time I pull into the patient parking lot at Emory, I still don't know what to write to PW147, but I have visualized her and Jack's entire future relationship, down to their three perfect children—the first two who will naturally attend Ivy League schools, while the third with her rebellious creative streak will go to a liberal arts school for a year before traveling abroad to find herself. It's a mental exercise that's both comforting and demoralizing. Pleasurable and painful. It's like a cerebral form of cutting or self-mutilation—something I didn't understand at all in my Psychological and Personality Disorders class but now suddenly makes perfect sense.

I continue entertaining my twisted fantasies through the MRI and the blood work and am wondering where the couple will retire—if she'll approve of Jack's dream to buy a beach house in Cape Cod where our, well, *their* grandkids can buy clam fritters from questionable roadside stands, and try to dig holes in the sand to China and fall asleep in exhausted heaps every night, their sunburned noses peeking out from a tangle of cool, crisp sheets—when Dr. Rankoff enters my exam room, holding a folder.

"How are you feeling?" she asks, studying my face with interest.

"Fine," I say, an automatic response that I've been firing at anyone who's asked the past month. But this time I pause, considering her question. She's not asking out of politeness, or even morbid curiosity. She's asking because it's important to the clinical trial to know how I am actually feeling. And after a quick mental inventory, I realize that I am feeling fine. Good actually. Ever since I got the stent, I've had more energy, I haven't had one headache and . . .

"Well, your skin looks much better than it did two weeks ago," she says. "Rosy."

"Thanks." I stuff my hands under my legs on the paper-covered table I'm sitting on, and chew the corner of my lip.

"Any shortness of breath? Pain in your extremities? Confusion? Forgetfulness? Headaches?" She ticks off a list like she's reminding me what to buy at the store.

I shake my head no and remind myself of the facts as I know them: I'm dying. I'm in a clinical trial not because it's going to miraculously cure my cancer, but because it could extend my life by mere months. Chances are, it won't even do that. But even as these sentences run on a loop in my head, I can't squash the glimmer of hope that's sprouted in my belly while I wait for my test results.

Maybe it's working.

Maybe the tumors are shrinking.

Maybe I don't need to send an email to PW147.

Maybe one day I'll live in Cape Cod.

Dr. Rankoff doesn't speak as she flips through my chart. The only sound in the airless room is the scratching of her pen on paper as she jots notations in the margins. When she finally opens her mouth, the glimmer of hope has blossomed into an all-consuming fireball and I know I won't be flattened by surprise if she says my tumors have all but disappeared. That I'm a walking phenomenon that will send shock waves through the scientific community.

But she doesn't say that.

"Your tumor markers are a little more elevated. The liver mets, especially, appear to be growing at a faster rate, but the stent should still be able to keep your bile duct free for the foreseeable future." She looks at me. "But there is good news. Your other tumors—brain, bone, breast, lungs"—as if I've forgotten where I'm harboring these cancerous criminals—"are progressing more slowly."

I know it's good news in the way that an arsonist not stealing your TV before he burns your entire house to the ground is good news. That it's just a nice way of saying that the trial isn't working.

I look down at my feet. Even though it's warm outside, I realize I shouldn't have worn sandals. My toenails are yellowed beneath the chipped pink polish from hibernating in heavy footwear through-out the winter. I'm suddenly embarrassed for their disheveled ap-pearance.

"Listen," she says, her tone changing from news anchor reporting the facts to sympathetic friend. "It's early, you just started. Let's give it a chance, huh?"

I nod, and wonder if I have time to get a pedicure before I go to my mom's house for dinner.

"WELL. IT'S BLACK," I say, poking at the piece of charred catfish on my plate.

"I'm sorry. It said to get the pan really hot," Mom says. "Guess I overdid it."

I choke down a bite, following it with a sip of water. Then I stab a vegetable with my fork.

"The Brussels sprouts are good."

She brightens. "I'm glad you like them."

After dinner, we clear the dishes and go into the den, where I sit on the same brown paisley couch that we've had forever. In fact, the entire house looks exactly the same as it did in my childhood—although a little more cluttered, since I'm not around anymore to make sure everything is returned to its precise location at the end of the day. I used to think Mom didn't buy new furniture or redecorate because she didn't have the time or money, but now I wonder if it has to do with Dad. Like she subconsciously keeps the house the same way it was the last time he was in it. Some psychological time warp that makes her feel closer to him.

Alex Trebek's voice fills the room, and if I wasn't looking at his cobwebby hair on the screen, I would swear I was in a time warp. I watched *Jeopardy* religiously in middle school while waiting for Mom to get home from work.

I sink back into the worn sofa, stroking Mixxy's fur, as the chubby guy on-screen buzzes in.

Who is the Marquis de Sade?

Right, Trebek says. *Go again.*

Strangely, it wasn't until my sophomore year in high school that I realized just how depressed Mom had been for most of my childhood. When she wouldn't get out of bed on her days off, I chalked it up to the exhaustion of working two jobs. When she picked at the micro-waved vegetables or frozen chicken nuggets I had made for dinner, I thought it was my cooking that had failed her. But intrinsically, even if I didn't know the depth of her depression, I did intuit her loneliness. Because I felt it, too. How hollow a tiny house can feel when some-one is missing from it. No matter how hard we each tried to fill his shoes, I couldn't be her husband and she couldn't be my dad and that's just how it was.

Now, remembering that ache—that hole—that my dad left be-hind, my heart seizes. And I know it's not just someone to make the sandwiches and the bed and the dentist appointments that I want for Jack. It's someone to fill that hole.

George and his handlebar mustache did that for my mom, though it was years overdue. But she hasn't dated anyone seriously since.

"Was the sandpiper tattoo guy there last night?" I ask during a commercial.

When she doesn't respond, I look over in time to see Mom sniffle, a tissue clutched to her face.

"Mom?" I ask, alarmed. "What's wrong?"

"Oh, honey," she says, between gasps. "I'm just glad you're home. I miss you when you're gone." She tries to smile. "You know what a weepy willow I am."

I roll my eyes, playing into her charade. Pretending that it's not the announcement I made over dinner that the clinical trial wasn't working that's got her all choked up. "You really are. I can't believe you haven't cried your tear ducts off by now."

"You're lucky. You inherited your dad's strength."

I've always basked in these comparisons. *You have your dad's eyes. His laugh. His ability to read people.* Like I'm a quilt with patches of him sewn into me. And I've never questioned them. But now, in my stoic position on the couch, I wonder, if I really am so tough, then why am I overwhelmed with the urge to crawl into my mom's arms, to feel her fingers smooth my hair? I can't remember the last time I allowed her to really hold me. And I feel childlike in my craving for it.

I sit still until the feeling passes.

Then I turn my attention back to the TV where a contestant has just uncovered a Daily Double.

I'd like to bet it all, Alex.

OK, that's $16,200. Let's look at the clue.

He answers incorrectly. The audience groans.

But I silently cheer him.

I admire his courage.

WHEN I GET home, it's late, but Jack's car isn't in the driveway, and I hate to admit that my fingers loosening a bit on the steering wheel and the knots disappearing from my stomach are signs of relief. That I'm *relieved* that my husband isn't home. The tension that sprouted between us on the couch last night only grew stronger after I rebuffed his advances and it began to feel as if we were two strangers who inexplicably share the same bed at night.

As I walk up the back steps and slip my key into the kitchen door lock, guilt begins to overtake my relief. I know the distance between

us is my fault. That I've been pushing Jack away—maybe without in-
tending to—but pushing him away nonetheless. And I wonder what's
wrong with me. What's wrong with *us*? Isn't cancer supposed to bring
couples closer? Aren't we supposed to be spending all our time petting each other's fingers while we whisper I love yous and regrets and
hopes as recklessly as teenage girls whisper pieces of gossip?

I push open the door and step into the house, where Benny
greets me with his typical happy yips. I let him out into the yard,
and then scoop him up and carry him under the crook of my arm
to the bedroom. I turn on the light and walk toward the bed where
I intend to flop Benny on it and then my tired body, but I trip over
something on the floor and end up falling instead. Benny leaps out
of my arms and lands safely on the comforter, leaving my hands
flailing for something to break my fall. I grasp the corner of the bed
just in time, the weight of my forward motion jarring the mattress
and creating a chain reaction of items toppling to the floor.

I land awkwardly on my knees with a thud and lay there for a
minute, taking inventory of my body. When I conclude that nothing is
broken, I slowly push myself up, feeling much older than my twenty-seven years. I know it's the cancer making me brittle and weak and
I know I'm lucky that I didn't snap a bone in half, or worse.

I look at the floor behind me to see what caused my fall, but
there's nothing and I feel a flash of embarrassment at my own clumsi-
ness. Then I walk over to Jack's side of the bed where the mattress
collided with his nightstand, causing everything on it to crash to the
ground, including his lamp. I pick that up first and put it on the table,
straightening the crooked shade. Then I reach for his glasses and
place those in the same spot where he leaves them every night. Last, I
pick up a book that fell facedown and I know what it is without turning it over, because it hasn't moved since the day I placed it on his
nightstand.

Preparing for the Death of a Loved One

As I run a finger down the uncracked spine, I get a flash of irritation at Jack.

Why aren't you preparing? I want to yell at him. But he's not here to yell at. I glance at the clock: 1:23 A.M.

It's late, even for Jack.

Sighing, I set the book back onto Jack's nightstand and crawl over his pillow to my side of the bed, snuggling under the covers. Benny curls up behind me, warming my back, and I lie there thinking about Jack and the tension and the distance. And as much as I hate it, as much as I want us to be that couple that pets each other's fingers and faces down my Lots of Cancer like a couple of caped superheroes, I know that it's better this way. I'm pushing him away because I'm preparing him for the inevitable—even if he refuses to prepare himself.

Because I understand what's ahead for him, even if he doesn't. I think about my dad, and the truck that so swiftly erased him from our lives. And I wonder, had he known four months earlier about his fate in that intersection, if he would have prepared my mom. I buzz with the idea that it's something else we have in common. If he could have found George for my mom years earlier, if he could have mitigated her pain, wouldn't he have? Wouldn't anybody?

The sudden urge to email PW147 overwhelms me and I sit up trying to remember where I left my laptop. But then I hear Jack's car pull up to our house, and I quickly reach up to turn off my lamp.

I wait in the dark silence for Jack to open the back door and walk into our bedroom, but minutes tick by and he never comes. I start second-guessing myself. Was I hearing things? Was it not Jack's car that pulled up, but a neighbor? Maybe Sammy? I get out of bed and tiptoe out of the room and down the hall toward the den and its row of large, single-paned windows that face the street.

I pry apart two of the white wooden slats covering the glass, careful not to stir the entire set of blinds, and then laugh at myself for my attempts at being stealthy. Jack's obviously not out there or he would have come in by now.

I stop laughing when I see his car parked at the curb in front of our house. Just ten yards away from me sits Jack in the driver's seat of his Ford Explorer. At first I think he must be on the phone, dealing with some emergency back at the clinic, but in the soft light shining from the streetlamp, I can see that there is no phone. His hand isn't up to his ear. He's just sitting. Staring straight ahead into the dark night in front of him, the light reflecting off the corneas of his eyes. And I'm struck, not just by his stillness, but by how tired he looks. No, not tired—he's always worn out after a long day at work. He looks . . . defeated.

And it occurs to me for the first time that maybe Jack doesn't want to be home any more than I wanted him here when I pulled into the driveway tonight. And even though I can't blame him, I still find myself indignant at this information. I'm *dying*! Shouldn't he want to be with me?

I take a deep breath, willing myself to calm down and be logical. I'm the one who's been pushing him away—eventually that's got to cause someone to start pulling, right? I can't very well expect him to keep trying, like a mangy dog following a kid home no matter how many times he's been told to scram. And shouldn't that make me happy? That Jack's *preparing*, even if he's not reading some stupid book?

Yes, it should.

So I can't explain why for the next twenty minutes I stand at the window quietly willing him with my mind to come inside and erase the distance between us.

sixteen

THE LETTER BOARD planted in front of Lexington Elementary School announces the date of a PTA meeting that has since passed, a Congratulations to the Student of the Mont (the "h" mysteriously missing), and the Kindergarten Open House on Tuesday at 6 P.M.

Jack checks his phone with one hand as he maneuvers the car into the parking lot with the other. I know he's anticipating a call about a bluebird that someone brought into the vet hospital after finding it flopping around in their backyard. Jack set the injured wing, but for two days has been unable to get the bird to eat. He left it in Charlene's care with explicit instructions to call him if she had better luck.

I know all these details because Jack told me Sunday night when he got home from a long day at his office. It was the only real conversation we had all weekend.

"Thanks again for coming," I say. "Kayleigh insisted and I know it means a lot to her."

He nods and pushes the gearshift into park. "Speak of the devil—"

I look up to see her making a beeline toward us. Jack's cell rings as I open the door. "Gotta take this," he says, already sliding his thumb across the screen. "I'll catch up to you."

"I was supposed to be here thirty-five minutes ago," Kayleigh says, grabbing my arm before I even have a chance to shut the car door behind me. "If anyone asks, we've been chatting in the parking lot."

I follow her to the front door and when we enter the lobby, Kayleigh's eyes dart around, taking in parents and teachers in name tags, chatting to each other.

"OK, I think we're good. If anyone approaches, just ask me something about the school," she says.

"Like what?"

"I don't know. If we teach Mandarin or something."

I nod, and as I take in the sea of faces around us, I notice the smaller humans weaving in and out of the crowd. "Is it weird that we don't have a kid with us?"

"No," she says. "Babysitter."

Of course. Jack and I have an about-to-be-kindergartener and he or she is with the babysitter. Got it. I glance around at other parents to glean cues of how they stand, carry themselves, like I'm in a method acting class. My eyes light on a woman carrying a baby strapped to her chest like a bomb. Her lithe hand clutches the wrist of a purple-frocked girl who's whining and struggling to get out of the wrestlerlike hold, and without warning the entire scene unfolding before me is like a serrated knife in my heart.

Before, when I used to see an obnoxious, demanding child, I'd feel a quick breath of relief that it wasn't mine. That I still had time and freedom and years before that was my burden to bear.

But now.

Now, I'll never have a child, whiny or otherwise. I'll never know the warmth of those tiny fingers in my palm wriggling to get free of my motherly hold. And the unfairness of it all threatens to liquefy my body until I'm nothing but a puddle on the linoleum floor. I try to swallow the lump in my throat that sits there like a ball of wet cotton, while Kayleigh drones on about other programs the school offers and questions I could ask, while the child's whining becomes more shrill, its pitch matching the emotion swelling in my body.

It's so all-consuming that I don't understand how Kayleigh hasn't noticed it. How she's still talking.

"Daisy," she says.

I exhale. She has noticed it. She's recognized the mistake in asking me to come here. "Yeah," I say, already forgiving her. How could she know how I would react to all of these kids? I didn't even know.

"Did you email her?"

She hasn't noticed.

"Who?" I ask, trying to come back to myself. To push the purple-frocked girl and her tiny fingers to the far corners of my mind.

"Seriously? The girl you've been mooning over all weekend. You're like a lovesick puppy."

"No. I still don't know what to say." I spent the last four days typing at least thirteen different drafts of emails—and berating myself for signing up for online dating without thinking it through. If I sent her a missive pretending to be Jack, then eventually the two would have to meet, and he would have no idea who the woman was. If I emailed her as myself and just explained the situation, she would probably think I was clinically insane, hopelessly pathetic, or both.

I shake my head. "It was a stupid idea."

"I'm telling you. The fake profile thing. It will work."

On Sunday, Kayleigh suggested that I create a bogus profile ("Find a pic of a hot guy online") and set up a date with PW147, then somehow get Jack to be at the same place at the same time. When she inevitably gets stood up because the guy doesn't exist, she and Jack will meet.

"I don't know. It's a little too *Catfish* for me. Too deceitful." Not to mention it's a lot of work with no guarantee that the two will actually speak to each other.

Kayleigh scoffs. "You're setting up your husband with another woman behind his back, but *this* is too deceitful."

I shush her as I see Jack walk through the front door. I wave at him.

"Sorry," he says when he gets closer.

"How's the bird?"

Two kids dart between us, playing chase. "Fine," he says, bending his knees sideways to avoid collision.

"Really? Is he eating?"

"Oh." He looks from the kids to me, and I wonder if he also sees in them the future we won't have. If he does, his eyes don't show it. "I don't know."

I'm confused. "Wasn't that Charlene?"

He opens his mouth to speak but gets interrupted by a staticky woman's voice blaring through the air, followed by high-pitched feedback. I wince as the chatter in the crowd goes still.

The offender, a tall, plump woman with gray roots betraying her otherwise black hair, is standing in the center of the room, struggling with her microphone. "Sorry about that," she says into the mouthpiece and this time the sound rings clear. "Ah, that's better." She smiles. "Welcome to Lexington Elementary's kindergarten open house." She pauses and scattered applause fills the empty space. "I'm Principal Woods, and we are thrilled that you all are here and interested in learning more about our award-winning educational facility."

I feel, rather than see, Kayleigh rolling her eyes beside me. The principal gives a brief overview of the kindergarten program—the academic curriculum, the enriched learning environment, the extracurricular activities. By the time she gets to the focus on global citizenship through their comprehensive world languages program, even I have to keep myself from snickering. Is this elementary school or college?

Kayleigh elbows me in the rib cage as if to say, "See? You thought I was exaggerating."

"There are four kindergarten classrooms that we'll be touring this evening," the principal continues. "Please feel free to ask the co-teachers in each room any questions you have at all about the learning environment here. Assistant Principal Perkins and I will also be milling around to answer any questions. Thank you again for coming."

She switches off the mike and parents start herding like cattle toward the back of the school, where Principal Woods indicated the kindergarten classrooms were. As we shuffle along, it dawns on me why Kayleigh was late. "You were with Bradley Cooper, weren't you."

She flushes, an involuntary grin spreading across her face.

"Wow. He must be really good," I say.

Jack groans. "Seriously?" I can almost hear him thinking: *This* is why I don't like to hang out with you two. His cell phone rings. He holds it up and squeezes my arm. "I'll be right back."

As Jack steps his way to the side of the crowd and ducks into an empty classroom, Kayleigh leans into me and says in a conspirator's voice. "He really is."

"Well," I say, giving in to Kayleigh's infectious happiness, the familiar roller-coaster high she rides at the beginning of every new relationship, "he is hot."

"You have no idea," she says, launching into a detailed description of his most chiseled body parts. At "carved obliques," I stop listening. I might even stop breathing. I know I've stopped moving because I'm ever so slightly aware of being jostled a bit from behind by parents jockeying to get through the doorway I'm standing in.

I'm a stone in a river and my body is ice-cold.

"Daisy." I hear Kayleigh's concerned voice floating toward me. "Are you OK?"

She takes my arm and pulls me out of the door frame and into the classroom, but I don't take my eyes off the woman with toffee-colored hair.

"It's her," I say, my voice dry.

"Who?" Kayleigh follows my gaze.

"PW147." She's more alive in person, which shouldn't make any sense—isn't everyone more alive in the flesh than in photos? But as soon as I light on the description, it fits. Her Pantene hair shines under the fluorescent bulbs. She's wearing a navy blue cardigan and bright yellow ballet flats that match her brilliant smile, and I understand why there's a child wrapped around her as if he's made of steel and her leg is a magnet.

"Where? The only person I see is Pamela."

Upon hearing her name, PW147 breaks the gaze of the parent she's talking to and looks in our direction. "Kayleigh, there you are! Do you mind showing Mrs. . . . I'm sorry, tell me your name again?"

The woman murmurs something.

"Yes! Mrs. *Beckwith*—the emotions chart? I promised to take a few parents"—she waves to a group of adults standing behind her—"through our typical work cycle."

Kayleigh looks from me to Pamela and blinks. "Um . . . yeah. Sure." She steps forward and directs Mrs. Beckwith toward the back of the classroom. "Right this way."

Kayleigh turns with narrowed eyes, mouthing something to me over her shoulder, but I'm too busy staring at PW—or Pamela—and trying to reconcile the fact that the woman in the profile is the same woman that Kayleigh's been bitching about since she started working here in August.

"Ma'am?" The word snaps me to attention as I realize that everyone is staring at me.

"Yes?" I manage, locking eyes with Pamela. There's such genuine kindness in them that I start to wonder if Kayleigh's poor judgment of men extends to other people in her life. Or maybe it's me. Maybe I've concocted this impossibly perfect woman in my mind based on her 173-word profile and have been rendered unable to find any possible fault with her.

Going forward, I must be shrewder.

"I was just asking if you wanted to join us in observing the children's work cycle."

"I do," I say. "Thank you."

She smiles, nods, and turns to the rest of the adults flanking her, asking us to take a seat in one of the pint-sized plastic blue chairs at our feet. Then she starts to unravel the boy from her leg. "Hudson, why don't you go get the seashell work and you can show them how you wash it?"

He scampers off on stubby legs to a shelf lining the side of the room, and I force myself to look away from his tininess, which threatens to clench my heart as tightly as the whiny girl's palms did. We each awkwardly lower our bodies into the molded seats and I turn my focus back to Pamela. "Each child gets to choose what he or she will work on when they come in for the day," she begins.

I lean forward on my knees—uncomfortably close to my chin— hanging on to every word. Her voice is firm, but melodic. It's apparent she's the kind of teacher who won't take any crap from her students, which makes them love her all the more.

I shake my head. But there must be something wrong with her. I try to think back. What did Kayleigh hate about her? The pearls. She was thoroughly offended by Pamela's pearls, launching into a diatribe that started with "Who wears pearls?" and ended with something about sorority girls and Jackie Kennedy.

My gaze travels to her neck—she's not wearing them tonight. Regardless, it's hardly a crime to own outdated jewelry. Maybe they're a family heirloom—passed down from her dead grandmother or something. I'm sure Kayleigh never thought to ask.

The other complaints I recall had to do with Pamela's overeager-ness in the classroom—constantly coming up with new bulletin boards, adding extra tasks into lessons at the last minute, sucking up to Principal Woods. I can see how that would be irritating to Kayleigh, but all it says about Pamela is that she's dedicated to her work, passionate about what she does.

Like Jack.

"Excuse me," I hear Kayleigh's voice break in, interrupting Pamela's explanation.

"I'm just going to grab Dais—er . . . Mrs. Richmond. I promised I would show her the, um . . . sandpaper letters."

"Of course," Pamela says, nodding at me as if to dismiss me. Kayleigh beckons me with her hand, and I have no choice but to get up from the chair and follow her. Pamela launches back into her speech behind me.

When we're a safe distance away and clutching large white cards with raised gritty characters on them, Kayleigh hisses one word: "*Pamela?*"

"Keep your voice down," I whisper back, peering around to make sure we're alone. And then: "I just don't understand what's so bad about her."

"Where do you want me to begin? She wore a reindeer sweater at Christmas. And she was not being ironic." Kayleigh stares at me as if she's just told me that Pamela strangles kittens for fun.

I stare back. "So?"

"*So?*" Kayleigh repeats. "She's *that* girl. Everything is sunshine and daisies and—oh! She puts contact paper on *everything*. Pencil holders, the inside of drawers, bulletin boards. If she lived in your house, she would contact paper the walls. Think about that."

I do. Not the contact paper bit—I already have it on the inside of every cabinet in my kitchen and bathroom—but Pamela living in my house. Looking around the classroom at all the neat cubbyholes, organized shelves, and immaculate desks, I have no doubt she would keep my home in perfect order—and she'd always know where Jack's scrubs were.

"What are you guys whispering about?" I jump at Jack's voice behind me.

"Nothing," I say, rearranging the sandpaper letters in my hand.

"Do you need us here much longer?" Jack asks Kayleigh. "I gotta get back to the clinic."

"Oh. No, I think we're good. I made sure Principal Woods saw me talking with you guys in the lobby," she says.

Jack nods and turns to me. "Are you about ready to go?"

"Uh, yeah," I say, darting my eyes over to where Pamela is still sitting in the half circle of chairs, watching Hudson use a toothbrush to scrub a conch shell in a shallow Tupperware filled with water. How long does it take to clean a freakin' shell? "Let me just tell Kayleigh's co-teacher thank you."

"OK, well, I'll go ahead and start the car."

"No! I mean, just, it'll take two seconds. Come with me."

As I walk toward Pamela, my thoughts stumble over themselves—I can introduce Jack easily enough, but how can I keep the conversation going? And even if I can get the two of them chatting, then what? I can't just ask for her phone number. Or say, hey, interested in marrying my husband? I curse myself again for being so foolish. For thinking I could pick a wife out for Jack as easily as I might buy him a pair of shoes. What did I think, that I would just bring a girl home and put her in the closet for safekeeping?

When we arrive at the blue chair I left empty, I'm defeated. I decide to just thank Pamela, because that's what I told Jack I was there to do, and leave, my tail between the cancerous bones in my legs.

As I take a deep breath to speak, Pamela looks up.

Her eyes widen.

And before I can say a word, she beats me to it.

"Jack?"

Confused, I glance around, wondering if one of the boys weaving through the class is named Jack. But then I look back at Pamela and see that her gaze is fully locked on my husband. So I turn my head to stare at him, too. And imagined or not, it feels as though the whole room—the whole world, perhaps—has gone still and is waiting for him to speak.

His response is a statement: "Pamela."

The thoughts in my mind that had been so jumbled just moments before dissipate, and I am left with one coherent sentence: they know each other.

But it's hard to focus on that information. Because there's something about the way he says her name that—for the briefest of seconds—makes me hate her as much as Kayleigh does.

Maybe even more.

april

seventeen

I DON'T EAT CHILI.

I've never liked it. I think the cans of it that I buy for Jack to slather onto his hot dogs look like dog food.

Yet I'm inexplicably standing in front of a table lined with Crock-Pots in a church basement, holding a Styrofoam bowl full of slow-cooked ground beef and spices. Orange puddles of oil have begun to congregate on top of the meat, and as I stare at the offending concoction, all I can think is: how did I get here?

Not literally. I know that I rode with Jack and we walked in together and now here we are, standing on top of linoleum and beneath cheap ceiling tiles.

And I know that it's because I said yes. That I agreed that we should come.

At the open house, after the revelation that Jack and Pamela were not meeting for the first time, Jack offered me the missing puzzle piece: "Pamela volunteers at the Small Dog Rescue, too."

He turned back to her. "But I didn't know you worked *here*," he said at the exact moment that Pamela said: "I didn't know you had kids."

Kids. Shit. Jack and I were supposed to be parents. Panicked, I glanced up at Kayleigh, her wide eyes meeting mine.

Following an awkward beat of silence, Jack spoke, easily explaining away our lack of children and therefore unnecessary presence at an elementary school open house: "We don't. My wife is best friends with Kayleigh. She's always wanted us to see where she worked."

Wife.

I basked in the noun. Smug at the possession it implied.

And then, as they continued chatting about the dog rescue and last weekend's adoption day at PetSmart, I silently scolded myself for my ridiculous overreaction to this entire situation. So they already knew each other. This was a good thing, no? Just minutes before, I had been trying to scheme their meeting. That part—though unexpected—took care of itself. I should have been relieved, elated. Not acting like a possessive schoolgirl who doesn't want to share her Oreos at lunchtime.

But if I was honest, I didn't really like the way she was looking at my cookies. Like she might eat them all, including the crumbs. And leave me without even one.

I forced myself to tune back into their conversation.

I heard the word "chili."

And then Jack and Pamela were looking at me expectantly.

"Huh?" I said.

"Do you want to go?" Jack said.

"Where?"

"The fund-raiser for the shelter. Pamela was just talking about it."

"Oh, sorry. Yes. That sounds great."

And now it's Saturday and I'm at a chili cook-off. Holding a bowl of chili that I don't intend to eat.

"You coming?" Jack says, grabbing two plastic spoons and a couple of napkins from a table covered in a red checkerboard cloth.

I follow him as he weaves through the crowd, past the dessert table, laden with homemade frosted cakes, chocolate chip cookies, lemon bars, and cherry pie. Though sugar has strictly been on my Do Not Eat list for years, I slow down and eye each goodie, surprised how easy it is to conjure the memory of its taste in my mouth.

The carrot cake reminds me of my first Christmas with Jack's family in Indiana. It was so normal it made me uncomfortable. Like I was in the middle of a Publix commercial, but someone forgot to hand me a script. I smiled a lot. At his mom when she offered more turkey and stuffing. At his three little sisters when they all wanted to braid my hair and paint my face with lipstick and glitter. At his uncle who said I hadn't lived until I ate a piece of Jack's mom's carrot cake. "Aren't you going to have any?" I asked Jack as his mom passed out slices on good china. "I don't really like sweets," he said, pouring coffee into a delicate cup.

"Who doesn't like *sweets*?" I raised my voice, forgetting my demure composure, shocked that I had known him for eight months without learning this significant piece of information. The family erupted in laughter. "He's the milkman's son!" His dad banged his fist at the head of the table. "It's unnatural," his mom tutted.

Jack doesn't eat dessert. As I slide into a folding chair, I make a mental note to add it to the list I started for Pamela. Things she should know about him, like how he'll never voluntarily get a haircut or how he keeps a box of Trivial Pursuit cards next to the toilet and reads them for fun, or how, if an animal dies on his surgery table, he needs to be left alone for a few hours that night—no hugs, no consoling "It wasn't your fault," no suggestions for distraction.

"I like your sweater."

I look up across the table that Jack has led us to into Pamela's round eyes and then down at my navy and white striped top. Jack calls it my boat captain shirt. He usually salutes me when I wear it, but when I came out into the living room this morning, he just looked at me and said, "Ready to go?"

"Thanks," I say, sitting down, while scanning her torso so I can return the compliment. "I like your . . . hair."

It's pulled straight back into a full ponytail. No muss, no fuss. And I know it's not the style I'm complimenting her on, but more her whole low-maintenance attitude. And how she can still look impossibly, irritatingly beautiful with her hair up and no mascara.

She smiles and then looks at Jack, already inhaling his chili beside me. "You like it?"

"Killer," he says, using his napkin to catch a grease dribble running down his chin.

"It's my grandma's secret recipe."

Jack pauses long enough to say, "You made this one?"

She nods. "Make sure you vote for it. I mean, you know, if you think it's the best." She glances at my untouched bowl. Then she adds, in a serious voice: "There's a plastic trophy on the line here."

Out of reflex, I pick up my spoon and start picking at the meat. "Sorry," I say. "I had a really big breakfast."

"Daisy hates chili," Jack says.

"I don't *hate* it. I just don't really like it." I offer Pamela a smile. "But yours looked the best out of all of them."

"Thanks." She laughs, and there's something pleasing about the sound. Or maybe I'm pleased with myself for eliciting it. Like I'm in high school and thrilled that the popular girl thinks I'm funny.

She straightens her back and clears her throat. "So, um . . . I have a confession to make."

She nervously glances at Jack and my spine goes rigid. The word "confession" is so personal, suggestive, intimate. I lean closer, wondering what the next sentence could possibly be. Is this when the popular girl tries to steal my boyfriend? Right in front of me? Or have I been watching too many *Gossip Girl* reruns on TBS?

"Jack, I've been wanting to ask you something all day."

"What?" he says, putting his spoon down, giving her his full attention. I stare at his face staring at her and wish I knew what was going through his mind. Does he think she's pretty? Of course he does. She's indisputably beautiful. But—does he think she's prettier than *me*?

"It's about Copper."

I wait for Jack to ask what I'm thinking: *Who's Copper?*—but he only nods.

"How's he doing?"

"Not good. They had to remove the sling this week because he was developing laminitis in his right hoof."

"From bearing too much weight," Jack says.

"Exactly. But his broken leg isn't completely healed and the vet says there's nothing else he can do. He recommends putting him down." She takes a deep breath. "But I just . . . I can't."

Jack nods again. "You want me to come take a look?"

She brightens and the water rimming her eyes glints in the light, and I know immediately that she's one of those rare girls who's pretty even when she cries. "Could you? I know you're so busy, but you were talking about all that prosthetics research—"

"It's really come a long way in the past few years, but I don't want you to get your hopes up," he says. "Leg injuries are tricky with horses."

"I know," Pamela says.

She continues speaking, but I'm stuck in what she's already said. Or not what she's said, but in what her words infer. Pamela and Jack really know each other. They have had actual conversations about her horse and about his job and I wonder what else they talk about. And I wonder how long they've been volunteering together. And I wonder why he's never mentioned her. Has he? I search my memory bank. Did Jack ever come home from PetSmart and say, "Remember that girl Pamela I was telling you about? She did the funniest thing today." But I don't think he ever did say that. And I wonder what it means that he didn't.

I try to stay involved in their conversation, but it's a tennis match and I'm very much just a spectator. So I observe. Their bodies are hunched toward each other, Jack's eyes bright and eager as he expounds the details of his prosthetics research. Pamela's a fervent listener, devouring every word that falls from his lips. And I wonder if I'm imagining it or if I can actually hear the buzz of the electric current that invisibly flows between them.

Jack loops me back into the conversation. "Is that OK with you? If I go up there tomorrow?"

I pretend to think. I pretend that our once-full calendar isn't completely blank except for my every-two-week Friday doctor appointments. I pretend that I'm still in control, that everything is going according to my plan, that Jack isn't slipping through my hands, but that I'm pushing him. Letting him go.

I nod my head. "It's OK."

Pamela stands up. "Great," she says. "Do you guys want anything? I'm gonna get a cookie."

My eyes are drawn to her stomach. It's so flat it looks like it's never seen a cookie, and I try to swallow my envy. "Get two," I want to say. But then a sentence from Pamela's dating profile jumps out at me.

"You don't want the pie?" I ask.

She tilts her head.

Why did I say that out loud?

"I just . . . it looked really good."

"Oh, do you want a piece? I'll bring you one."

"No, I'm fine."

She nods. "Jack?"

We both look at my husband, whose mouth is full of cornbread.

I speak for him: "He doesn't eat dessert."

But then, I wonder if maybe she already knows that and is just being polite.

ON THE DRIVE home it's still light outside. More cars than usual line our street, which can only mean—

"Must be a baseball game today," Jack says.

"Mmm," I say, still lost in thoughts about Pamela. But part of me inexplicably waits for him to say more. To ask if I want to go to the game with him. Right now. Grab a blanket and go sit on the hill, a grassy slope behind right field where students without tickets gather to drink cheap beer and heckle the opposing team's outfielders. Jack and I went once when we first moved in to our house. It was fun, until an obnoxious frat boy sitting next to us started pitching his empty Miller Lite cans onto the field and then unbuttoned his pants and let a long stream of piss fall onto the patch of dirt three feet from where we were sitting. The splatter came within inches of our blanket.

And even though it was disgusting and I swore I'd never go again, now I want to. And I want Jack to want to, too.

But he doesn't say anything else.

So I take a deep breath and ask, "How long have you known Pamela?"

Jack blinks while he expertly steers the car until it's hugging the curb in front of our house. "I don't know," he says, shifting the gear into park. "Six months?" Then he looks at me. "Why?"

"You've never mentioned her before, and it just . . ." I try to choose my next words with precision, keep my tone steady and light. I don't want to sound like a nagging wife. Or insecure. Or jealous. Or portray any of the real emotions I'm actually feeling. "I guess it seems like you guys know each other pretty well. I was surprised is all." I open the car door. "No big deal."

I hop out of my seat, crafting my body language to match my carefree demeanor. Jack steps out into the road and walks a pace behind me toward the front door. When my foot grazes the third step of the stone porch, I feel his hand fall on my waist. He tugs the belt loop on my jeans.

"Hey," he says. I pivot to face him. With his feet planted firmly on the ground and mine teetering on the middle step, we are the same height. We are literally seeing eye to eye. I wait for him to speak, but instead, Jack leans in, closing the gap, and firmly plants his lips on mine. I pucker my mouth automatically, returning his kiss out of instinct, years of habit shaping my mouth to meet his.

"Mwah," I say, ending the familiar peck, and force my mind to move on to the evening's activities—the bath I want to take, the flannel jammies I'm looking forward to snuggling in—and not the fact that it's the first time we've kissed on the lips in weeks. Or that the skin where his cheek stubble scratched my face is still tingling.

But before I can turn back toward the door, his hand is on the back of my head, pulling me forward. Our lips meet again, this time with a grave force that snaps me out of my conditioned response and reminds me instantly of those first kisses we shared in doorways and parked cars. The weak bellies. The trembling knees.

And though I've had no desire to have sex in weeks, a primal urge blossoms in my belly and spreads like wildfire.

I want my husband.

And I know it's some biological instinct reacting to the threat of competition, a symbolic way to drive a red flag through his chest and stake him as *mine*, but I don't care.

We stumble up the last few steps still kissing, our hands groping, neither one of us wanting to risk breaking the connection. Jack unlocks the front door and I start unbuttoning his jeans before it's fully closed behind us.

He digs one hand in my hair and the other roams over the curves of my sweater and then glides underneath it. He stretches his fingers across my bare stomach, kneading them into my flesh and I freeze. An image of Pamela's flat abs flashes through my mind. I sharply inhale, concentrating all my efforts on sucking in my rounded belly that has never been taut, despite the endless hours of hot yoga and number of kale smoothies I subjected it to.

"Are you OK?" Jack whispers, his hands as still as my breath. "Did I hurt you?"

"I'm fine," I say, unzipping my pants and shrugging them down my legs. I give my head a shake, willing myself to stop thinking about Pamela and why I shouldn't be taking my clothes off with my husband. To stop ruining this moment. To exhale.

But as hard as I try she's still there.

When Jack kisses a trail down my neck.

Falls on top of me on the couch.

Moves inside of me.

I close my eyes tight and dig my fingers into his shoulders, proving to myself that he's there. Mine. But even with my eyes closed I still see her face.

With all my strength, I pull Jack to me. Closer. Deeper. I want us to become one in every sense of the word. But then, the full weight of his upper body is on mine, crushing my chest, my lungs, and I can't breathe.

I can't breathe.

I really can't—

"Jack!" I gasp, pounding his back with my fists.

But he mistakes my frenzy for passion and buries his head in my neck. "Daisy," he rasps.

"No!" The giant fist clenches tighter around my lungs and panic has taken hold of me. "Get—off!" I push at his face, shoulders, anything I can get purchase on, with my fingers, my palms.

"Daisy?" He immediately sits up, his eyes mirroring the wild look that I know is in mine. "Daisy! What's wrong?"

I struggle to sit up, to respond, but there's a weight on my chest. I rake my fingers across my breasts in a desperate attempt to remove it. I suck in air, but it gets caught in my throat; there's no place for it to go. I hear a noise far off that sounds oddly like a baby seal. And then I realize that it's me. My heart is pounding in my ears and I'm vaguely aware of Jack's hands on my shoulders, pulling me up to sitting, as I open and close my mouth like a fish on land, searching for water. But I'm searching for oxygen.

"Daisy. Look at me," Jack is gripping my chin. "Look at me!"

I do.

"Now. Relax," he says, in a steady voice. "Just calm down." He gently rubs my arms. "Breathe," he commands.

As if it were that simple. I open my mouth to tell him I can't, but all I do is wheeze, and my head is light and I wonder if this is what dying feels like. And then I think how nice it is for Jack's face to be the last thing I see.

"Close your mouth. In through your nose." Jack follows his own directions as if he's teaching a class on breathing techniques. *Like this.*

I obey. And we both sit there sniffing like dogs, until my heartbeat slows and I can match his inhales. Air fills my lungs with sweet relief and I open my mouth to gulp more.

"Slowly," he says. I nod, my eyes never leaving his. Silence fills the room as we breathe in unison.

In.

Out.

Deliberate.

"Better?" he asks.

"Yes," I manage.

And for a moment neither one of us moves, even though I'm clad only in a bra and Jack's boxers are absurdly wrapped around one ankle.

I don't notice that I'm trembling until Jack gets up to drape the afghan around me. He sits down beside me and I can feel his hand heavy on my shoulder. I cover my face with my hands, because I feel the tears welling up in my eyes, and unlike Pamela, I'm not a pretty crier. My face gets blotchy and puffy and my nose turns shiny and red. On top of that, I'm half naked and hotly embarrassed and I just don't want Jack to see me like this. I shrug his hand off me without looking up.

"Daisy," he says.

I shake my head into my palms. "Just go," I whisper, my voice threatening to crack if I raise it.

"What?" he asks. I can feel him leaning closer.

"Just go!" I croak, thrusting my hands to my side but keeping my eyes clenched tight. I don't want him to bear witness to my further humiliation. I crumple away from him and roll myself into a ball in the corner of the sofa, pulling the blanket around me tight like a cocoon. "I just want to be alone," I say in a small voice, spent from my outburst.

The room fills with silence and everything is so still I wonder if he already left and I missed it. But I'm scared to open my eyes and check. So I lie as still as the air, until finally I feel the couch shift beside me when he stands up. I hear him slowly tug on his clothes. And then I hear his heavy, burdened footsteps as he retreats out of the den, down the hall, into his office.

But I still can't open my eyes. I lie there, hot, salty tears leaking from them, as I replay the last few moments in my head—the craving, the urgency, the familiar touching that somehow, miraculously, felt new again. And then the sheer panic that took hold when the fire in my belly moved to my lungs. And then I reach up and clutch my dry throat, marveling at how quickly—and without warning—everything can go to shit.

THE NEXT MORNING when I pad out into the kitchen, I'm nearly knocked over by Jack's lanky body rushing past me back to the den. "Sorry," he calls over his shoulder, and then: "Have you seen my keys?"

"On the dresser," I call back, opening the refrigerator and pulling out my smoothie ingredients.

When he reenters the kitchen, I'm stuffing kale into the glass pitcher of the blender. I turn it on. The jet-engine-like whirring drowns out his next sentence.

When it goes silent, he repeats himself: "I'm late. I'm gonna go."

I wonder if he is late, or if he's just eager to leave. Not that I can blame him if he is.

"OK," I say, not turning to look at him. The embarrassment of the evening before flames hot on my cheeks again. Jack doesn't move and a thick silence settles in the air.

"Daisy?"

"Yeah?" I say, and for a second I have a crazy hope that he'll just rush over to me and throw his arms around me, that I could melt into him and forget last night and Pamela and the Lots of Cancer and just remember Jack. Me and Jack.

But he doesn't.

"I think you should call Dr. Saunders."

At this, I turn and look at him. "Why?"

"You know," he says, shifting his gaze to the floor. "Last night. Your, uh, episode."

My *episode*? Is he talking about my *crying*? I feel the heat in my face explode, as irritation overtakes my embarrassment. Jack has always been terrible at dealing with emotions, but Jesus, I think I have a right to be upset once in awhile. I'm *dying*.

When I don't say anything for fear of crying again—this time out of anger—Jack speaks up. "I just think you should make sure it's not something to do with your lungs."

Oh. He's talking about the whole not-being-able-to-breathe thing.

"I'm sure it's fine," I say, even though I'm not sure of this at all.

"Still," he says, not moving, and even though seconds before I wanted him to envelop me, now I just want him to be gone already.

"OK. I'll call him."

"OK," Jack says.

I raise my eyebrows at him. "I thought you were running late."

"Oh. Yeah," he says, and takes a few steps toward me, closing the gap between us. He leans in to kiss me and I turn my head at the last second so he gets part of my ear and a mouthful of hair.

He takes a step back and I can feel him looking at me, so I busy myself pouring the smoothie into a cup.

"Daisy?"

"What," I say, not looking at him.

The silence stretches as I will him to stop staring at me and just leave.

And then—after muttering a quick "nothing" under his breath—he does.

I stand at the counter for a minute, my hand clutching the cup. I concentrate on my breathing.

In.

Out.

In.

Out.

Then I walk over to where my cell phone sits and unplug it from the wall. I sit at the kitchen table with my thick drink and call Dr. Saunders. As it rings, I half hope he won't answer. It is Sunday morning, after all. Maybe he's at church. Wait. Does Dr. Saunders go to church? It stuns me how little I actually know about him.

"Hello?" he answers on the fourth ring.

"It's Daisy," I say. And then after a few pleasantries, I tell him about the fire in my chest and how I couldn't breathe and how I kind of sounded like a baby seal.

"Uh-huh," Dr. Saunders says, and I picture his eyebrows nodding. "And what were you doing when you experienced this shortness of breath?"

"Um, what?" I ask, my face flushing for what feels like the thirtieth time in the past twelve hours.

"You know, were you at rest, lying down, active, walking?"

I get a flash of Jack's naked body hovering above mine. I can feel him breathing in my ear.

"Um . . . active," I say, hoping Dr. Saunders can't hear the embarrassment in my voice. "I guess I was active."

After a few more questions, he concludes that it was most likely a panic attack, but that it's also consistent with symptoms of pleural effusion—a fluid buildup around the lungs often experienced by people with malignant tumors. He said to call if it happened again, otherwise he could run some tests on Monday.

I hang up after making yet another doctor appointment for the next morning, even though I know I should have asked more questions about pleural effusion, if only because I'm sure Jack will ask me more questions tonight and it would be nice to have the answers. But I can't be bothered to care about my most likely panic attacks or possible pleural effusion, because all I can think about is Jack being on his way to see Pamela. And how I can't properly kiss my husband good-bye. And how for weeks now I've been a walking bingo cage, my emotions tumbling around on top of each other like balls of numbers and I never know which one is going to come out next.

I take a deep breath and try to deal in facts. Logic. Jack is on his way to see Pamela. He is going to help her with her horse. They are going to talk and probably laugh and Jack's crooked tooth is going to peek out of his lips at something clever she says. I remind myself that this is exactly what I wanted to happen. That it's the perfect opportunity for Jack and Pamela to let the potential spark between them grow. That Jack deserves someone who can breathe. And who's not actively dying.

But slowly, those logical thoughts give way to the image that's been plaguing me since Pamela invited Jack to her horse farm. It's all romantic rugged cowboy and wind through toffee-colored hair and Hallmark movie scene, and it's utterly absurd, but it still pangs my heart and threatens to compress my lungs all over again.

I take a deep breath to reaffirm my airways are still open.

Then I look at the green, thick sludge in my cup and find that I've lost all desire to drink my smoothie.

I hear Jack's voice echo from an earlier time. A pre-Lots-of-Cancer time: Why are you still drinking those things?

And sitting here, I begin to nod in agreement to his repeated question. *Why* am *I still drinking these goddamned things?*

I pick it up and watch my hand curiously—as if it's a rebellious, petulant child that's acting of its own accord—and heave the entire plastic cup, green liquid and all, across the room where it *smacks* the cabinet beneath the sink. Green slop sprays the maple, the fake Saltillo tile, the baseboards. The cup then hits the floor where it rolls to rest at the foot of the refrigerator.

And in the silence that follows, the stupid therapist's voice from the stupid first time I had stupid cancer once again rings in my head:

Your anger is grief wearing a disguise.

I slump back against my chair.

My anger is all over my kitchen floor.

eighteen

AFTER CHEST X-RAYS and more blood work and breathing into a ridiculous plastic tube connected to a loud machine, Dr. Saunders confirms that I have a small amount of excess fluid on my lungs.

"We'll keep an eye on it, but I don't think that's what caused your labored breathing," his bushy eyebrows inform me.

"OK. So what did?" I'm sitting on a tissue-paper-covered exam table. It crinkles loudly with even the slightest movement, so I try to stay absolutely still.

Dr. Saunders sets the manila folder he's carrying down beside me and takes his glasses off. "What you're dealing with right now is stressful, anxiety inducing."

Stressful.

I try not to scoff.

Stressful is when you have two final exams in one day. Or when your basement floods on the same morning that your in-laws are getting in town.

This is not stressful.

This is something else.

He fixes me with a serious stare. "I think it would be helpful for you to see a specialist. Learn some breathing techniques."

I stare back at him. "A specialist. That sounds like code for a therapist."

The left side of his mouth turns up. "A respiratory therapist." He
taps his chest with his index finger. "Not a head one," he says, moving
his finger to the side of his skull. "There's a difference."

"OK," I nod. "As long as it's not some trick to get me to see a
shrink."

"I wouldn't do that. I know how you feel about it," he says, then
fixes me with a pointed stare. "But that doesn't mean I don't think you
should see one of those, too."

"I'm sure you do," I say, remembering it was Dr. Saunders who re-
ferred me to the single therapy session I agreed to go to the first time
around. I resisted then, too, which prompted him to ask: "Don't you
want to *be* a therapist? I would think you of all people would understand the benefits of going." I wanted to tell him that I do understand
the benefits—for other people. But for me? I'm already so self-reflec-
tive, introspective, so overanalytical about everything I say and do that
there's nothing a stranger could ask me or tell me that I haven't already asked or told myself. And really, who wants to go to a therapist
who needs therapy? It's like being examined by a physician who's sniffling and sneezing and coughing. Not very comforting. But I didn't
know how to explain all of that to Dr. Saunders without sounding
hypocritical and arrogant, so I just shrugged.

Now I look at Dr. Saunders, who's looking back at me, his forehead crinkled, and I sigh. "The last thing I need right now is someone
asking me how I feel every five seconds or trying to tell me what my
anger *means*."

The last word hangs in the air and Dr. Saunders' wooly brows furrow together in concern.

"Are you angry?"

I pause for a minute and stare at my jean-clad knees, silently
cursing myself for saying too much.

Then I look up at him: "Wouldn't you be?"

Dr. Saunders holds my gaze for twenty long, silent seconds. Even the paper beneath me remains quiet. Then he reaches into his pocket and pulls out a handful of business cards. He looks down and shuffles through them until he finds the one he wants. He hands it to me.

"Patrick's part of our extended patient care team," he says. "He works in the Pulmonary Center next door. Just call the number on the bottom there."

I take the card, stuff it into the side pocket of my bag, and tell him that I will, even though I think the notion of paying someone to teach me how to breathe is about as ridiculous as it gets.

I'd almost rather see a shrink.

AS I DRIVE home from the cancer center, I roll down my window. The breeze blows my hair back and feels good, almost good enough to make me ignore the exhaust fumes that are also gusting in my face. I search for the electric up button on the side of the door with my index finger, but before the glass meets the door frame, a new smell wafts in the open gap and up my nostrils.

Grease.

Cheeseburgers.

The Varsity Jr.

While it usually makes my stomach turn—the thought of all that processed meat, chemical-laden bread and cheese and potatoes—the scent is currently having the opposite effect on my belly. It's growling.

Maybe it's nostalgia. A yearning for the time when Jack would turn to me on the way home from a late-night movie with a devilish grin: "I could go for a burger." I would agree, because in that heady beginning of our relationship, it never occurred to me to say no. And in the front seat of his Explorer we fed each other French fries out of a grease-spotted bag, exchanging oily kisses and secret grins, reveling in the thrill of our spontaneity.

Without thinking about it, I turn my car into the parking lot and pull into an empty space. The restaurant is set up like an old-fashioned drive-in burger joint, complete with carhops. A voice crackles out of the box outside my partially open window. I can't make out the words, but I know it's the standard Varsity Jr. greeting—"What'll ya have?"

I open my mouth to say "Nothing," but stop when I realize how crazy that would sound. Why else would I have pulled into the spot if not to order something? Then I chastise myself for caring what a fast-food waitress thinks about my mental health.

The voice repeats itself, and I panic. The engine is still running and my hand is on the gearshift. All I have to do is move it to reverse and press the gas. But instead, I turn my head to the electronic box.

"Burger," I say. But the word comes out soft and broken and squeaking, as if I've just learned how to speak.

"Naked? Glorified? Chili?" The rapid-fire questions unnerve me and I don't remember what they mean, so I just go with the first one.

"Naked," I say, which is how I feel. Exposed.

"Strings?"

A neuron fires somewhere in my brain, recalling the knowledge that strings equals fries, and I picture Jack feeding them to me, one by one.

"Please."

Minutes later a woman in a paper hat appears at my window. I hand her my credit card, which she runs through a handheld device, and she gives me a paper bag. I set it on my passenger seat and then move the gearshift into reverse.

Driving home, I glance over at the bag, as if it's a puppy I've adopted on a whim, and now what am I supposed to do with it? I try to remember the feel of the food in my mouth, that pleasing first bite that's all steamy bun and fatty beef, but I resist opening the bag, my strange bout of spontaneity waning.

And by the time I pull in my driveway, the odorous sack has morphed from appealing to utterly disgusting, so I pinch it between two fingers and carry it up the back steps, through the kitchen door, and deposit it directly in the trash can under the sink.

IT'S JUST PAST eleven when I hear Jack's car pull up that night. I'm lying in bed, forcing my eyes to stay open because I want to see him. Not to say anything or do anything. I just want to lay my eyes on his untamed, shaggy hair, and his asymmetric face, and his impossibly long arms. It will be the first time I've seen him since he left for Pamela's farm yesterday morning, as he was called into the wildlife clinic on his way home and didn't get in until long after I had fallen asleep, and he left for work before I got up this morning. Part of me wonders if he's doing it on purpose, if it's easier not to be around me. I roll my eyes. Of course it's easier. I've not exactly made him want to be home with my loving gestures and kind words.

When the back door creaks open, Benny jumps down from the bed to go greet him, and I sit up a little and run my fingers through my hair, smoothing it over one shoulder. Jack's boot-clad feet clop down the hallway, and it feels like they're keeping in time with my heartbeat.

And then he's there.

"Hey," he says, his eyes locking with mine.

"Hey," I say.

He turns toward the dresser and deposits his keys and wallet, then starts peeling off his scrubs.

The air feels thick and I know it's still there. The tension. I search my mind for something to say, but every sentence sounds ridiculous, like a line from some after-school special, and I dismiss them one by one.

Can we talk about this dying thing?

What's happening to us?

Do you still love me?

The questions themselves are juvenile, stemming from my own recently acquired insecurities and selfishness. Like bait on a fishing rod, I've cast Jack off, and now I feel the need to reel him in, tug on the line, make sure he's still there.

Of course he's still there. He's Jack. He's my Jack. And I know all it would take for me to reach him is a couple of words.

I'm sorry.

I know I've been impossible.

I love you.

I open my mouth to speak and then close it.

And then I ask him about Pamela's horse.

He looks up at me, as if he'd forgotten I was there and my voice reminded him. "I've been working on it all evening," he says, and I can see the strain in his eyes as he walks, hangdog to the bed. "The good news is, artificial limbs for horses have come a long way since Midnight."

I stare at him, confused.

As Jack pulls down the comforter and crawls in beside me, he looks up and notices my expression. "The miniature horse that was first fitted with a prosthetic a few years ago?"

I shake my head. "Never heard of him. Him?"

"Yeah. Anyway, some vets even fitted a quarter horse up in Washington with a prosthetic last year, but it was her back leg, just like Midnight's. Hind leg injuries are better suited for prosthetics because they bear less weight. Copper's injury is in his front leg."

"Oh, well, that sucks," I say, trying to be sympathetic.

But Jack's lip curls up on one side. "It's exactly the type of case

Ling has been having me research. And I found this vet named Redden in Kentucky who developed a pin-cast technique that Ling thinks we can replicate—"

I don't understand much of what he says after that, but his eyes have brightened and I know it means the news is good for Pamela. That Jack has figured out a way to save Copper.

"Pamela won't ever be able to ride him again, but if the amputation goes smoothly and we can get him to bear weight on his new prosthetic directly after surgery, I do think he'll live."

"That's really great," I say. And then, because this may be the longest conversation we've had in a few weeks and I don't want it to end, I ask: "What's the farm like?"

"Gorgeous," he says, yawning. "Did you know that Pamela helped build most of it?"

It's a rhetorical question, as there's no reason for me to know that. But it still grates. Or maybe it's the admiration in Jack's voice that strikes a nerve. "Really?" I say, concentrating on keeping my voice steady. Calm. Interested.

He nods and reaches up to turn out his light. "Crazy, right? Her parents bought it about five years ago. Major fixer-upper. Pamela and her dad bought a bunch of books—*Carpentry for Dummies*, stuff like that—and the two of them did most of the work."

Pamela and her dad. Just one more thing to envy her for.

As Jack burrows under the covers, I picture Pamela and her perfect family. I wonder if Jack met her parents yesterday. Would they be his in-laws one day? And then I think of Pamela meeting Jack's parents. I wonder if they would like her. I wonder if they'd like her more than me. I wonder if Jack's mom would teach her how to make her "famous" green Jell-O salad with celery and pineapple and marshmallow fluff and if Pamela would lie to her and tell her how delicious it looked.

I turn to Jack to say something else. Keep the conversation going somehow, but his back is to me and his breathing is deep. I wonder if he said good night and I missed it.

I pull the chain on my light and lay down in the dark, blinking up at the ceiling and trying to attach a word to the feeling in the pit of my stomach.

I can only come up with one: empty.

I picture the greasy Varsity burger and fries rotting away in the trash can in the kitchen and my stomach lurches. I close my eyes and try to clear my mind, but Pamela's face is there, staring at me like a . . . like a . . . like a woman that my husband could fall in love with.

I slide out of bed, taking care not to jostle the mattress, even though Jack's a sound sleeper. I tiptoe out of the room and down the hall, where I open the cupboard under the sink and reach into the trash can, feeling for the paper bag in the darkness. Then I lower my butt to the floor, clutching my treasure.

The tile is cold through my thin pajama pants, but I don't care. I don't care about anything but getting the wrapper off the dense layers of bread and meat in my hand. When the barrier is gone, I stuff the burger into my mouth as far as it will go and bite, and even through the cold rubberiness, I can taste the burst of flavors that I've denied myself for so long, but I don't linger or savor or relish the moment.

I just keep chewing, moving my mouth up and down, trying not to gag on the thick pieces of oily bread and fibrous meat. In between bites of the sandwich, I stuff cold hard strings of fries into my mouth by the handful.

And then the burger is gone and the fries are gone and my stomach is full and slightly queasy. So I close my eyes and lean my head back against the cabinet door. It's firm and unyielding. And this comforts me.

OVER THE NEXT four days, Jack and I manage to have many real conversations, which at first feels like a breakthrough. That maybe we're no longer tiptoeing on glass around each other. Until I realize they all seem to somehow revolve around Pamela. It started on Tuesday evening, after he returned from spending the afternoon with her and Ling and Copper at the farm. We were sitting on the couch stuffing ivory envelopes with Jack's graduation announcements.

"Pamela really has a way with animals," he said. "Ling even noticed. He called her the horse whisperer."

"Kids, too," I said, remembering the boy on open house night who was glued to her leg.

Then on Wednesday, while Jack was cleaning out Gertie's cage in the kitchen, it was: "Did I tell you Pamela's brother is a total hippie? He lives in Arizona. In a yurt commune."

"Interesting," I responded, stroking Gertie's swirls of black and white fur with one hand and feeding her a carrot with the other. "Does she ever visit him?" I try to picture Jack learning to whittle around a campfire and sleeping on the ground.

Thursday, I grilled salmon steaks and made Jack's favorite yogurt dill sauce to go with them. But when he came home a little after eight, he wasn't hungry. "Sorry," he said. "Pamela brought dinner up to the clinic for me and Ling as a thank-you." He patted his belly. "I'm stuffed."

I covered his plate with plastic wrap and stuck it in the fridge.

"Thoughtful," I murmured, but my heart wasn't in the compliment. Something was bothering me.

That Jack didn't call to say he didn't need dinner? No, he had missed plenty of meals over the course of our years together. But he always ate the food, either late when he got home, or for lunch the next day. Was it that Pamela took him a meal at work and I was feeling territorial? OK, yes, but I was also glad that she was proving to be the caretaker I had pegged her for, the caretaker Jack would need when I was gone.

It's not until I'm driving to Emory on Friday that what's bothering me becomes clear. It's something Kayleigh said to me when Jack and I were first dating. I had just told her that Jack played the trumpet when he was in elementary school and that he could still play part of "Boogie Woogie Bugle Boy."

"Oh my God. Would you please stop?" she said.

I looked at her. "Stop what?"

"Talking about Jack. You say his name every two seconds."

I hadn't realized I'd been doing it.

But now, Jack is doing the same thing. With Pamela.

And maybe it's nothing. Maybe it's just because he always tells me about his days at work, and this week, his days have involved Pamela and her horse whispering and her considerate cooking.

And if it's something, well, then, isn't that what I wanted? I mentally repeat the Martha Stewart–ish mantra that I've been rolling over in my head this week every time I think about Jack-and-Pamela, Pamela-and-Jack: it's a good thing.

But if it really is a good thing, then why do I suddenly feel like I can't breathe?

Goddamn it.

Not again.

I grip the steering wheel with white knuckles and glance in the rearview mirror before swerving across three lanes of traffic to pull my car to a screeching stop in the emergency lane. I gasp for air, but it has nowhere to go. My lungs are blocked off like a street under construction, and they burn like someone just coated them with hot tar. My heart thumps wildly, panicking of its own accord, even as I try to convince myself to remain calm. Sweat dribbles from my forehead into my eye, and only then do I notice how uncomfortably hot I am.

And light-headed. Yet somehow I still manage to open the car door in time to deposit my half-digested breakfast smoothie on the asphalt.

When my body stops heaving, I lean back and gratefully breathe in through my now-acidic mouth. My heartbeat slows. Tension drains from my shoulders and I inexplicably feel weepy. I look at the clock on the dashboard and urge myself to pull it together. I don't want to be late for my trial workup. But I know there's something I must do first. I reach over to my purse on the passenger seat and pull out a white business card and my cell phone. And with trembling hands, I dial Patrick, the respiratory therapist, to make an appointment.

"YOU'VE LOST WEIGHT." Dr. Rankoff frowns as she looks at my chart. "Have you been eating?"

I immediately think of the cold, greasy Varsity burger and French fries and feel guilty that I was so reckless with my diet. I picture the cancer as a cartoon monster, greedily feeding on my irresponsibility, growing exponentially in just a few days' time, causing my body to shut down, shedding pounds like a tourist sheds layers of clothing when they reach their balmy destination.

When I don't answer, she peers at me, studying my face more intently. "Are you feeling OK today?"

There's that word again. OK.

I know I don't look OK. I caught a glimpse of my reflection in the automatic glass doors on my way in. My hair is disheveled. My face sallow from my "episode" in the car. I only had time to smooth a few errant locks behind my ears before my name was called in the waiting room.

"I'm all right," I say.

She waits. Allows the silence to grow.

"I . . . uh. I guess I've been having panic attacks?"

She nods. "Dr. Saunders mentioned something about that."

I pause. They talk about me?

"Have you made an appointment with the respiratory therapist?"

I tell her I have. And then I steel myself for her news, which isn't really news.

The tumors are still growing. "Slowly," she adds, but her voice is not filled with hope.

I now picture my Lots of Cancer as the tortoise in the fable race with the hare. Slow and steady. And I know Dr. Rankoff doesn't sound hopeful because, in the end, the tortoise always wins.

"DID YOU KNOW Pamela's brother lives in a yurt?" I ask Kayleigh as we're sprawled on her couch half watching a weekend marathon of *The Rachel Zoe Project* on Bravo.

"What's a yurt?" Kayleigh asks. She's been furiously texting on her phone for most of the morning, so I know she's not really paying attention to me.

"I don't know. Some kind of teepee, I think."

"Huh," she says.

"Did you know she makes her own jam?"

I only know this because I spent most of my free time last week poring over her Facebook page and Pinterest board and LinkedIn profile. Other things I learned:

She has 684 friends.

She attended college in Florida.

She went skydiving on her thirtieth birthday.

She watches *Grey's Anatomy*.

"Huh," says Kayleigh.

"And I think Jack likes her," I say. "I mean, really likes her. He's mentioned her a lot this week. Of course, they have spent a lot of time together, because he's trying to save her horse. But still. It feels like he's a little fixated. You know, like a kid with a new toy."

I'm just rambling now, giving voice to my thoughts, more to sort them out than to get Kayleigh's opinion, because I know she's not really invested in the conversation. So I keep talking. About how Pamela's ex-boyfriend looks a little like the football player with the Mohawk from *Glee*. Except he didn't have a Mohawk. And how she sometimes reposts those Facebook statuses that promise good luck if you share them within ten seconds of reading them. And how she ate at the new Wildberry Café downtown for dinner on Tuesday night. Herb-crusted chicken and prosciutto-wrapped green beans.

She had posted a picture and the food looked really good. So good that I started to regret turning down Jack's suggestion a few weeks earlier that we go check it out.

I glance at the TV where a Ford Motors commercial is touting some spring sale. It reminds me of something else I learned about Pamela.

"Oh, and did you know she drives a pickup truck? A gray one with an extended cab. She got it a few months ago."

I pictured her as a Honda Civic kind of girl, so it caught me off guard. But even I had to admit, there was something sexy about a woman behind the wheel of a big rig. I know Jack thinks so. When we visited his parents for Christmas last year, I offered to run out for eggs for his mom and I had to drive his dad's old Bronco to the corner store because Jack's car was blocked in. He came with me.

"You look so hot," he said, and reached over and squeezed my thigh from the passenger seat.

I smiled at him.

"You know there's an abandoned parking lot up here on the right," he said, with a naughty grin.

"Jack! We're not doing it in the backseat of your dad's car," I said, keeping my hands at a very responsible ten and two on the wheel, even as Jack's began wandering up my blouse.

"Who said anything about the backseat?" He leaned over and nuzzled my neck.

"Behave," I said, cocking an eyebrow and gently pushing him away.

Now I wish I had pulled him closer.

"Anyway, I guess it comes in handy when she's working on her parents'—"

"Daisy!" Kayleigh interrupts me. I tear my eyes away from Rachel Zoe's brittle frame on the television where she's fingering a red silk gown that's "bananas" and look at my best friend.

"What?"

She shakes her head and scoffs. "Do you even hear yourself? Pamela this. Pamela that."

"So?" I raise my eyebrows, challenging her. Doesn't she get it? She could be Jack's *wife*.

"I'm just saying," she says, her voice softer. "I don't think it's Jack that's obsessed with her."

nineteen

ON TUESDAY MORNING, I'm twenty minutes late to my appointment with the respiratory therapist. Instead of paying attention to the seven-mile route to Athens Regional, I had been going over my mental to-do list for the day:

> Grocery store to buy Greek yogurt, organic baby carrots, rice chips, toilet paper
> Post office to mail Jack's graduation announcements sitting in a box in my trunk
> Clean bathroom

And one more thing—what was it?

As I was trying to conjure the missing task, I looked and realized bewilderingly that I had somehow taken a wrong turn and was on a street in Athens that I had never been on before. I slowed down, looking for clues as to where I was, my heart thudding in my chest and my lungs tightening. If I hadn't been so frightened I would have laughed at the irony of having a panic attack on my way to learn how not to have panic attacks anymore. Finally I saw a sign that said the university campus was five miles straight ahead and it reoriented me. I took two rights and was back on Milledge and the familiar path to the hospital.

I park next door to the cancer center in the lot for the Pulmonary, Allergies, and Sleep Center, and even though I'm late, I sit in my car for a minute, hoping the motivation to walk into another doctor/specialist/cancer appointment will gather like clouds for a storm and propel me through the afternoon.

In the waiting room, I check in at the front desk, apologize for my tardiness to a woman with large gold earrings that look like spaceships, and sit down in an uncomfortable wooden chair. I grab a magazine off the table beside me, but I have no interest in reading, so I look around the room.

There are just two other patients besides me. In the corner sits a birdlike woman with reading glasses perched on the point of her nose, a beaded chain drooping from the ends of them and around her neck. And directly across from me, a balding man with a rotund belly and skinny legs taps on a BlackBerry. He's wearing a checkered button-up that—

Shit.

He looks up at the exact same moment that I look at him. Accidental eye contact.

Don't talk to me don't talk to me don't talk to me.

He talks to me.

"Pretty day outside, huh?" he says. There's a gap so wide in his front teeth you could fit a jelly bean through it.

I nod and smile and look back at my magazine, hoping to convey that I am not available for conversation.

"Dr. Brunson's running behind today," he says. "Been here thirty-five minutes. Don't know why I have to be on time, but they never are."

If I were to respond, I would tell him that I'm not here to see Dr. Brunson, but I don't want to encourage him. So I smile again to acknowledge that he has spoken, but that I'm so involved in this ESPN article on ultimate Frisbee that I couldn't possibly tear myself away from it to chat.

"You got allergies? They're terrible this time of year."

I look at him and sigh at his inability to grasp social cues. I offer one sharp shake of my head and two words: "Panic attacks."

"Hmm," he says. "Woulda pegged you for allergies." He rests his hands on his pregnant-looking stomach. "I've got sleep apnea myself. Lost fifty pounds ever since I died, but Doc says that's not enough. Gotta lose fifty, sixty more."

I'm not sure that I heard him right. "Ever since you *died*?"

He grins like a fisherman who just got a tug on the line. "Yep. Heart attack. Was gone for seven minutes until the EMT started up the old ticker again."

I find myself grinning back at him, surprised that my annoyance has dissipated and genuine affection has taken its place. This is his cocktail party story, like my scar is my cocktail party story. And it's a good one.

The door to the waiting room opens up. "Michael?" says a nurse in blue scrubs.

"Just Mike," he says, hefting himself out of his seat with a groan. He winks at me. "You have a real nice day now, ya hear?"

"You, too," I say to the first man I ever met who had died. It's not until the door closes behind him that I wish I had asked him what it was like.

WITH BICEPS AS big as footballs and a buzz cut, Patrick looks like he'd be more at home in army fatigues and dog tags shouting derogatory orders than in a crisp polo and khakis talking about finding your center.

But here we are.

"I subscribe to a holistic method of stress relief," he tells me in a voice so gentle it's as if he's reading me a children's book. "Panic attacks are really about a loss of control. Life gets so overwhelming that your body literally can't process it and you become paralyzed by the fear or anxiety."

I'm trying to be a good audience, but all I can think about are the angles of the hard plastic chair I'm sitting on and how they're pressing into my bones, making it impossible to get comfortable.

"Think of it like a pot of water boiling over on the stove. What I try to do is turn down the burner in your life. If we can keep it on low or medium-low, you won't boil over. Of course, we'll go over some techniques on what to do if and when it does. But let's first work on reducing the overall level of anxiety in your life. Now, what seems to be your biggest stress factor?"

I stop shifting in my seat and stare at him. He has my chart. He knows my medical history. Shouldn't it be obvious what my biggest stress factor is?

But Patrick remains silent, forcing me to tell him.

"Dying," I say, but my voice cracks in the middle, like I'm in the desert and haven't had a drop of water in days. I clear my throat.

"What's that?" Patrick raises his eyebrows.

"I'm dying," I say, with more force than I intended.

"Ah, yes," Patrick says, unruffled. "A cancer diagnosis can be particularly stressful, but I find that it's all about perspective. I mean, we're all dying, aren't we? I could walk out of here and get hit by a bus this evening. Really, none of us have any control over when we die and that's the frightening part, hmm? The loss of control."

He smiles, obviously proud that he's brought his lecture full circle, while I grind my bones further into the seat to keep from screaming. If I've learned anything from Patrick so far, it's that there's nothing more patronizing than someone who is not dying telling someone who is how to feel about it. And why do people always say they could get hit by a bus? Like life is just one big game of Frogger and people are getting struck left and right by dangerous city transport. I don't think Patrick *could* leave here tonight and get hit by a bus. First, he would have to be walking, and I bet he drove his car here. Second, you'd have to be an awfully careless pedestrian not to see a twelve-ton rectangular van barreling in your direction.

Third, I don't like Patrick.

I silently curse Dr. Saunders for sending me to a respiratory therapist who fancies himself a real therapist after all.

"Hmm," I say, pretending to mull over Patrick's little speech. "Maybe we could move on to the breathing techniques? I think that would be most helpful."

His face falls and I wonder if he really expected me to jump up and say: *"Yes!* Oh, thank you! Here I was completely worried about the fact that I'm *dying*, but I could get hit by a bus tomorrow, so there's no need to worry! I feel so much better now."

He lifts his right leg and settles the sock-clad ankle of it over his left knee. "Sure, of course," he says. "But think over what I said, hmm? You might also find it helpful to look for other areas of your life that you can loosen your hold on. The more we accept we're not really in the driver's seat, the better. You gotta let go, you know?"

"Let go," I repeat, through clenched teeth. "Got it."

He stares at me a beat longer, as if to let that tidbit of wisdom sink in, then he nods once. "All right, then, let's get started."

He tells me that deep breathing is actually the worst thing you can do to stop hyperventilating. He tells me to hold my breath in ten-second bursts when I feel a panic attack coming on. He tells me the AWARE technique is an acronym for Accept the anxiety, Watch the anxiety, Act normal, Repeat, and Expect the best.

But I can't stop thinking about getting hit by a bus.

And if, just maybe, that's a better way to go.

I CAN'T FIND the baby carrots.

I know I bought them at the store yesterday, but they have inexplicably disappeared from the crisper in the refrigerator.

"Jack!" I yell from my bent position, my eyes scanning each shelf, as if the bag of orange vegetables will magically appear in front of me.

"Yeah," he says, the word so loud and clear I jump and nearly hit my noggin on the closed freezer door.

I turn around and find him standing behind me in his scrubs.

"Have you seen the carrots?" I know it's impossible that he fed them all to Gertie last night when he got home, but maybe he left the bag by her cage or . . . or . . . I can't come up with another plausible explanation.

"Nope," he says, grabbing his brown lunch bag off the counter.

"Wait! It's just the sandwich. Here," I grab an apple out of the drawer and hand it to him. "Take this."

"Thanks," he says, and squeezes my arm. "Have a good day." With his lunch sack in one hand he heads out the back door, the screen slamming shut behind him.

I stare at the door that's still vibrating from his hasty retreat and realize that he didn't kiss me good-bye. And really, who can blame him? It's not as if I've exactly been receptive to his recent advances. But still.

Still.

Gertie starts squealing. I know she heard me rummaging in the fridge and wants to know where her carrots are.

"You and me both," I mutter, grabbing a cucumber out of the crisper and slicing it for her. After feeding her, I go into our bedroom to strip the bed. I carry the sheets to the basement and stuff them into the washer with detergent and turn it on. Then, I stand there, the whole day stretching out in front of me like an ocean.

I have things to do. I need to get more carrots, for starters. And I could always go to class, even though I haven't been in a few weeks.

Or I could wash the baseboards. And sweep the dog hair from where it's accumulated beneath the bed and call to get a quote on how much it would be to stop the porch from running away from the house.

But my feet are firmly rooted to the cement floor. I look at the closed washer and, for a second, lament that I put the sheets in there. I'd like nothing more than to crawl back into bed. But it's not because I'm tired.

I'm bored.

I roll the words over in my head. It's been so long since I've not had something to occupy my time—classes, even searching for a wife for Jack kept me busy. Now what am I supposed to do?

Bored people are boring. Are you boring? My mother's response when I would whine from the couch on a lazy Saturday that there was nothing to do rings in my head. And now I'm afraid that she's right. That that's exactly what I am. And I wonder if Jack thinks so, too.

It's all the motivation I need to go upstairs, pull on a pair of jeans, and leave the house, blinking at the bright sunshine as it taunts me from its perch in the sky. I'm not sure where I'm going, but I want to have something to tell Jack at the end of the day that's more exciting than "I washed the baseboards."

I wind up downtown and am surprised to see the throngs of people walking around on a Wednesday morning. Then I remember that it's farmer's market day, and am pleased that I'll be able to pick up carrots while I'm here.

But first, I think I'll have a cup of tea. I park in front of the coffee shop and walk in, my head held high. There are no constraints on my time, nowhere that I have to be, and now, instead of mourning my loss of planned days and activities, I attempt to conjure the twenty-one-year-old version of myself and carpe diem. What was it that Patrick said? Let go. Give up control.

I take my tea to the back couch, the one I think of as Jack's and my couch, and sit down on the worn cushions. For five minutes I sip the hot liquid, soaking in the atmosphere and trying to enjoy the moment. But I can't.

I'm bored.

And I hate Patrick.

I turn to the door and begin watching the students and professors trickle in and leave, grabbing quick jolts of caffeine between classes. They all walk with an enviable purpose and I try to guess what they're studying. The guy with a baseball hat and khakis I peg for a frat guy majoring in business. The girl with streaks of pink and blue in her hair? Liberal arts. Probably sculpture. Then I see a familiar face.

"Dr. Walden?"

The short woman turns from the cashier where she's paying for her coffee in my direction. Her eyes light up.

"Daisy!" She walks over to me. "I've missed you in class. How are you?"

And instead of giving her my standard "fine," I'm suddenly unloading on Dr. Walden exactly how I've been, the clinical trial, my still-growing tumors, and now, my inescapable boredom. At some point during my soliloquy, she takes a seat on the couch beside me.

"Oh my God, I'm so sorry," I say. "You probably have a class to get to and I'm just going on and on." My cheeks get hot and I'm not sure why I've chosen to confide in Dr. Walden, except that she's easy to confide in. One time when I went to her office to go over a paper that I got a B on, when I felt sure I should've gotten an A, I ended up telling her that my father had died when I was little and that I was inexplicably terrified of fireworks. I left feeling empty, light. And with the idea that perhaps Walden missed her calling as an interrogator for Homeland Security.

"Oh, Daisy," she says. "You're going through a lot." She pauses. Pats my hand. "You know, my mom had breast cancer."

I tense, preparing myself for the story. The unsolicited advice of the Chinese herbalist or type of chemo her mom got that really helped. But Dr. Walden remains silent and I realize that she was simply offering me the information, a bridge of empathy.

"I'm sorry," I say.

"Me, too." And then her eyes brighten as if she's just gotten an idea. "You know what," she says, "I'm really overwhelmed this semester and could use a graduate-assistant type to help grade papers, assist in research, that kind of thing. What do you think? Would you be up for it?"

I know there are only three weeks left in the semester and that Dr. Warden is only trying to be nice. But I grab on to her offer like a life vest in the open sea.

"Yes," I say, instantly hating how overeager I sound. *Desperation makes a terrible cologne,* I can hear Kayleigh saying. If that's the case, I reek. I try to tone it down. "I mean, if you think I'd be helpful."

"You were one of my most promising students. You'd be perfect."

The "were" stings, but I choose to ignore it, and focus on her compliments. Even if she is just being nice.

"Come by my office tomorrow and we'll talk details. Set up some hours."

I hesitate. Though I only have set doctor appointments every other Friday, I've been managing to see health-care professionals much more often. I don't want to let Dr. Warden down by being unreliable.

"Don't worry," she says, using what I'm now convinced is voodoo magic to read my mind. "We'll make it flexible."

THE SUN BAKES my face, warming me from the inside out as I walk down the sidewalk toward the farmer's market booths. I choose to ignore the malevolent part of my brain that's telling me I am officially a charity case. That Dr. Walden doesn't really need the help. That she pities me. And I try to focus on the fleeting sense of pride that swelled like a wave in my chest when she said I'd be perfect. *Perfect.* I haven't felt perfect for anything lately.

Booths pepper the closed-off street in front of city hall and I take my time perusing them. I sample the season's first strawberries, inhale clutches of wildflowers, savor the scent of fresh-popped popcorn sold by a street vendor. I buy four long carrots with big leafy green stems and a slice of crustless vegetarian quiche and sit on the brick steps to eat it. The same steps where Jack and I first emerged as husband and wife.

I bite into my eggy lunch and picture the two of us walking toward the exit, arm in arm, after our short ceremony. I can almost hear my laughter when he leaned in and whispered, "Was it just me or did that judge smell like he bathed in gin this morning?" Then he held open the door and gestured me to walk through it with a deep and goofy and grand: "After you, Mrs. Richmond." And in that moment, all my qualms and feminist reservations about taking his last name melted away and I was left with nothing but pure giddiness at my new moniker. The one that meant that I belonged to Jack and he to me.

"Daisy?" A voice jolts me back into the present. I look up and into the eyes of Charlotte. No, wait. Caroline? I'm fairly certain the name of the limber blonde standing before me starts with a C. I know she's limber, not only because she looks so flexible in her black stretchy pants and tank top, but because I've actually seen her in action in Bendy Mindy's hot yoga class.

"Hi!" I say, shielding my eyes from the sun to better see her, and that's when I notice how intently she's staring at me. I wonder if I literally have egg on my face. I reach up to discreetly wipe the corners of my mouth with the napkin that came with the quiche.

"I haven't seen you in a few months," she says. "Have you, um, been going to a different studio?"

I stand up, because it feels rude not to, and she reaches out to grab my arm, as if she's afraid I'm going to topple over any second.

I stare at her and realize the intent look dripping from her eyes is concern. I know I've lost some weight, but do I look *that* bad? As if I need to be supported, like a little old woman crossing the street?

I look down at her hand where it's grasping my wrist and she quickly removes it. But my eyes remain glued to my arm as if I'm seeing it for the first time—and I'm shocked at just how brittle it looks.

"No, ahh . . . I've just been really busy, you know? End of semester stress and all that." I force a chuckle. "I've been meaning to come back."

She nods, but can't seem to close the gap between her lower jaw and upper lip. I start fidgeting under her scrutiny, self-consciousness overwhelming me.

"Well, it was really good to see you," I say. "But I've got to run to class." I glance at my watch for effect.

"Yeah, OK," she says, finally making her lips meet. "Maybe I'll see you soon?"

"Mm-hmm," I mumble, grabbing my shoulder bag from where I left it on the step and giving her a little wave. I turn on my heel and concentrate on walking slowly, when my legs are urging me to run.

Jack. I need to see Jack.

Or maybe, I need him to see me.

THE LOBBY OF the animal hospital is scattered with a few dogs on leashes, a couple of cat carriers and their owners, and the cacophony of barks and hisses greets me as I walk through the sliding glass doors. It's a much more welcome reception than the screaming girl who last welcomed me to the clinic and I say as much to Maya. She smiles, then glances at the standard-issue school clock on the wall. "Jack may be at lunch, but you can go on back and check."

I thank her and trace the familiar path toward the offices, leaving the chorus of animal noises behind me. But as I approach Jack's door, the silence in the hall is broken by a loud, feminine laugh that stops me in my tracks and makes my blood run cold.

Pamela.

Pamela is in my husband's office.

But what is she doing here? I know that Jack's helping her with Copper, but isn't she supposed to be at school? What could be so important that she couldn't wait until later this afternoon to see him?

I move toward the wall and inch closer to the door. My heart races and my stomach heaves at the thought of getting caught eavesdropping on my own husband, but I ignore it.

I can't quite make out what they're saying, but a burst of giggles overflows into the hall again, and this time I hear Jack's bellow joining in. I'm struck dumb by the sound—not just because he's laughing with another woman—but because he's laughing, period. Hearing it reminds me that I haven't heard Jack so much as chuckle in weeks. Months? I'm not sure. I lean my head back against the wall and close my eyes, reveling in his momentary joy. And then wishing I could be the one sharing it with him.

I add it to the list of things I know about Pamela: she makes Jack laugh.

And I hate her for it. I hate her with a black, liquid hate that starts in my belly and burns to the ends of my fingers and toes. I want to burst into his office and tell her to stop talking to my husband and stop making him laugh and stop being so damn alive, while all I'm doing is dying.

But then, Patrick's gentle voice comes floating into my mind, and even though I hate him, too, I know he's right about one thing: I have to let go.

I stay, standing in the hallway, until my fists unclench and my breathing returns to normal. And then I tiptoe back down the hall, the full sound of Jack's laugh following me like a shadow.

WHEN JACK GETS home that evening, I'm lying on the couch with a cool wet washcloth on my forehead and my eyes closed. He walks into the living room and I hear him shush Benny and tiptoe across the scuffed wood floors. He thinks I'm asleep.

I open my eyes and spy him at the bar, attempting to quietly pour a few fingers of scotch into a glass. "Hey," I say.

He turns. "Hey. I thought you were asleep."

"Nope. Headache."

He frowns, transforming his face into someone who has the weight of the world on his shoulders. And it seems impossible that this is the face that elicited the careless joy that I heard just hours before. This is what I do to Jack now. This is what I bring out of him. Pamela makes him laugh. I make him frown.

I shrug him off. "It's no big deal. I took some Excedrin. How was your day?"

"Good," he says. "Ling finished the prototype for Copper's prosthetic. We'll do the amputation next week."

I wait for him to tell me that Pamela came by the office. He doesn't. Last week, he couldn't stop talking about her and now he doesn't mention her? I can't decide which feels worse. Or what it means.

Our eyes lock in silence, and it's like we're positioned on either end of a tightrope twenty stories high. We have no idea how to reach each other.

Finally, he speaks up. "Do you want to watch TV?"

I shake my head no.

And I know I'm not imagining the look of relief that washes over his face as he picks up his glass of scotch and carries it out of the living room, down the hallway, and to his office. And I know I should be relieved, too. About the distance between us and how it's making room for Pamela. But I'm not relieved. I'm aching. I remain on the couch, marveling at how thoroughly I can miss my husband, even though he's in the next room.

Later, I wake up in our bed when I feel Jack ease into his side. Still half asleep, I reach over and graze my fingers along his warm back. His body tenses at the touch, then slowly relaxes under my hand. Oh, God. What am I doing? I need to move my hand away. To roll over and go back to sleep. But the heat of his skin feels so good on my fingertips. And when I breathe in, all I can smell is Jack. He smells like my husband. And don't I deserve to touch my husband? To be with him, like this, just one last time?

But my hand freezes. What if he doesn't want to be with me?

He turns to me in the dark and I can just make out the light in his eyes, his white teeth. A warm hand cups my face and the touch is like someone finally taking a pebble out of my shoe that I've been walking on for months.

"You're awake," he breathes.

"I'm awake," I agree.

And then under the cover of darkness, we find each other. And at some point in the middle of the strained breathing and desperate touching and pretzel tangle of our limbs, I realize I'm leaking tears, along with perspiration. And I know it's because something in me is mending, at the exact same time that it's breaking.

THE NEXT MORNING I wake with a smile playing on my lips. In my groggy state I can't quite figure out why. Was I having a good dream?

And then all at once I remember. Jack. And the breathing. The good kind of breathing, this time.

I slowly roll over and turn to Jack, anxious, as if I've traveled back to the morning after our first time, and I don't know what to expect from him. But he's not there. His side of the bed is empty, rumpled. I glance at the clock. It's only 6:15 A.M. I lean back in the pillow. He must be in the kitchen, eating cereal. Silently, because I don't hear the spoon hitting the bowl.

I take a deep breath at the small reprieve, and allow delight to elbow its way back in. I replay every touch, every murmur from our encounter like a sixteen-year-old girl who's been kissed for the first time.

I sit up a little and pull the sheets around my breasts, allowing myself to wallow for a few more moments in the memory, not wanting to pack it away with the rest of them in the far corners of my mind just yet.

"Jack?" I call out, a little too eagerly. And I know I'm being greedy. In my desire to see him. To share this moment together, knowing it could be one of our last.

But there is no response.

"Jack," I yell a little louder, not wanting to believe what I already know to be true.

I lean forward, listening to the silence in the house, straining to hear something, anything. Benny lifts his head beside me as if he's listening, too. But the air is still. Quiet. Empty.

Jack is gone.

twenty

WHEN I SEE the stack of ungraded papers and exams on Dr. Walden's desk, I concede that maybe she wasn't simply asking for my help out of pity.

"Some midterms may even be hidden away in there," she says, waving her hand over the towering pile. "Answer keys to exams are in the bottom left file cabinet. Papers are mostly freshman-level stuff, opinions of how women are portrayed in advertising, media, etcetera. If they make halfway compelling arguments that seem somewhat thoughtful, give them an A. You'll be shocked at the drivel you have to sift through."

Leaving me with a red pen and a jumble of keys, one of which unlocks her file cabinet, Dr. Walden rushes off to begin her Monday classes. Alone in her office, I take a deep breath, inhaling the heady scent of school—computer paper, ink, books. I'm nearly giddy with feeling useful, important, needed. But lying just on the edge of that contentment is a raw pain, a reminder that while these freshman have their entire college lives ahead of them, career paths yet to be traveled, my own academic progress has ground to a complete halt, likely to never be restarted.

I dig into the papers with gusto, barely taking time to eat or breathe or get lost in my own downward spiral of thoughts.

Later that afternoon, my mom calls my cell. I put down the pen and stretch, then slide my thumb over the screen to answer it.

"What's the date of Jack's graduation?" she asks.

"Second Saturday in May," I say. "Whatever that date is. I'm not in front of my calendar. Didn't you get the announcement?"

"No," she says. "When did you send it?"

I roll my eyes. She probably did and it's sitting in a pile of unopened mail on her counter.

She says her bird-watching club is going to St. Simon's Island for a weekend in May and she wants to make sure it wasn't the same one. "I mean, I'm not sure that I'll go," she says. "I probably won't."

And then her breath catches in that familiar way and I know she's crying again. And I know she didn't call to ask about the graduation or tell me about St. Simon's.

"You should go," I say gently. "It would be good for you. Fun. You deserve to have some fun."

She sniffles and I picture her dabbing her nose with a rumpled Kleenex.

"Yes," she says. "It would be fun."

She inhales a wheezy breath and then speaks again. "Do you want me to come up this weekend? We could do something fun. Go to a movie or something."

I hesitate. I don't want to hurt her feelings, but I also know I can't bear the weight of her sadness for an entire weekend. "We'll see. I've started helping out a professor and I may have too much work to do."

"Oh, Daisy, that's wonderful," she says, a little too animated. "I don't want to keep you from it."

"It's OK," I say, but then we just sit in silence until I pretend I have a call coming in and tell her I have to go.

When I hang up, I walk down the hall toward the water fountain. My eyes are strained from staring at all the black type on bright white paper and my brain throbs from the exertion.

I take a long pull of cool water and stretch my legs, walking slowly up and down the linoleum passageway, turning the conversation with my mom over in my mind.

Jack's graduation.

Jack.

Any concerns—or hopes—I had about our night together bringing us closer quickly vanished. We've barely spoken since the night we made love, as if we broke down walls only to have them be replaced by ones taller and thicker, like stubborn hair that returns with a vengeance after you shave it. And I've tried to ignore it, but there's something else in Jack's eyes on the rare occurrence that we are in the same room. It's an emotion I haven't wanted to attach a name to, for fear of making it real. But now, the word comes screeching into my head unbidden.

Guilt.

And I wonder if guilt is what drove him out of our bed so early the morning after we had sex. Was he thinking of Pamela when he was with me? Or worse, was he wishing I *was* Pamela?

The thought stops me, and I put my hand on the white-painted cement-block wall to steady myself. Then I straighten my spine and walk back into Dr. Walden's office, burying myself in her mountain of paperwork.

FOR THE NEXT few days, my view consists of the four yellow walls of Dr. Walden's square office and the back of my eyelids. I leave before Jack gets up in the morning, and when I get home, he's either still at work or shut in his study, and I drop into bed without disturbing him. I know I'm pushing my body too hard, but it's easier this way. To not see my husband. To not wonder why he doesn't want to see me.

On my breaks from paperwork, I add to my lists. More things Pamela should know about Jack: the way he leaves empty shampoo bottles and shaving cream canisters on the counter, as a signal that I need to pick up more the next time I go to the store; his tendency to misplace his keys, wallet, and cell phone within five minutes of coming home; how he sometimes gets so lost in his work that he forgets to call to say he'll be late. I get flashes of resentment as I recall some of these less-than-desirable traits, and I sit with the anger, preferring it to other emotions.

Then I flip the page of my notebook and stop short at a notation I made weeks ago, when I was in Jack's office contemplating cremation. And I know it's a task I've been putting off for too long.

THE MCARTHUR FUNERAL HOME looks more like a southern plantation house where you'd go to drink mint juleps in the parlor than a place you'd go to "arrange burials with dignity, caring, and compassion." Their Web site also said their consultants could help you "plan your own funeral in four easy steps," as if it was as simple as sewing your own drapes or baking bread.

"I always thought this was a sorority house," Kayleigh says when we pull up the long driveway and park in front of the tall white columns. I laugh, grateful that Kayleigh is keeping the mood light, but when I open my door to get out of the car, she doesn't move. I look at her. "Coming?"

"I don't know if I can," she says, staring straight ahead, her tight curls billowing around her face. "I know I said I would, but"—she shivers—"oh my God. I just. I can't."

"Seriously? You're going to sit in the car?"

"Daisy. There are dead bodies in there. Right now." Her voice is a whisper, as if she doesn't want the deceased to hear her.

"You don't know that. They don't stockpile them in the basement. Maybe no one has died this week."

"Do you *read* the obituaries?"

"Do *you*?" I've never even seen Kayleigh with a newspaper.

"No, but I've seen them and they take up at least an entire page in the paper every week—sometimes two pages. People have died this week. And they are in there." She raises her eyebrows and points at the house, as if I wasn't sure which funeral home she was referring to.

I begin to think bringing Kayleigh wasn't a good idea.

"Anyway, where's Jack?" she says. "Shouldn't he be the one doing this with you?"

"He's in class," I say. I don't add that asking him would have required us to speak to each other, something we weren't doing much of recently.

When Kayleigh still doesn't budge, I sigh. "It's fine. I'll go in by myself," I say, and let the car door slam shut. But as I walk toward the house with my shoulders straight and my head held high, staring at the dark clouds above the trees that have been threatening rain all day, I know I'm acting braver than I feel. I wanted Kayleigh to come because this place creeps me out as much as it does her, but I don't want to admit it.

When I reach the brick steps, I hear the passenger-side door open and I let out a small sigh of relief. "Sorry!" she calls out. "I'm coming, I'm coming."

We're greeted by a woman who smiles and leads us down a hall into a back room where leather chairs surround a long black table. I'm relieved it looks like a bright, sterile office conference room, and not the dark, musty *Addams Family*–esque room I had been envisioning. "Can I get you anything? Tea? Coffee?"

"No, thanks," I say.

She gives a pleasant nod. "John Jr. will be in shortly."

I wait for Kayleigh to make fun of his name—to say something like *Junior? Are we meeting with a four-year-old?*—but she just sits there, pale-faced and twitching.

Her silence makes me even more anxious, so I say the first thing that comes to mind.

"How's Harrison?"

She looks at me blankly, and I wonder if I've misspoke his name. No, I'm fairly certain the nineteen-year-old is Harrison.

"What?" I ask.

"Uh, we broke up?" she says.

"Oh, I'm sorry."

"Daisy, you know this. I've been seeing Greg. For a few weeks now."

It's my turn to stare at her blankly.

"You know, Bradley Cooper?"

"Oh, right," I say, even though I'm still not sure exactly whom she's talking about or when she stopped seeing Harrison and I feel bad that I haven't been a better friend. That I've been so absorbed in my own life—or death, I suppose—that I haven't been there for her.

We sit in silence, because I don't want to betray any more of my lack of knowledge of her romantic life. I'm relieved when Kayleigh speaks up.

"How are Jack and *Pamela* doing?" She says Pamela's name with a sneer, and my guilt turns into a flash of annoyance. Ever since I realized PW147 was Kayleigh's reviled co-teacher, she hasn't exactly been a good friend either.

"You know, I could use a little support in this."

Kayleigh's eyes grow wild. "Support? Look where I am. You think I'm not supporting you?" She pauses. "But you know how I feel about *her.*"

My annoyance quickly turns to anger. "God, Kayleigh, yeah, I get it! You don't like her. But can you just take *your* feelings out of it for a second? She's a good person. She would be good for him. He deserves to be happy."

I'm expecting a snide retort, but instead, Kayleigh looks down at her fingernails, and I know she's trying to decide which one to start gnawing on. I sit back, smug that I've put her in her place. She starts chewing on her thumb thoughtfully, and then, in a tiny voice, says: "What about you? Don't you deserve to be happy, too?"

I scoff. How typical for Kayleigh to not get what it means to really be someone's partner, to not understand what it is to love someone more than yourself. "So selfish," I say, under my breath.

She turns to me. "What did you say?"

It's all the prompt I need. "You're selfish!" I explode. "You sleep with married men and boys young enough to be your nephews without ever considering the consequences! You make Jack and me come to your school and pretend to be *parents* when we'll never have any children of our own. Ever. You didn't even think for a *second* how that might make me feel. You hate Pamela—because she makes *you* look bad! And you wonder why you're terrible at relationships?"

I know I should stop there, but words keep tumbling out as if they're a flood of water that's broken through a dam and can't be stopped.

"And you have your whole life ahead of you and you're just *wasting* it. Do you know what a slap in the face that is? I won't ever be a therapist. Ever. I won't get my master's. I'll never have my own counseling practice in New York or Georgia or anywhere, for that matter! But you, you could be *anything*. Anything you want. But no, you just wake up every day and go to that stupid job that you hate and just accept it. And what for? To spite your parents? God forbid you *succeed* at anything, lest they compare you to your perfect sister and you don't live up to it. Better to just not try, right?"

I slump back in my chair, feeling like a weight has been lifted off my chest.

Until I see Kayleigh's face. There's so much pain in her dark eyes it makes my bones hurt.

I put my hand over my mouth, as if I can somehow go back in time and prevent the words from coming out. I didn't mean them. Not really. I know I'm just a tornado of emotions and Kayleigh happened to be in the path of my storm.

I wish I could take it all back. But I can't.

"I'm wasting *my* life?" Kayleigh asks. Her voice is steady, eerily calm. "What the fuck do you call what you've been doing?"

Before I can respond, the door to the room opens and John Jr. walks in. He has television preacher hair, shiny wing-tip shoes, and a clammy handshake. And while he goes over the myriad of options for caskets, as if he's telling me the features of a brand-new Cadillac, I sit absolutely still and pretend that I'm ordering a car and that my best friend doesn't have every reason in the world to hate me.

THE SKY HAS opened up and it's raining thick pellets of water when I drop Kayleigh back off at her car in the elementary school parking lot. The only sound in the air is the music coming out of the radio. It's some Sarah McLachlan song and I reach up to turn it off. I've hated Sarah McLachlan ever since my freshman roommate played the *Surfacing* album on rotation for three straight weeks when she broke up with her high school boyfriend.

But now I wish I hadn't turned it off because the silence just underscores that I can't find the words to convey the depth of my remorse to Kayleigh. As she reaches for the door handle, we both speak at the same time.

"Kayleigh, I . . ."

"You know . . ."

I force a small chuckle, relieved that the silence is broken, even if she's still angry with me. I forge forward with my unprepared speech. "I'm so sorry for what I said. I didn't mean—"

She cuts me off. "It's fine," she says, but it's not, because there are tears in her eyes. "You know, maybe I am selfish. The school thing . . . I didn't—"

"No! I know. You couldn't have."

She sniffs. "But I've tried to be there for you. I really have." Her voice is wobbly. "You asked me to be normal. To not be polite, remember? I've just been trying to do what you want."

What I want.

I almost laugh at this.

I want to not have Lots of Cancer.

I want to take back everything I said to Kayleigh.

I want my husband to not be possibly falling in love with another woman.

"It's just . . . I guess . . ." She takes a deep breath and pushes her next words out with force: "You're my best friend! And sometimes I wonder if you even realize or care—that Jack's not the only one losing you."

I'm stunned. Embarrassed by how right she is. That I haven't thought about her feelings. How this has been affecting her. But Kayleigh's always been so tough, so unruffled by the nuisance of emotion.

"I gotta go," she says, opening the door, allowing the full sound of rain hitting the pavement to break the muted air in the car. I know it's because she doesn't want me to see her cry. She never wants anyone to see her cry. I reach out my hand to stop her, but words are caught in my throat and the door slams between us.

As I watch her walk across the dim, wet parking lot, I want to go after her, but I'm weighted down by guilt. And by how hard it is to properly die.

WHEN I GET home, Jack's car is already in the driveway, so I park at the curb, run across our yard through the downpour and up the stairs, jamming my key into the front door. I'm emotionally spent, my head is pounding, and I can't wait to crawl into bed, but I stop short when I see Jack sitting on the couch, staring at me. He's not locked in his office. In hiding.

"Daisy," he says, his face so grave, I wonder for a brief and ludicrous moment if I've already died and he's in mourning.

"My mom called this afternoon."

Oh my God. A series of possibilities flies through my mind, each one worse than the last—Ruggles, their eleven-year-old family German shepherd was put down; his sister Rachel, who just got her license, was in a car wreck; his father had a heart attack.

"She didn't get her graduation announcement."

I look at him, waiting for the terrible part. *Because thieves stole it, along with all the family's silver. Because their house burned down. Because terrorists bombed the postal service's air carrier.*

He doesn't say anything.

"Huh," I say, walking toward the sofa. I'm trying to decipher why the situation is so serious and what my appropriate response should be. "Well, I'll send her another one?"

I sit down on the opposite side of the sofa as he reaches into his bag on the floor beside him. He pulls a handful of ivory envelopes out of it and sets them on the cushion between us.

"What are those?" I ask.

"My graduation announcements."

"Well, obviously. I can see that. I meant, where did you get them?"

"They were sitting in the trunk of your car. I found them last night."

I blink. I put his announcements in the mail weeks ago.

Didn't I?

I try to let out a little laugh, but it sounds hollow. "Well, that explains why my mom didn't get one. I guess I've been under more stress than I thought."

Jack continues to stare, his face painted with concern.

A flash of annoyance runs up my spine. "Jack, I'm sorry! But really, it's no big deal. We'll mail them out again."

"It's not just the announcements, Daisy."

"What do you mean?" I cross my arms and wait for him to tell me what this is all about, but a part of me thinks I might already know, and I have to force my butt to stay in my seat and listen to him.

"You've been off, lately. Absentminded. At first, I thought it was stress, too, when it was little things—like forgetting to lock the back door when you're the last one that goes to bed. But now it's other, weird stuff. Like in my lunch bag last week, you packed a stick of butter. And I found four pairs of my neatly folded boxers in the drawer beside my bed, instead of the dresser."

I want to lash out, tell him that he's lucky I make his lunch, that I fold his laundry at all, but I know it's a defense mechanism, another way to avoid the truth that's been gnawing at the pit of my stomach since the day I got lost on the way to Athens Regional.

Jack's cell rings and he looks at the screen. Then at me. "I've gotta take this," he says. I wait for him to answer the phone, but instead, he stands up. Leaves the room. Jack never leaves the room for a phone call, unless we're around other people and he doesn't want to be rude. And what could possibly be more important than this conversation?

I hear a hushed "Hey" as he heads toward his office.

Pamela.

I know it's her like I know what time it is when I wake up in the middle of the night without looking at the clock. I just know.

What I don't know is why she's calling. If it was just about Copper, why would Jack leave the room? Graphic and horrific images spill into my brain involving Jack and Pamela in various stages of wanton undress. I give my head a sharp shake to rid myself of them.

Then I stand up and walk into the kitchen with more confidence than I feel. So I've been a little forgetful lately. It happens. Maybe I've been working too hard for Dr. Walden and the stress really is getting to me. Stress does all kinds of kooky things to your body. And I haven't been doing my yoga. Or even walking. I'll start walking again. Exercise has been proven in numerous studies to reduce stress.

I turn on the tap and rinse the few dishes that are in the sink and load them into the dishwasher. Then I straighten my back and stare at the rain falling outside the glass panes. I cock my head. Something's different. I look closer.

Even though water is coming down in buckets, none of it is coming in through the cracks in the windows.

Because there *are* no cracks in the windows.

Bewildered, I turn back into the den and approach the window nearest the door. I run my finger over the fissure between the pane and the frame that's no longer there. It, too, has been caulked over.

My legs begin to shake and I know they won't hold me upright for much longer. I wobble over to the couch and sit down, tears forming in my eyes, confusion and panic churning in my stomach, threatening to explode.

All of my windows are caulked.

And I don't remember doing it.

I try to take deep breaths and then I remember what Patrick said and I attempt to hold one big gulp of air in my lungs.

Maybe Jack's right.

Maybe I'm very literally losing my mind.

But when a piece of his voice comes floating down the hall from his office, where he's in hushed conversation with another woman, all I can think is: haven't I lost enough?

twenty-one

INSTEAD OF DRIVING to Emory the next morning for my biweekly appointment, I find myself back in Dr. Saunders' office, sitting next to Jack, waiting for the bushy eyebrows to deliver their news. The déjà vu produces a shudder in my spine.

The only difference between a couple of months ago and today is that I'm noticeably less anxious. What news could I possibly get that's worse than *You're dying*?

Dr. Saunders takes off his glasses and sets them on the desk. He looks at me. "Brain tumors are funny things," he says. "Where yours is positioned"—he uses a pen to point to the glowing orange and yellow orb on the computer screen—"we might typically expect to see some balance issues, interruption in motor coordination, things like that." I think of tripping over nothing in my bedroom a few weeks ago and swallow, while he continues. "But yours is causing a considerable amount of swelling in the brain, which appears to be the culprit for the confusion, memory loss. You've been getting headaches?"

I nod.

"That, too," he says.

Jack clears his throat. "OK, so what can we do about it?"

"Well, I can prescribe some steroids to reduce the pressure. It should take care of the headaches and hopefully the other symptoms will abate as well."

"*Hopefully?* So it might not go away?" I blink. "Could it get *worse?*" Before I even give him a chance to respond, my panic level shoots to ten. A five-alarm fire. And I hold my breath to keep from hyperventilating. I remember the cold fear that gripped me for the few minutes I got lost that day and how much worse it would have been if I had driven around for hours. Or what if I start forgetting whole chunks of my life? Or Jack. I don't want to forget Jack.

"That's always a possibility. Like I said, brain tumors are tricky."

I want to point out that he didn't say "tricky," he said "funny," and that those seem like more appropriate adjectives for magicians at children's birthday parties than brain tumors.

"You could also get surgery," he says, steepling his hands, his elbows propped on the desk. "It hasn't grown very much in the past two months and would still be easily removable."

"But I thought you didn't recommend surgery unless I was doing the whole nine yards of treatment, chemo, radiation."

He nods patiently. "I did say that, but that was when you were asymptomatic, when the tumor wasn't causing you any problems—"

I try not to laugh. As if the side effect of imminent death wasn't a *problem*.

"—Now, it's something you may want to consider. For quality-of-life purposes. But there are still plenty of risks involved. Maybe even more so. Your body is in a battle right now; it's in a weakened state. Surgery may be more difficult to recover from. It's not an easy decision."

Finally, I latch on to something I can agree with Dr. Saunders on. It's not easy. None of this has been easy. My head is now swelling with information, along with the pressure, and I'm not sure that I have the energy to make one more decision when it comes to my health, my life, my death.

I'm relieved when Jack speaks up.

"Dr. Saunders," he says, addressing him with the new gravity that I've come to expect in his voice these past few months. "What would you do? If this was your wife, I mean. What would *you* do?"

Dr. Saunders looks at Jack over his steepled hands and then at me. He's silent for so long that I think maybe he forgot the question. Maybe he has a brain tumor, too.

Finally he takes a deep breath. "The surgery," he says. "I'd want her to do the surgery."

Jack turns to me and raises his eyebrows. I know the ball is in my court. I take a deep breath.

"OK," I say, turning back to Dr. Saunders. "I'll do the surgery."

I LEAVE THE cancer center with a prescription for Decadron, a preop appointment with a neurosurgeon in Atlanta for Monday, and the actual surgery scheduled for Tuesday, ever amazed at the speed with which Dr. Saunders can get things done.

In the car, Jack fiddles with the radio until he lands on a Lynrd Skynrd rock ballad. I open my mouth to thank him for coming with me, even though I did my best to protest that morning, but he speaks first.

"I'm coming with you to Atlanta."

"No," I say, fervently shaking my head. "You heard Dr. Saunders. I'll be in the hospital for at least three days. You cannot take that much time off from clinic. Ling won't let you graduate."

"You're getting brain surgery," he says in his quiet, pragmatic way. "Ling will understand."

"No," I repeat. "My mom will take off work, she'll be by my side the whole time—"

"DAISY!" The word is a roar that reverberates through my body and causes my heart to stop for a full two seconds. Maybe three.

I glance at Jack out of the corner of my eye and see his hands gripping the steering wheel so tightly it looks like the white bones of his knuckles have broken clear through the skin. He takes a breath and loosens his fingers slightly and then speaks in a quiet, low voice, enunciating each syllable.

"I am coming with you to the surgery. End of discussion."

I let out the breath I didn't notice I was holding and I sit back in the bucket seat. I want to argue with him, reiterate that it's not necessary. That my mom can handle it. That I'll be fine. But I can't ignore the warm fuzzy growing in my belly from Jack's dogged determination to be there for me. *With* me. Then again, part of me wonders if it's just Jack's sense of obligation and loyalty that's driving his determination. It's like one of those conditionals we learned in ninth-grade geometry: *if* a wife has brain surgery, *then* the husband must go with her.

As I gaze at Jack's profile, his BlackBerry rings from the cup holder it's sitting in and he grabs it with his right hand. And I'm not sure if I'm imagining it, or if he's turning the screen from me on purpose. He pushes a button on the side of the cell, silencing it, and places it back in the cup holder.

It takes all my effort to keep from picking it up and ending my curiosity.

"Who was that?" I ask, hoping I sound indifferent, and not as if the balance of my entire world hangs on his answer. I keep my eyes trained on the trees and telephone poles passing outside my window.

He hesitates for a split second before he answers. "Work," he says, and the one word coupled with the hesitation makes my heart plummet to the pit of my stomach, and the warm fuzzies that had just bloomed there grow cold and steely.

Because I know he's lying.

ON SATURDAY MORNING, Jack gets called in by his Wildlife Treatment Crew to help treat a flock of poisoned ducks from a local pond. "And then I might head up to the farm to check on Copper, since I won't be at his surgery on Monday," he says before he leaves the house in his scrubs, and my heart falls, because I know it's not just Copper he'll see.

I swallow my trial pills, a yun zhi, and the tiny white pentagon of a steroid with a glass of water, and then settle into the couch with my laptop. I need to email Dr. Walden and let her know about the surgery and apologize that I won't be able to continue helping her. But when I open my computer it's dead. And I can't remember where I left the charger.

Stupid brain tumor.

After a futile search of my shoulder bag and every socket in every room of the house, I decide I must have left it in Dr. Walden's office. Sighing, I walk into the study and sit down at the desk, giving the mouse a shake to wake up Jack's computer.

His school email fills the screen and before I click on the X to close out of it, a subject line catches my attention. I hesitate for a second—just enough time to suppress the sliver of guilt from snooping—and then click on it.

Subject: Absences

Jack,

I'm sorry to hear about Daisy. I certainly understand that you need to be with her. But I hope you understand I can't make an exception to the absence policy, as it wouldn't be fair to the other students. If you're not in attendance next week, your total of absences for this semester will far exceed the three allotted. (You've already missed six, if my records are accurate.) When you return, we will discuss whether we can set you up to graduate in December or if you'll need to wait until next May.

Best,
Dr. Samuel Ling

The blood in my veins runs cold. When was Jack going to tell me this? But I know the answer before I even formulated the question in my head: he wasn't. I sigh. Part of me is touched. I know Jack thinks he's doing a Nice Thing. A Husband Thing. That he thinks being with me at my surgery is more important than graduating. But it's not. And the rest of me is annoyed that Jack has made this executive decision without telling me. That the Lots of Cancer is ruining one more thing and I have no control over it.

I email Dr. Walden and then go into our bedroom to pick up Jack's socks and make the bed. And then I notice the accumulation of Benny's hair rolling like tumbleweeds across the hardwood and I get out the broom. And then the mop. And then I can't stop cleaning. I wash the baseboards and scrub the bathroom grout with a toothbrush and spray every mirror and window in the house with vinegar and water and do four loads of laundry. And in the silence of my dusting and washing and scrubbing, my irritation at Jack rises.

I've only asked him for one thing—*one thing!*—since my Lots of Cancer diagnosis. I want him to graduate on time. To not let the sacrifices we've made—*I've* made—go to waste. And he can't give me that? Worse, he's *lying* to me, telling me Ling will understand, allowing me to believe that he will still graduate in a few weeks. What, was he hoping I'd just die before then and would never know?

But you're having brain surgery, a small voice pipes up. *And Jack just wants to be with you.*

I tell that voice to shut up and forge forward with my anger because Jack's with Pamela and her Pantene hair and I'm alone with wrinkled fingers and a bucket of bleach water that I'm now crying into. I lie down on the half-wet floor and let the tears roll off my cheeks, tickling my earlobes before they drop into the hair sprawled out behind my head.

I stare at the ceiling in the hallway and practice breathing until the floor dries and my face dries and my heart hardens a little bit more.

WHEN JACK COMES home that evening, I'm sitting on the couch waiting for him, calm and collected. Before he can open his mouth to say hi, I tell him that I found the email from Ling and that he can't come with me to the surgery.

His face goes stony.

"You have to graduate," I say.

"I will," he says.

Oh. I lean back. I didn't expect it to be that easy.

Then, he adds: "In December. Or next May."

"No!" I sit back up. "Don't you get it? I won't *be* here in December or next May."

He shakes his head. "You don't know that—"

I cut him off. "I *do* know that. And you do, too. You just don't want to admit it." I take a deep breath and fix him with a pointed stare. "Jack. I'm dy—"

"*I know you're dying!*" he thunders, and I feel as though I've been slapped across the face.

Everything goes still. Even Benny sits like a statue at Jack's feet, no longer whining to be petted or acknowledged.

And in the hollow silence that follows, I'm surprised to find not only did I expect Jack to deny it, I *wanted* him to deny it. Because maybe Jack believing I was going to live was the only thing that was keeping me alive.

His voice is raspy and quiet when he speaks again: "Sue me if I want to be there for you while you do it."

It's so sincere and he looks so broken, like a marionette without its puppeteer, that I waver. So what if he doesn't graduate on time? I shake my head. No. He has to. And I have to be there to see it. And though I've sat in this conviction for months, it's only now that I really begin to understand why. Because everything in our life the past seven years has revolved around and been hurtling toward this one moment.

We'll spend more time together *when Jack graduates*.

We'll go on vacation *when Jack graduates*.

We'll have babies *when Jack graduates*.

And I have to know that all those moments we didn't share, that all the time we didn't spend together—that it meant something. We were working toward a goal, and I need to check it off my list.

But I don't know how to explain that to Jack. So I just repeat what I've already told him, with as much conviction as I can muster.

"I don't *need* you to be at the surgery," I say through gritted teeth. "I *need* you to graduate."

He shakes his head and opens his mouth and I know in the split second before he speaks what's coming—the inevitable push back, the beginning of hours of circular conversation this will turn into before someone finally caves. The anticipation of it exhausts me, and I have the overwhelming urge to end it before it begins.

"Daisy, I—"

"*I don't want you there!*" I yell. The harsh words cut Jack off as sharply as a guillotine blade.

It's mean. I know it's mean as soon as I say it. But I also know, in the moment after it leaves my mouth, that it's true. I don't want Jack at the surgery, not just because it will keep him from graduating, but because I don't want him to see me woozy and gauzy and brittle. I want him to remember me—the real me. The pretty me. The strong, capable me. The me that he fell in love with.

But again, I don't know how to explain it. How to give voice to the insecurities that have blossomed in my once confident brain, seemingly overnight. How to admit how deeply inadequate I've felt next to Pamela's aliveness.

So I wait for Jack to break the sharp silence, but he just stares at me. I search his eyes for an emotion, expecting to see pain, defiance, or even defeat, but what I find is more terrifying. There's nothing. His eyes are empty, as he offers a simple nod and palms his keys and leaves the house without saying a word.

I've won.

But when I lean back into the sofa and turn on the TV and wait for the feeling of triumph to wash over me, it never comes.

twenty-two

T HAT NIGHT, I lay awake in bed straining to hear Jack's car pull up out front, the key in the door, but before I do, night overtakes me. And when I wake up the next morning, he's not there.

I walk into the kitchen, rubbing sleep out of my eyes, half expecting to see Jack sitting on the counter in his boxers, slurping a bowl of Froot Loops, but the room is empty.

I stand in the doorway, stunned by his absence.

Where is Jack? Why didn't he come home?

It's so unlike him, I think fleetingly that my brain tumor is to blame. Surely he called last night to tell me about a squirrel or a skunk or a sparrow that he needed to nurse every two hours and wouldn't be coming home, and I just don't remember. I check my phone, but his number doesn't appear in my call log.

I set it down on the counter and let the full weight of what I've done settle on my shoulders. My words from last night haunt me on repeat in my brain:

I don't want you there.

I don't want you there.

I don't want you there.

But I know what Jack heard was: *I don't want you.*

And I know it was the last straw. That I've pushed him away so thoroughly that he's out of my grasp, like the moon or the stars.

Still, I spend an hour packing, refolding T-shirts, taking a pair of shoes out, only to put it back five minutes later. I know I'm drawing it out, expecting him to come home at any second, laughing that he fell asleep on his desk right in the middle of working late. *Ha-ha-ha! Can you believe it?* But when I finally close my suitcase, I shut the lid on my hope.

WHEN I GET to my mom's house that afternoon, she's still at work. I let myself in the front door, drop my suitcase in my old bedroom, and walk into the den to lie on the couch. And remember throwing myself onto this sofa in tears the day Simon Wu turned down my request to go to the school dance and crying until nightfall. By the time Mom got home, my eyes were red and swollen, but when she asked me what was wrong, I mumbled *nothing* and sulked off to bed. Now, as I pull a blanket over my legs, suddenly exhausted, I wish I had confided in her.

What feels like seconds later, I wake up in the dark to a hand smoothing my face.

"Mom?"

"Yeah," she whispers.

I sit up mildly confused until I remember where I am and why. I squint at Mom's face in the dark and see that it's eye level with mine and I realize that she had been holding my head in her lap.

"Why didn't you wake me?"

"You have a big day tomorrow," she says in a way that makes it sound like I have a prom or my first job interview—not major surgery. "I wanted you to rest."

"What time is it?"

"Around ten, I think."

I sit up even straighter and wonder if Jack called while I was sleeping. But I know without checking that he didn't, and the truth weighs heavy on my heart. I want to lay back down.

"Come here," Mom says.

And though I haven't willingly laid on my mom in years, I'm overwhelmed by the urge to wrap myself back in her arms. To be held. To be loved. I'm like a neglected houseplant that's just been offered water. It's impossible to resist. I lay my head on her chest and curl my knees up tighter, pushing them against her stomach as if I'm trying to crawl back into her womb.

Be reborn.

Get a mulligan.

Then I wonder, if I knew it would turn out the same, would I want to do it all over again? This life. This body. This Lots of Cancer.

I think of Jack.

And realize I knew the answer before I had fully thought the question: Yes. I would.

Mom squeezes me closer and sighs into my hair. I know she's crying again. And normally I would stiffen, or ignore it, or make a joke, but I'm just too tired to do any of those things. So I squeeze her back and let her cry.

DR. NELSON BRAUNSTEIN is a diminutive man with a large nose and intelligent eyes. And he makes removing my tumor sound as easy as plucking a splinter out of my thumb.

"It's really in an ideal position," he says, pointing to the black-and-white film of my brain hanging on a wall-mounted light box. And I wonder if I should say thank you. If I should take responsibility for this portion of my cancer being so considerate in its placement.

He says I'll need to have one more MRI that afternoon and fill out some paperwork and then be at the hospital bright and early the next morning to get checked in and prepped and then he shakes my hand, as if we've just struck a bargain, but I'm not sure what my end of the deal is. "Get your rest tonight," he says with a grin. "See you tomorrow."

"Well," Mom says after he leaves. "He was efficient."

Then we sit in the sterile room in silence until a woman named Sheila enters with a stack of papers and I sign my name and address and social security number and insurance information on a thousand different papers while she drones on about what each one means.

"And this," she says, holding up the final paper while I massage a cramp out of my hand, "is your medical directive, which just states your preferences about end-of-life care in the event of cardiac death or a coma during or as a result of the surgery."

I stare at her. My preferences?

I force a chuckle. "Um . . . I *prefer* not to have cardiac death or coma be a result of the surgery."

She offers a courtesy laugh in return and then holds out the paper for me to take.

I shy away from it, the word "death" growing bolder and larger until it threatens to overtake every other word on the page, like a beauty queen who refuses to share the spotlight.

I could die. I mean, I knew I could die—*know* I'm dying—but this surgery could actually be the thing that kills me. Tomorrow.

I feel my lungs tighten, panic gripping them with its steely fist, and I suddenly understand what Jack meant when he said, "This is *brain* surgery."

It's the complete opposite of what people mean when they say *It's not brain surgery.*

Because this actually is. Brain. Surgery.

And I could die.

THE NEXT MORNING, I'm surprisingly calm as I lay in a hospital bed hooked up to an IV, clad in nothing but a hospital gown and my Jockey briefs. Which is probably because of the Xanax I've been eating like jelly beans since Sheila gave me one shortly following my panic attack while signing the medical directive yesterday, and then sent me home with five more to "take as needed."

"You're OK?" Mom asks me for what feels like the thirty-fifth time.

"Never better," I say. And then I laugh. And I know I sound a little crazy, which makes me laugh some more.

Then Sheila comes in and announces that it's time to "take a ride," which I gather means she's going to wheel me to surgery. "Are you ready?" she says with a bright smile.

I look from her face to my mom and then back to Sheila, because I swear she asked if I was ready *to die*, and I'm wondering why no one else thinks that was an entirely inappropriate question.

"No," I say, the effects of the Xanax suddenly dissipating. "No, I'm not."

Shelia's smile turns into a frown and Mom steps forward.

"Daisy?"

"Mom," I say, desperately studying her familiar face—the lines that I've watched emerge over the years; the kind, sad eyes; the mole on her cheek that she's always called her "supermodel mark"—just in case I don't ever see it again. But as much as I love my mom, I know it's not her face I want to see. And even though I told Jack not to come, all but forced him to stay home, I have the sudden hope that he'll come bursting through the door like a hero in a romantic comedy, to hold me one last time in his long arms.

"Jack," I say. "I need Jack." And I know in that instant that it's true.

Mom nods and digs into her jeans for her tiny cell phone. She takes her glasses from their perch on her head and slides them over her eyes, squinting at the buttons to dial my husband's number. Then she hands it to me.

I put it up to my ear and it's already ringing.

Please pick up.

By the fourth ring, I'm all but casting spells to entice him to answer. *Pick up the phone, Jack.*

And then he does.

"Daisy?" he says, his breath strained, as if he ran to get the phone.

"Jack," I say, but my husband's name catches in my throat. And we sit there on opposite ends of the line, listening to each other breathe. Sheila touches me on the shoulder, and I know I have to go, but I don't want to hang up. To not hear him breathe.

"Do you need me?" he asks.

Yes.

"Do you want me to come down there?" His voice is steady, calm, but it's underlined with traces of anger. And even though I usually hate when Jack is angry with me, I'm relieved to hear it. It means he still cares. "I'll leave right now."

I grip the phone tighter. There's nothing I'd rather see than his face, but it's too late. I'm already headed into surgery and it would be pointless for him to miss clinic—to not graduate—just to sit in the hospital when I can't look at him.

"No," I say. "No. Stay there. I just wanted to . . ."

The nurse taps me again. My mom steps forward.

"Daisy," she says as she reaches for the phone.

"I love you," I say in a rush of words, even though it feels so inadequate. I once heard that Inuits had sixteen words for love, and I suddenly wish that at some point I had memorized them all, just for this moment. "Jack, I *love* you."

I wait for his response. His automatic return of my affections that used to be as natural as the sun following the moon.

I love you.

I love you, too.

But all I hear is silence.

"Jack?" I ask.

I hear a deep, ragged breath from his end of the phone, and then: "I love you, too." But his voice is no longer steady and calm. No longer Jack. It's fractured. Broken. Split. Maybe he, too, has realized the gravity of my situation. That I could die. That this surgery could kill me. That this could be the last time we speak.

Or maybe, just maybe, it's his emotions that are fractured. Broken. Split.

Not all directed toward me.

I listen to him inhale and exhale one more time, and then hand the phone to my mom. I close my eyes and choose to focus on Jack's words, and not the way he said them.

He loves me, too.

For now, it's enough.

I turn to the nurse. "I'm ready."

twenty-three

I WAKE UP.

I squint my eyes at a bright light and hear a groan, which I soon realize is coming from me, and I remember that I'm in a hospital and that I had brain surgery.

And I woke up.

As I silently cheer myself for this accomplishment, my mom's face comes into view. "Honey?"

I open my mouth to speak, but my mouth is dry. She holds a cup of water up to it and I gratefully take a sip.

"How do you feel?"

I try to nod to indicate that I'm OK, but my head feels heavy and I move my hand up to it, gingerly touching the turban of gauze I'm wearing.

And then I remember Jack and his fractured voice, and realize that I'm not OK. I have so much I need to say to him. So much I regret. So much I wish I could do over. And I just hope I'm not too late.

As if reading my mind, Mom speaks again. "I called Jack to let him know it went well. He said to call later if you feel up to it."

"He did?" I push the words out of my raspy throat.

She nods. "I'll go get the nurse and let her know that you're up."

"OK," I say, closing my eyes and drifting back to sleep.

I'M NOT SURE what time it is when I wake up again, but my mom's steady breathing and the shadows that fall across the room indicate that it's night.

"Mom?" I say, my voice a little stronger. She immediately opens her eyes and is by my side.

"I need my phone."

She squints at the watch on her wrist. "Daisy, it's six in the morning."

"I don't care," I say. "I have to talk to him."

"OK," she says, and walks over to the counter where my bag sits. She digs inside it, retrieves my cell, and gives it to me.

"I'm going to get a coffee," she says, stuffing her feet into her Keds.

Jack picks up on the third ring.

"Jack," I breathe.

"Daisy." It's a statement, and I search for an emotion in it, but I can't find one.

"Did I wake you?"

"No," he says. "I couldn't really sleep."

I hang on to the admission, allowing myself to believe his restlessness was over missing me, worrying about me, *loving* me.

"That's funny. All I've been doing is sleeping," I say, trying to lighten the mood. "Brain surgery is hard work."

"I've heard that," he says, and I think maybe I detect a smile in his voice. It's all I need.

"Jack, I'm so sorry," I say. "I should've let you come. I should've *asked* you to come. I did need you and I was wrong to tell you I didn't."

He doesn't say anything so I keep talking.

"God, I was so scared. They made me sign all these papers and kept talking about how I could *die* and all I could think about was—"

He cuts me off.

"Daisy."

"Yeah?"

"It's OK," he says, and I hear him exhaling. "Just . . . It's OK."

I hold the phone to my ear, waiting for him to say something else, anything else. But he doesn't.

"OK," I say. "So, do you—"

I'm about to say *forgive me*, but I hear something on Jack's end of the phone. It's not Jack.

Where do you keep your sugar? the voice that's not Jack's says.

My heart stops beating and I wonder if this is what Sheila meant when she said *cardiac death.*

"Daisy, are you there?" Jack's voice is full of concern and I can't decide what he's more concerned about—if I heard her voice or the fact that I'm suddenly very much dying.

My mom opens the door to my room holding a steaming Styrofoam cup and I look at her.

She stops when she sees my face. "Should I leave?" she mouths.

I shake my head no.

"Jack, I gotta go," I say.

And I hang up the phone before he—or Pamela—can say another word.

"LOOK TO THE left . . . Good . . . Now right . . . Good . . . Up."

I follow the occupational therapist's instructions as she shines a penlight in my face. My entire morning has been a flow of doctors and nurses and specialists testing all of my basic functions: speech, movement, memory, ability to follow instructions, and now vision. So far I have passed all of the tests, which would typically fill me with pleasure, a sense of achievement. I am top of the class when it comes to recovering from brain surgery. But I don't care.

Jack is with Pamela. Or he was with her. For a night. Or a morning. And then I wonder if he was with her the night he didn't come home, which is stupid to wonder because of course he was with her. And who could blame him? I told him I didn't need him—didn't *want* him. Worse, I told myself that I wanted him to be with Pamela. I plotted for it, planned for it, *wished* for it. Now my only wish is that I could click the button on my motorized bed and hold it down until it folds completely in half, swallowing me whole. What have I done?

What *have* I done?

The question has been running on a loop since I hung up the phone with Jack, going from a soft-spoken whisper to a full-on fist-pounding wail inside my head. I got Lots of Cancer, and instead of running directly into my husband's long arms, I pushed him into someone else's.

And he went.

In between my constant barrage of self-flagellation, this is the bare fact that keeps popping up like insistent puppets in a game of Whac-a-Mole.

Jack went.

And it's this information that I can't bring myself to accept. It's like dropping a plate that you think is unbreakable plastic, only to have it shatter into a thousand pieces when it hits the ground. Has our relationship always been so fragile? I think back to my announcement to Jack on our third date—that love isn't real. It's a notion I quickly dismissed when I realized that science could point to the hormones and chemicals that made me feel tingly and reckless and safe, but it couldn't explain why I felt tingly and reckless and safe *with Jack*. Science can't explain why two specific people are magnetically drawn to each other instead of repelled. Only love can. And though I never believed in fairy tales or soul mates or any of those other purely romantic notions, I believed in Jack. I believed in Jack and me.

And I realize that even though I was searching for a wife for Jack, that I wanted him to have somebody, to not be alone when I was gone, I never really believed he would love another woman. That he *could* love another woman. Not the way he loved me.

But now, that belief is shattered.

And simmering beneath my turmoil of emotions at this stunning revelation is anger.

At Jack.

For shattering it.

How could he do this to me? To us? I know I haven't been a perfect wife. OK, so I've been a terrible wife, shutting Jack out, pushing him away, pushing him *toward* Pamela, even. But still, I am his *wife*. Whatever happened to *in sickness* and health? I picture Jack repeating those words to me in front of the gin-soaked judge and it turns my stomach.

"Great," the occupational therapist says. "Your vision checks out perfectly."

Sheila chimes in. "That's all the tests for today. If you're feeling up to it tomorrow, we'll get you out of that bed. Try taking a few steps." She's taken to speaking to me like I'm a child, and it sounds like she's promising me chocolate cake if I'm a good girl. "Until then, get your rest. Buzz if you need anything."

I need you to go get my husband so I can strangle his lying, cheating neck. I take a deep breath and close my eyes, trying to defuse my anger. Be reasonable. Rational. This is my fault. It's all my fault. But as much as I try to tell myself that, all I can picture is perfect Pamela in my kitchen, opening my cabinets, using my sugar, talking to my husband, and petting my goddamned dog. And I can't for the life of me remember why I wanted Jack to be with her in the first place—or what he could possibly see in her.

She wears animal sweaters, for Christ's sake.

LATER THAT EVENING, Mom says she's going home to freshen up and feed Mixxy. A few minutes after she leaves, there's a knock at my door.

"Come in," I say, expecting to see another nurse or therapist of some kind ready to poke and prod me, but it's not.

"Kayleigh." It's the first time I've seen her since I dropped her off at her car after the funeral home. "How'd you know I was here?"

"Your mom called," she says, then walks over to the bed and swats me on the arm.

"Ow!"

"I can't believe you didn't tell me you were having fucking brain surgery. What the hell's the matter with you?"

"I'm sorry," I say. "It all happened kind of fast."

"S'ok. I'm just glad you didn't die or anything. I would never have forgiven you."

Despite the storm of pain still swirling through my heart and mind over Jack, I grin. Because she's here and she's Kayleigh and I know we're OK.

"So, any hot doctors?"

I shake my head. "Not a one."

"Damn. Well, I guess I'll go, then."

"No, you're sitting down. I'm so bored I'm about to go crazy." I don't want to tell her what's really driving me crazy. I'm not ready to hear *I told you so.*

"I would have been here earlier but your precious Pamela rushed

out the door at three today, leaving me to do four parent-teacher conferences by myself."

At this I sit up a little. "She did?"

"Sorry, I know I'm not supposed to talk bad about her, but it was
so last-minute and I stayed up really late with Greg and I was a tad
hungover and was *not* prepared to stay late, much less talk to those
annoying par—"

"Do you know what for?"

"What?" she asks.

"Do you know why she left early?"

Kayleigh squints her eyes as if she's trying to remember. "I don't
know. Maybe it had something to do with her horse? Didn't Jack fix
its leg on Monday? I never pay attention to her. Anyway, apparently
it's got her all discombobulated, because she was late this morning,
too. Just came in right when the kids started arriving as if I didn't
need her help getting the classroom ready—"

Kayleigh keeps talking while my heart sinks as quickly as the *Ti-
tanic*. Because I know Pamela was with Jack this morning, not with
Copper. And my heart squeezes tighter, because I know that's what
made her late. I know what it's like to be with Jack in the morning. To
wake up in bed with him and wish that we had been snowed in overnight or that a bomb threat had shut down the entire campus, just so
I'd have an excuse to lay next to him for a little bit longer. But I never
gave into my impulse, always dragging myself out of the warm covers,
dutifully going to class. Now I wish I had. I wish I had woken up one
of those mornings and never left the bed. Never left Jack. I wish I was
still beside him now.

"What's wrong with you?" Kayleigh cuts into my thoughts. "Your
face is all screwy." She scrunches her nose at me and then looks
alarmed. "Are you going to cry?"

I bite my lip because I do feel like I'm going to cry. And then I take a deep breath and tell her about the phone call and the sugar and the vows that Jack has broken.

Kayleigh listens and then furrows her brow. "I'm confused. I thought that's what you wanted."

"I thought so, too," I say. "I was wrong."

Kayleigh nods slowly, thoughtfully. "Well, what are you going to do about it?"

I look up at her. "What do you mean? What *can* I do about it?" It's so apparent in her question that Kayleigh's never been in love. Not really. And my heart breaks for her at the same time that I long to be in her shoes. To not know the irreversible rush of emotions that overtakes everything when you first are falling in love. It's like trying to stop a flood with a chain-link fence. Impossible.

"You could fight for him," she says, shrugging, as if it is the easiest thing in the world.

"What, like challenge Pamela to a duel?" Even though I'm joking, I instantly picture facing Pamela with a saber in hand. I would skewer her without hesitation.

"Yeah, if this was 1874. Or, you could just tell him how you feel. Jack loves you, Daisy. This doesn't sound like him."

"I know, but he's different now. I just kept pushing him away. And we just—everything just fell apart. And now . . ." I shake my head, searching for words to explain how Jack is now. But I can't find any, and I know it's because I don't know how Jack is now. That's how much we've fallen apart. My eyes sting and I take another deep breath. "You know, maybe I should just let it go. I do want Jack to be happy. But . . . but—" I'm not sure what the but is, what has exactly changed to make me abandon my plan to let Jack move on with Pamela. With his life. Except I just know that I don't want him to. Move on. Not yet.

"But you want to be happy, too." Kayleigh finishes for me.

"Yeah," I say, my voice tiny.

"You should be," she says. "You're not fuckin' dead yet."

JACK CALLS AROUND seven forty-five while I'm watching *Jeopardy*, but I ignore it. I don't want to hear him lie about how he spent his day or pretend to be the obligatory caring husband—not while he cares for someone else. I put my phone on silent and push a button on my mechanical bed to turn out the light. Kayleigh is gone and I told my mom to stay home so she could get a good night's sleep in her own bed, but now I wish I hadn't because I feel impossibly alone. I pump an extra shot of Vicodin through my IV and close my eyes, letting Alex Trebek's familiar voice lull me to sleep.

The next day I traverse the nine steps to the bathroom door and back to the bed by myself, impressing the physical therapist who's come to screen me. "Beautiful!" he says. "Think you're up for stairs this afternoon?"

I agree that I am, and ace those, too, and when Dr. Braunstein visits me just before the hospital dinner service he says I'm well enough to be discharged the next morning. "But you still need plenty of bed rest," he adds. "And no strenuous activity for at least two weeks. That's when I'll see you for a follow-up, unless there are any issues between now and then."

He pats my leg and I thank him for removing the tumor, which feels like a silly thing to say once it's out of my mouth. "Happy to do it," he says.

Then I call my mom to tell her the news, and when I hang up with her I just stare at my phone. I know I should call my husband to tell him I can come home. That's what wives do, right? Let their husbands know when they're coming home from the hospital? But then, husbands don't go falling in love with people who aren't their wives. Or they're not supposed to, anyway.

I dial his number.

He picks up on the first ring.

"Daisy," he says. "I've been trying to call you."

This, at least, is true. When I picked up my phone this morning to turn the ringer back on, I had three missed calls from him and ignored two more during the day.

"Sorry," I say. "I've been meeting with a lot of therapists and stuff."

"Yeah, that's what your mom told me. But everything is going well, right?"

"Yeah. They said I can go home tomorrow."

"Tomorrow?" I hear the surprise in his voice, but it's more of horror than of delight, and it drives the knife deeper into my chest and brings my bitterness directly to the surface.

Sorry to break up your little love nest.

But then, I'm not sure I will break up his love nest, because I'm not sure I'm ready to see him just yet. "I think I might just stay at my mom's, though. Rest up there."

"For how long?" he asks, and I wonder if he's calculating how many more nights he'll have with Pamela.

"I don't know. When do you want me home?" It comes out more heated than I anticipate, but, well, I *am* heated.

"I want you home now," he says, and it sounds so sincere I almost believe it. And for a second I have a flash of sympathy for Jack. It must be hard to have a dying wife and a healthy lover waiting in the wings. But at the word "lover," the bubble of sympathy bursts, and my anger flares again.

Jack keeps speaking, oblivious to my warring emotions. "But you probably should get your rest. How about I drive down and get you on Sunday? We'll just leave your car at your mom's. Figure out how to get it later."

"That's fine," I say. And even though we haven't been fighting, haven't really been talking about much of anything, the conversation is exhausting me.

"OK," he says. "And, Daisy?"

"Yeah?" I ask, but the only sound on the other end of the line is Jack's steady breathing.

And then he speaks. "G'night."

"'Night, Jack." And for a split second I'm back home in our bed and there's nothing between us—no miles of road or Lots of Cancer or Pamela—but the sheets.

twenty-four

I AM SIX YEARS old.

Well, I feel six anyway, tucked into my twin bed, watching my nineteen-inch TV while Mom fiddles with the rabbit-ear antennas. "How's that?" she asks after she has made the squiggly lines slightly less squiggly with her expert maneuvering.

"Good enough," I say. "I think I can still grasp what's happening on *The Price Is Right.*"

She smiles. "I'll go get you something to eat."

"Thanks," I say, and turn back to Drew Carey and his pencil-thin microphone.

I fall asleep at some point during the Showcase Showdown and wake later to find a tray on my nightstand with a plate of sliced oranges and a bowl of cold chicken noodle soup. It immediately reminds me of Jack and the night that I yelled at him. I should have just eaten the damn soup. And then curled up on him and looked him in his imperfectly perfect face and told him I was lucky to have him.

But now Pamela is lucky to have him.

No. I shake my head, determined to stay angry with Jack. He lied to me. He betrayed me.

But as hard as I try, I can't muster the energy to be mad at him.

And I know it's because I love him. And because I betrayed him first.

I turned away from him when I should have turned toward him. I spent the last three months looking for a wife for him, telling myself I was doing it because I loved him, because I didn't want to leave him alone. But all I was doing was leaving him alone.

And then I remember what Kayleigh said to me at the funeral home. That I was the one wasting my time. And I know for once she was right. I've been wasting my time. I think of all the hours, minutes, seconds that I could have spent petting his fingers, tracing his face, kissing his crooked smile. All the days that I should have spent with him, just talking to him about algae and hip pins and how I was terrified to die, to go somewhere without him.

A sound erupts from the pit of my stomach and out through my mouth that sounds like a cat being tortured.

The thought of being away from Jack for one second longer is more than I can bear. And I can only hope that Kayleigh is right again. That it's not too late.

"Daisy?" I hear my mom call from somewhere in the house and then the sound of her footfall in the hallway as she comes rushing to my room.

"Are you OK?"

"No," I say. "I need Jack. I have to go get Jack." If I started it, maybe there's a chance I can end it. Maybe Kayleigh's right and it's not too late.

"Honey, he'll be here on Sunday."

"*Now!*" I say, putting one sock-clad foot on my bedroom floor.

"Daisy, lay back down. You're in no condition—"

"I'm going," I say, standing up and ignoring the fact that the room is slightly off-kilter. "If you won't take me, I'll drive myself."

"OK! OK," she says. "I'll get my keys. But stay right there. I'm helping you to the car."

❧

DURING THE NINETY-MINUTE drive to Athens, I practice what I'm going to say to Jack. How I'm going to convince him to forgive me, come back to me, be mine. But it's hard to concentrate with the pitching of the car and the intense throbbing in my head. I'm lying with the seat fully reclined and my mom keeps shooting me worried sidelong glances that she thinks I can't see.

"Stop looking at me like that," I say through clenched teeth. "I'm fine."

By the time we pull up in front of my house, I consider just living in my mom's car for the rest of my days, as I'm not sure I even have the strength to open the door. But I somehow manage to slowly raise myself up in the seat and look out the windshield. The first thing I see is an unfamiliar car in our driveway. Not a car, but a truck. A gray pick-up truck. And something clicks.

I saw that truck on Facebook. On Pamela's home page.

And suddenly I find a store of energy that I didn't know I had. I throw open my mom's car door and stomp across the yard to the front steps and then I'm at the front door, swinging it open and looking for Pamela like a lion stalks a gazelle.

I'm barely registering the disarray my house is in—where the hell is my couch?—when I see Pamela standing in the hall, staring at me, her perfect mouth locked in an O.

"Daisy," she says.

"What the hell are you doing here?" I growl, surprised at my own venom, like I'm a mama bear and she's an evil hunter who's just shot one of my cubs. But it's kind of an apt analogy, because really, what kind of woman dates someone's husband? Even if his wife *is* dying.

Before she can answer, Jack appears behind her.

"Daisy," he echoes, his feet glued to where he stands. "What are *you* doing here?" His eyes are already big, shocked at the sight of me, but then they widen more as he takes me in, and it's only then that I realize what I must look like—my head wrapped in gauze, my sallow-just-had-surgery complexion, a pair of my mom's gray sweatpants that have ridden up on my calves during the ride here. And I'm sure I look especially dreary compared to perfect Pamela, who still looks put together in a white T-shirt and a pair of ripped-up jeans. What the hell is she wearing?

"Daisy?" My mom appears at my side and her eyes dart from me to Jack to Pamela, trying—like everyone else in the room—to decipher what, exactly, is happening.

"Can't you wait in the car, Mom?" I say through clenched teeth, crossing my arms in front of me. "I'll be right out."

"Honey, I really think—"

"Mom." I cut my eyes at her, but she hesitates, looking at Jack, Pamela, and then me once more. Then she nods and turns to go.

When she's gone, I point at Pamela, but my energy is considerably sapped. "What is she doing here?" I ask again, in a weak voice.

He hesitates, and a look passes between him and Pamela before he looks to me. A secret look that two people who have a secret share. A flash of jealousy and anger stings my belly. He takes a deep breath, and when he exhales, he says: "You should sit down."

He walks toward me and gently places his hands on my shoulders. And even though I came with the explicit intention of grabbing on to him and never letting him go, I want to shrug him off, because I suddenly can't stand the thought of him touching me. Or where else his hands have been. But my head feels light and the room is spinning a little and I know he's right. I need to sit. He steers me through the living room and into the kitchen, because it appears to be the only room that has any furniture at all right now.

"Jack?" I say, as I collapse into a chair, worried that the surgery was unsuccessful, that the screenings were wrong, that my brain is malfunctioning.

He studies me. "Are you OK?"

"No," I say. "What is going on?"

"I didn't want you to find out," he says quietly. And I stare at him with a mix of horror and anger. That he's so readily admitting to it. I mean, I guess he doesn't have much of a choice, since Pamela's here, but I realize now I was still holding on to a sliver of hope that I had been wrong.

"Well, I know all about it," I say as angrily as I can muster, which isn't very, considering the short walk from the car to the house—and the confirmation of Jack and Pamela's relationship—has left me shattered.

"You do?" He furrows his brow.

"Yeah," I spit, wondering how he can be so calm. How he can sit there looking at me with his deep dimples and his mock expression of concern.

He shrugs. "I guess I've never been a great liar."

At this, I find one more inexplicable store of energy and explode. "You've never been a liar at all, Jack! I don't even know who you are anymore. How you could do *this*."

It feels good to yell at him—to blame him—even though I know it's not entirely his fault.

We sit in silence staring at each other and he looks so sad that I fight the urge to reach out for him, to hug him. And it makes me hate him as much as I love him.

But then, in an instant, his countenance changes, and instead of sadness, his eyes burn with something else. Something that looks like fury. "What else was I supposed to do?" he shouts. "Tell me! You wouldn't let me come to doctor appointments, I couldn't postpone school. God forbid I try to *be* with you."

I know he's right. That this is my fault. But his words burn. So I latch on to the last thing he said, and lash out with it. "Seriously, Jack? This is all because I wouldn't have *sex* with you?"

"What? No!" he says. "What is wrong with you?" He looks at me with his forehead crinkled, and then it relaxes, as if he's thinking *Oh right, you've had brain surgery.* And it inflames me even more, because *he's* the one who's cheating, but somehow *I'm* the one who's crazy. When he speaks again, his voice is quieter, more level. "I just . . . I thought it would make you happy."

It's my turn to furrow my brow, confused. Did he somehow find out my plan to set him up with Pamela? How *could* he have? Kayleigh's the only one who knew and I know she wouldn't have told him. She's never betrayed me, and she wouldn't start now.

I narrow my eyes at him. "What *exactly* did you think would make me happy?"

"You know, not having to worry about it anymore. I know it's a big stressor and I just wanted to help. I had to do *something* to help."

Wait, *it*? Doesn't he mean *him*? Not having to worry about *him*?

"Jack," I say, putting my hands on the table in front of me, as if that will stop the room from revolving and bring some clarity to my muddled mind. "What are you talking about?"

He tilts his head and gestures back to the living room. "Uh . . . the house?" he says, dragging out both words, as if he's talking to a child.

I just stare at him, waiting.

"You know, how I got Pamela to work on it?"

I think of the bare living room and Pamela's unkempt clothes, and pieces of a puzzle begin to slowly connect to one another in my pulsing head. All the things I know about Pamela race through my mind— the sky-diving, *Grey's Anatomy*, her ability to make jam—but suddenly one tiny fact emerges above the rest. Something that Jack told me: Pamela and her dad built most of the farm themselves.

"What is she doing to it?"

"All the stuff that I wasn't able to do," he says. "She just finished the beams in the basement. Today she's starting on the floors."

I try to wrap my head around this new information. Pamela is not only my husband's girlfriend, but she is, apparently, our new contractor.

"How much is this going to cost us?" I ask, my head swimming with numbers—prices that we can't afford.

"Nothing," he says. "Well, I mean, materials. And we had to rent a sander. But the labor is free."

I take this in, trying to slow down the flood of information, to sort out what I've learned so far, to understand it. But a question still leaps to my lips: "Why?" I regret it as soon as it's out of my mouth. I know I don't really want to hear the answer. I know it's because she loves Jack. That this is the kind of thing you do for someone you love.

"I did save her horse's life," he says, as if this is the only explanation needed. But it's not. I need more. So I wait.

He fills the silence. "She wanted to do something in return. She overheard me telling Ling about the other stuff I was working on, the landscaping, the caulking, and asked if she could help out. We've been talking about it, planning it, for weeks, but I wasn't sure when we'd be able to get it done. Then you wouldn't let me come to the surgery and—"

He shrugs.

He's trying to spare my feelings. To not rub his relationship with her in my face. But I need the truth.

"And you're"—I take a deep breath, not wanting to finish the sentence, but I don't have a choice—"*with* her?"

"What do you mean *with*?" he says, and then his eyes grow wild, as it dawns on him exactly what I mean. "Wait. *With* with? With Pamela? Why on earth would you think that?"

I shake my head, trying to organize my thoughts, and then remember his all-nighter and, of course, the phone call. "Sunday night, when you didn't come home. And then when I talked to you the other morning, I heard her voice in the background. She was here."

He nods. "Yeah. I couldn't tell if you heard. She came over early to get started on the beams. I didn't want to ruin the surprise, so I didn't say anything in case maybe you didn't hear her."

I nod, absorbing this.

"And the other night," Jack says. "I didn't come home because I didn't think you wanted me here." He pauses, as if he's wondering how much to tell me, how honest to be. Then he shrugs. "And I was furious." He glances into my eyes. "At you."

The raw honesty of his emotion takes me aback because it's so unlike Jack. But then, he does have every right to be mad.

"So where'd you go?" I ask.

"The clinic. Pamela did meet me there," he says, and I prickle. "She was worried about Copper's surgery the next morning, but she left around eleven and I stayed up late working and then slept on the couch in Ling's office."

I nod again. "So all those times you left the room to talk to her, or said it wasn't her calling, even when I knew it was, it was because of *this*? You were talking about our house?"

"Yeah," he says, and then as if the full weight of my accusation has dawned on him, he sputters, "You really thought . . . ? Oh, God, Daisy—no. I could never . . . I *would* never." He reaches out to put his hand on my face and the warmth of his palm is everything.

I want to revel in his touch, but my head is still thudding. I close my eyes, trying to absorb this completely unexpected turn, when something else he said jumps out at me. *All the stuff he wasn't able to do.* "Wait—the front garden." I open my eyes. "Was that Pamela?

The right side of his mouth turns up, as he slowly shakes his head no.

"It was *you*?"

His crooked tooth peeks out at me.

"And *you* did the caulk?"

"Yep."

"Jack, I thought I was going crazy."

He pauses, as if he's considering this. "Well, you kind of were."

I smack him on the arm and he grabs my hand.

"But why?" I ask again. "The house has always been my thing."

He squeezes my fingers. "I told you. You wouldn't let me do any-thing else."

I think back to every time the past few months that I shut Jack down, pushed him away, and I know that most men would have given up—that I thought Jack *had* given up. But he hadn't. I sit back and let the enormity of his gestures sink in. He didn't just plant some flowers or fix a couple of windows—he found a way to love me when I was doing everything I could to not let him.

I nod, a smile creeping across my face. "I guess I have been a lit-tle hard to live with."

"Hard?" He scoffs, and a flash of anger lights his eyes again. "Try impossible. You're so goddamned stubborn and independent." He shakes his head, and I think he's done, but then more words tumble out. "You stopped telling me things—not just big stuff, like how you were feeling, but little things, like what you ate for lunch or how you bought a new laundry detergent because it was on sale." He lowers his head. "I thought—I don't know what I thought. That you were fac-ing your mortality and taking stock of your life, and I don't know—regretted spending it with me or something."

My heart, which has already been through so much, nearly cracks at this information. "*What?* Oh Jack, no. No, no, no," I say. "You are the thing—maybe the only thing—that I've ever gotten right."

And for the first time in months, I see Jack's shoulders visibly relax as he takes this in.

But then he furrows his brow, as if he still can't figure something out. "So what are you doing here? You really need to be in bed."

I close my eyes and rub my temples. "Well, I really did think . . . I mean, you and Pamela . . . And, you know." I search, but I can't find the right words, so I just end with: "I didn't want you to be."

But it's not enough, because I still can't shake the feeling that maybe there's more to their relationship than friendship, that maybe Jack does harbor some attraction to her—how could he *not*?—even if he hasn't done anything about it, so I say, "You don't . . . I mean, you're not . . . Do you have any feelings for her?"

Before Jack can respond, I hear laughter from behind me. "Oh my God," she says. "Me and Jack? We would kill each other."

I turn around to see Pamela standing in the doorway. I had forgotten she was here.

She smiles. "I mean, have you *seen* his office?"

I put my hand over my face to try to hide the flames of color that are spreading up my cheeks. "Oh, Jesus, did you hear all that?"

She nods, ducking her eyes. "Daisy, I—"

"No, stop. You must think I'm completely crazy."

"No," she says, but I know she's just being nice, because that's what she is—no matter what Kayleigh says about her.

JACK WALKS ME out to Mom's car, where she's sitting in the driver's seat, her lips a thin line of concern.

"You need to go home and get some rest. You shouldn't even be out of bed right now."

"I know," I say. "I just . . . I had to see you. I was so afraid that I messed everything up."

"Daisy, c'mon. We can talk tonight," he says, moving to open the door.

"No!" Since my surgery, I'm now all too aware that anything can happen, that I might not ever get this chance again. That I need to tell him how I feel and keep telling him and never let a day go by without him knowing it. That I can't waste any more time. Not a second of it. And then, for some reason something Patrick said pops into my mind. "I could get hit by a bus when I leave here."

"What? I don't think there's a good chance of that happening."

I hide a smile, confident that Jack would have hated Patrick as much as I did. "I know. I just want you to know that I'm sorry. I haven't felt like I've done anything right since all this started, especially when it comes to us."

He nods. "I haven't either. There's so much I wish I could go back and do differently. Like not take no for an answer when you wouldn't let me come to your doctor appointments."

"I guess there's not exactly a handbook for this kind of thing, huh?"

He stares at me. "You're kidding, right? You bought me the handbook."

I stare back at him, confused, until I remember the self-help book I picked up for him at Barnes & Noble.

"You read that?"

"Isn't that why you got it for me?"

"Well, yeah, but—I didn't think you actually *read* it."

He laughs, and then throws back his head and laughs some more, and the sound warms me from the inside out like a cup of hot cocoa.

"God, Daisy," he says, shaking his head. "Only you."

may

twenty-five

"IT'S NOT SUPPOSED to be this hot in May," Kayleigh says, fanning her face with a paper program.

We're sitting in Sanford Stadium, and I'm leaning forward, straining to find Jack's lanky body in the sea of doctoral candidates wearing white square caps.

I finally spot him, and a flood of warm fuzzies fills my body. Jack is finally done with school, the checklist on our house is complete thanks to Pamela, and we have days, maybe weeks, maybe months to spend together, rubbing noses in the sunshine of my favorite season. Maybe even more—who knows? At my last clinical trial checkup, Dr. Rankoff said that my tumors hadn't made any progress—they were the same size they'd been a full month earlier. She said perhaps I was finally responding to the medicine, or that removing the brain tumor somehow shocked the other ones to behave, at least for now. And I've never been so happy to hear that some part of me was underachieving, not living up to its full potential. But I know they will, one day.

When the students in Jack's section stand up and move their tassels from one side of their caps to the other, my mom hoots and Kayleigh leans over to me.

"You husband is officially a doctor. Twice over."

I laugh. "And he still has no idea how to make canned soup."

"He's hopeless."

"Nah," I say, thinking of the door handle and the windows and the garden that he fixed. I know that Jack can take care of himself, even if he may not pick up his socks as much as I want him to, or know how to make anything other than cereal for dinner.

But there is one thing that still gnaws at my heart in the middle of the night. And there's only one thing I can think of to fix it.

"Promise you'll check in on him," I say to Kayleigh.

"If you mean go over there and do his laundry, it's not happening," she says.

"No," I say. "Just spend time with him. Make him get out of the house. I just—" I bite my lip and look up until my eyes feel dry again. Then I look back at Kayleigh. "I don't want him to be alone."

She squeezes my hand.

"He won't be."

I nod, satisfied that Jack is going to be all right on that inevitable day that my tumors decide to rebel again. To live up to their full potential.

I turn my face toward the sun, letting it warm my face, and allow myself to take comfort in the one other small fact I know to be true: today is not that day.

may

one year later

jack

DAISY'S GONE. IT'S the first thing I notice when I wake up in the dark and roll toward her side of the bed. It's empty. Is she in the kitchen? I strain to listen for the telltale sound of the fridge door opening, or the pad of her slippered feet in the hall, but all I hear is Benny's light wheezing snores drifting up from the foot of the bed. I stop just short of calling out her name when it hits me.

Daisy's gone.

I lay in bed, wondering when I'll stop waking up like this. I used to be a sound sleeper when Daisy was here. But I don't think I've slept a full night since her funeral.

It's been five months since I sat wedged between a misty-eyed Kayleigh—I think it was the first time I've ever seen her cry—and Daisy's sobbing mom, listening to a preacher who didn't even know Daisy talk about what a kind person she was. I wasn't sure what made me madder, him calling her kind when he didn't even know her, or him saying *was*.

And then they played that stupid Sarah McLachlan song, and I thought I was going to explode until Kayleigh leaned over and said, "Wherever she is, Daisy is *pissed*." And it lifted my anger and grief and sadness just for a moment, because she was right. Daisy hated Sarah McLachlan.

Now it's become a catchphrase whenever we talk about her. *Wherever she is.* And I like it because it makes me feel like she's just at the farmer's market or yoga and she's forgotten to leave me a note saying which one.

For six days after the funeral, I didn't leave the house. I didn't even walk Benny. Not that he seemed to mind. He spent most of his time curled on Daisy's pillow, his eyes big and sad and accusing, as if I had something to do with her absence. I lied to my mom when she called and asked if I was getting out. I definitely didn't tell her that I was turning on the blender because it filled our empty house with the sound of Daisy in the morning. It had the added bonus of drowning out my childish weeping.

And then one rainy afternoon when I was sitting at my desk, staring at the photo of Daisy from our final vacation together—standing in front of that strange, rusty bicycle stuck in the middle of a massive tree that she insisted we go see, even though it was an hour outside of Seattle and we had to take a ferry to get there—Kayleigh appeared. She didn't even knock.

And seeing her reminded me of the first of the two things Daisy made me promise her before she died—that I stay in touch with Kayleigh.

When I'm gone, she won't have anyone, she said to me. *I just don't want her to be alone.*

So I let her stay. We watched an episode of *Game of Thrones* in silence. I had never seen the show before, but sitting on the couch staring at the TV with someone else was infinitely better than sitting on the couch staring at the TV by myself. And for a moment, I was even able to pretend it was Daisy sitting beside me, which loosened the viselike grip on my chest that had been ever-present since the night she died.

Kayleigh came back the next weekend. And the weekend after that, she informed me that Daisy's mom was coming, too, and that we would all have dinner together.

"I don't cook," I told her.

"Neither do I," said Kayleigh.

We ordered pizza.

I was glad we ordered two, because Daisy's mom showed up with some burly guy in a leather biker hat. I vaguely remembered him from the funeral, holding Daisy's mom up like a trellis holds a vine. He seemed nice enough, except I noticed a strange tattoo on his neck of a spindly-legged bird, and I wasn't sure what to make of it.

At first it was awkward, the four of us sitting together at Daisy's and my kitchen table. It seemed for the first hour or so that Daisy had just run to the bathroom and she would be back any second to relieve the tension. Daisy was always so good in social situations. I loved watching her when she didn't notice me watching her. And I loved watching her even more when she did—she seemed to shine brighter, tell a story with more gusto, smile wider, as if it was solely for my benefit.

After we'd each had a few glasses of wine, conversation flowed more freely and we took turns telling stories about Daisy. Her mom cried at all of them. Even the happy ones.

"How'd you two meet?" Bird Tattoo asked me, and it stopped me cold, because it's the one thing I wish I had told Daisy before she died. I had planned to, but I was waiting for the right moment—one of those movie scenes where the girl is holding on to life and the guy is telling her how much she means to him. That's when I was going to tell her this story. But Daisy died in her sleep and our final conversation was about whether she wanted to sip any more orange juice through a straw.

So I told the story to them—how we met at the bus stop when I saved her from a bee, and how she didn't know that bumblebees could sting you and how I told her it was a common misconception. And how, when she laughed, it challenged my belief that I was born to be a veterinarian and made me suspect I had been born with the sole purpose of finding ways to make her laugh again.

But what Daisy and my captive—and somewhat drunk—audience didn't know was that I had actually seen her at that bus stop six weeks before meeting her and I went to it every day, even though my classes were clear on the other side of campus, hoping to see her again. And then I did. And then I had no idea what to say to her. And then the bee buzzed her head. And I have never been so grateful to see a potentially dangerous insect.

After that dinner, it became easier for Kayleigh and me to talk on her weekly visits and I even began to understand why Daisy liked her so much, although the one thing she used to complain about was true—Kayleigh has terrible taste in men.

She began confiding in me the things I suspect she used to tell Daisy, although thankfully with much less clandestine detail, and I would listen and give her terrible advice, and then I started telling her the things I used to tell Daisy.

Like how I'm afraid that I laugh at inappropriate times constantly these days. It's as if Daisy's death threw my nervous system out of whack and I don't know how to respond to normal social situations. Not that I've ever been good in normal social situations.

It's something I would have told Daisy late at night right before I turned off the light to go to sleep. As an aside, so she didn't think I was really worried about it. Or that I thought it was a big deal.

But Daisy's not here to tell. So I told Kayleigh last week when she stopped by the house with a bag of enchiritos from Taco Bell.

"Your wife died," she responded. "You're allowed to laugh whenever you fucking feel like it."

It's not what Daisy would have said. But it did, somehow, make me feel better.

Now, laying in the dark, my heart is heavy once again—I've realized that's what grieving is, a constant cycle of feeling better and feeling worse, and I'm hopeful that one day I'll feel better more often than I feel worse—so I think of the second promise I made to Daisy before she died.

"Please, for the love of God," she said while we were sharing a wedge of Manchego cheese underneath our lone tree—a dogwood, not an olive tree as Daisy once hoped—in the backyard, "pick up the socks beside the bed and put them in the hamper."

"OK," I said.

"Every morning," she said, fixing me with her Daisy stare.

"Every morning," I said.

But I lied. On the floor beside me right now is a pile of at least ten pairs of dingy white athletic socks. I leave them there, not because I forget to pick them up, or because I'm too lazy, but because now it's our inside joke. My final connection to Daisy that I can't sever.

And wherever she is, I hope she's laughing.

acknowledgments

Heartfelt gratitude to the following people, without whom this book would not have made it to completion in its current form:

My agent extraordinaire, Emma Sweeney, who changed my life forever with one phone call. And Noah Ballard for his patience holding my hand through this new-to-me experience.

Karen Kosztolnyik, my amazing and possibly clairvoyant editor, and all of the supportive staff at Gallery Books/Simon & Schuster, especially my hard-working publicist Stephanie DeLuca, the incomparable Jennifer Bergstrom, the dynamic Wendy Sheanin and the best assistant in publishing, Paige Cohen. Thank you all for loving and believing in this book.

Rich Barber, my publishing mentor and friend.

Dr. Chad Levitt, for graciously spending numerous hours explaining complicated medical procedures, tests, and diagnoses in words that I could understand, and answering my hundreds of questions and e-mails with unwavering enthusiasm. Any mistakes or inaccuracies are mine.

Lisa Shore, for introducing me to Chad and for your writerly friendship and support over the years. Thank you.

Dr. Leo Sage, for sharing his experiences as a dual DVM and PhD student at the University of Georgia. Again, any inaccuracies in this experience are mine. Go Dawgs!

My sister, Megan Oakley. In *On Writing*, Stephen King says that each novelist has a single ideal reader and keeps that person in mind in every sentence they write. You are who I write for. Thank you for always being willing to read—even at three in the morning, when you'd rather be sleeping.

My mom, Kathy, for your brilliant edits, and, along with dad, your unconditional love. Thank you both for everything.

My grandmother, Marion, for reading the first draft and then immediately reading it again. You and Grandpa have always been my biggest cheerleaders and I wish he was here to see this.

My grandparents, Penny and Jack, for their relentless love and support.

My brother, Jason, for his unique method of encouragement ("Aren't you done with that novel yet?"), my brother-in-law, Matt, for his unorthodox advice ("Add a high-speed car chase"), and the rest of my large, supportive family (Wymans, Oakleys, Tulls, etc.—you know who you are). As Dad would say: You guys put the "fun" in dysfunctional.

My trusted circle of friends/sounding board, who all read various drafts and gave me priceless insight, criticism, and encouragement: Brooke Hight, Kelly Marages, Kirsten Palladino, Jaime McMurtrie, Caley Bowman, Laurie Rowland, and Shannon Jones. Thank you.

Seasoned authors who kindly shared wisdom, encouragement, and support along the way: Allison Winn Scotch, Catherine McKenzie, and Nicole Blades. Thank you.

Henry and Sorella, for reminding me of the precious beauty in the world outside the fictional ones I create. You are my reason for everything.

Finally, my husband, Fred. There aren't enough words, so I'll leave it at two: Only you.

Before I Go

Colleen Oakley

Introduction

As a twenty-one-year-old college student, Daisy Richmond's answer to the question "If you knew you were going to die in one month, what would you do?" was full of adventure and travel to exotic lands. As a twenty-seven-year-old woman who is faced with a recurrence of breast cancer, her answer is very different. *Before I Go* is the poignant story of Daisy's journey to navigate the unexpected twists and turns of life, and the painful process of letting go of everything but love.

Questions and Topics for Discussion

1. At the beginning of the story, Daisy describes herself as stubborn, independent, organized, and definitely not indecisive. What words would you use to describe her at the beginning of the story?

2. After receiving the news from Dr. Saunders about the probable recurrence of her cancer, Daisy waits twenty-four hours before telling Jack. Why do you think she waited? What do you learn about Daisy and Jack's relationship from the way they navigate the conversation when she tells him the news?

3. Daisy describes her observation about people from her work at a credit card call center by saying, ". . . most people just want to talk. To be heard. Even if it is by a stranger. Or maybe, especially if it's a stranger." Do you think she wants this for herself? Is this observation true for you? Why or why not?

4. On page 78, Daisy says: ". . . there's only one thing that's worse than actually having cancer, and that's having to tell people you have cancer." What do you think makes talking about cancer (or any other serious illness) so awkward for most people? How would you want people to respond if you were in Daisy's situation?

5. How is Daisy's response to the question "If you knew you were going to die in one month, what would you do?" different at age twenty-seven than it was at age twenty-one? How did she use the first month following the news about her cancer's recurrence? What did you feel toward her as you read the story of how she was spending her days? How would you answer the question?

6. How would you describe Jack's response to Daisy as she pushes him away? Do you think he represents a typical partner's response? Why or why not? How would you respond to someone you knew had a serious illness and seemed to be pushing you away?

7. What do you think Daisy is trying to avoid by focusing on planning Jack's future before she dies?

8. Describe Daisy's friendship with Kayleigh. In what ways are they similar? How are they opposite? Do you relate to the kind of friendship they share? Describe.

9. What do you think were some of the factors that precipitated Daisy's panic attacks? Have you ever experienced a panic attack or known someone who has?

10. Describe the bargain Jack and Daisy made about each other's schooling when they learned about the extent of her cancer recurrence. Why do you think Daisy was so intent on Jack continuing school in the midst of her cancer treatments? Would you have made the same decision? Why or why not?

11. What role does Pamela play in the story? How does she serve a similar function for both Daisy and Jack?

12. Based on what you learn about Daisy's life as a young girl, what are some of the ways she has learned to cope with pain and disappointment in her life? How do those strategies serve or hinder her when she's diagnosed with Lots of Cancer?

13. On page 219, Daisy quotes a therapist she saw once who said, "Your anger is grief wearing a disguise." Do you agree? Why or why not? Do you think Daisy would agree at the end of the story?

14. How do you feel about the way the story ended?

Enhance Your Book Club

1. Invite someone you know who is a cancer survivor to share their story at your next book club. Spend time discussing the question "If you had a month to live, what would you do?"

2. Make a bucket list. Spend time thinking about the things you want to experience before you die and write them down. Make plans to start crossing things off your list, one at a time. Discuss your lists at your next book club.

3. Think of someone in your life who is dealing with a chronic or terminal illness. Make a list of a few ways you could encourage and demonstrate care for them during this time. Make a plan to do at least one of the things on your list for them. Discuss what this was like at your next book club.

4. Notice the things that make you angry in the course of a week and write them down. Spend some time reflecting on what griefs your anger may be disguising. Share reflections at your next book club.

A Conversation with Colleen Oakley

What was your inspiration for writing *Before I Go*? Have you ever walked through a terminal illness with someone?

About six years ago, I was assigned an article where I had to interview a woman who was dying of metastasized breast cancer. It was a powerful interview for many reasons, but what struck me the hardest was the fact that she was around my age—late twenties at the time—so I couldn't help but put myself in her shoes. I was a newlywed and it surprised me that my first thought wasn't *What would* I *do if I was dying*, but *What would my husband do?* My husband is the kind of guy who thinks cooking a meal means opening a box of Rice-A-Roni and a can of tuna. Would he eat boxed meals for the rest of his life? Would he date again? Would his new girlfriend or wife be like me? The idea evolved from there. I think most couples have had the conversation "Would you remarry if I died?" And I thought it would be interesting to take that one step further—what if you could hand-pick who your husband married?

What did you enjoy most about writing this story?

I had so much fun creating Jack and Daisy's relationship—particularly the beginning of their love story. Who doesn't love those first few months of falling in love with somebody? Of course, that just made it so much harder for me to write the ending, because I was invested in them as a couple, and I hated tearing them apart.

Have you always dreamed of writing a novel? When did you first know you were a writer?

I've been writing stories since I first learned to hold a pencil. I think my mom still has some of the books I wrote in elementary school (I bound them and everything!) in a box in the attic. So yes, I've always dreamed of writing a novel, but like most writers, I have a hard drive full of unfinished manuscripts, so I wasn't always sure I would actually realize my dream.

What was the most challenging part of writing this story?

There were so many challenges, but I think the hardest thing was to strike the right tone. The subject material is obviously fraught with emotion, but I didn't ever want it to be too maudlin or depressing. I hope that I achieved a good balance.

Even though the story of Daisy's Lots of Cancer is filled with sadness, your writing style conveys a lighthearted, humorous tone. What role does humor play in your life?

I've never been great at dealing with very serious, grave situations. I'm usually the person in the corner cracking a joke or trying to say something witty or clever to lighten the mood. Sometimes I'm probably wildly inappropriate, but sometimes I think it's really necessary. I remember when my grandfather (who was a very funny man) died, my entire family sat around telling the most hilarious stories about him and laughing until we cried. So maybe I come by it naturally, but I really do believe that laughter is the best medicine.

Do you think Daisy is a picture of someone who refuses to grieve?

That's a good question. I think I've always seen Daisy as someone who's in denial, but refuses to admit she's in denial. She uses Jack—and finding a wife for him—as a way to avoid processing what's really happening to her. I also think grief is partly about accepting that not everything in life is within our control, and that's something Daisy obviously has a really hard time with.

Is there a message you hope readers take away from reading *Before I Go*?

My favorite books are those that touch me in some inexplicable way. I do hope the book reminds people to love hard and live their lives fully in the present. But I think my biggest hope is that readers find something in my book that they connect with emotionally—whether it makes them laugh, cry, or throw the book across the room in frustration.

When you're not writing novels and essays, what are some of your favorite ways to spend time?

Laughing with (and sometimes at) my husband and my unbearably cute kids, throwing dinner parties, and watching clips of Jon Stewart and Jimmy Fallon online (I'm never awake late enough to watch them live). I'm also a reluctant runner—I'm often training for some type of race that I have no hope of winning.

Your Twitter bio says you are a margarita enthusiast. What is your secret to making a fantastic margarita?

Jalapeño tequila. My website designer (the fabulous Maria Palladino) introduced me and now I'm hooked. Try it! You won't be disappointed.

Which character in the book was the most fun to develop?

The easy answer is Kayleigh, because she's so wry and her character really allowed me to bring comic relief to some tough scenes. But I probably enjoyed writing Daisy's mom the most. I love her quirks—the obsessive bird-watching, the incompetence with technology—and I really enjoyed writing her full-on emotional outbursts. She doesn't hide her sadness, and it was somewhat of a relief to write her, since every other character is so guarded with their feelings.

Do you have a "bucket list"? If so, what are some of your favorite hopes on your list?

To learn to ski. To master one magic trick that baffles adults and children alike at parties. To have a first-person encounter with the Loch Ness monster. I realize these aren't all completely realistic. Skiing is hard.

What can we expect from you next?

I'm working on a book about a young girl who's a medical marvel—she's allergic to other humans. It's going to be amazing. Or really terrible. Depends on the day you're asking.